Waltzing

with the

Light

MARNIE L. PEHRSON

ISBN 0-9729750-5-5

Acknowledgments

I would like to thank Dr. Jack M. Morton, Marvin E. May and my late, great-aunt, Thadda Springfield Moody for sharing their recollections with me and reviewing this work to make this portrayal of Daisy, Tennessee in the late 1930's as accurate as possible. I'd also like to express my appreciation to my mother, Betty Morton, for her proofreading and assistance in making the language of the time authentic, my friend Cathy Nattress for her support, encouragement and help in tweaking the manuscript, Tamara Ingram for her cover design, and Granite Publishing & Distribution for their cover assistance and editorial suggestions.

For Jenette
who taught me that it's all about
sowing seeds,
loving patience,
and holding hope…

Preface

This historical fiction novel is written with love for the town I grew up in, Daisy, Tennessee, and for the people of that community. While the primary characters of this story are purely fictional, several of the secondary characters are my relatives who were born and raised in Daisy. Within the pages, you'll find my father, Jack Morton, as a child and my great aunt Thadda Springfield Moody as a young woman. You'll read about my pioneering grandparents, Sherman and Edna Morton, and my great-grandmother Maude Springfield.

Two other characters you will meet in this story are Francis "Fanny" Snodgrass and her sister Lillian Karrick. These two remarkable ladies are real women who kept the Church going in the Chattanooga area during volatile times when the branch vacillated between a small branch to a Sunday school and back. When the lack of priesthood leadership persisted, LDS Church leaders considered dissolving the little unit completely, but Sisters Snodgrass and Karrick stepped forward and kept it going. Through their pioneer efforts the large geographic area covered by their tiny group has rolled forth like a stone cut out of the mountain without hands into the Chattanooga, Tennessee Stake of Zion with thousands of strong and valiant members.

This work is a tribute to their vision and to the faithfulness of all those early members of the Church who traveled thirty to fifty miles just to attend church on Sunday. It is a tribute to my forebears who embraced the restored gospel in the 1960's and 1970's and to the home of their youth.

I hope you enjoy this work as much as I have enjoyed researching and writing it!

Marnie L. Pehrson

Chapter 1

Beads of perspiration glistened on Jake Elliot's bronze muscular biceps as the ax descended in a heavy blow, splitting the log in two and cracking loudly through the hot early autumn air. Mikalah Ford stood at the kitchen window, dunking a ceramic cup into the sudsy water as she stared mesmerized by the man her mother had hired to chop wood, help with the apple harvest and perform much-needed repairs.

Mikalah's father left nearly a year prior when he found work as a telegraph operator in Athens and sent most of his paycheck back to his wife to clothe their four children and pay the debts that he had accumulated through speculating before the stock market crash. Laurana Ford was a strong woman who never let her children see the tears that watered her pillow at night as she lay awake missing her husband Bill. Seventeen-year-old Mikalah was an incredible help to her mother. She cleaned, cooked and tutored the twelve-year-old twins, Hank and Hannah, with their homework every night and made sure that five-year-old Matilda got her bath and stayed out of trouble.

Mikalah dried her hands on a dish towel and brushed back a stray strand of strawberry blonde hair. Mikalah's thick locks hung in naturally curly ringlets to her shoulders, and her baby blue eyes remained riveted on the workman as he sauntered toward the house, buttoning up his plaid shirt to cover his white undershirt. Unconsciously, she brushed at her skirt making sure she was presentable as he approached.

Jake stood outside the open kitchen door and tapped on the wooden frame with his knuckles.

"Come in, Mr. Elliot. I bet you're thirsty. Would you like some lemonade?" she offered.

"Oh, yes, thank you, Miss Ford," his voice was rich and deep. He ran his fingers through his dark brown hair and his emerald green eyes twinkled in

7

appreciation. She handed him a tall cool glass of lemonade, and he gulped it down.

He extended the glass to her, "Thank you, Miss."

"You're welcome. Would you like another?"

"Ya know, I'd really appreciate that," he smiled and thought to himself what a pretty girl she was. There was something about her big blue eyes and long eyelashes that drew him in.

Mikalah turned toward the counter and poured him another glass. His eyes followed her as she turned from him. She was tall, nearly five foot nine, with long shapely legs and a tiny waist that was further accentuated by the way she filled out her blouse. Jake caught himself and quickly looked down at his feet fumbling with his shirt, buttoning a couple more buttons.

"Here you go," Mikalah extended the glass to him, and he took it gratefully. As his hand brushed against hers, Mikalah felt a warm shiver run up her spine, taking her by surprise.

"Thank you, Miss," he nodded and sipped the lemonade slower this time.

"Would you like to sit down and rest a spell?" she offered pointing to the kitchen chair as she held a glass of lemonade for herself in her other hand.

"I probably shouldn't. I'm pretty smelly," he mumbled.

"Oh, have a seat. It's hot out there, and you need to rest," she offered.

Jake hesitated, and Mikalah motioned again toward the chair, "Go ahead, Mr. Elliot, rest yourself."

Jake pulled out the chair, sat down and crossed his long leg over his knee. His dungarees were patched at the knees, and he wore large leather boots that laced up to his calves. "Is your mother around, Miss? I need to ask her if I've chopped enough wood or whether she'd like me to do some more." Mikalah sat down at the table across from him.

"Mama's out back in the garden. She'll be in shortly, I suspect. She doesn't like to work too much in the heat of the day."

Mikalah found herself staring across the table at him. She was curious about this tall, strapping young man. His wavy brown hair was neatly trimmed, his square jaw and dimpled chin clean-shaven. She found him so incredibly different than the men who normally came around looking for work. Besides being the handsomest man she believed she'd ever seen he also had an air of honesty about him that seemed to radiate from his countenance. Maybe that's why her mother had hired him when she never would hire the others. Laurana was a generous woman and would gladly share what she had with the men who stopped by, giving them a meal and sending them on their way, but she never hired them to stay. She didn't want strange men boarding in her house. But when Jake had appeared at her doorstep this morning and asked if he could help her in exchange for room and board, she agreed.

Mikalah had been flabbergasted, raising her eyebrows in disbelief as her mother told the young man, "I do need some wood chopped. There's some loose roof shingles, and the house needs painting before winter hits. Can you do those types of repairs?" Jake informed her that he could, and she immediately set him to work chopping wood to stock the wood pile for winter.

"So where are you from originally, Mr. Elliot? You don't have a Southern accent, so you can't be from 'round here," Mikalah quizzed him as he sat sipping his lemonade slowly, enjoying his second glass.

"I'm from Utah," he answered.

"Utah? How in the world did you manage to get all the way out here to Tennessee?" she asked incredulously.

"My father owned a general store in St. George, and he let too many people buy on credit. When times got hard, he lost everything – the store, the house, the land – everything. So he moved the family to Oklahoma where his family's from. He got a job with my uncle doing road work. There wasn't enough work there for me too, so I started doing odd jobs for people and have gradually worked my way across the country, helping a lot of folks like your family – where the man of the house has left to find work and the women need help." His eyes took on a far away look as if he were replaying a memory, "I've enjoyed traveling the country and meeting nice folks along the way." Mikalah liked the way the dimple in his chin deepened when he smiled. In spite of her conscious decision not to let this handsome stranger get to her, she was completely unnerved by him.

"When was the last time you saw your family?" she asked.

9

"Let's see here, I was twenty when I left, and I'm twenty-two now, so two years, yep, two years since I've been home – well, since I saw my parents anyway. Oklahoma doesn't really feel like home to me. It's been about three years since I was in St. George."

"Do you plan to go back?"

"I miss my family, but I really like it here in the South. People are friendly, and there's so much color. It's so beautiful here that I just might stay," he mused aloud.

Laurana Ford appeared at the kitchen door, brushing her feet on a mat outside the door with her three blonde-headed children behind her. She entered, carrying a basket full of beans. Her children followed her carrying bowls of squash and okra.

Jake's back was to her as she entered, and he turned around and stood facing her, "Afternoon, Mrs. Ford. Your daughter was kind enough to offer me some delicious lemonade." He raised his glass and nodded at Mikalah with a smile, "I've chopped the wood and piled it outside in the woodshed. Would you like me to chop down those two dead trees that are standing by the entrance to your property? They might make some good firewood."

"Yes, those two trees are an eye sore. Please do that," she nodded her head in agreement.

Mikalah peeked in the oven to check on her casserole. She grabbed a pot holder and pulled the pan from the oven and placed it on top of the stove, "Everyone ready for lunch?" she asked.

"Boy, that sure smells delicious!" Jake marveled, "I don't believe I've smelled anything that good since I was back home."

Hank, Hannah and Matilda poured into the room setting their bowls of produce on the kitchen counter and gathering around Mikalah, "I'm starved!" Hank rubbed his hands together anxiously awaiting his plate of food.

"Settle down, children. I'll get you some," Mikalah scolded. She counted six plates, pulled them from the cabinet and began dishing out casserole and garnishing the plates with sliced garden fresh tomatoes and cucumbers.

"Wash up," Laurana directed.

The children and their mother gathered around the sink as she poured water to wash their hands. Mikalah handed each of the children a plate first to get them out from under her feet. They grabbed forks, clanging them onto their plates and plopped down at the kitchen table while Jake washed his hands and forearms. Mikalah served Jake a large portion and then served her mother and herself. As everyone gathered around the table, Hank started shoveling his lunch into his mouth.

Jake cleared his throat and ventured, "Mrs. Ford, would you mind if I offered a blessing on the food?"

Laurana Ford patted her hand on the table, motioning for Hank to put down the fork of food he was about to shovel into his mouth, "That would be nice, Mr. Elliot," Laurana answered, "We haven't had a man in the house to offer grace in so long, that I'm afraid we've gotten out of the habit. But if you'd like to, go right ahead."

Jake began to pray, offering a blessing not only on the food but also on the Ford family, including Mr. Ford and asked for special protection for Mrs. Ford and each of the children by name. After closing the prayer, Laurana's eyebrows raised as she looked at Mikalah and then turned to smile at him, "Thank you Mr. Elliot, that was – that was lovely."

"Can Hannah and I go swimmin' at the creek, Mama?" Hank tapped excitedly on the table as he looked hopefully toward his mother, his blue eyes twinkling with anticipation. His twin sister Hannah matched his anxious expression and shared his same wavy blonde hair, fair countenance and sparkling blue eyes.

"That's fine. Just a few hours though," Laurana agreed.

"Can I go too? Can I go?" begged Matilda, bobbing her little blonde head.

"Mikalah, why don't you go with them? You've been cooped up in here all day, and you can keep an eye on Matty."

Mikalah looked up from her lunch toward her mother and grinned at her baby sister, "That sounds fun, let's go."

After lunch, Jake smiled as the children scampered from the table gathering their swim clothes and towels. He wished he could tag along. A swim on this hot afternoon would be refreshing, but there was too much work to be done.

Soon, Mikalah and the children came down the stairs carrying their towels and headed toward the door.

"We'll be back in a few hours, Mama," Mikalah waved at her mother.

"Race you to the end of the road," Hank called out. "The last one there's a rotten egg." Everyone took off running as fast as they could – including Mikalah. She lifted her skirt slightly and ran toward the end of the road. Mikalah was a fast runner. She had played basketball at Daisy High School and often ran in races at the county fair. She soon passed up Hank and Hannah as little Matty trailed behind. When she reached the end of the road, she leapt around to face them.

"Aha, Matty's the rotten egg!" Hank teased.

"Am not!" Matilda's bottom lip puckered.

"Are too! You're slower than a turtle stuck in molasses!" Hank jeered.

"Micky, make Hank stop callin' me names!" Matilda whined.

"All right, 'nough o' that Hank, let's try to get along today. It's too pretty to fuss." Mikalah scolded.

Hank rolled his eyes, "She's such a baby!"

Mikalah picked little Matty up like a sack of potatoes and plopped her onto her hip as she placed her other arm around Hank's shoulder, "Come on Matty, give me a smile," Mikalah kissed her little sister's rosy cheek. Matty smiled back at her big sister and returned her kiss.

Mikalah set her down, and the four of them walked along Highway 27 toward Chickamauga Creek. One rarely saw a car drive up Highway 27 in the afternoon and this day was no different. The highway sliced through the open fields of farmland, and the occasional farmhouse dotted the landscape. Mikalah smiled at the sea of long stemmed daisies and vibrant orange black-eyed-Susan's that swayed in choreographed rhythm to the melody of the autumn breeze. Enjoying their last days of life, they stretched their colorful heads skyward, basking in the vibrant sunlight. As the children turned the corner and descended the embankment to the creek, the breathtaking beauty of the stream appeared before them. Crystal clear water leading back to the green mountains babbled over creek rocks rounded smooth from years of wear. Several little cabins nestled amongst the woods on either side of the creek.

Matty pointed down into the water, "Look Micky, somebody's weft their meowk and buttow down in the cweek."

"That's Mrs. Morton's things, Matty. She lives over yonder, and she keeps her milk and butter down in there to keep them cool." Mikalah looked toward the Morton's little house and saw five-year-old Jack running toward them.

"Why doesn't she just buy ice for her icebox?" Matty asked quizzically.

"Ice can get expensive. If we lived this close to the creek, Mama would be havin' us put ours down in there too." Mikalah explained.

As Jack trotted toward them, he waved, "Hi Matty! You goin' swimmin'?"

"Yep, you wanna come?"

"Sure!" he dropped in stride with the Ford children, and they ventured further down the creek where the water was a bit deeper. Hank, Hannah, Matty and Jack hopped from rock to rock as Mikalah drank in the beauty of the autumn colors that exploded from the trees on the unseasonably warm fall afternoon.

The children tossed their towels that were made from old feed sacks down on the rocks and skipped into the creek, splashing and squealing with delight. Mikalah sat down on a large boulder, removed her shoes and socks and let her feet dangle in the cool water.

Matty gathered brightly colored stones from the bottom of the creek bed, collecting them in her pocket. She carried them to the large rock slab where Mikalah sat and laid them out in the sun to dry, and ran back to the other children to play.

"My daddy's buildin' a big new house up the road," Jack stated proudly as he balanced himself on a small creek rock in front of Mikalah.

"He is?" Mikalah asked, "When will it be done?"

"Daddy says in a few weeks," he answered.

"Are you excited to move?" she asked the blue-eyed child.

"It's big an' fancy, even got 'tricity, but I'm gonna miss bein' on the creek - 'specially gonna miss my stump," he seemed a bit melancholy all of a sudden.

"Your stump?" Mikalah could hardly keep from giggling.

"Oh, yeah, I have the best stump in the whole wide world. Rain water gets in it, and it gets all musty smellin' and I can stir it with a stick, hide treasures in it and even collect frogs there."

"Now that sounds like somethin' you're gonna have a hard time doin' without, Jack," Mikalah affected a sympathetic expression of concern. "Maybe you'll find a stump at your new place."

"I hope so, but I've looked all over up there and ain't seen one yet," Jack flung a rock into the water, emphasizing his frustration over losing his stump.

"I'm sure you'll find lots of other fun things to do – nice big house like that with 'tricity an' all."

"Daddy says there's not many people in Daisy's got 'tricity in their house. Did ya know that, Miss Micky?"

"That right?"

"Yep. Mama's all 'xcited cause we're gonna have indoor plumbin' and a telephone and everythin'," Jack related the details as if there wasn't much to it all in his opinion.

"Really? A telephone!" Mikalah was impressed. While larger cities in 1938 had electricity, the little town of Daisy lagged behind.

"Nobody else in Daisy's got one a them in their own house," Hank chimed in.

"You gonna let me come visit and see this new house o' y'all's, Jack?" Matty asked.

"Sure, come on over any time," he grinned. Jack covered his eyes to shield them from the sun and peered off in the distance behind where Mikalah sat, "Who's that a comin'?"

Mikalah looked back over her shoulder and nervously began straightening her skirt and hair.

"Why, it's Hal Craig, Mikalah's beau," Hannah answered.

"You got yourself a beau, Miss Micky?" Jack asked.

Handsome brown-eyed, brown-haired, Hal Craig was a stocky fellow about the same height as Mikalah. All the girls in Daisy had a crush on him, but he only had eyes for Mikalah.

14

"Good afternoon, Micky!" he called as he strode determinedly across the rocks along the side of the creek.

"Afternoon, Hal!" she called back.

He came up behind her and put his hands on her shoulders, leaned over and gave her a peck on the cheek. "Care if I join ya?"

Mikalah scooted aside on the rock making room for Hal to sit down next to her, "Please do."

Hal seated himself, pulled off his socks and shoes, rolled up his pant legs and plunged his feet into the icy water, "Oh, now that sure feels good! What's up with this hot weather?" he asked boisterously.

"Indian summer," she answered. "What ya doin' at the creek in the middle of the day, Hal? You're usually at work 'bout now."

"Got too hot. I gave the workmen a long lunch and most of 'em headed over to the Blowin' Hole to cool off, but I spied you over here and figured I'd come see my girl."

"Oh, let's go to the Blowin' Hole, Micky!" Hank suggested excitedly.

"We told Mama we'd be at the creek, not the Blowin' Hole."

"Come on, Micky, let's go! It's close by!" Hannah begged. Matty and Jack shook their heads in delighted agreement as they saw Mikalah's determined expression begin to weaken.

"Why not? Let's go!" Mikalah grabbed her shoes and stockings and stood up on the rock. The children were jumping stone to stone, crossing over to the other side of the creek before she could barely stand. Mikalah and Hal followed behind them. Hal grabbed her hand and helped steady her as she crossed. The group traveled along the creek and then back toward the mountain, into the woods a bit to the cave that everyone called the Blowin' Hole. A group of men sat around the mouth of the cave. The chilly air coming from inside wafted out, cooling the weary laborers who had come to rest for a spell.

The children ran ahead into the cave, and Mikalah called out, "Now, no goin' down deep in there and gettin' lost! You know how ya can't hear a thing back in there. When I say it's time to go, you've gotta get out o' there quick and come along home."

"All right, we won't go too far," Hank called back to her as the children giggled and ran into the cave.

Mikalah and Hal walked hand in hand to the cave, passing the men outside who turned their heads, gawking at Mikalah. One of them, the son of a prominent moonshiner, whistled in her direction, and Hal glanced over his shoulder. A confident yet amiable look in Hal's eye told Jeb Bailey that Mikalah was Hal's girl. A hair-raising tremor shuddered along Mikalah's spine. The moonshiners made her nervous. They somehow managed to rise above the law in the little town of Daisy. Their feudal rampages went unchecked by local county authorities, and many felt it a matter of time before innocent people were harmed in their vengeful shootings.

The pair entered the cave a few yards and crossed to a small alcove. Hal motioned for Mikalah to sit on a rock, and he scrunched in next to her.

The cool breeze wafted through Mikalah's curls. The cave was nearly twenty degrees cooler than outside, and the chill of it caused her to rub her bare arms warming them in the friction of her hands.

"Boy, this sure feels good!" Hal kicked his feet out in front of him, wiggling his toes. Mikalah laid her shoes down on the ground beside Hal's.

"Jeb Bailey gives me the willies," Mikalah muttered.

"Ah, Jeb won't hurt nobody unless they're a Richards," Hank soothed.

"I don't know about that. All of 'em make me nervous. They're merciless," Mikalah insisted.

"Ah, you're worryin' for nothin'. You know good 'n well that the Richards and the Baileys have always kept their goin's on between themselves. They don't bother the rest of us. Heck, they've been feudin' for years. Only time they stopped was when they got on that big radio show, shook hands and agreed to put it all behind 'em."

"Yeah, those silly radio people thought they could stop a feud like that. That lasted about a week!" Mikalah rolled her eyes in disgust. "Then they were back to shooting each other. They love killin', Hank, and I say that kind of meanness isn't selective."

"You needn't worry your pretty little self over such matters, Micky. If we stay out o' their way, they'll stay out o' ours," he reached over, put his arm

16

around her shoulder and leaned in to kiss her. She returned his kiss that soon became more heated and demanding than she found comfortable. She put her hand to his chest and pushed him back, "Stop, Hal."

He pulled her closer. "Oh, come on, Micky" he almost whined as she quickly stood up and retreated a few steps with her back to him.

Before she had a chance to say anything, Jack and Matty ran up to her. Matty chased Jack as he ran behind Mikalah's skirt, dodging Matty who tried to grab hold of him.

"Save me Miss Micky!" Jack giggled.

"You're gonna need savin'" Matty scolded.

"What's up you two?" Mikalah grabbed Matty by the shoulders.

"Jack stow my pwetty wed wock I found at the cweek,"

"I did not steal it. I was just a lookin' at it! I was gonna give it back," he held a small red stone in the palm of his hand extending it to Matty who quickly snatched it.

"A likely stowey, Jack Mowton!" Matty stuck her tongue out at him.

"Now, now, Matty. If Jack says he was gonna give it back, then he was gonna give it back. You need to learn to share." Mikalah's hands went to her hips as she scolded her little sister.

"You're always takin' his side," Matty rolled her eyes and stomped away.

"Where are Hannah and Hank? It's time we got home," Mikalah rounded up the children. She wanted to put some distance between herself and Hal. While she found him attractive and fun to be with, he made her uneasy when he got too close to her. Mikalah was no prude, but something in his kiss made her uncomfortable and nervous.

"Hank! Hannah! Come on, we're leavin'!" Mikalah called, and the two came running.

As Mikalah led Jack and Matty out of the cave – a child holding each hand, Hal called after her, "We're goin' to the ball game tonight – right, Micky?"

Mikalah's head hung down momentarily as she closed her eyes, "Oh, that's right." She tried to hide the frustration in her voice, "Sure, yes, pick me up at seven." She exited the cave and accompanied the children home.

17

Jake spent the afternoon chopping down one of the old dead hickory trees in front of the Ford property. He was unloading the last few logs onto the woodpile as Mikalah and the children passed him. The children paid him no mind, but raced into the house. Mikalah followed them at a slower pace and studied Jake as he unloaded the logs. Something about him made butterflies flutter in her stomach. He nodded at her as she passed and wiped the perspiration from his brow with his shirt sleeve, "Have a nice swim, Miss Ford?"

"Yes, we did. Looks like you've been workin' hard. I can smell Mama's bread bakin' from out here. Come on in and have a bite."

"Thank you. I will in a few minutes - as soon as I finish unloading these last few logs."

As Mikalah entered the house her mother pulled two loaves of homemade wheat bread from the oven. The Fords typically prepared a big breakfast and lunch and then ate only bread and milk for dinner each night.

The children gathered around their mother anxiously awaiting the bread, "Run along upstairs and change out of those wet clothes."

Mikalah came up behind them, steering them along toward the stairs, and then turned toward her mother, "Hal asked me to go to the ball game with him tonight. Is that all right?"

"That's fine dear," her mother answered as she sliced the bread and placed it in a basket.

Mikalah turned and retrieved some butter and milk from the icebox and placed it on the table next to the basket of bread. Soon the children came tromping down the stairs and gathered around the table grabbing slices of bread and drinking glasses of sweet milk.

Jake tapped on the door frame as he watched the family gather around to eat.

"You don't need to knock every time you enter, Mr. Elliot. Start makin' yourself at home here," Mrs. Ford wanted him to feel welcome. There was something about him she liked, something about him she felt she could trust. "Come on in, get washed up and have some bread and milk."

18

"Thank you, Ma'am," Jake entered, washed his hands, sat at an empty chair, poured himself a glass of milk and buttered a piece of bread. Mikalah found herself staring at him again until his eyes met hers, and he smiled nervously.

She quickly looked away, finished her bread and turned to her mother, "Mama, may I be excused? I need to get ready."

"Yes, dear."

Jake helped Mrs. Ford clear the dishes and then sat down in a chair to rest after his long work day.

Matty pranced up to him, "Lookie, Mr. Ewiot, lookie what I found at the cweek." The child started pulling the creek rocks from her pocket and placing them in Jake's outstretched palm.

"Huh," she let out a frustrated sigh.

"What is it, Matty?" he asked.

"They ain't near as pwetty and shiny as they was when I found 'em. Ain't nothin' special 'bout 'em now, 'tall."

"I bet they're shiny when they're wet," he patted the little girl's head and then took her hand. "Let's go over here to the sink and put some water on them. I bet that'll make 'em shine again." He led the child to the kitchen, doused the rocks, and handed them back to her. "See there, all nice and shiny again. They're beautiful, Matty."

"Oh, thank you, Mr. Ewiot!" she exclaimed excitedly and ran to her mother, "Lookie at what I found at the cweek. Mr. Ewiot made 'em shine again."

"Those are lovely dear," Laurana caressed the child's chubby cheek.

About that time, there came a knock at the front door, and Mrs. Ford opened it to find Hal standing outside, "Why come on in, Hal. It's good to see you!"

Hal nodded at Mikalah's mother and entered the house, "Evenin', Mrs. Ford."

Jake rose to his feet, and Mrs. Ford introduced him, "Hal Craig, this is Jake Elliot. Mr. Elliot is boarding with us for a spell and helping us with some repairs. Mr. Craig helps supervise a group of farm hands at the Springfield place." Jake extended his hand to shake Hal's.

"Is Micky ready?" Hal asked as he released Jake's handshake.

"She'll be down in a minute."

Jake was a bit surprised to hear Hal refer to Mikalah as "Micky." The graceful and feminine young lady, who descended the stairs to join them, certainly didn't look like a "Micky" to him. He felt a twinge of emotion as he watched her leave the house on Hal's arm. If he didn't know better, he would have thought the feeling was jealousy, but what right did he have to be jealous? And why would he be jealous of a girl he didn't even know? He shook it off and walked to where Hannah and Hank were playing checkers.

"Ah checkers, how 'bout I play the winner?" he suggested.

Hank's bright eyes looked up at him, "Sure - and that will be me, of course."

Hannah rolled her blue eyes, "Oh gimme a break, Hank. You are the bragginest boy I've ever known. I've beat you plenty o' times."

"When?" he protested.

"All right you two, just play the game without the fussin'," Laurana scolded.

~*~

Jake sat down on the cot in the storage room where Mrs. Ford had cleared a place for him to sleep. He unbuttoned his shirt, removed his shoes and socks and reached down into his bag to pull out a book. He sat up on the cot with his head propped against the wall and began reading by the light of an oil lamp. Jake read for about an hour and then heard Mikalah and Hal talking outside the kitchen door.

"All right now, Hal, I've gotta go! Tomorrow's Sunday, and I need my beauty sleep for church," she giggled.

"I don't think you could get any more beautiful," he flattered.

Jake tried not to pay attention to their conversation, but their voices carried clearly into the storage room that was directly off the kitchen. He studied his book more intently, but found himself only gazing at the words without comprehending their meaning.

There was silence for a minute and then he heard a loud smack, "Hal Craig! That was entirely improper. I'm going inside," anger seethed from Mikalah's voice.

"Oh, come on Mikalah," Hal whined.

"No, Hal. If you can't keep your wanderin' hands to yourself, then I can't see you anymore," she scolded sternly.

Jake's eyebrows rose, and his eyes widened. Without thinking, he put his feet to the floor, stood up and walked toward the kitchen. As he reached the doorway, he saw the kitchen door fly open and Mikalah hurry to push it closed. Jake could see Hal's hand in the door, that narrowly escaped before Mikalah slammed it, shut and bolted it. Jake leaned against the doorway, his muscular arms folded across the chest of his white t-shirt, his right bare foot crossed over his left leg and propped on his toes.

"Everything all right, Miss Ford?" his deep voice asked softly.

She jumped and turned toward him, "Oh! You scared me!"

"I'm sorry" he whispered.

She stared at him, almost forgetting what they were talking about, so distracted was she by him standing there with his tousled hair and concerned handsome expression. Her eyes moved to his well defined arms that were still folded across his muscular chest. "Uh - Everythin's fine, Mr. Elliot. Hal can just be a bit of a tease," she understated.

"Let me know if you ever need help. Men like that…"

"Oh, Hal's a good fellow. He's just a bit full o' himself," she wondered why she found herself defending Hal in front of this stranger.

"Uh huh," Jake agreed. He couldn't help but notice that her dress was slightly pulled down to expose her shoulder, and her hair was mussed.

She followed his gaze and quickly pulled her dress back onto her shoulder, "If you'll excuse me, Mr. Elliot, I need to get to sleep. It's late."

"Yes, Ma'am," he nodded and watched her as she ascended the stairs. Then he turned and went back to his cot. Mikalah glanced back over her shoulder to see him enter the room and shut the door behind him. *How's a body supposed to sleep with somethin' that good lookin' under the same roof?* she thought to herself and then shook her head, *What in the world are you thinkin'? Shake it off, Mikalah!* She shut her bedroom door softly behind her.

Chapter 2

      Mikalah lay in her bed, awakened by a deep melodious voice outside her bedroom window. She listened, enthralled by the richness of the melody, the words, and the expression in the singer's masculine voice. She'd never heard the song before,

A poor wayfaring Man of grief
Hath often crossed me on my way,
Who sued so humbly for relief
That I could never answer nay.
I had not pow'r to ask his name,
Whereto he went, or whence he came.
Yet there was something in his eye
That won my love; I knew not why.

      Mikalah lay listening to the verse, thinking of the stranger from whose lungs it came. She thought about the words and realized that there was "something in *his* eye" that was winning her over.

Once when my scanty meal was spread,
He entered; not a word he spake,
Just perishing for want of bread.
I gave him all; he blessed it, brake,
And ate, but gave me part again.
Mine was an angel's portion then,
For while I fed with eager haste,
The crust was manna to my taste.

      Jake continued to sing all seven verses of the song. Tears streamed from Mikalah's eyes as he concluded:

Then in a moment to my view
The stranger started from disguise.
The tokens in his hands I knew;
The Savior stood before mine eyes.
He spoke, and my poor name he named,
"Of me thou hast not been ashamed.
These deeds shall thy memorial be;
Fear not, thou didst them unto me."

Who is this stranger, and why is he here? she pondered. Something told her that this was no ordinary man who sang outside her window and that because of him her life would never be the same.

Mikalah tossed the covers back and went to the window, looking down at the barn where Jake tended the cows. He picked up two steaming pails of milk and carried them toward the house. Hank followed him carrying two more pails. He smiled, evidently pleased that his morning chore took half the time with Jake's help.

Mikalah could smell her mother's sausage, gravy and biscuits cooking downstairs. She changed into a pretty blue Sunday dress, fixed her hair and went downstairs.

"Mmm… something smells good, Mama," she put an arm around her mother's shoulder and gave her a kiss on the cheek.

"Good mornin', Mikalah," she handed her daughter a plate, and Mikalah filled it with biscuits, sausage, gravy and eggs. When she turned around, she bumped squarely into Jake's chest.

"Oh, excuse me," she mumbled as she lifted her gaze slightly and stared into his magnetic emerald green eyes. She lost a few moments before she realized she had met his gaze for too long. He smiled, "No, please excuse me, Miss Ford." She moved aside toward the table, and he ladled food onto his plate.

He turned to join the family around the kitchen table. The children started to eat, and Laurana shook her head indicating they should stop. "Mr. Elliot, would you mind offering one of those beautiful prayers of yours for us this morning?"

24

"Yes, ma'am, I'd be happy to," he smiled. He seemed a bit surprised that she would ask.

Jake blessed the food, and Mikalah's curiosity piqued, "So tell us, Mr. Elliot, where did you learn to say a prayer like that? I don't believe I've ever heard anyone pray quite the way you do."

Laurana started to scold her daughter for being so bold, but quite frankly she was curious herself. So she looked toward Jake in anticipation.

"Oh, it's just the way my parents taught me to pray," he shrugged his shoulders.

"You must have some remarkable parents, Mr. Elliot," Laurana observed.

Jake smiled, "Thank you ma'am. I think so."

When Jake had finished the last bite of his biscuit and gravy, he pushed his chair back slightly from the table and patted his stomach, "Mighty fine breakfast. Thank you so much."

"You're welcome," Laurana smiled then turned to Mikalah, "Since you're ready for church, can you please help Matty get dressed? We need to leave in about twenty minutes."

"Yes, Mama," Mikalah finished her breakfast, rose from her chair and took Matty's hand to lead her upstairs. She turned toward Jake before ascending the staircase, "Will you be joining us for church this mornin', Mr. Elliot?"

"Well, I uh – "

"Oh yes, you must join us for church this mornin'," Laurana's voice grew insistent. "We've been going to the Daisy Methodist."

"You're Methodists?" Jake asked with interest.

"My husband is a Baptist, but since he's been away, the children and I have been going to the Daisy Methodist. I enjoy the ladies there – Mrs. Morton and Mrs. Springfield and her girls go there, and they are always so friendly."

"Are you a Methodist, Mr. Elliot?" Laurana asked.

"No ma'am."

"Baptist?"

"No ma'am."

"Congregational?"

"No ma'am."

25

This conversation grabbed Mikalah's attention so she stood holding Matty's hand as she stared at Jake and her mother. She wondered if her mother would name every denomination before she found one that Jake belonged to.

"There ain't nothin' else," Hank interjected.

"I don't believe you'll guess the church I belong to," he smiled, his eyes twinkling. "Not too many of us around these parts."

"Now you've got my attention. What church do you attend?" Laurana asked.

"I belong to The Church of Jesus Christ of Latter-day Saints," he stated clearly and distinctly so she could absorb the entire name.

"I've never heard of that one," she returned a puzzled expression, "But I heard Jesus Christ in there somewhere, so that's all that matters to me," she grinned.

"Yes, He is the most important part, isn't He?" Jake's eyes twinkled and the dimple in his chin deepened with his smile.

"I don't believe you'll find one of your churches in Daisy, Mr. Elliot. So if you'd like, we'd love to have you join us," she offered.

"I suppose I could do that. Thank you for the invitation, Mrs. Ford," Jake rose from his seat, "If you'll excuse me, I'll go get ready."

The children were actually dressed and ready in plenty of time so Laurana suggested that they walk to church since it was such a pretty morning. Jake joined them, and they all went out the door and down the road to Highway 27. They passed the house Sherman Morton was building on their right.

"Look Mama, there's Mr. Morton's house. Jack says it's gonna have 'tricity," Matty chattered excitedly.

"That's what Edna told me. That's really somethin', isn't it?" Laurana agreed.

Matty tugged on her mother's skirt, "Mama, what *is* 'tricity?"

Hank started laughing, "You don't even know what 'lectricity is? You're actin' all excited about it, and you don't even know what it is!" Hank doubled over laughing.

"Mama, make Hank stop makin' fun o' me!" Matty cried.

26

"Hank, leave your sister alone." She turned to Matty, "Electricity is what makes the lights go on at the home store. It's what makes Mr. Morton's radio work and what makes the movie pictures show on the big screen down the road. It means that Jack and his family will have lights in their house."

"Ooh!" understanding lit up Matty's face.

They trudged up the steep hill, and as they descended the other side Hank took off running. The landscape leveled out, and they traveled passed the ball field on their right, then the clay pit, general store, and service station on their left before they came to the Methodist church.

Edna Morton and her mother, Maude Springfield, greeted them as they entered the building.

"Hello, Laurana! So glad you joined us today," Edna welcomed.

"And who is this fine lookin' young man at your side, Mikalah?" Edna's sister Thadda strode up alongside her.

"This is Mr. Jake Elliot. He's boarding with us and doing some work around our house this season," Laurana answered.

Jake shook each lady's hand. As he did so, Laurana introduced each of them, "Jake, this is Edna Morton. Her husband Sherman is the one buildin' the new house we passed. And this is her mother, Maude Springfield, and her sister, Thadda."

"It's a pleasure to meet you fine ladies," he smiled that smile that won over anyone who met him.

"Nice to meet you Mr. Elliot," Edna took a step backward, "If you'll excuse me, I better get to the piano." She turned away from the group and crossed to the front of the sanctuary where she began playing *Bringing in the Sheaves*.

The Fords found their seats, and Hannah and Matty fought over who would have the privilege of sitting next to Jake. "You can both sit by me," he chuckled.

Mikalah slid in next to Matty. Hal and his family sat two pews behind the Fords. Hal fidgeted nervously as halfway through the sermon, someone came in late and squeezed in next to Laurana. Mikalah pulled Matty up onto her lap and scooted next to Jake to make room.

Mikalah felt her arm brush up against his, and her heart fluttered nervously. Jake patted Matty's cheek, and she climbed over onto his lap and nestled her blonde head into his chest as he put his arms around her shoulders. Mikalah couldn't help comparing how good Jake was with children - how quickly they took to him - in contrast to Hal who paid little attention to them.

This sent her mind off to thinking about the two men. While Hal attended church with his parents, he did so more for show than driven by any spiritual connection to God. There's no way on earth he'd offer to say a prayer, much less give one as touching as Jake's. Then there was the honesty and integrity that Jake exuded in contrast to Hal's constant desire to push the limits of propriety. She felt comfortable with Jake, exhilarated, excited, but somehow comfortable at the same time. Hal was fun and cute, but there was something about him that made her uneasy. She wasn't completely sure she could trust him. Then again, Hal had a reputable job that paid cash money, and Jake was just a drifter.

Mikalah felt an elbow in her side as her mother nudged her to stand for the closing hymn. She'd been so wrapped up in her thoughts that she'd gotten very little from the preacher's sermon. She looked over to see that Matty had fallen asleep, and Jake stood holding her with her head on his shoulder, drool running from her mouth onto Jake's shirt. Mikalah smiled and looked up to meet Jake's gaze. As he returned the smile, his eyes met hers, and once again she found herself oblivious to everything around her.

Hal cleared his throat and clenched his fist as he observed the moment between them. The chorister motioned for everyone to be seated, and the minister offered a closing prayer. As soon as the meeting concluded, Hal leapt to his feet and strode boldly toward Mikalah's pew, the starch in his white pants crackling as he walked. Hal always dressed impeccably. Jake rose, still holding Matty sound asleep on his shoulder.

"I'll walk you home, Micky" Hal stated more than asked.

"I uh..." she glanced at Jake.

"Why certainly, Hal, you come along home with us. We've got plenty of food for you to join us for lunch," Laurana offered. Oblivious to Hal's recent actions toward her daughter, she still saw him as the finest catch in town.

Jake cleared his throat, but didn't say a word. Hal grabbed Mikalah's hand and all but drug her out of the sanctuary, into the vestibule, and out the front door. Hannah and Hank ran along following them, and Jake took up the rear. Laurana stopped to talk with her lady friends.

"Can we walk a little slower, Hal? The church ain't on fire," Mikalah gave Hal a perturbed look.

"Sorry," he mumbled and slowed his pace. Soon Hank and Hannah caught up to them.

"Wait up for Mr. Elliot and Matty," Hannah said as she tapped Mikalah on the back.

Mikalah stopped walking, and turned to look back at Jake who still carried Matty asleep on his shoulder.

"Mr. Elliot, Matty can walk. There's no need to carry her the whole way," she called back. Hal still held her hand tightly and tugged it for her to continue. Irritated, she yanked her hand from his clutches and shot him a stare that told him in no uncertain terms that she wouldn't be yanked along down the road for one more second.

Mikalah turned completely around toward Jake with her fists shoved to her hips, "Mr. Elliot, put her down. She weighs a ton."

"Oh, she's as light as a feather. I hate to wake the poor little thing. Your Mama said Matty didn't sleep much last night – was up with nightmares."

The irritation began to melt from Mikalah's expression, "Oh, I didn't know that. It's very thoughtful of you to carry her."

Hal rolled his eyes and waited impatiently for her to turn around and continue walking. But she didn't. She stood still waiting for Jake to catch up and then folded her arms and continued home at Hal's side.

When they reached the house, Jake carefully carried Matty up to her bedroom and laid her on her bed, covering her lightly with a blanket. He returned downstairs just as Laurana opened the door.

Mikalah had started cooking lunch, and Laurana joined her, "Go on into the parlor with Hal, honey. Hannah and I can take care of this."

"That's all right, Mama, I'm happy to help," Mikalah wasn't in the mood to fool with Hal and hoped to hide behind the stove for awhile.

"No dear, you run along and be a good hostess," Laurana instructed.

Reluctantly, Mikalah went out into the parlor. Hal sat on a loveseat and patted the spot next to him indicating she should sit there. Instead, she sat down in a chair opposite him.

Hal hung his head, "I'm sorry Micky. I didn't mean to make you mad."

"What's the big idea draggin' me half the way home?" her voice rose in an agitated whisper.

"I don't know – I – I'm sorry," he wasn't about to say that he was jealous of the way she sat next to and looked at Jake in church.

Jake entered the parlor and plopped down in a vacant wingback chair. He crossed his legs in front of him, "Matty's still sleeping soundly. Poor little girl must have been totally exhausted."

"Thanks for takin' care of her, Mr. Elliot," an expression of gratitude spread across Mikalah's face. Hal noted the contrast in the way she looked at Jake opposed to the irritation she showed him only seconds before. He felt his blood pressure rise, and he really just wanted to throw a fist in Jake's face, but he clutched the arm of the loveseat instead and looked up at the ceiling.

Hank came into the room and stood in front of Jake, "Mr. Elliot, would you like to play a game of checkers with me?"

"I will, if everyone stops calling me, 'Mr. Elliot.' Makes me feel old. Just call me Jake please." He waved his hand from left to right, "That goes for all of you. Please just start calling me Jake."

"It's a deal," Hank agreed, "Now get over here so I can beat you at checkers," he chuckled.

Hank and Jake crossed the room between Mikalah and Hal and sat facing each other at a small table by the fireplace. They began their game. Their presence in the room put a crimp in Hal's afternoon, but was a welcome relief for Mikalah who was still in no mood to fool with him.

Laurana left a pot roast with potatoes and carrots in the oven to cook while they were at church, so after making a bit of gravy from the broth, and cooking a batch of biscuits, a delicious lunch was ready to serve with little time or effort. Like most of their neighbors, having a farm with cattle, hogs, chickens and a garden kept the Fords well fed. Many people also obtained flour and cheese from the commodity truck that came into town every now and then. People would stand in long lines to get their portion of the commodities the government provided as part of FDR's social programs. Being too proud, Laurana refused to take handouts. She insisted on trading her milk and butter for the commodities she needed at the general store.

"Come and eat, everyone," she called.

Hank jumped three of Jake's checker pieces and hopped up, "Looks like I've got ya Jake."

"Hmmm... you do, you little stinker." While Hank ran off to eat lunch, Jake sat scratching his head wondering how the boy managed to beat him. Mikalah and Hal rose from their seats and walked to the kitchen. Laurana normally let everyone just grab what they wanted from the stove, but today she instructed Hannah to set the table, and she spread everything out on the kitchen table for easy access. She only did that when they had guests and in this case, it was for impressing Hal.

Hal pulled Mikalah's chair out for her, and she sat down. He and Jake waited for Laurana to be seated and took their places on either side of Mikalah. She felt like she was sandwiched between two men as different as white bread and wheat. One of them was pretty, tasty but devoid of all nutrition while the other was golden crusted, hearty, substantial and utterly delicious. She found herself giggling at the wit of her own analogy, and quickly bit her lip. Both men looked at her wondering what she had suddenly found so humorous.

"What?" Hal asked smiling at her, relieved that her good mood had returned.

"What?" she shook her head as if she didn't know what he was talking about and then reached forward to spoon a helping of potatoes and carrots onto her plate. By now everyone expected their mother to ask Jake to say the blessing, so they sat quietly, their hands in their laps.

Mikalah noted the reserved manner of her otherwise ravenous brother and suggested, "Hal, would you like to say grace?" She couldn't resist the opportunity to get back at him. She knew he wouldn't want to.

"I uh..." he stammered, totally taken by surprise.

31

"Of course, if you don't feel comfortable saying a prayer, I'm sure Jake here will say it for us," Mikalah suggested. She couldn't resist twisting the knife.

"No, I'd be happy to say it," Hal interjected. He wasn't about to give Jake a single opportunity to get anything over on him.

He bowed his head, "Lord, bless these victuals and them that prepared it. Amen."

Mikalah bit her lip and covered her face with her hands. She fought to keep from laughing. She knew she shouldn't laugh at someone's prayer, but it only further proved to illustrate the contrast between the two men sitting on either side of her. She could hardly contain herself, so she pretended to have something in her eyes.

"Are you all right, Mikalah?" her mother asked.

"Yes, I just have something in my eye, I think," she continued to rub them as she got hold of herself. "There, I think it's out," she smiled.

Hal assumed the smile on her face indicated that she was pleased with his prayer. He had no idea that he had just dug one more shovel of dirt from the pit into which he was already sinking.

Everyone pitched in and helped clean the dishes after lunch and then relaxed on the front porch enjoying the cool breeze and perfect temperatures. They watched the people take their Sunday strolls up and down Highway 27 while Hannah and Hank sat on the porch railing counting cars. Hannah counted the ones that came up the road while Hank counted the ones that went down.

"That's two!" Hannah called out.

Jake relaxed in a rocking chair while Mikalah and Hal shared the swing. Laurana went upstairs to take a nap with Matty since the child had kept her up most of the night. Soon Jake had dozed off himself.

When he awoke a couple hours later, Hank and Hannah were playing jacks on the porch but Mikalah and Hal were no longer there. Jake rubbed his eyes and looked at the children, "Where'd everybody go?"

"Mikalah and Hal went inside. Mikalah made a cherry pie. We already had some, but we didn't want to wake you," Hannah explained.

"Go get some, Jake, it's delicious," Hank suggested.

Jake rose from his seat and yawned as he stretched his arms high above his head and rose up on his tip toes to stretch his calves. He entered the front door to see Hal sitting with his arm around Mikalah as they talked on the loveseat. He nodded at them and walked into the kitchen, grabbed a plate from the cupboard and scooped out a piece of cherry pie. He sat down at the table and began eating. As he finished he rose from his seat, put his plate on the counter, and went back to the parlor, "You sure make a fine cherry pie, Miss Mikalah," he grinned, "I could eat a whole one myself!"

"Thank you, I'm glad you enjoyed it," she grinned.

Hal put his arm tightly around her shoulder and tugged her toward him, "My girl's a good cook, ain't she, Mr. Elliot?" he beamed. Mikalah knew his words were given more in an effort to mark his domain than to pay her any form of compliment.

"Mikalah does indeed make an excellent pie," Jake agreed, but he felt almost sick to his stomach by Hal's possessive remark.

"What was the name of your church again, Jake?" Jake's head popped up suddenly by Mikalah's out-of-context question. "I was just tellin' Hal about Mama tryin' to guess your denomination earlier this morning. I thought that was so funny." She was trying to turn the attention onto someone besides herself.

He wasn't particularly interested in letting Hal know what church he belonged to since not everyone in the South took too kindly to members of his church. He had the distinct feeling that if Hal learned that he was a "Mormon," the ramifications might get ugly. Nevertheless he answered the question, "It's The Church of Jesus Christ of Latter-day Saints."

"Never heard of it," Hal stated flatly.

"Not many people around here have," Jake replied.

"Is that a more popular faith where you're from?" Mikalah asked.

"Yes, it's very common where I'm from," he answered.

"Where *are* you from anyway? You talk funny," Hal quipped, and Mikalah punched his ribs with her elbow.

"What?" he asked as he looked at her innocently with his palms up.

"I'm from Utah," Jake could feel it coming.

"Utah – I remember readin' about Utah in school. Ain't that where they have all them wives?" Hal questioned, and Mikalah's eyebrows rose.

"Not anymore," Jake replied, "That was over sixty years ago."

"Why would anyone want more'n one wife? Seems like it only takes one to nag ya clean to death," Hal laughed, and Mikalah gave him an irritated stare.

"I wouldn't know," Jake hopped up, "Mikalah, would you mind if I had another piece of that delicious cherry pie of yours?"

"Go right ahead, help yourself."

Jake walked back to the kitchen, grabbed his plate from the counter and served himself another piece. He pulled out a chair and sat at the kitchen table to eat it.

The sun was starting to set outside, and he could hear Hal from the other room, "Hey, Micky, how about a walk?"

"Oh, I don't know," she hesitated.

"Come on, let's go for a little walk 'fore it gets dark," he stood up and tugged on her hand.

"I guess so," she rose from her seat, "Let me go get my sweater; it's been turnin' cold at night." She stood up and walked around to the kitchen and up the stairs to her bedroom.

"I'll wait for you on the porch," Hal called after her and then strode out the front door.

When she came back down the stairs, she felt a hand firmly grip her arm and pull her aside toward the stove.

Startled, she bumped into Jake's chest as he pulled her to the side and out of the line of sight of the front door.

"What are you doing?" he asked her.

"Gettin' ready to go for a walk," irritation flooded her features.

"After what happened last night, do you really think that's wise?" Jake's anxious expression bordered on scolding.

"Oh, Hal's just a tease," she shook her head and then grew more irritated, "and what business is it of yours anyway?"

"I just don't think it's wise for you to be out with him alone, much less this close to dark. It doesn't feel right," he whispered.

"Mr. Elliot, I think you've forgotten for a moment who you are. You're a laborer in my mother's home. You aren't a relative. You aren't my big brother, and you ain't my daddy. I can do durn well whatever I please," she pulled her arm from his hand and spun around to leave.

"I – uh – I didn't mean to – I'm just worried about you," he didn't know what to say. He just knew that he had a bad feeling about her leaving the house with Hal.

She looked back over her shoulder to him as she stomped away, "It's not your job to worry about me, Jake Elliot. I can take care of myself."

Jake ran his hands through his hair and then shoved both of them into his pockets as he watched her walk out the front door and away with Hal.

~*~

After everyone was in bed, Jake stayed awake sitting in the parlor reading by lamp light. He was anxious to make sure that Mikalah got home all right. He had his Bible and Book of Mormon open on either side of him as he sat on the loveseat studying and cross referencing the two. A few minutes before ten o'clock he heard rustling at the front door. He could hear their conversation.

"I just feel it's best if we take a little time to see other people," Mikalah explained.

"I don't wanna see other people. I've already dated 'nough girls to know that you're the only one for me, Micky," frustration simmered in Hal's voice.

"I haven't dated anybody but you really, Hal, and I think it's better if I have more time to discover what I want from life," she tried to reason with him.

"Dang girl, you're nearly eighteen! Half the girls in Daisy's married by the time they're your age. Ain't you figured out what you want by now?"

"No, I haven't, Hal," she snipped, "Maybe I'm just slow."

"Oh, don't gimme that, Micky! You're the smartest girl in your gradiatin' class," he spat.

"Look, Hal, I just need some time, and I'd like you to give me that, please?" she tried to speak sweetly.

35

"This wouldn't happen to have anythin' to do with that feller in there would it?" Hal's jealousy was starting to seep out.

"Who?"

"That Jake fella. I saw the way you two were lookin' at each other at church this morning.'"

"Pardon me? I don't even know what you're talkin' about. You're the one who's been pushin' me to get physical, and all I'm sayin' is that I'm not ready for that yet," she was tired of this conversation and just wanted to go inside and get away from him. She jiggled the doorknob and started to open it.

Hal pulled her to him, "Lookie here, girly, I've invested a lot o' my time and hard earned money in you and all you've done is tease and egg me on and then push me away when I get close. Don't be actin' like you weren't askin' for it."

Mikalah's mouth dropped, and she slapped him across the face, "Well, Mr. Craig, you won't be needin' to spend any more of your precious time or money on me. This little friendship is over!" With that she flung open the door, closed it and bolted it behind her before Hal knew what happened.

He knocked on the door from the other side, "Oh come on, Micky," he whined, "I didn't mean it that way. I'm sorry. Don't leave me. You're the only one for me."

"Go home, Hal. I'm too mad to talk to you anymore tonight," she leaned her back against the door and closed her eyes. She didn't notice Jake sitting on the loveseat.

"Micky?"

"Go away, Hal," she breathed heavily and tears streamed down her face. Had she egged him on? Had she led him to believe that he would get physical favors by spending time and money on her? She didn't know. She certainly didn't mean to.

Jake saw Hal mope away through the parlor window, "Uh hum," he cleared his throat when Hal was gone. Mikalah startled and turned toward him, "Oh great! You!" she whispered loudly and quickly brushed the tears from her cheeks.

"I – I'm sorry. I didn't mean to eavesdrop. I was just sitting here reading my books." He lifted his scriptures that sat on his lap.

36

"Guess you heard all that then?" she asked.

"I'm afraid so. You all right?"

"Oh, I'll live," she sighed. "I just threw away the best catch in Daisy, and my Mama's gonna think I'm crazy, but I'm all right," she shook her head, chuckled and then flopped down in the chair next to the loveseat, leaning her elbow on the chair arm and resting her head on her fist.

"I'd hate to see what the worst catch would be," Jake mused aloud.

She chuckled, "Now that was funny!" She brushed the tears from her cheeks. Why did she even have tears? It wasn't like she was heartbroken. Her pride was just bruised. She was aggravated that she even had to perform the distasteful task of sending Hal away.

"Whatcha readin'?"

Jake took a book in each hand, "This is the Bible – King James Version, and this is the Book of Mormon"

"The Book of what?" she asked.

"The Book of Mormon," he repeated.

"Never heard of it. What's it about?" she yawned.

"It's a historical record of a group of people who left Jerusalem around 600 BC – during the reign of King Zedekiah. A prophet named Lehi lived in Jerusalem, and he was warned to flee the city with his family because it was about to be destroyed. He took his family into the wilderness, and they built a boat and sailed to the Americas where they continued to believe in God and record His dealings with them." Mikalah continued to listen intently so he ventured on, "After Jesus was resurrected, He appeared to them, and the account of His visit to them is recorded in this book."

"Really? So is this a fiction novel?"

"No, it's a real history book, kept by the inhabitants of the American continent – the ancestors of the Indians. It was translated by a man named Joseph Smith. It's a religious book – like the Bible," he explained.

Mikalah didn't know what to think, "So if Jesus came to America after his resurrection, how come this is the first I've heard of it?"

Jake chuckled, "It's not exactly common knowledge. No one knew about it until the 1830's when Joseph Smith translated the original historical records and printed them in book form."

"Now that's interesting," Mikalah wasn't sure what to make of this new information, "So where did Mr. Smith get the records to translate them?" She shifted her head, leaning her right elbow on the chair and her head on her fist.

"You see they engraved these records on thin sheets of golden metal and bound them together with a few rings on the end," Jake motioned with his hands to describe how the plates would have been shaped and bound on the end by rings. "They couldn't keep the records on paper cause that wouldn't have lasted through the centuries. The last prophet who kept the ancient records hid these golden plates in a hillside in New York. He showed Joseph where they were and gave him instruments to help him translate it by the power of God."

"So you're saying this ancient prophet lived on up into the 1800's, visited Joseph Smith and showed him where the records were? There were Indian prophets around in the 1800's?"

"Oh no, Moroni – the prophet who gave the records to Joseph – died about 400 years after Jesus appeared to the people."

"Then how in the world did he give the records to Mr. Smith in the 1800's?" Mikalah jumped in with her question before Jake could continue explaining.

"Moroni appeared to him as an angel and showed him where they were," Jake answered.

"An angel!" she raised her head from her fist, laughed and slapped her knees, "Oh, Jake, you're tellin' me tales. I thought you were serious there for a minute, but you're just tellin' me a bedtime story." She chuckled, "You are the funniest thing."

Jake smiled but shook his head, "No, I'm serious. I'm not telling you a bedtime story. This really happened, and I've got the book to prove it." He lifted the book up into the air. He scooted over on the loveseat and pulled his Bible onto one knee and the Book of Mormon onto the other and then patted the spot next to him, motioning for her to join him, "Come on over here, and I'll show you."

She thought he was still kidding her so without fully thinking it through she stood up and quickly sat next to him on the loveseat. She giggled, "All right, show me."

He thumbed through his Bible turning to John 10:16 and handed the Bible to her, "Could you please read that out loud for us?"

She glanced at him and then looked down and started to read, "And other sheep I have, which are not of this fold: them also I must bring, and they shall hear my voice; and there shall be one fold, and one shepherd." Mikalah looked back up at him puzzled.

"Now who's that talking there?" he asked her.

She looked back down at her Bible. "Jesus," she answered.

"Right, it was Jesus, and what is he telling them in that verse?"

Mikalah looked down and read it again, "It sounds like he's telling them that there are other people besides them who he's gonna visit."

"Right, all right, now hold on a second, and I'll give you another one," Jake thumbed through his Book of Mormon until he came to third Nephi. "This is Jesus talking to ancient Americans when he visited them. They all gathered around him by a beautiful temple that they had built, and he told them this." He handed her the book and pointed to two verses in chapter fifteen, "Please read twenty-one and twenty-four aloud."

She put the Bible on her left knee and the Book of Mormon on her right, "And verily I say unto you, that ye are they of whom I said: Other sheep I have which are not of this fold; them also I must bring, and they shall hear my voice; and there shall be one fold, and one shepherd. But behold, ye have both heard my voice, and seen me; and ye are my sheep, and ye are numbered among those whom the Father hath given me."

She flipped through the book, "Where did you get this?"

"We use the Bible and the Book of Mormon in my church," he explained.

She wasn't sure what to make of it. It was all too much information to process in one night – breaking up with Hal and then being sideswiped by Jake with a story about prophets in America – Jesus in America – and an angel, "You know, it's late. I think I better go to bed," she handed him the two books and stood up.

He extended the Book of Mormon back toward her, "Do you like to read? You want to take it, and read it yourself?"

She hesitated a moment and then had to admit that the curiosity was killing her. Not only was the story intriguing, but also it was doubly unsettling since the man she felt a growing attraction for was the one sharing this farfetched story as if it were truth.

"You mind?" she extended her hand to take it.

"I don't mind at all. I've got another one. I always keep an extra one for people to borrow," he explained.

"I guess you get a lot of people wantin' to borrow it after you tell 'em that story?"

"Actually, not as many as you'd think," he winked.

"Hmm – well 'night Jake," she yawned, covered her mouth and carried the book upstairs with her.

While Mikalah felt totally exhausted, she still laid in her bed for an hour thinking about Jake and his book. The episode with Hal was long gone from her memory. She was too busy wondering how a grown man could believe in such fairy tales about angels and golden sheets of metal. It sounded totally crazy to her. Yet – there was the book sitting on her dresser, *Of course, anyone can write a book – don't make it the truth.* Then again, she had a tough time matching up the preposterous story with the levelheadedness and compassion of the man who shared it with her. The man exuded honesty, why would he be telling her a pack of lies? *Then again, are you lyin' if you really believe it? People on the mountain believe that if a bird flies into your house, somebody's gonna die. Don't make it true, but they ain't lyin'.*

But Jake was too refined to be like the moonshiners on the mountain. He may be a drifter, but he sure didn't act, talk or think like one. Even his warning about Hal when they left for their walk turned out to be prophetic. What Jake didn't know was that Hal had pressed her again. He touched her in ways and places he had no business touching her, and she'd pulled away, running as fast as she could home. He'd caught up with her at the front porch, and the fact that the lamp was on in the parlor was probably the only thing that kept him from taking advantage of her further. It didn't add up, and her head was tired of thinking about it so she rolled onto her side and tried to push it all out of her mind.

Chapter 3

Mikalah awoke to Jake's melodious voice as he sang the same tune from the previous morning. She tossed her covers back, put her bare feet to the cool hardwood floor and crossed to the window. She stood staring down at him. He wore overalls, and his plaid shirt sleeves were rolled up slightly, exposing the arms of his white long johns. His hands worked to express the cow's milk as the melody wafted effortlessly from his vocal chords:

Stripped, wounded, beaten nigh to death,
I found him by the highway side.
I roused his pulse, brought back his breath,
Revived his spirit, and supplied
Wine, oil, refreshment – he was healed.
I had myself a wound concealed,
But from that hour forgot the smart,
And peace bound up my broken heart.

Jake sensed that he was being watched. He stopped, looked around and then glanced up to the window where she stood in her nightgown. She smiled and waved at him, and he nodded, grinning back at her. She backed away from the window toward her dresser to where the book he'd given her lay. She traced the engraved lettering on its cover. It was Jake's personal copy for his name was also engraved in the lower right corner: *Jacob Allen Elliot.* She ran her finger along his name, *What in the world am I doing? He's crazy, that's all there is to it. He's got bizarre beliefs, and he's pulling me into his delusions.*

She tossed the book onto her bed in frustration, grabbed her comb and started fixing her hair and changed into her work dress. As she started to leave the room, she noticed that the book had landed open. She sat on the edge of her bed, pulled the book onto her lap and read the marked passage on the open page:

41

"And when ye shall receive these things, I would exhort you that ye would ask God, the Eternal Father in the name of Christ, if these things are true; and if ye shall ask with a sincere heart, with real intent, having faith in Christ, he will manifest the truth of it unto you, by the power of the Holy Ghost. And by the power of the Holy Ghost ye may know the truth of all things. And whatsoever thing is good is just and true; wherefore, nothing that is good denieth the Christ, but acknowledgeth that he is."(Moroni 10:4-6)

Mikalah sat pondering on the passage, *just and true – whatsoever is good is just and true. Those words fit Jake – just and true.* She closed the book and unconsciously ran her fingers along his name. She gently placed it beside her on the bed, stood and walked downstairs.

By the time Mikalah made it to the kitchen table everyone gathered around eating breakfast. Jake glanced briefly in Mikalah's direction and then his eyes turned to her mother, "Would you like for me to chop that last hickory tree into firewood? Or do you have something else you'd like me to do today?"

"The wood choppin' can wait 'til another day. We've got so many apples ready for pickin' out there, we could use another hand. Would you join us in the orchard this mornin' so we can get the apples in?

"I'd be happy to."

"Wait until you taste Micky's apple pie, Jake! It's the best thing ever!" Hank chimed in.

"I don't know how it could be any better than what she made yesterday!" Jake smiled at Mikalah, and she felt that familiar flutter she always felt when his gaze was directed at her.

"Micky's apple pies win first prize every year at the county fair," Hannah bragged on her older sister.

"That's right the fair is this Saturday!" Mikalah smiled

"The bus is comin'!" Matty stood watch at the front door. Hank and Hannah kissed their mother simultaneously on either cheek, grabbed their books, and ran out the door and down the drive.

"You're gonna love the fair, Jake. Hank always enters one of his hogs, Mikalah makes pies, and I enter preserves. There's races and games and good food," Laurana described.

"I'm lookin' forward to it," he smiled.

"I bet you could win the strongest man contest," Matty squeezed Jake's bicep, "You're the biggest, strongest man I ever seen."

Jake brushed her cheek with the back of his hand, "And you're the prettiest little girl I've ever seen." He winked at her, and her smile brightened from ear to ear.

"Let's get these dishes done so we can get out there and pick some apples," Laurana instructed. Laurana scraped the scraps from the breakfast plates into a bucket, "Here, Jake, give this bucket of scraps to the hogs for me, please."

"Yes Ma'am," Jake took the bucket from her and walked outside, his boots clomping across the hardwood floor.

"So how was your date with Hal last night, Mikalah?" her mother asked excitedly. "You weren't home until late. Is that boy about ready to pop the question?"

"No, Mama," Mikalah shook her head.

"Why not? He won't find anybody prettier or smarter than you!"

"That's not it, Mama. We – we broke up," Mikalah's face remained emotionless.

"He broke up with you?" her mother was incredulous, "That boy must have rocks for brains!"

"No, *I* broke up with *him*," Mikalah closed her eyes bracing herself for her mother's rebuttal.

"What? Why in heaven's name would you break up with the most eligible bachelor in town? Why, that boy makes cash money, Mikalah!"

"I don't love him," she answered.

"You don't love him? Do you think I loved your daddy when I married him? Why no! He was a good provider. I thought he'd make a good daddy for my children, and he treated me right. That's why I married him. Love came later. You can learn to love anybody, Mikalah," her mother lectured.

"Mama, Hal doesn't treat me right. He won't make a good daddy to my children, and I don't think I could ever learn to love a man I don't respect. Frankly, I don't see why I should have to!" Mikalah was angry now.

43

Her mother could only stare, her steel blue eyes widening, her mouth dropped open as Mikalah stormed out of the kitchen leaving her mother to do the dishes alone. She scooped Matty up from her game of jacks on the front porch and carried her to the barn.

"Let's go pick some apples, Matty," she set Matty down, selected three buckets from the barn, gave one to her little sister and carried the other two toward the apple orchard.

Jake noticed Mikalah stomping off to the orchards as he came back into the house. He found Laurana with her elbows on the kitchen table, and her head in her hands.

"Everything all right, Mrs. Ford?" he asked.

"Oh, that girl o' mine – don't ever have daughters, Jake. They'll drive ya plum crazy." She rubbed both her graying temples with her fingertips and then stood up and sighed, "Let's go pick some apples."

Jake followed Mrs. Elliot out to the barn where they each selected two buckets and headed toward Mikalah and Matty in the orchard. Mikalah had already climbed high up into a tree and was putting apples in the bucket hung in the crook of her arm. Matty sat at the bottom of the tree eating an apple. Jake patted her head, "Those good apples, Matty?"

"Yummy!" the child grinned from ear to ear.

While Laurana found a tree as far away from Mikalah as she could, Jake climbed up into the tree beside Mikalah's and started putting apples in the bucket that hung on his arm. He could see that she was still irritated, "You all right, Mikalah?"

"Oh, I'll live," she huffed.

"I didn't figure you were dyin'. But you sure look mad enough to spit nails," he chuckled.

A smile started to form on the corners of her mouth. She enjoyed just looking at him. *"What a specimen of manliness!"* the phrase her grandmother always used when she saw a handsome man floated through her mind. "Mama's just mad that I broke up with Hal," she confided.

"Ah, did you tell her why?" he asked.

"I told her I didn't love him," she answered.

44

"And what did she say?"

"She basically told me that I was a fool for throwin' away the best catch in town and that I could learn to love anybody. She said she didn't love my daddy when they married and that she grew to love him. You think that's true, Jake?"

"What? That your mother didn't love your daddy at first?"

"No, do you think it's true that love doesn't matter when you're decidin' who to marry 'cause you can learn to love anybody?" she personally found the whole idea totally unromantic.

"I think that people can learn to love each other, but I would like to think that the girl I ask to marry me will agree to it because she loves me, not because of any possessions or prospects I may have," Jake answered honestly.

"Thank you!" she flung her hand, palm side up, into the air as she held onto the tree limb with the other. "I'm so happy that someone sees things the way I do!" she rolled her eyes and shook her head. "This whole idea of marryin' for money or property just seems so – so – what's the word I'm looking for?"

"Cold," he offered.

"Yes, *exactly* – cold and heartless. I mean really, did Jesus say, "I'll love you *if* you dress fine or I'll love you *if* you have money or *if* you take me places and buy me things?"

"No, he didn't," Jake agreed. He liked the way this girl thought. He looked down to the base of the tree, "Where's Matty?"

Mikalah looked around, "I don't know. Maybe she went back to the house?"

"There she is, she's climbed up in a tree over yonder," he pointed to a tree about three rows over. "Should she be climbing that high?"

"She does it all the time," Mikalah shrugged her shoulders. Then she and Jake both gasped and instantly Jake descended the tree in one drop. He let the bucket fall from his arm, tipping apples along the ground, as he ran to where Matty lay at the base of the tree.

"Matty! Matty! Mama, come quick! Matty's fallen!" Mikalah screamed as she ran to join Jake at Matty's side. Laurana approached the little lifeless body, "What happened?" she cried.

45

"Matty's fallen from the tree," Mikalah knelt next to Matty who lay flat on her back, a half eaten apple lying on the ground next to her little hand.

"She's not breathing," Jake's face was ashen as he looked up at Mikalah. He knelt holding Matty's head in his hand. He began to pray in his mind for help to know what to do. Then he tipped her on her side and rubbed her stomach and her back. As he applied pressure, Matty began to cough and expelled apple pieces that had been blocking her air passage. She gasped, coughing and breathing.

"Thank the Lord!" Laurana looked heavenward as she knelt next to her child. But Matty was still unconscious. Jake tapped lightly on Matty's cheeks, "Matty, honey, wake up – Matty." When she didn't stir, Jake looked to Laurana, "Is there a doctor in town?"

"Yes, Dr. Allen," she answered, "Mikalah, run as fast as you can to where Mr. Morton's working' at his new house, and ask him to ride over in his truck and fetch Doc Allen."

Mikalah brushed the tears from her eyes, stood and started running toward the Morton's. Jake examined Matty's arms and legs. "I don't believe there's anything broken. But there's already a lump forming on the back of her head here."

Jake picked Matty up into his arms and carried her inside the house, "Take her on up to her bedroom, Jake" Laurana directed, wiping the tears from her cheeks.

Jake and Laurana sat on either side of the bed and held Matty's hands, but the little girl didn't stir. The minutes dragged on until finally they heard Mikalah call out from downstairs, "Mama! Where are you? The doctor's here!"

Laurana stood and walked to the doorway, "We're up here in Matty's room!"

Mikalah ascended the stairs – taking two at a time, "Did she wake up?"

"No, she's still out cold," the anxious expression on Laurana's face made her look significantly older than her forty years.

Jake stood as Mikalah and the doctor entered the room. Dr. Allen sat on the edge of Matty's bed and pulled back her eyelids to examine her eyes. "Mikalah told me what happened," he checked her limbs and torso. "Nothing seems to be broken."

46

"She's got a nasty bump on her head," Jake pointed.

The doctor felt her head, "Let's put some ice on that. Mrs. Ford, do you have a water bottle?

"Yes."

"Fill it with ice and hold it to the back of her head for a while," the doctor stood.

"Aren't you gonna do anything for her?" Laurana was frantic.

"There's not much we can do but wait until she wakes up. Let's give her a few hours to see how it goes, and if she's not awake by this afternoon, we'll take her to the hospital in Chattanooga. Right now, I think it's best to move her as little as possible. I'll stay here at your house, and we'll watch her for a while."

Mikalah, Laurana and the doctor took shifts watching Matty and holding the ice to the lump on her head. When it was Mikalah's turn, Laurana went downstairs to make lunch, and the doctor joined her. Mikalah sat on her bed, propped the ice to Matty's head with a pillow and held her hand, "Come on Matty, wake up." Tears rolled down her cheeks. Matty was Mikalah's little pet. She doted on her, dressed her up and felt like she was practically her own little girl. It was killing her to see Matty this way.

Jake stood watching them in the doorway. His left arm hung by his fingertips on the door frame above his head as he leaned on his right shoulder. He quickly turned and went downstairs to find Laurana cooking in the kitchen as the doctor sat in the parlor reading a newspaper.

"Mrs. Ford," he spoke softly.

"Yes, Jake," she turned to glance up at him and then looked back to the tomatoes she sliced.

"Would you mind if I gave Matty a – if I prayed over her?" he asked.

"Oh, how kind of you, Jake! You are a good boy," she put her hand on his arm. "Go right on up there and say a prayer for our little Matty. I have a feeling the Lord listens intently to your sweet prayers."

"Thank you, ma'am," he nodded and strode up the stairs, taking two at a time.

He walked into the room where Mikalah still sat holding her little sister's hand. He knelt in front of Mikalah and brushed the tears from her face with the back of his hand, "I asked your Mama if I could give Matty a blessing, and she said it would be fine."

"Give her a blessing?"

"Yes, it's a prayer of healing."

He pulled a small vile of oil from a pocket in his overalls and put a dab on the top of Matty's head.

"What's that?" Mikalah asked.

"It's olive oil. It's been consecrated for the healing of the sick," he explained.

Then he placed both of his hands on top of Matty's head and began to pray aloud. He blessed her with healing, strength and a speedy recovery along with a long and happy life. His prayer was so beautiful that there were fresh tears rolling down Mikalah's face by the time he finished.

As he concluded, he lifted his hands from Matty's head and turned toward Mikalah. He brushed the tears from her cheeks, "She'll be all right, Mikalah. She's going to be just fine." A warm feeling spread throughout Mikalah's body from head to toe. She didn't know why, but she knew what he said was true. From that point forward she felt a peaceful assurance that Matty would recover.

Jake stood, "I'm going to go pick some apples. Let me know when she wakes up." She watched him walk out of the room and thought about what an unusual man he was – handsome, strong, sensitive and spiritual. She'd never met anyone like him, and yet she wondered about his odd beliefs. In practice they were so sweet and soothing – like the blessing he just gave Matty, but in theory they still seemed strange.

Mikalah moved from Matty's bedside to sit in a chair next to her. She leaned over and rested her head on her folded arms on the side of Matty's bed. Soon, she drifted off to sleep.

Mikalah awoke to someone stroking her hair, "Micky, whatcha sleepin' in here for?" Mikalah looked up to see that the tiny voice that addressed her came from her little sister.

"Matty!" Mikalah flung her arms around Matty and embraced her, "You're awake!"

48

"Uh huh," Matty expression puzzled at all the fuss.

"Do you remember falling out of the apple tree?"

Matty searched her memory, "No, I wemember climbin' up and weachin' for a big juicy wed apple, but I don't wemember nothin' 'bout fallin'"

"Honey, you fell out of the tree, and we thought we'd never wake you!" Mikalah straightened up so that her voice would carry through the house, "Mama! Jake! Come quick! Matty's awake!"

Footsteps pounded up the stairs, and Laurana appeared in the doorway, "Matty!" She ran to her little girl and hugged her, kissing her cheek, "My sweet little Matty! How do you feel?"

"She doesn't remember fallin', Mama," Mikalah explained.

"You don't?" Laurana shook her head.

"No," Matty answered.

"That's just as well. No need for a traumatic memory rattlin' around in your pretty little head," Laurana breathed a sigh of relief as she continued to hold Matty in her arms. "Do you hurt anywhere?"

"My head hotes."

"How 'bout your arms or legs or anywhere else," Laurana patted Matty's limbs as she spoke.

"No, just my head," she answered.

"Where's Jake?" Mikalah asked.

"He's outside in the orchard. Sweet boy's trying to make sure we have some apples to put up," Laurana answered, "Why don't you go get him? And send the doctor up. He stepped outside for a few moments."

Mikalah rose from her seat, bent down to kiss Matty's cheek and then left the room. After letting the doctor know that Matty was awake, she went to the orchard and found Jake high in an apple tree, a bucket full of red apples hanging on his arm. She strode to the base of the tree and looked up at him, "Jake, come on down. Matty's awake!"

"She is?" joy filled his countenance. "I'll be right down." He descended the tree with as little effort as someone stepping off a stool. He sat on a lower limb and leaned down to hand Mikalah the bucket, "Here take this, please, so I don't spill it."

She grabbed the bucket from him and placed it on the ground, "Boy this is heavy!"

He hung upside down from the tree limb by his knees and then flipped over onto the ground, landing on his feet. He put his hands on Mikalah's shoulders, "So she woke up? Is she all right?"

"She seems as right as rain," she smiled.

He was so happy that without thinking he wrapped his arms around her, giving her a big hug, "I just knew she'd be all right!" he chuckled.

Mikalah hugged him back and then looked up into his emerald eyes, "Thank you Jake. Thank you for all you did for her – for saving her life and for the prayer."

His eyes smiled into hers as he continued to hold her in his arms, "Don't thank me. Just thank the Lord for his goodness and mercy. He did all the work."

"I think he had a little help from a mortal man," she winked. *At least I think you're mortal* she thought to herself.

"Let's go see her," he released her, and they walked side by side to the house.

~*~

The doctor prescribed bed rest for Matty and instructed that someone check on her every hour. Laurana stayed in the house, and Mikalah and Jake went back to the orchards to bring in the crop. They worked together gleaning the apples, enjoying each other's company. Hours passed as she quizzed him about what it was like to grow up in the west, and he asked her about her father and what life was like with him at home.

They chatted at great length without their conversation turning to anything of a religious nature until finally Mikalah broached the subject, "So, how did you come to believe in angels and the Book of Mormon?"

"I was raised to believe it so it doesn't seem odd like it probably does to you, but I do remember a time when I was about fifteen when I had a bit of a crisis of faith."

Mikalah's eyebrow rose in curiosity.

50

"I started looking at our beliefs from the perspective of say — someone like you. I tried to imagine what it would be like not to be raised in our faith, and I began to see how hard it all might be to take – how hard to swallow it might be."

She nodded her head. She knew what he was talking about.

He continued, "The more I thought about it, the more I realized that I just believed it all because I'd always been taught to believe it. I decided that I really didn't know if it was true or not."

She was surprised, "So what did you do?"

"I did what it says to do in James 1:5, *If any of you lack wisdom, let him ask of God, which giveth to all men liberally and upbraideth not and it shall be given him.* I read the Book of Mormon, I studied and pondered on it. Then I knelt down in my bedroom one night and prayed and asked God if it was true or whether it was just something I'd been fed my whole life."

He looked over at her as she sat on the next limb, her eyes riveted on him. "And…" she coaxed anxiously.

"I got my answer."

"What was it? How do you know you got an answer?" She wanted to know how one could be certain God was really speaking to him.

"I just knew it was true. It was as if pure light flowed through me, and I was warmed from head to toe as if someone poured hot chocolate through my soul," his eyes glistened as he remembered the occasion. Mikalah thought how she had felt earlier that day. She'd felt the very same sensation.

"So how do you know that that feeling is God speaking to you and not you just wanting to believe that somethin's true?"

"Well…" he began.

"I mean I felt that way today after you prayed over Matty, and you told me she would be all right. I felt that same warm feeling and I – I just knew that it was true. But how do I know that wasn't just wishful thinking that happened to work out?"

"Have you every felt that feeling before, Mikalah?"

"Not that I can recall."

"Have you ever wished and hoped something would happen and felt good about it? Maybe even if later on it may or may not have happened the way you hoped?"

"Yes"

"Did it feel the same way that it did today? Did you have the same warm feeling when you only wished something was true?"

"No, it's not the same."

"Did you have an overpowering knowledge when you only wished for something?"

"No," she answered, a light of recognition flickering in her eyes.

"The Book of Mormon says that *by the power of the Holy Ghost you may know the truth of all things.*"

"Yes! I read that today," she smiled at the impressed expression on his face. He was surprised that she'd read anything from the book already.

"Then if the Holy Ghost tells you the truth of all things, then it's important to know what the Holy Ghost feels like – right?"

"Yes" she agreed.

"We find that out in Galatians 5:22-23 where it says, *But the fruit of the Spirit is love, joy, peace, longsuffering, gentleness, goodness, faith, meekness, temperance: against such there is no law.* So if you feel any of those things, then you know that the Holy Ghost is present and is testifying of the truthfulness of whatever you are seeking an answer for."

"You make it all sound so simple," she smiled.

"You know, it really is. We make it all a lot more complicated than it has to be," his eyes twinkled as he dropped two more apples into the bucket. He looked down as he ran his hand along the ripe fruit, "Looks like my bucket's full."

"Mine too," she noted. "Let's take these inside and see how Matty's doin'," she suggested. "Hank and Hannah should be gettin' home from school soon, and they can help."

~*~

After a long day of apple picking, Hank, Hannah, Jake and Mikalah sat on the front porch surrounded by buckets of apples. Hank and Hannah sat on the floor of the porch sorting those that had worms or blemishes from those of higher quality. Mikalah and Jake took the better apples, wrapped them in newspaper and stacked them in baskets.

"This basket's full," Mikalah noted.

"I'll take it on down to the cellar," Jake hefted the basket onto his shoulder and carried it into the house. Apples would keep this way all winter. The ones with blemishes would be cleaned, cut and canned in jars to make applesauce, pies and cobblers throughout the coming year.

"Can you believe how he lifted that huge basket of apples like it was nothin' more than a sack o' flour?" Hannah commented after Jake left hearing range.

"I know! I believe he's just about the strongest man I've ever seen," Hank agreed.

"I think you need to marry Jake," Hannah giggled as she winked at her older sister.

"What? Now you're just bein' silly!" Mikalah acted as if Hannah's idea was totally preposterous. Yet she had to admit to herself that something about the notion appealed to her.

"Yeah, Jake's ten times the man a' that wimpy Hal Craig," Hank scrunched his nose as if he'd caught a whiff of a skunk.

They could hear Jake's heavy boots as he strode across the hardwood floor toward them.

"Shh — you two," Mikalah shot them a stern look.

Jake sat down in his rocker next to Mikalah, grabbed an apple, wrapped it and placed it in the basket, "How many days does it usually take to bring in all the apples and preserve them?"

"Oh, it takes several. We'll can these tomorrow morning, and then we'll spend the afternoon pickin' more. Mama usually likes to dry some of them too. We'll probably be workin' apples for a week or two."

"I get so sick of apples by November every year, but I'm always happy to have them again come fall," Hannah chuckled.

"Jake can you help me load Big Ed into Mr. Donaldson's truck on Saturday for the fair? He's the biggest hog I've raised yet. I bet I'll have a chance o' winnin' a blue ribbon this year with him."

"I'd be happy to. He is a monster. You must be putting something special in his slop!"

"He likes Micky's cherry pie," Hank snickered.

"Hank! You're not givin' that hog my cherry pie?" Mikalah exclaimed. A mischievous smile spread across the boy's face.

"Hank, that borders on sin, my boy," Jake shook his head.

"Nah… I ain't givin' Big Ed the cherry pie. You think I'd share a piece o' that perfect pie with a hog?!" Hank teased. "I just like to get Micky's goat."

Mikalah reached out and flicked the back of Hank's head with her finger.

~*~

Mikalah picked up the Book of Mormon and tossed it gently to the foot of her bed, pulled down her comforter and sheets and nestled in for the night. She grabbed the book from the foot of the bed, opened it to the introduction and began reading.

~*~

The sights, sounds and smells of the county fair hit Mikalah's senses as she stepped off the school bus, and the gravel crunched under her feet. Throngs of people descended on the Chattanooga Fair Grounds for the big event. The odor of fried pies, hay, and livestock combined to create the distinctive fair aroma. Mikalah carefully held a freshly baked apple pie in her hands. Hannah held Matty's hand, and Laurana followed close behind with her jars of preserves in a brown paper sack tucked snug under her arm. Jake and Hank left early with Mr. Donaldson who owned the Home Store in Daisy. Mr. Donaldson kindly agreed to give "Big Ed" a ride to the fair along with his own livestock. The girls would meet Jake and Hank later at the hog pen.

The ladies made their way past a myriad of booths displaying handmade crafts and furniture to the tables where the pies and preserves would be judged later that afternoon. Mikalah filled out the entry card for her pie and handed it to the volunteer who assigned it a number and included it with a group of other entries in the apple pie category. She thanked the volunteer and turned to amble through the booths, admiring the work of artisans and craftsmen.

As she strolled past a storage tent, Mikalah suddenly felt a strong hand grab her from behind, covering her mouth. A second arm bound her arms tightly to her chest and pulled her into the storage tent.

"Well, well, fancy meetin' you here, Micky," the familiar voice chuckled. "How about a little kiss?" Still holding her from behind, Hal kissed Mikalah's neck and shoulders as she wiggled to free herself.

"What? Don't want my kisses anymore Micky?" he feigned disappointment.

Mikalah stomped his toe with her heel, and he released his grip on her mouth, "Let me go, Hal Craig!" she demanded.

Hal regained his composure, his toe still throbbing with pain. He seized her by the shoulders and spun her around to face him, pulling her against him.

"Let go of me Hal. I told you it's over between us," she struggled to free herself, but to no avail. His strong arms held her bound against him.

The evil glint in his eye startled her, and she screamed for help as he flung her against a stack of crates. She screamed one more time, and he clamped his hand over her mouth.

"If you can't be quiet..." he pulled a scarf from his pocket and shoved it in her mouth. She struggled and gasped to spit it out as he pulled down the shoulder of her blouse. "Now, Micky, you know you're mine. I've pert near bought and paid for ya. So you just stop your strugglin' and enjoy yourself."

As Hal's sickening kiss made its way over her shoulder, the flap of the tent flung wide, and Jake stormed straight toward them. He pulled Hal off her and plunged his curled fist squarely into Hal's nose.

Hal fell backward onto an adjacent stack of crates, his hands clutching his nose. Shock, fear, then anger crossed Hal's face as blood poured into his hands, "You broke my nose!" he whined angrily.

"You better get outa here before I break every bone in your body," fury rose in Jake's expression as he curled his fist again and made his way toward Hal. Hal put up his hand, "I'm goin', I'm goin'"

As Jake allowed him to pass, Hal turned and punched Jake forcefully in the stomach. Jake bent over and then leaned into Hal with his head, driving him across the tent and onto the floor. Jake sat on top of Hal's chest and punched him in the face, busting his lip.

"All right! All right! I'll leave!" Hal pleaded for mercy.

"You're right you're leavin'!" Jake stood, yanked Hal up off the floor by his shoulders, carried him to the door and flung him onto the ground outside the tent, "If I ever – ever see you lay a finger on Mikalah again, you'll find your dinner served through the bars of a jail cell."

Jake stood over Hal as he fell on his hands and knees, wiping the blood from his nose and mouth. He crawled a few feet and then pulled himself up to slink away.

Jake rushed back to Mikalah. He adjusted her blouse to cover her exposed shoulder, and held her arms in his hands as he searched her eyes, "Are you all right? Did he harm you?"

"I'm fine. But if you hadn't come in when you did — I think, I think he meant to…"

"Don't even think about it," he gazed into her baby blue eyes as he dried the tears from her cheeks and then hugged her. "It's all right now, nobody's going to hurt you," he whispered into her ear.

In the warmth of his embrace the fear began to evaporate and a sense of security spread throughout her body.

"You're trembling. Are you sure you're all right?" he pulled back to search her eyes.

"I'm – I'll be fine," she stammered. He kissed her forehead as he continued to comfort her in his arms. Mikalah leaned back, staring up into his emerald eyes. At that moment she realized that this was the first time in her life that she wished a man would kiss her. Every other kiss she'd returned was because she felt it was expected, not because she wanted it. But now —

Time seemed to stand still for Jake as he gazed into Mikalah's face. Her blue eyes welcomed him and the strawberry blonde curls framing her porcelain features further accentuated her lips. Their color reminded him of the bright red apples they'd been picking all week. In that moment, Jake forgot that he was a laborer in her mother's home. He didn't care that he'd just given Hal a bloody nose and lip. He forgot everything but the way this girl made him feel – the melody of her voice, the sound of her laughter, the way she climbed an apple tree and the feel of her arms clinging to him for security at that moment.

He leaned forward and gently kissed the tears from her cheeks. She turned toward him as she sought out his mouth with her own. He instinctively met hers, and his kiss was just as she knew it would be – perfect, warm, and loving. It was nothing like she had experienced before, and for the first time in her life she allowed herself to truly return a kiss and not simply be the object of one. She slid her arms around his neck and ran her fingers through his wavy brown hair.

Reluctantly Jake pulled from her, "I'm – I'm sorry, Mikalah. I shouldn't have," he closed his eyes and shook his head.

"Why?" the word came from her mouth before she had time to think about it.

"After what you've just been through – I just shouldn't have." Mikalah's heart pained with the expression of guilt on his face. How could something that bound up and healed her heart make him feel so guilty?

Her hands slipped from the back of his head to his cheeks, "Jake, I'm fine. It's all right."

"I'm sorry, I shouldn't have taken advantage of your vulnerability," he continued.

"Please…please don't apologize," she pleaded.

Mikalah's heart sank as she saw the resolve infuse his chiseled features. He thought it was a mistake. The one man she felt connected to and respected – the one man whom she'd ever been able to thoroughly kiss - felt it a mistake to have touched her.

"We better find your family," he mumbled as he released himself from her embrace and guided her to the door with his hand lightly touching her arm. Mikalah still tingled from the warmth of his lips on hers, but she doubted she would ever feel them there again. The look on his face was too resolute. What was for her a moment of bliss was for him only a moment of weakness. Another tear rolled down her cheek, and she brushed it away as the sun hit her eyes.

Chapter 4

As Jake and Hank helped Mr. Donaldson unload the last of the livestock back into their pens, Mr. Donaldson turned to Jake and pulled his wallet from his back pocket, "You boys were a big help to me today. I'd like to give you a little somethin' for helpin' out." Mr. Donaldson was impressed with Jake as he'd spent the morning and afternoon with him.

Hank eagerly put out his hand to receive the coin. "Wow, thank you, Mr. Donaldson!"

Jake waved his hand, "No thank you, Mr. Donaldson. I just appreciate you giving us a ride for Big Ed."

"Oh, that was nothing. You boys worked hard loading and unloading. I want to repay you somehow," Mr. Donaldson started back into his wallet to insist that Jake take something for his work.

"Well…" Jake hesitated to ask for what he really wanted.

"Go ahead, Jake," Donaldson coaxed.

"Would it be too much to ask to let me borrow your truck sometime on a Sunday? My church is in downtown Chattanooga, and I haven't been able to attend in so long because the buses don't run to Chattanooga on Sunday."

"I'll do one better, Jake. You stop by my house tomorrow morning, and I'll let you borrow my Chevrolet," Donaldson offered cheerily.

"Oh, I don't want to take your good car. The truck would be fine."

"Nonsense, Jake, take the car," Donaldson insisted.

"Thank you so much Mr. Donaldson. I really appreciate it." It had been months since Jake had been to his own church, and there was no amount of money that could replace what Mr. Donaldson had just offered him.

~*~

Jake sat on his cot and pulled off his boots, letting them drop to the floor. He unbuttoned his shirt and tossed it on the chair next to him. He leaned his elbows on his knees and ran his fingers through his hair. What had he been thinking? He never should have kissed her. Now everything was complicated. How would he ever shield his heart now?

After the last family he introduced to the gospel – the O'Neals — decided to stay with tradition, his heart had broken. They were so close – so close to embracing all the blessings the restored gospel had to offer. Even though they were receptive to the things Jake taught them, family tradition and old habits were too hard to break. In their minds, it was easier to leave things as they were than to commit to a new religion – a new way of life – especially with so little support for them in Tennessee where the Church was so weak. But Jake still hoped that one day –

When it was time for him to leave Athens, he headed toward Chattanooga and felt led to the little town of Daisy. Jake thought of that first day he passed the Ford's two-story yellow house with the white trim and shutters. While the yard was neatly kept, Jake noticed the two dead hickory trees and that the house could use a coat of paint. He felt drawn to the cozy home and strode boldly to the door and offered his services in exchange for room and board.

As Jake became familiar with the family, he determined that this time would be different. If the opportunity presented itself to share his beliefs, he would. But he wouldn't get tied to any outcome. This time he wouldn't allow his heart to feel the pain of watching people he loved refuse the gift. It would have been one thing if the O'Neals hadn't believed it to be true, but they knew it was. They just weren't willing to change. That fact broke Jake's heart. From now on he determined that he would see himself as a sower of seeds. Seeds take time to grow, and he couldn't – he wouldn't expect them to bear fruit overnight – not this time.

Jake's mind returned to the Sunday night that Mikalah came home late with Hal. It all flowed so naturally and effortlessly to explain his beliefs to her. Then there was the day Matty fell and the long talks he'd had with Mikalah in the orchard or as they sat out on the front porch each night for the last week working on apples. Mikalah had been reading the book he'd given her. She was asking questions and learning. Jake could see the transformation in her eyes – doubt was gradually turning into consideration and in many respects belief.

Now today, he'd muddied the water by kissing her. He scolded himself – what was he thinking? He wasn't thinking. He was feeling. Her simple presence in the room energized him. He loved talking with her for hours on end, listening to her perceptions of what she was learning and sharing insights with her.

Jake's determination to shield his heart had failed. Today's actions showed him that he'd already started to give his heart to Mikalah without even realizing it. But he had resolved long ago that he would never become romantically involved with someone who did not share his beliefs. He wouldn't pressure her to change her belief system for him, yet at the same time he wouldn't let the relationship go further if she didn't. At that moment he realized just how selfish he was being – it was Mikalah's heart that was at risk.

It was a fine mess he'd made of the situation. Both of them were bound to get hurt unless a miracle happened. But experience had taught him not to hope for overnight miracles where other people's agency was concerned. His decision was made. It wouldn't be right for him to lead her on in hopes that she would accept his beliefs. He'd guard his impulses better from now on. He could talk with her, but he could never touch her again.

~*~

Mikalah laid her first place blue ribbon on her dresser. Her pie had won again this year, and Big Ed earned Hank a blue ribbon as well. Laurana's preserves received a second place ribbon. She still hadn't perfected her pear preserves to beat Mrs. Samples from Ooltewah. But Laurana was happy nonetheless. Overall it was a day of victories, but Mikalah couldn't shake the melancholy feeling that washed over her all afternoon and into the evening.

She lay on her bed replaying the events in the storage tent – avoiding the memories of Hal and focusing on Jake. She'd never experienced anything like what she felt for Jake, but somehow it was tainted by the look of guilt and sorrow on his face after their embrace. Why had he pulled from her in such an odd way?

All afternoon he was his usual charming self, but she noticed he kept his distance from her. He didn't so much as brush against her arm, but carried Matty around the fair grounds on his shoulders most of the time. Hank and Hannah had even talked him into seeing how strong he was. He slammed the hammer and rang the bell three times in a row and gave Matty the small stuffed animal he won. He barely made eye contact with Mikalah all afternoon.

Maybe he didn't care for her the way she did him? Perhaps it was just a moment of weakness – after all she really instigated the kiss. He might not have given her more than a peck on the cheek. Maybe he was feeling bad because he'd given into physical desires when he really didn't see her in that way?

Her thoughts were interrupted by a light tap on her door.

"Yes, who is it?" Mikalah asked.

"It's me – Jake," his deep voice spoke from the other side.

"Jake?" was he really outside her bedroom door now? Her heart leapt into an accelerated rhythm.

"Yes, don't open your door. I just need to ask you something that I forgot," he stood there barefoot with his plaid shirt hanging open loosely over his long johns.

Mikalah threw back her covers and walked to the door, but didn't open it, "Yes?"

"Mr. Donaldson is letting me borrow his car tomorrow so I can attend the Latter-day Saint church in Chattanooga. Would you like to go with me?"

"I'd love to. Thank you for asking," she answered, excited to see what the church she was learning about was like.

"Great, I'll go get the car in the morning, and we'll leave around eight," he explained.

"I'll be ready," she smiled.

"Good night, Mikalah,"

"Good night, Jake," she hopped back into her bed excited not only for the opportunity to see what the church was like, but also to ride into Chattanooga and spend the morning with Jake.

Mikalah's mind was a whirl. So many thoughts, feelings and questions were running through it that it took a full hour to find sleep.

~*~

Jake rose early to feed the animals and milk the cows without waking Hank. As he milked Bessy, Hank joined him, "You're up early!"

"I wanted to get the chores done so I could ride into Chattanooga for church this morning. Mikalah said she'd like to go, do you think the rest of the family would like to join us?"

Hank's eyes lit up, "Yes! Ask Mama, Jake. I'd love to go for a ride in Mr. Donaldson's car!"

Jake chuckled. He realized that Hank didn't care about where they were going. He just wanted to go for a ride. "I'll ask her then." Jake carried a pail of steaming milk to the kitchen, "Good morning, Mrs. Ford."

"Good morning, Jake!"

"Mr. Donaldson is letting me borrow his Chevrolet today to go to church in Chattanooga. Mikalah and Hank said they'd like to go. I'd be happy to drive the whole family if you'd care to go," Jake offered as Hank strode up beside him and anxiously awaited his mother's response.

"That would be an awfully lot of us to cram into Mr. Donaldson's car. Why don't you take Mikalah, Hank and Hannah, and I'll take Matty to church here in Daisy."

"Oh, we can squeeze in, Mama. You don't want to pass up a chance to ride in Mr. Donaldson's car do ya?" Hank coaxed his mother.

"It's a long ride to Chattanooga. Just being there yesterday, I really don't feel up to ridin' back all crammed in. Maybe another time."

"All right. I'll get dressed and then go get the car," Jake turned and walked to the storage room. "Hank, please make sure Mikalah and Hannah know we need to leave at eight."

"Will do!" Hank ran up the stairs to wake Hannah and Mikalah.

~*~

After breakfast, Jake approached a loaf of bread on the counter, "Mrs. Ford, would you mind if I took a couple slices of bread?"

"Why heaven's, Jake, take anything you want! No need to ask."

"Thank you, ma'am," Jake wrapped the slices in brown paper and slid them into his coat pocket. "I'll go get the car now," he said as he walked out the door and toward Mr. Donaldson's house.

Soon he returned and before he could even reach the house, Hank and Hannah were waiting outside ready to go, "Come on Micky!" Hank called to her. They ran to the car and slid in the back seat.

Mikalah walked outside, and Jake opened the passenger side door for her to sit in the front seat next to him, then walked around and climbed behind the wheel.

"Everybody ready?" he asked.

"Yep!" Hank bounced in the seat, "Let's go!"

Jake chuckled and put the car into gear. It took about forty minutes to reach the Cadek Conservatory where the small group of Saints met. Jake parked the car on the street, and the four made their way inside the building.

Two refined, friendly Southern ladies - Francis "Fanny" Snodgrass and her sister Lillian Karrick – met them at the door. Lillian was in her forties, well dressed and draped in costume jewelry. Her sister, Fanny was older and somewhat heavy, probably from her excellent cooking. Lillian was a schoolteacher at Hixson High School who had never married. Fanny, an excellent seamstress, was married, but never had children.

"Welcome!" Fanny greeted, "We're so happy to have you with us this morning! I'm Fanny Snodgrass and this is my sister, Lillian Karrick."

"Good morning, Sister Snodgrass, Sister Karrick," Jake extended his hand to each lady, and they returned his firm handshake. "I'm Jake Elliot and these are my friends from Daisy – Mikalah, Hannah and Hank Ford. This is their first time to attend a Latter-day Saint meeting," Jake explained.

The ladies shook each of the young people's hands and expressed their gratitude for their joining them. Lillian guided them down the isle toward the front of the conservatory where three other women, a little boy and two little girls sat. Jake was the only grown man there. Lillian introduced them to the small group of members.

As Hannah, Hank and Mikalah filed into the row, Lillian Karrick tugged on Jake's jacket sleeve, "Brother Elliot, do you happen to hold the priesthood?" she whispered.

"Yes ma'am."

"Oh, that's wonderful!" she exuded. "Would you be willing to conduct our meeting? And perhaps we could find some bread somewhere to have the sacrament,"

"Yes, ma'am," Jake was a step ahead of her and pulled the brown paper from his pocket.

"I realized you had very few priesthood leaders here and thought it wise to come prepared," he smiled as he slightly pulled back the paper to reveal the bread.

"Heaven bless you, Brother Elliot! You're an answer to prayer! It's been months since we've been able to partake of the sacrament."

"I'd be happy to conduct. Have you assigned anyone to speak?" he inquired.

"My sister, Fanny has prepared something," she answered.

"Do you have someone who can play the piano?" he asked.

"No, I usually lead, and we just sing without a piano."

"That's a shame since there's this fine instrument on the stage," he gestured to a shiny black baby grand piano behind him.

"I know," she shook her head disappointedly.

"I play a little. Would you like me to see what I can remember?" he offered.

"Oh, you are just a bundle of blessings, Brother Elliot. Please play for us," she smiled.

"I'll need a bit of warming up. It's been a while. How about if I play a little prelude music before we get started?" he suggested.

"Please do!" Sister Karrick radiated enthusiasm.

Jake hopped up on the stage and opened the piano to expose the keys. He interlaced his fingers, stretching them back, and began to play *Lead, Kindly Light*. After playing it through three times from memory, he rose and stood before the little group.

After welcoming everyone and offering a prayer, Jake returned to the piano. Sister Karrick led the little group, and Jake's voice carried as he played,

> *Lead, kindly Light, amid the encircling gloom;*
> *Lead thou me on!*
> *The night is dark, and I am far from home;*
> *Lead thou me on!*
> *Keep thou my feet;*
> *I do not ask to see the distant scene –*
> *One step enough for me.*

When they had sung all three verses, Jake rose and offered a prayer. He then asked Sister Snodgrass and Sister Karrick if they had any announcements. They announced an upcoming Relief Society meeting to be held through the week. Jake made the piano come alive with a moving and reverent rendition of *I Stand All Amazed*, and then knelt to offer the prayer to bless the sacrament bread. Since there were no deacons to pass it, he did that as well. He then offered the prayer to bless the water and passed it to the tiny congregation.

Sister Snodgrass brushed tears from her eyes, she was so overjoyed at the opportunity to partake of the emblems of the Savior's sacrifice and remember Him. Mikalah thumbed through her Book of Mormon and turned to Moroni chapters 4 and 5 which Jake had shown her earlier. She read several times the commitment and promise associated with the sacrament, "*that they are willing to take upon them the name of thy Son, and always remember him, and keep his commandments which he hath given them, that they may always have his Spirit to be with them.*" (Moroni 4:3)

To always have his Spirit to be with them. She wondered what that would be like. She had a feeling that she wouldn't have gotten herself into quite so many scrapes with Hal if she'd always had the Lord's Spirit to be with her. She figured she would have detected his true intentions much sooner had she been led more closely by the Spirit.

Jake sat down next to Mikalah, and Sister Snodgrass spoke on faith and how it grows like a seed. She read from Alma 32 and explained it in great depth. As Mikalah listened, the things she heard began to make even more sense. She felt that warm "hot chocolate" peaceful feeling that Jake described in the orchard. She could have stayed there forever and wanted to learn everything there was to learn about God and His plan for her life. She never wanted to leave, and she was thrilled when Sister Snodgrass suggested that Jake say a few words before closing the meeting with a song.

Jake didn't speak long, but what he said had a deep impact on her. He said he felt impressed to read from Mosiah 18. He spoke of Alma and how he taught the people repentance, redemption and faith on the Lord Jesus Christ. Then he read verses eight through eleven.

'As ye are desirous to come into the fold of God, and to be called his people, and are willing to bear one another's burdens, that they may be light; Yea, and are willing to mourn with those that mourn; yea, and comfort those that stand in need of comfort, and to stand as witnesses of God at all times and in all things, and in all places that ye may be in, even until death, that ye may be redeemed of God, and be numbered with those of the first resurrection, that ye may have eternal life – Now I say unto you, if this be the desire of your hearts, what have you against being baptized in the name of the Lord, as a witness before him that ye have entered into a covenant with him, that ye will serve him and keep his commandments, that he may pour out his Spirit more abundantly upon you?'

'And now when the people had heard these words, they clapped their hands for joy, and exclaimed: This is the desire of our hearts.' (Mosiah 18:8-11)

Mikalah asked herself, *Is this the desire of my heart?* At that moment she was filled with love for everyone in the tiny group – even though she didn't even know them she loved them. And that love seemed to radiate out to her family and everyone she knew. *Yes, this is the desire of my heart!* Tears welled in her eyes as Jake concluded, returned to the piano and played *The Spirit of God*. Mikalah wished she knew the words to the songs. Her heart wanted to sing along, and by the end of the third verse she'd picked up the chorus and joined in,

> We'll sing and we'll shout with the armies of heaven,
> Hosanna, hosanna to God and the Lamb!
> Let glory to them in the highest be given,
> Henceforth and forever, Amen and amen!

67

Tears continued to stream from her cheeks as a woman offered the closing prayer. Jake stepped down from the piano, and shook several people's hands before he returned to his seat next to Mikalah. Noting her brushing the tears from her eyes, he smiled for he knew what they meant.

"Everybody ready to go?" he asked.

No! Mikalah thought to herself. She didn't want to leave. She loved the feeling she experienced and wanted to bask in it a little longer. But she stood, and Jake offered her his arm as he led her out of the conservatory. Hank and Hannah followed. The two sisters met them at the door, thanked them for attending and asked that they return. Jake told them that he would do his best, but that he had borrowed a friend's car that day and wasn't certain how often he'd be able to attend.

"Come as often as you can, Brother Elliot. You brought a sweet spirit of authority to the meeting that we sorely miss. Not to mention we enjoyed meeting your guests. We just love having guests," Sister Snodgrass smiled affectionately at Mikalah, Hank and Hannah and shook their hands as they left.

As Mikalah stepped outside, she marveled at the warmth she felt from the sun in contrast to the coolness of the autumn air. Her mind immediately drew the symbolic comparison to the Spirit which filled her with warmth and peace even when only yesterday she'd realized how cold and cruel the world could be. Instinctively she clutched Jake's arm tightly. He looked toward her and smiled, and she whispered to him, "Thank you!"

A flicker of puzzlement washed across his face, but then an understanding smile quickly replaced it. He opened the car door for her. Hannah and Hank climbed in the back.

"That was different," Hank broke the silence as Jake walked around the outside of the car. "Yes, it was," Hannah agreed.

When Jake climbed behind the wheel, Hank chuckled, "You were a regular one man show today, Jake."

Jake smiled at him through the rear view mirror.

"I didn't know you could play the piano too," Mikalah was impressed.

"Oh, it's been a while, but I guess it's like riding a bicycle. Comes back naturally."

68

"You play beautifully," Mikalah added.

"My mama insisted that I learn. She played and taught all of us to play. Always said, 'You never know when they might need you to play in a meeting.' I guess Mama was talking about days like today," he smiled as he thought of his mother.

"You play almost as good as you sing, Jake," Hannah flattered, and Mikalah shook her head in agreement.

"You two sound like you're butterin' me up for something," he teased.

"They're hopin' you'll take the scenic route home so we can ride for a little longer," Hank laughed.

"I thought we *were* taking the scenic route," Jake smiled.

The four chatted and talked through the forty minute drive home, but no one said much about the meeting. Jake didn't want to push it. As they entered Daisy, Mikalah suggested, "Jake, why don't you drop Hank and Hannah off at the house, and I'll walk back with you from Mr. Donaldson's. I'd like a good stretch of the legs."

He glanced at her and gathered from her expression that what she really wanted to do was talk, "Sure, I'd enjoy the company."

Hannah winked at her brother. The two of them were playing matchmaker whenever they could. They had decided that they wanted Jake for their brother-in-law. So they were pleased to see that the pair would have some time alone.

Jake stopped the car at the end of the Ford's driveway and let the twins out. "Enjoy your walk," Hannah called back.

"Yeah, take your time," Hank smiled. The two took off racing to the front door.

He put the car back in gear and drove up the road to Mr. Donaldson's house. "So what did you think?" he glanced toward her.

"I thought it was beautiful," she replied.

He glanced at her and smiled, "I'm glad you liked it."

"I'd like to talk with you about a few things, Jake. If you don't mind," she ventured.

"Sure, go right ahead."

"Let's drop off the car, and then we can talk uninterrupted as we walk home," she suggested.

"Ok"

Jake turned into Mr. Donaldson's driveway, parked the car and walked around to open Mikalah's door. "I'll let Mr. Donaldson know I've returned the car." He trotted to the door and knocked. Mr. Donaldson opened the door, and Jake thanked him for the use of the car and returned the keys.

"Anytime, my boy," Mr. Donaldson shook his hand, and Jake jogged back to Mikalah's side. He slid his hands into his pockets, and she slipped her hand into the crook of his arm.

"So what did you want to talk about?" he asked.

"I think – I think I would like to be baptized," she looked up into his emerald eyes as he stopped and turned toward her. "Really?"

"Does that surprise you?"

"Yes – no – well, yes sort of," he stammered. "Why do you want to be baptized?"

"Lots of reasons but mainly, I've read nearly all of the Book of Mormon, and I really believe it's true. There is a power in the book. It makes me feel warm inside when I read it. And then today when you were talking about the people of Alma being baptized and whether it was the desire of their hearts… I … that's the desire of my heart, Jake. I want to have the Spirit with me all the time. I don't want to make foolish mistakes anymore. I want to know that the course I'm pursuing in my life is what God wants for me. I want the constant companionship of the Holy Ghost."

Jake could hardly contain his elation. It was all happening so fast! He'd never had the opportunity to serve a mission due to the economic conditions of their times, but he had shared the gospel with enough people in his travels to know that it was rare for anyone to recognize truth so quickly. He also knew from experience that Satan's ugly head would soon rear itself at this first whiff of a budding testimony. Would Mikalah be able to forge ahead? Was her testimony strong enough to withstand persecution? Or would she be like the O'Neals and lose courage?

"I think that's wonderful, Mikalah," he finally spoke. "I would be happy to baptize you if that's really what you want."

"It's really what I want," she smiled.

"Mikalah, I want to be fair with you," he started uneasily. She looked at him puzzled. "I want you to realize that not everyone is so kindly disposed to our beliefs. A lot of folks won't like it if they find out that you want to be a 'Mormon.' People you thought were your friends will turn on you. They'll call you crazy or say that I've duped you somehow."

"I don't care what other people say. I never have cared," Mikalah's expression grew resolute.

"You've never faced anything like this, Mikalah. It can - it can get ugly," he warned.

"I've faced ugly too," she stated solemnly.

"Yes, I suppose you have," a slight smile turned up the corners of his mouth. "What I'm trying to say is that I want you to be absolutely certain that you are ready for this commitment, because it won't be easy to stand alone."

"I don't have to stand alone," she grabbed his arm again and started walking.

"What do you mean?" he was afraid she was leaning too much on him.

"I have God on my side –right?" she beamed.

"You're absolutely right," he smiled, "You do indeed. Very well then, if you really want to be baptized, let's make certain you get a good solid confirmation. Finish your Book of Mormon and put it to the test. Pray about it as Moroni directs, and when you have your definite answer, then we'll arrange a time and a place."

"I can finish it this afternoon. I'm in Ether."

"You're a fast reader," his eyebrows rose in surprise.

"I've always loved to read, but I can't put this down. I've been up late every night. Perhaps you've noticed the bags under my eyes," she chuckled.

"No, hadn't noticed any bags, but I have noticed you just about falling asleep over the wash tub as you're doing laundry," he winked, and she laughed.

"How old are you Mikalah?" Jake suddenly realized something.

"I'm seventeen. I'll be eighteen in three weeks. Why?"

"You'll need a parent's permission to be baptized if you're under eighteen. You can either get your mother's permission or you can just wait until after your birthday," he explained.

"I don't want to wait. I'll ask Mama," she was so excited she could hardly contain herself. Her enthusiasm was contagious, and Jake found himself hoping, actually believing, that this time would be different.

~*~

Jake sat in the parlor reading by lamp light as was his usual nightly habit. Mikalah crept down the stairs and peeked around the corner to see that he was indeed just where she hoped he would be. Tears trickled down her cheeks as she watched him for several moments. She dabbed the tears from her eyes with her handkerchief.

As she approached him, he looked up from his reading. Noting her bloodshot eyes he asked, "Mikalah, what's wrong?"

"Nothing," she sniffed, "Everything is perfect." She smiled, "I got my answer." Mikalah sat in the chair next him. "I can't believe it's only been a week since I sat here and laughed at you for telling me fairy tales, and now I'm sitting here telling you that I know it's true. I *know* it, Jake. I really do." She seemed awestruck by the miracle of it all.

Jake's eyes were now glistening, and he wanted with all his heart to rush over, scoop her up into his arms and give her a big hug. But he'd made a promise to himself that he would not further taint Mikalah's conversion experience with anything that could be construed as romantic involvement.

He scooted closer to her and took her hands, "That's so wonderful, Mikalah! Even though the promise is there for everyone who'll test it, it still strikes me with such wondering awe when someone puts it to the test and gets their answer."

"Why is that?" she asked.

"I think it's because there are so few people who will read, study, and ask with a sincere heart. I'm always struck with wonder at the beauty of the soul who does. A testimony isn't just God telling you something, it's you putting in the time to study, ask and really want to know. That's the miraculous part of it – you are the miracle, Mikalah."

Mikalah flung her arms around his neck and kissed his cheek, "Thank you, Jake! I believe that's the nicest thing anyone has ever said to me!" He gave her a quick hug in return and then stood and rubbed his hands together. Smiling, he asked, "So now what do you want to do with this testimony of yours?"

"I'm going to ask Mama tomorrow if I can be baptized," she beamed.

"What do you think she'll say?"

"I have no idea. I know what my father would say," she frowned. "But he's not here, is he?" she smiled. "I think Mama likes you, and she'll factor that into her decision. No matter what she says, I'll be eighteen in three weeks, and I can do whatever I want then."

"But it would be nice to have her blessing," Jake noted.

"Yes, that's true. Would – would you be there with me when I ask her, Jake?"

"Hmmm… I'd be happy to help you answer any questions she may have, but I think it would be best that I not be there when you ask."

"Why?"

"Because if I'm there, she may get the idea that I've talked you into this."

"But this has all been my decision. You didn't pressure me to do anything!" she defended.

"You know that, and I know that, but your mother doesn't know that. And if I'm there, she may not feel comfortable speaking freely with you. I think you better talk with her alone."

"Will you at least stay nearby so that if she has questions I can get you?"

"Sure, just let me know when you plan to ask, and I'll make sure I'm in the area," he smiled.

Mikalah jumped up from her seat and threw her arms around his neck. He stood there with his hands shoved in his pockets and couldn't help but smile at her enthusiasm, "I'm so excited I'll never go to sleep. She tugged his head toward her and kissed his cheek. "Thank you, Jake. Thank you so much!"

She turned and trotted off toward the stairs. "You're welcome, Mikalah," his deep voice whispered. It was such an odd, exhilarating blend of emotions for Jake. He always loved those he taught, especially those who were receptive, but there was something more with Mikalah. He couldn't deny that there was definitely something more.

Chapter 5

Jake set a stack of logs on the wood pile and nearly bumped into Mikalah as he turned around. "Oh, you startled me," he stepped back a little.

"Sorry, I'm getting ready to go speak with Mama," she whispered, "Will you please stay around?"

"Sure, I'll be right here if you need me," he winked and patted her on the shoulder.

"Thanks!" she turned and walked back to the kitchen door.

Laurana was kneading bread dough when Mikalah entered the kitchen, "Can I help?" she offered.

"Sure, you can help me knead," Laurana smiled and gave her daughter a blob of dough to work.

"Mama, there's something I'd like to talk with you about," Mikalah began.

"Go right ahead dear," Laurana looked at her expectantly.

"I've been studying and reading a lot about Jake's church, and I would like to join it."

This was not what Laurana expected to hear her daughter say, and she wasn't prepared with a response. All she could say was, "Really?"

"Yes, I'd like to be baptized as a member of The Church of Jesus Christ of Latter-day Saints," she smiled.

"Mikalah, you already have a church. Why do you need to join another one?"

"Because I believe there's more truth in Jake's church."

"Jake's church?" Laurana gave a knowing nod, "Oh – I get it. I've noticed the way you two look at each other. You've got a crush on Jake. That's what this is about."

"Mama, everything isn't about love and romance. This has nothing to do with how I feel or don't feel about Jake. This has to do with what God has told me through study and prayer," Mikalah tried not to let her frustration show.

"God has told you something? What has He told you?" Laurana asked.

"He's told me that the Book of Mormon is true and that The Church of Jesus Christ of Latter-day Saints holds the truth of Jesus Christ's restored gospel."

"Ok, dear, I didn't understand much about what you just said, but I do know one thing and that's that your father would never approve of you joining any other church. He's a very devout Baptist, and he would have a fit if I let you join another church," Laurana's voice was firm.

"But Mama, since Daddy's been gone, we haven't even been going to the Baptist church. We've been going to Daisy Methodist. Do you think he'd be happy about that?"

Laurana knew that Mikalah had a point, "That's different."

"How is it different, Mama? You've chosen to attend another church while Daddy's gone. Why can't I choose to attend a different church while he's away?"

"I don't mind you attending Jake's church honey, but joining it is different. What are you going to do when Jake moves on, and you're left alone in this new faith? How are you going to attend church with it all the way in Chattanooga?"

Jake move on? The thought had never occurred to Mikalah before that moment, and it threw her. She hesitated, "Mama, I can cross that bridge when I come to it. The Lord will provide a way. The Lord has told me that this is what I should do, and I know He'll provide a way somehow."

"Let me think on it."

Mikalah threw her arms around her mother's neck, "Oh thank you, Mama!"

"And I think I better read what you've been reading so I know what you're getting yourself into. People in town say Jake's got some strange beliefs."

"Mama, please keep an open mind. Remember what Jesus said about 'by their fruits ye shall know them.' Look at Jake's fruit – the kind of man he is. Isn't he good? Doesn't that prove that his beliefs can't be bad if they produce good fruit?"

"I'll think about it, Mikalah. That's all I'll promise right now."

When they finished kneading the dough and placed it in bowls to rise, Mikalah turned to her mother, "I'll go get that book." She climbed the stairs and returned shortly holding Jake's copy of the Book of Mormon. She walked directly to the door and put her head out to look for Jake. He was still working at the woodpile. "Jake, can you please come in here for a moment," she called.

Jake dropped what he was doing and walked toward the kitchen door and Mikalah's hopeful expression. She went outside to meet him halfway. "Mama says she'll think about it but she wants to read what I've been reading to make sure it's all right. Would you please come in and tell her a little about the book like you did for me. I think it will help."

"Sure, I can do that," the two of them entered the door and went into the parlor where Laurana sat darning socks. Matty played outside on the front porch.

"Mama, I thought it might help if Jake explained a little about the book before you read it."

Jake took the book from Mikalah and asked her to get a Bible. Mikalah returned shortly, and Laurana set aside her darning to take both of the books from Jake. He opened them each to the same two passages he had originally shown Mikalah and explained about the book and where it came from.

Discomfort grew evident on Laurana's face, and she shook her head, "I don't know about this Mikalah. This sounds really - different."

Mikalah knelt in front of her mother, "Please mother, all I'm asking is that you give it a chance. I thought it was fairy tales when Jake first told me. I thought he was completely mad. But Jake isn't mad, is he Mama? He's a perfectly sane upstanding man. And that made me want to read – just out of curiosity really. I wanted to know how a grown man could believe such fairy tales. But as I read and prayed about it, the words of the book sank into my soul, and I know that it is true. God has told me that. I have felt His Spirit bear witness to me that it is true."

"I don't know, Mikalah," her mother hesitated.

"Please, Mama, just do it for me. Study it. Have an open mind. Just ask yourself – what if? What if it's true? And then pray about it."

"All right. I'll read it. Your daddy would tan my hide if he knew I was…"

"But wouldn't daddy be upset if you didn't really research what I'm *going* to do? I mean, I need your permission to be baptized right now, but in three weeks, I'll be eighteen, and I won't need anyone's permission. This is something I'm going to do, I would just like to have your understanding and blessing."

Laurana's eyebrows rose.

"Don't you think Daddy would want you to really understand what I'm doing?" Mikalah reasoned.

"Yes, I suppose he would…" but in her heart she knew her husband would be angrier with her for reading it. But he wasn't there, and it was her decision to make in his absence. This was her daughter, and she felt it better to understand her than to alienate her. "I'll read it and pray about it just as you suggest. Then, I'll make my decision."

Mikalah put her arms around her mother's neck, "Thank you so much, Mama! You are so good to me!" She kissed her mother's cheek.

"Thank you, Mrs. Ford," Jake smiled.

"All right, you two, it's time we got some things done around here." She pulled a piece of paper and a few bills from her apron pocket. I need some things from town. Jake, please take Mikalah and help her get these supplies. She handed the list and the money to Mikalah.

"Yes, ma'am, happy to," he smiled.

"You'll need to take the wagon because I've got too many heavy items here," Laurana explained. "And Mikalah, take the butter and eggs I've rounded up on the kitchen counter and swap them for the items we need at the general store."

"Yes ma'am."

The pair grabbed their jackets, and Jake brought the wagon around to the front of the house as Mikalah carried the butter and eggs. Jake helped her up into the wagon. As he climbed into the seat, he looked to Mikalah and winked, "That went fairly well."

"Yes, I think it did too," she smiled.

They pulled out onto Highway 27, and Mikalah rubbed her arms, shivering, "Brrrr... it's really cold out here this morning."

Jake pulled a blanket from the back of the wagon and put it around her shoulders, "Here you go."

"Thank you!" she smiled. He pulled her toward him and rubbed her shoulder in an effort to warm her. She loved the way she felt nestled next to him, and she felt deflated when he pulled his arm from around her and used both hands to steer the team. She pulled the blanket tightly around her shoulders and nudged closer to him so she could feel the heat from his body.

Orange, yellow and red foliage blanketed the ridge of mountains to their left and open fields lay along their right. They rode past the Morton's house, and the horses slowed with the strain of the steep hill. Jake held the reins steadily as they made their descent toward the ball field on their left. Roy London's Garage lay across from it. They traveled a little further until they came to the bright orange clay pit gouged out of the mountainside. Near it was the mountain road and the spring. Poe's Restaurant and the Blacksmith shop lay opposite the mountains.

Daisy was a clean rural little town. "Sleepy" might be the best way to describe it at a superficial glance. But appearances were deceptive. Daisy had its moments when it could be anything but sleepy; the moonshiners saw to that. Out of nowhere the feuding lawless bands could send the little town into a panicked state of disarray.

"We'll need to go to the general store, the feed store and the home store. Why don't you drop me off right here over on the left at the general store while you go on over to the feed store? Then we can meet up the road at Donaldson's Home Store," Mikalah suggested.

"Sounds fine," he said as she tore off the list of items that they needed from the feed store and handed it to him along with some money. He dropped her off at the general store and turned the wagon around.

As she entered the establishment Mr. and Mrs. Ketner met her.

"Good morning, Mikalah!" Mrs. Ketner welcomed.

"Good morning, Mrs. Ketner. You sure look nice this frosty morning," Mikalah greeted.

"Thank you, dear. Did you hear about what happened last night at the clay pit?"

"No, I didn't. What happened?" Mikalah's brow furrowed at the anxiety on Mrs. Ketner's face.

"They found one of the Bailey boys over there shot in the head."

"No!" Mikalah felt a sick twirling deep in the pit of her stomach as she envisioned a bloodied corpse lying amidst the bright orange clay.

"More of those moonshiner killin's," Mr. Ketner shook his head. "Won't be long before those two groups annihilate one 'nother at the rate they're goin'. Yep ever since Ed Bailey shot Pop Richards over moonshinin' territory, Daisy's been a hotbed of violence."

"Why some days I'm terrified to even come to town!" Mrs. Ketner exclaimed. "You never know what they'll do next."

"Oh, I don't think we've got anything to worry about," Mr. Ketner tried to soothe his wife and wide-eyed Mikalah who was beginning to wish she'd stayed with Jake. "They're just out for each other. I don't think they'd hurt the rest of us."

"You don't think so? Really?" Mikalah asked.

"Nah, I think they're just after one another. We're all safe as a babe in its mama's arms."

"I don't think you grasp the seriousness of the situation." Mrs. Ketner argued. "Last time they shot somebody it was right here in broad daylight in the middle of town!"

"Oh come on now, Violet. You're scarin' the girl. She didn't come in here to hear gossip anyway. She came to get somethin'. Didn't ya?"

"Oh, yes, here's the list. And I have butter and eggs that Mama wanted to swap for them."

Mr. Ketner counted the eggs, weighed the butter and studied Mikalah's list, "Yep, you've got enough here for the items you need." He handed the paper to his wife and carried the butter and eggs back to where he stored them.

80

Mikalah drummed her fingertips nervously on the store counter and peered out the window. Something in the stillness of the air sent a foreboding shiver along her spine. She tended to think like Mrs. Ketner. The moonshiners were loose cannons. The police didn't try to stop them, and either band of renegades would just as soon shoot you as ask questions if you got in their way. It was just a matter of time before some innocent person got caught in their crossfire.

Lost in her own thoughts, Mikalah didn't notice Mrs. Ketner put her purchases in a sack and extend them toward her.

"Here you go dear," Mrs. Ketner offered cheerily.

"Oh, thank you, Ma'am," Mikalah smiled absently and took the bag.

"Thank you for coming in, dear," Mrs. Ketner waved as Mikalah walked out the door. "You be careful, now!" Mrs. Ketner called out as her husband rolled his eyes.

Mikalah walked up the road to the home store. Jake had just pulled up out front with the wagon and hopped down to meet her. He took the bag from her arms and put it in the wagon. The hair on the back of his neck stood on end, and he looked around to see why he had such an eerie sensation, but saw nothing.

As they turned to enter the store, they could hear a car speeding up the road. Mikalah turned toward the black Ford barreling down the street. Before she knew what happened, Jake threw his arms around her, flinging her to the ground, shielding her with his body. Repetitive shots fired from a Thompson submachine gun mounted in the missing back window of the car.

The car sped off. Silence. Then the hum of murmuring voices followed as people trickled onto the street from the stores.

Jake's heavy body lay on top of her, "It's over, Jake. Get up, I can't breathe." She pushed at his shoulder to remove him, but he didn't budge. She pulled back her blood drenched hand and screamed in terror, "Jake! Help! Somebody help me! Jake's been shot!" she screamed as her trembling hands inspected his wounds.

Within seconds, Mr. Donaldson and another man were standing over them. "Oh, my, Miss Ford! Be still, and we'll lift him," Mr. Donaldson's voice was low and comforting. The other man grabbed the blanket from the top of the wagon and tossed it over Jake. It took both men to pull his lifeless body from her.

"Let's get 'im inside," Mr. Donaldson directed, and the two men carried Jake into the home store. Mikalah followed with tears pouring down her cheeks. She began to pray in her mind, *Please, Heavenly Father, not Jake, not Jake. Please let him be ok.*

"Let's lay him on his left side," Mr. Donaldson directed as they stretched him out on a cot in the back room. Mr. Donaldson lifted the blanket, "Oh my! What a mess!" he gasped.

Mikalah put her hands over her eyes. "Is he- is he alive?" she whispered.

Mr. Donaldson put his fingers to Jake's neck, "Yep, he's still alive. Good thing he's a big ol' boy. If anyone's strong enough to survive this type of thing, Jake is. Nelson, run for Doc Allen." Nelson bolted from the store, started Mr. Donaldson's car and sped away in search of the town doctor.

Donaldson patted Jake's cheek, "Jake, boy, wake up, Jake."

Jake groaned, and his eyes fluttered, but he slipped back to unconsciousness.

Mr. Donaldson ripped away Jake's blood soaked shirt and examined the wound. His shoulder had been hit by one bullet and grazed by two others.

Mikalah gasped, "Oh Jake!"

Mr. Donaldson stood and put his arm around her. "He'll be ok. The doctor will be here soon."

Donaldson returned to Jake and examined his head which was also bleeding profusely. "I'm more worried about his head. He must have slammed it really hard when he fell. Hand me that towel over there." Mikalah gave Mr. Donaldson a towel, and he placed it against Jake's head. "Hold this here and apply pressure, Miss," he directed.

Mikalah held the towel in place as Donaldson walked out of the room and spoke to one of the people in the store, "Did anyone see who they were after? Has anyone else been shot?"

"No one else," the man shook his head.

"Did anyone see who did it?" Donaldson asked.

"No, all I heard was that it was a black '36 Ford with a Thompson submachine gun hanging out the back window. The driver and the gunman were both wearing hats and scarves.

"Great, those blamed moonshiners again!" Donaldson shook his head in disgust. "I knew one day they'd miss their mark and hurt an innocent bystander. The person they were after probably got away."

Mikalah hovered over Jake wiping the blood from his pale face with her handkerchief. "Could someone please bring me some warm water and towels to clean off this blood?" she called from the back room.

Donaldson returned shortly carrying a bowl of warm water and several towels.

As Mikalah lovingly cleaned his face, she remained oblivious to the fact that she was covered in his blood and had skinned up her own elbows and arms from the fall. She didn't even register the pain.

"Did someone call the police?" Mikalah asked Mr. Donaldson.

"I don't know. Doesn't much matter anyway."

She rose involuntarily, "What do you mean it doesn't matter? Jake's been shot and could die and you say it doesn't matter?" She became incredulous with anger.

"Now settle down, Miss Ford. All I mean is that they're long gone, and the county police are slower than molasses in February about showin' up when they think it's moonshine related."

"Why? Why wouldn't they come quickly?" she didn't understand.

"They're hopin' those ol' moonshiners will just kill each other off, I suspect."

"I think they're scared of 'em," Nelson commented as he came in the door with the doctor.

"Someone should have to pay for what's been done here!" Mikalah furiously insisted.

"Settle down, now, Miss Ford. Nelson, go call the police," Donaldson felt it better to humor her by doing what he could, even though it would make little difference in the long run.

"Thank you!" she huffed.

Everyone moved aside, letting the doctor through to the cot where Jake lay on his left side. "Hmmm," the doctor muttered as he sat beside Jake and pulled a syringe from his bag.

Mikalah stood facing Jake, watching the doctor's every move. She was convinced that every man in town was clearly incompetent if they wouldn't even know to call the police after a crime. "What's that you're giving him?" she asked as Doc Allen flicked the air bubbles from the syringe.

"It's a tetanus shot. We don't need him gettin' lock jaw. You never know what those moonshiners fill their weapons with," he gave Jake the shot, and Jake stirred a little, moaning. "Good, he's startin' to come around. Donaldson, please bring a bag of ice for his head."

Mr. Donaldson darted from the room as the doctor began examining Jake's back. Donaldson returned with the ice and handed it to the physician.

"Dear, I don't think you're gonna wanna watch me remove this bullet. Why don't you go outside for a spell," the doctor suggested.

"I'm not leaving him," she knelt down beside the cot and stroked his face with her hand.

"All right, but just sit down there and don't watch," Doc Allen pulled out his scalpel and tweezers and started to work on Jake's back.

Jake moaned, and his eye lids fluttered. Mikalah grabbed his hand and held it in hers. "It's ok Jake. You're going to be fine," she comforted.

The doctor worked to remove the bullet. Mikalah was thankful that Jake remained unconscious throughout most of the ordeal. He stirred occasionally when the doctor probed into the wound, and he gripped her hand tightly.

"Good thing the Thompson machine gun is known for its lack of penetration. The bullet didn't go too deep," Doc Allen observed as he held the bullet between his tweezers for her to see.

As the doctor cleaned and bandaged his back, Jake began to awake. "Oh, I feel like someone used me for a pin cushion," he mumbled. "What happened?" he groaned.

"You saved my life," Mikalah answered. "You shielded me when the moonshiners rode by and shot their machine gun at us."

"A machine gun? Why would someone shoot us with a machine gun?" he mumbled.

Mikalah shook her head and looked up at the doctor who answered, "Don't know boy. I 'spect they were shootin' at someone else who escaped, and you were just in the way. Or maybe they mistook you for someone else."

"Does he need to go to the hospital?" Mikalah asked.

"Don't see why he'd need to. I've got his back taken care of here and since he's conscious, I think he can go home and rest there. I'll check on him each day. How'd you two get to town?" the doctor asked.

"We rode in the wagon," she answered.

"He doesn't need to be ridin' in a wagon right now. I'll give you two a ride to your house." Doc Allen turned to Mr. Donaldson, "Could you please have someone take their wagon home?"

"Sure, Nelson can do that," Donaldson turned to Mikalah, "Miss Ford, were you two comin' into the store when you were shot? Do you need somethin'?"

"I completely forgot." The moment she reached down to pull the list from her pocket, she noticed her bloodstained dress and hands. "My goodness, Mama's gonna have a heart attack when she sees us."

Donaldson took the list from her hand and pointed to a washroom, "Why don't you go in yonder. There's a mirror, and you can wash your face and hands a bit while I get your things together."

Mikalah pulled the money from her pocket and handed it to Mr. Donaldson, "Thank you."

He waved his hand, "Honey, with what you two have been through today, this is on me."

"Oh, no, Mr. Donaldson. This had nothing to do with you. You don't need to do that."

"I insist, it's on me," he shook his head.

"Mr. Donaldson, if anything we owe you," Jake groaned.

"Jake's right," Mikalah thrust the money out for him to take it.

"No thanks, dear. You run along, and clean yourself up a bit, and I'll get your things together," Mr. Donaldson turned and walked back into the store.

"Thank you, sir! You're much too kind," Mikalah called after him and then turned toward the wash room.

There wasn't much she could do. No amount of scrubbing her face and hands could make up for the blood that covered her coat and dress.

She stepped out of the room as Mr. Donaldson and Doc Allen braced Jake on either side, helping him to the doctor's car. Jake wore a new shirt that Mr. Donaldson had given him, and they had wrapped him in a clean blanket. They put Jake in the back of the car, and Mikalah rode up front with the doctor.

Jake dozed in and out. When they reached the house, Laurana stepped outside, surprised to see them getting out of the doctor's car. When she saw Mikalah's blood stained dress, her hands flew to her mouth, and she ran toward her daughter, "What on earth? Mikalah? Are you ok?" Mikalah winced as her mother put her hands on her arms, and it was then that she realized she had wounds of her own.

"What is it dear? I'm sorry!" Laurana realized she'd hurt her.

"Oh it's nothing," Mikalah rolled up her sleeves and saw that her elbows and arms were bruised and scraped. "I just have a few scrapes. Mama, Jake was shot outside the Home Store." Mikalah whispered.

"Shot! By who? How?" her mother exclaimed.

Doc Allen stepped out of the car, "Moonshiners, Ma'am. They're gettin' more lawless by the day."

"Moonshiners? In town?" Laurana gasped.

"Jake saved my life. He jumped in front of me and took the bullets that would have hit me," tears began to well up again in Mikalah's eyes.

"Oh dear, how horrifying!" Laurana patted her daughter's hair and cheeks.

"They shot up the poor boy's shoulder pretty bad. But I cleaned him and removed the bullet. He'll need to rest for a week or two, I'd say. But he'll be ok."

"Mama, Jake can't sleep on that uncomfortable cot in his condition. He can have my room, and I'll sleep with Matty," Mikalah suggested.

"I guess that is a good idea," Laurana agreed.

"He's pretty groggy, I'll need both of you to help me get him in the house and up those stairs," the doctor opened the back door of the automobile.

"Where's the wagon?" suddenly Laurana realized that it was missing.

"Mr. Donaldson is having Nelson bring it home with our things," Mikalah explained.

"Wake up, Jake. You're too heavy for us to carry," the Doctor patted Jake's cheek. His eyes opened, and he winced as he scooted over to get out of the car. He stood, and then his knees buckled. The doctor and Mikalah supported him on either side. He put an arm around each of their shoulders, and they guided him into the house and up the stairs. Laurana opened the door to Mikalah's room, pulled back the covers on the bed, and they helped him sit down.

"I can't take your room, Mikalah!" he protested.

"Nonsense. You can't sleep on that cot when you're wounded," Mikalah insisted.

"But where will you sleep?" he asked.

"I can sleep with Matty. She's so little I'll have plenty of room in her bed."

"I don't know. I don't feel right taking your room," he shook his head and started to rise, but he grew dizzy and light headed all of a sudden and flopped back down.

"Lie down, boy. This is where you're stayin'," Doc Allen commanded in an authoritative tone.

"Yes, sir," Jake obeyed, grimacing as he lay down on his left shoulder. His eyes closed, and he lost consciousness as his head hit the pillow. Laurana and the doctor left the room and went downstairs. Mikalah started to follow them but turned back. She knelt in front of Jake, gently ran her fingers through the locks of his hair, and bent over to kiss his cheek.

"Thank you, Jake," she whispered. He didn't stir as she stood and left the room.

~*~

The scent of her filled his senses. It was the sweet perfume of apple blossoms in autumn. She stood before him dressed in white, her strawberry blonde curls perfectly framing her face and her baby blue eyes gazing into his. He slipped his arms about her small waist and pulled her to him, kissing her without reservation or restraint. Her arms slid around his neck, and her fingers lovingly toyed with the locks on the back of his head. He looked up and a feeling of love and warmth filled his heart as the magnificent structure of the St. George temple came into view.

"I love you, Mikalah," he mumbled as he pulled her pillow tighter. Mikalah's wide eyes lifted from her reading to study him. Was he awake?

"Jake," she leaned forward and whispered. But he didn't stir. "Are you dreaming?" she asked softly. She reached forward and gently stroked his hair.

"I love you too, Jake," she whispered and kissed his cheek.

~*~

Jake slept until the next morning and awoke to the pangs of hunger as the scent of sausage and biscuits filled the air. He winced in pain as he rolled over and remembered that he was wounded. He struggled to sit up, rubbed his temple and moaned from the pounding in his head as the room started to fade in and out. About that time Matty skipped by his room and darted in.

"Jake! You're awake!" she bubbled. "I was wowied about you!"

"You were?" he smiled at the little child. "You don't need to worry about me, Matty. I'm as tough as a grizzly bear," he patted the child's cheek with his fingertips.

"That food sure smells good. Could you please tell Mikalah that I'm awake and as hungry as one of those grizzly bears?"

"Yep!" she smiled.

"I'd go get it myself, but the room's spinning," he explained.

"The woom's spinnin'?" Matty looked around to see if the room was indeed moving in circles.

"Well, it feels like it's spinning to me," he chuckled.

"Oh! I'll go get Micky!" Matty skipped off to find Mikalah.

Mikalah returned shortly with a tray of food.

"Thank you! This smells wonderful!" he smiled.

"Matty said the room was spinning. Are you all right?" Mikalah put the back of her hand on his forehead and then leaned over to test his temperature with her cheek, "You don't feel hot."

"I'm all right, just a bit light headed when I make sudden movements."

"Probably from all that blood you lost," she sat in the chair next to him. "Is there anything I can get for you?"

"No, this is perfect, thank you," he smiled. "I feel bad that you have to wait on me hand and foot. Give me another day to rest, and I'll be up and holdin' my own."

"No sir, you're resting for a week," she insisted.

"A week! I can't lie around for a week!"

"Doctor's orders. You lost a lot of blood, Jake. You can't just get up and start runnin' around here. Those wounds need time to heal."

"But a whole week?"

"Go ahead and eat your breakfast. Doc Allen will be here soon to check on you," she stood and walked to the door. "Just holler if you need anything. I'll be in Matty's room sewin'."

"Can't you sew in here and keep me company? I'm going to go crazy lying here all day with no one to talk to," he smiled pleadingly.

"I suppose I could sew as easily in here as in there. I'll go get my things," she walked out of the room and returned with Matty on her heels.

"The woom still spinnin', Jake?" Matty plopped on the bed next to him.

"Oomph" he gritted his teeth as the bed jarred.

"Matty honey, you're hurting Jake jostling his bed,"

"Oh, I'm sawee" she stood up quickly.

"That's all right, sweetie," he patted her cheek, and she sat as gently as she could next him.

"Are you sure you want us in here? You probably should get some sleep," Mikalah suggested.

89

"Please stay. I'm not sleepy," he ate his breakfast as Mikalah sewed. Handing the plate to Matty he asked, "Honey, could you take this downstairs for me?"

She grabbed the plate and silverware from him and trotted out of the room.

Mikalah set her sewing in her lap and looked at him intently, "Jake, I haven't had the chance to properly thank you for saving my life yesterday. I'm just so grateful for what you did for me....shielding me like you did and takin' that bullet for me." Tears began to well up in her eyes.

"Ah ..." Jake waved his left hand as if it were no big deal.

"No please hear me out. I could have died yesterday if it hadn't been for you. You could have died *because of me*! With saving my life and saving my soul, I'll never be able to repay you."

"I didn't save your soul, Mikalah," he spoke softly and shook his head.

"Because of you, it will be," she clarified. "I never would have understood what life was about. I wouldn't have known what God expected of me or how much He loved me or how I could return to live with Him again. I would have lived my life by fear instead of by faith."

Jake listened to her, watching her mouth as she spoke. Suddenly the dream he'd had the day before flooded into his mind, and he felt tingles go up his arms as a feeling of warmth filled his chest. He realized then that Mikalah would one day be his bride. He didn't know how or when, but he knew that this young woman would spend the eternities at his side.

"Jake, are you all right?" she asked.

"Uh, yeah, I'm ok. You're welcome Mikalah, and you don't owe me anything," he wiped the inside corners of his eyes with his thumb and forefinger.

"Oh yes I do. I've got to find a way to repay you," she insisted.

"Well, I – I think we might be able to find a way someday," he winked.

Mikalah smiled and then her brow furrowed in confusion. She wondered what he meant by that, but didn't venture to ask. She returned to her sewing, and then she remembered what he had said in his sleep the day before. Her eyes darted up toward him as she guessed at what he might be eluding to. Her eyes met his for he was still gazing at her. Jake grinned and turned his head toward the door as Matty pranced back into the room.

"Miss me?" she asked and started to pounce on the bed, but the look of apprehension in his face reminded her that she needed to be more careful. So she gently sat on the edge of the bed.

"Sure did, sweetie!" he answered.

"Hannah says you're gonna mawie Micky, but I want you to mawie me instead," she blurted out, and Mikalah's heart began to pound furiously.

"Hmm... that would be a hard decision, Matty," he winked. "But I think I'd be a wrinkled up old man by the time you're old enough to get married, sweetie."

Matty's expression fell, "Then mawie Micky, and you'll still be with us always." The child's face brightened, and Jake's eyes darted toward Mikalah who busily sewed and tried to pretend she didn't hear the conversation even though her face flushed crimson.

"Matty, honey, why don't you run along and play. All this chatter is probably making Jake's head hurt," Mikalah pointed to the door, and Matty reluctantly stood and moped out of the room.

Jake chuckled, and Mikalah rolled her eyes and shook her head, "I'm sorry about that, Jake. I don't know where she gets her ideas."

"They aren't bad ideas," he mumbled.

"Pardon?"

"Oh nothing," he shrugged, "Ouch!" he grimaced.

"What is it?"

"I gotta remember that I can't shrug my shoulders," he winced.

Light tapping interrupted their conversation. They turned to see Doc Allen standing in the open doorway. "You look quite a bit more alert today, Jake. How you feelin'?"

"Better... a bit light headed and really sore, but better."

"Have you heard anything about why this happened to you?" The doctor's eyes darted from Jake to Mikalah and back again. Jake nodded negatively and looked at Mikalah, anticipating an answer.

"The police stopped by yesterday afternoon and questioned me. Since Jake was sleeping, they said they'd send someone out today to talk with him. So far they seem to think that the Baileys were retaliating for the shooting the other night at the clay pits. Somehow in the confusion Jake and I got in the way. They consider it either a case of mistaken identity or that the person they were aiming for managed to get away. They even asked me if I knew where Jake was on the night of the killing, as if he could be involved!"

"What did you tell them?" the doctor asked.

"I told them the truth – that Jake was with us," Mikalah answered as her eyes met Jake's resolutely.

"I'm sure it was simply a case of being at the wrong place at the wrong time," the doctor shrugged. "It was bound to happen. It was just a matter of time before an innocent person was harmed in their mad frenzy for revenge," the doctor sighed. "Well, son, let's check on your bandages, shall we?"

Mikalah rose to leave the room. "No, Miss Ford, I need you to stay in here," the doctor directed. "He's gonna need his bandages changed every day, and I need you to stay here and learn how to do it."

"Me? You want me to change his bandages?" the thought of it made her woozy.

"Yes, your mother told me to show you how. She said she'll be too busy and needs you to learn to do it." The doctor motioned to Jake, "Take off your shirt, and flip onto your stomach"

Jake began unbuttoning his shirt with one hand, "Miss Ford, help him with that while I go get some water from downstairs."

Sensing her hesitation, Jake, tried to work faster with his left hand to unbutton his shirt, "That's ok, Mikalah, I can do it myself." But he wasn't making much progress so she sat gently next to him and began unbuttoning his shirt. He leaned forward, and she pulled the shirt from his left arm.

"Maybe we should just leave your right arm in it so you don't have to go through the discomfort of getting it back on," she suggested as she stood and stepped back.

"That's a good idea, thank you," he carefully rolled over onto his stomach with the side of his face in the pillow. Mikalah pulled his shirt out of the way so

92

that the doctor could work when he returned. She stepped nervously to the door to see what was taking the doctor so long. She wasn't comfortable being in the room with Jake's muscular chest exposed.

The doctor stepped into the room carrying a bowl of warm water. "Good, all right, now Miss Ford, I'm going to show you how to do this." Mikalah expected that she would stand back and watch, but instead the doctor made her remove the bandages, clean the wound and apply clean bandages as he instructed her step-by-step. After the initial shock of seeing the wound, she was glad he allowed her to learn by experience. Now she would know exactly what to do when the task was hers to do alone.

"Watch the wound closely. If it becomes inflamed or gets infected, you need to let me know immediately," the doctor instructed. "You should change the bandage morning and night. I'll leave you enough supplies for the week."

"Yes, sir," Mikalah stood back as the doctor helped Jake put his left arm into his shirt. Jake turned onto his side.

"How long do I have to lay here for?" Jake asked.

"Get help whenever you get up and move around so you don't pass out. You can judge yourself how well you feel, but I don't want you doin' any manual labor for at least a week."

"Doc, while you're here, would you mind helping me get up and to the outhouse?" he whispered.

The doctor chuckled, "Sure, I guess that is quite a trek." The doctor turned to Mikalah, "Maybe you should move him back downstairs to the storage room so he doesn't have to risk these stairs. I don't want him getting up in the middle of the night by himself and fallin' while he's trying to get to the outhouse."

Mikalah agreed. She hadn't considered the difficulty of the stairs.

~*~

Over the next eleven days Jake continued to recuperate and gained strength, working a little more around the house each day. The police stopped by to speak with Jake, but nothing further materialized. They wrote the whole incident off as Jake and Mikalah getting caught in the middle of the moonshiners' feuding. And since no one dared interfere in their battle, the investigation came to a stand still.

Friday afternoon Laurana stepped into the parlor holding the mail. She sat down next to Mikalah who sewed while Jake repaired one of Matty's broken toys. Laurana opened a letter, jumped up, and hugged Mikalah.

"Your daddy's comin' home!" she exclaimed excitedly.

"For a visit or to stay?" Mikalah asked.

"To stay! He's gotten a job with the railroad here in Chattanooga!" she darted around the house, "There's so much to be done!"

"When will he be here?" Mikalah laughed at her mother's disorientation.

"He says Saturday. That's tomorrow!" she exclaimed.

Mikalah rose and gave her mother a hug, "That's wonderful news, Mama! I can't believe after all this time Daddy's really comin' home!"

Matty joined in the hug and pranced around the house, "Daddy's comin' home! My Daddy's comin' home!" she sang.

Jake smiled at their jubilation, but knew that Mr. Ford's return meant it was time for him to leave. There wasn't enough work around the Ford household for two men. Jake had finished the tasks he was initially hired to perform.

As the women bustled around deciding on what needed to be cleaned, washed and straightened before Mr. Ford arrived, Jake stepped outside into the cool October air. He walked to the barn and slid a bucket on his arm and ambled toward the orchard. He collected apples that he could reach from the lower limbs as he weighed what he should do next.

He didn't want to leave town, but he knew it was time to leave the Fords. He began to pray in his mind about what he needed to do. The answer came and by the time he entered the house, he knew what he must do. In the end it would be best for everyone.

Jake set the bucket on the kitchen table, "I brought you some fresh apples. I thought Mikalah might like to make her daddy one of those award winning pies."

"What a wonderful idea!" Mrs. Ford exclaimed. "You are just so thoughtful, Jake!"

"Thank you ma'am." He paused, "Mrs. Ford, I wonder if I might be able to borrow the wagon and go into town for a bit this afternoon?"

Mikalah looked up at him, "Jake you're not well enough to go into town by yourself."

"I'm all right," he turned back toward Mikalah's mother, "May I borrow the wagon, Ma'am?"

"Sure, Jake, but maybe Mikalah should go with you just in case you get one of your dizzy spells."

"Oh, I haven't had one of those in four days. Besides you need her around here to make those pies," he smiled.

"Very well, Jake, if you feel you're up to it. Go ahead."

Jake gave no response to Mikalah's inquisitive stare. He thanked Laurana and stepped out the kitchen door toward the wagon.

"I'll be right back, Mama," Mikalah followed after him.

"Jake, where are you goin'?" she asked as he hitched up the team.

"I have a personal matter I need to tend to," he answered.

"What kind of personal matter?" she pressed.

"Don't worry, Mikalah. It's nothing dangerous. I just have an errand I need to run. I'll be back in an hour or so," he patted her cheek, circumvented her and climbed into the wagon.

Mikalah watched anxiously as he rode away.

~*~

After dinner the family sat on the front porch listening to the crickets. Hank and Hannah chatted excitedly about their father and all the fun things they'd be able to do with him when he returned.

"You're gonna like Daddy," Hank turned to Jake.

"Yes, I'm sure I will," he smiled.

"Daddy's gonna like Jake," Mikalah added, "He'll be happy to have an extra man around to help."

"Uh…" Jake saw this as his opening, and it was to Laurana that his eyes turned, "Ma'am I've been thinkin' about this, and I don't believe there's enough work around here for two men – especially not with the winter months coming on." Everyone's eyes were riveted on Jake. "I think it's time for me to go."

"What?" Mikalah exclaimed.

Matty leapt onto Jake's lap and flung her little arms around his neck. "You can't go Jake! You're supposed to stay and mawie Micky!" she cried.

Jake's eyes darted to Mikalah's stunned expression and back to Matty, "I'm not leaving Daisy, Matty. I just think it's time I found a job and somewhere else to live."

"We've got enough for you to do here," Mikalah insisted and looked to her mother who shrugged her shoulders.

"Honey, Jake is probably right. It's not like we have a huge farm here. I mainly hired Jake on 'cause there were certain things only a grown man could do, but now that your Daddy's comin' home …"

"Where will you go?" Mikalah interjected.

"That's why I went to town today. I got a job at B. Mifflin Hood."

"The tile factory?" Hank asked.

"Yes and I'm going to stay in the spare room in the back of Mr. Donaldson's store in exchange for keeping an eye on the store at night."

"Jake that sounds like a fine arrangement for you – a good job that pays cash money and a place to stay rent free," Laurana was impressed with Jake's initiative but Mikalah was still disappointed. She'd miss their long talks and working alongside him, and not to mention that his mere presence filled their home with an indescribable sweetness and peace that was never there before he arrived. Mikalah was glad that it was dark outside and that no one could see the tears brimming in her eyes.

"When do you start?" Hank asked.

"I start at the tile factory in the morning, and I'll start watching Mr. Donaldson's store tomorrow night."

Mikalah brushed the tears from her cheeks and tried to pull herself together. After all, he wasn't leaving Daisy and a steady job meant he intended to stay for a while.

"You're gonna come visit us – right?" Hannah asked.

"Every chance I get," he smiled.

"It's time for bed kids," Laurana stood and took Matty from Jake's lap and entered the house followed by Hannah and Hank.

Jake rose and motioned to Mikalah, "I'll be right back, Mikalah. I want to ask your mother something." He followed Laurana inside and returned after a few minutes. He sat down in the swing next to Mikalah, "I'm sure going to miss being here with your family."

"We're going to miss having you here. But I guess it's time you moved on and shared your light with someone else," she mused.

"You're a good friend to me, Mikalah," he took her hand in his and held it as they rocked in silence for several moments. "Actually, you're more to me than a good friend, and I think it's a good thing that I'm moving out."

"What…what do you mean?" she studied him as her heart leapt with the possibilities. Her mother lit a lamp in the parlor, and the light streamed softly onto the porch so they could see each other's faces.

"Now that we're not going to be living under the same roof, I – I wonder if you'd consider letting me court you? I asked your mother, and she said it would be all right for me to ask you."

"Jake, I can't think of anyone else I'd rather spend my time with."

"Then, how about I pick you up tomorrow night, and we'll go see the movie they're showing over on the hill."

"That sounds fun. I haven't been to a movie since…" she was going to say since she'd been out with Hal, but didn't want to taint the moment with his name. "In a long time," she finished.

He stood up, but still held her hand, "I guess I better get inside and pack my things. I'm going to get everything ready and drop it off at Mr. Donaldson's on the way into work."

"I'm so excited for you! It sounds like a great job opportunity for you!" Now that she knew he wanted to court her, his job and the move suddenly became a great blessing. Her mother and father would consider him a viable suitor now.

"I'm glad you're happy about it. I wasn't sure at first what you thought. But I think this will be the best thing for our relationship."

"I wasn't sure at first, but yes, I think you're right," she smiled.

"Good night," he leaned over and kissed her cheek and then reluctantly released her hand.

"Good night, Jake."

Chapter 6

Mikalah awoke to the familiar sound of Jake's voice as he milked the cows. A tear rolled down her cheek as she realized that this would be the last time she'd hear his beautiful singing first thing in the morning.

She rose and stood at the window watching him. The thought occurred to her that it may not be the last time she would awaken to his voice after all... maybe... no, she wouldn't dare hope. Jake carried the two pails of steaming milk to the kitchen, and Mikalah turned to dress.

"Good morning, Mikalah!" Laurana greeted her as she descended the stairs. Hannah, Hank, Matty and Jake were already gathered around the kitchen table for breakfast. Mikalah joined them as Jake offered the blessing.

"We're gonna miss those prayers of yours, Jake," Laurana smiled.

"I'm going to miss your delicious breakfasts, Mrs. Ford!"

"Mama, Jake asked me to go to the movie with him tonight. I was thinking he could join us for dinner before we go. What do you think?" Mikalah asked.

Laurana's eyebrows rose, "Oh, sure, come on for dinner, Jake, and you can meet Bill then."

"Thank you! I'm looking forward to it," Jake was going to miss the Fords, but he was a little nervous about meeting Mikalah's father. He'd heard that Bill Ford could be a stern man who was intolerant of other people's beliefs.

Jake rose from his chair and placed his dishes in the sink, "I guess it's about time I was off." He turned to face Laurana, "Mrs. Ford, I can't tell you enough how much I've enjoyed staying here with your family and how much I appreciate all that you've done for me while I was here – especially looking after me when I was injured."

Laurana stood and gave him a big hug, "You more than carned your keep. You're like my own son, and if anything we owe you a debt of gratitude for saving Mikalah's life."

Jake grabbed his bag from the floor by the door and flung it over his good shoulder. Hank, Hannah and Matty gathered around and clung to him, "Do you really have to go Jake?" Hannah spoke for all of them.

"Oh, come on now, kids, Jake's gonna be here for dinner tonight," Mikalah chuckled. "Let him get goin'."

He bent down and hugged each one of them and gave Matty a kiss on her cheek, "I'll see you tonight, sweetie."

Jake stepped out the door, and Mikalah followed him to the end of their driveway. She handed him a sack, "Here, I made you some lunch."

"Thank you, Mikalah!" he took it from her hand and gave her a hug, "See ya tonight around six." He started down the road.

"Good luck!" she called, and he turned back and waved as the school bus pulled in front of their house. Hannah and Hank raced to where Mikalah stood. She rubbed Hank's head as he passed. "You two have a good day."

"See ya!" they called as they climbed into the bus and Mikalah returned to the house. As she entered the door, her mother stood waiting for her with Jake's Book of Mormon in her hand.

"Mikalah, here's Jake's book. You can give it to him tonight," she held it out.

"Did you read it?"

"I read most of it," she still stood there holding it in her outstretched hand.

Reluctantly, Mikalah took it from her mother, "What did you think?"

"I think it's very interesting. Some sections are quite moving," Laurana turned to walk into the parlor, and Mikalah followed her.

"Did you pray about it?" Mikalah asked hopefully.

"I don't need to," her mother answered as she lifted her sewing.

"What do you mean?" Mikalah studied her intently.

"It doesn't matter whether it's true or not," her face remained emotionless.

"What do you mean it doesn't matter? How can you say that? If it's true, then God still speaks to us today. There are prophets living on the earth today. Everything takes on new meaning and direction if it's true!" Her mother's apathy was beyond Mikalah's comprehension.

Laurana sat down in a chair and placed her sewing on her lap, "Honey, if you believe it's true, then I think that's wonderful for you. But it's not something I can do anything with."

Mikalah knelt in front of her mother and put her hands on her mother's knees, "I don't understand, Mama."

"Honey, your father would never let me go to a different church. I know already that he'll make me stop going to the Methodist church where my friends are. He's not going to let me go to a church that believes in a totally different book than the Bible."

"We believe in the Bible too, Mama," Mikalah defended.

"I know, honey, but your father doesn't believe there's anything but the Bible – and only the Bible interpreted the way he's been taught. The Book of Mormon is just something I can't have in my life. But you...maybe you and Jake..."

"So, will you give me permission to be baptized?"

"Honey, I can't do that. Your father's coming back today, and if he finds out I gave you permission to be baptized into another church, I'll never live it down. Don't get me wrong, honey. Your daddy's a good man, but this is something he feels very strongly about. You need to just wait another week and get baptized when you're eighteen."

Mikalah's face fell. How could people be so closed minded? How could anyone keep someone from exercising her freedom of religion like this? Isn't that what our forefathers fought for – the freedom to worship as we please? She felt a sudden sadness and compassion for her mother.

"Since you're going to be seeing Jake, I think you should keep the fact that Jake's Mormon and your interest in Mormonism to yourself," Laurana suggested.

"You mean you want me to lie to Daddy?" Mikalah inquired with surprise.

"No, honey, I'm not telling you to lie to him, just don't mention it. If you do, it could mess up everything for you – not just your baptism, but your ... your relationship with Jake."

"Oh," Mikalah suddenly understood.

"Tell Jake not to mention it," Laurana instructed.

Mikalah nodded. She was grateful for her mother's kindness but simultaneously sad that her mother would never experience the joy she'd found. "Thank you, Mama," Mikalah leaned forward and gave her mother a hug and kissed her cheek.

~*~

Bill Ford stepped off the bus in front of the Home Store, straightened the hat on his salt and pepper hair, crossed the street and entered the store. A bell chimed. Mr. Donaldson soon greeted him. Donaldson was stocky and several inches shorter than Mr. Ford's thin six-foot frame.

"Hello Bill! It's been ages since I've seen you," a wide grin spread across the merchant's face and twinkled in his kind eyes, as he thrust out his hand and shook Mr. Ford's.

"How have you been?" Bill smiled at his old friend.

"Good, good, how 'bout yourself? Are you here to stay?"

"Yep, I'm home for good. Got a job on the railroad in Chattanooga," Bill unbuttoned his jacket, reached into his pocket and pulled out a few coins. "I'd like to get some candy for my little ones."

Donaldson stepped behind the counter, "Sure, what can I get for you?"

Bill selected some licorice whips and peppermint sticks and handed Donaldson the change.

"Your family's been in good hands while you were gone," Donaldson smiled.

"Oh really?"

"Yep, young man named Jake Elliot was stayin' at your house and helpin' out with things. Fine young man," Donaldson spoke of Jake with the pride a father would have for his own son.

"My wife said somethin' about a young man helpin' out with jobs around the house in exchange for room and board."

"Oh, Jake's a fine fella. You probably haven't heard, but last week he saved Miss Mikalah's life."

"He did? What happened to Mikalah?" Mr. Ford's eyes narrowed with worry.

"The moonshiners have gotten plum lawless around here, Bill. Last Monday they come speedin' down 27 shootin' a spray of submachine gun fire out the back window of their car. Jake shielded Miss Mikalah with his body and took a bullet in his shoulder."

"Was Mikalah injured?" Bill anxiously inquired.

"No, I think her arms got a bit scraped up from the fall. He had to throw her to the ground to get her out of the way, but she's just fine. Still the prettiest girl in town and blossomin' into quite the woman since you've been gone."

"Is the boy ok?" Bill asked

"Oh Jake's healin' up just fine. Now that you're back he's gonna stay here in my storeroom and watch the place for me at night. Also got a job over at B. Mifflin Hood."

"Sounds like you're mighty fond of him?" Bill smiled.

"I am. He's a good boy. Been a big help to me. And I believe you'll find that your family is very fond of him as well....especially one of them in particular," he winked.

"Who? You mean Mikalah?" Bill guessed.

"Maybe... but she'll have to fight little Matty for him first," Donaldson chuckled.

Bill's eyes lit up with the mere mention of Matty, "Speakin' of Matty, I've 'bout waited all I can stand to get home and see that little one. Thanks for the candy! I'm gonna run along."

"Good to have you back Bill!" Donaldson waved as Bill stepped out of the store.

Bill stood in front of his house amazed at the well kept yard and freshly painted house. Before he could even reach the door, Matty ran from the house to greet him. "Daddy, Daddy! Daddy's home," she yelled. Laurana ran from the house and threw her arms around her husband's neck and kissed him as Matty clung to his knees.

Mikalah stepped out onto the porch as her father and mother walked arm in arm up the steps. Mikalah tossed her arms around her father's neck and kissed his cheek, "Daddy! We've missed you!"

"My word, Mikalah! You've turned into a woman while I was gone," he pulled her back to arm's length and studied his oldest daughter.

Matty tugged his coat, "What about me, Daddy? Have I grown?"

He pulled Matty up into his arms and groaned, "Matty, you're heavy! You've gotten so big." He marveled, "And as pretty as ever!"

Matty hugged her father's neck, and he carried her into the house.

"The house looks great, Laurana," his eyes surveyed the home.

"Jake did it!" Matty beamed.

"I hear that you and Mikalah are fightin' over that boy," he pinched Matty's tummy, and she giggled delightedly.

"He's too old for me, so he's gonna mawie Micky," Matty announced as if it were a well known fact. Bill's eyebrows rose and studied Mikalah expectantly,

"Oh, Matty's just bein' silly, Daddy," Mikalah shook her head and waved her hand.

"Mikalah could do worse," her mother chimed in. "Jake's a fine boy."

"He's comin' for dinner tonight so you can meet him Daddy. Then he's takin' Micky to the movies," Matty chattered.

"Aren't you a wealth of information! Now I'll know who to come to when I want to know what everyone's up to," her father teased and carried her into the parlor and sat down with her on his lap.

Mikalah gave her mother a worried look, and Laurana smiled as she followed them.

~*~

Jake took a deep breath and sighed as he stood at the end of the Ford's driveway. He was doubly nervous. Not only was he meeting Mikalah's father for the first time, but also it was his first date with her. He looked down and brushed some lint from his coat and walked up the drive. As he stepped on the front porch, Matty ran out to greet him.

"Jake!" she squealed. He lifted her up and carried her toward the door. She put her hands on his cheeks, "I missed you!"

"I missed you too, sweetie."

Mr. Ford, who sat in a chair reading, draped his newspaper over the arm of his chair and stood to greet Jake.

"Daddy, this is Jake!" Matty introduced. Bill surveyed him. Jake was not what he expected. He was at least four inches taller than Bill, and his broad shoulders indicated that Jake was no boy, but a full grown man.

Jake shifted Matty onto his hip and shook Mr. Ford's hand, "Nice to meet you, sir."

"You too - I've heard a lot of good things about you," Bill's handshake was warm and friendly and his eyes twinkled. Inside Jake breathed a sigh of relief. This didn't seem like the stern man Mikalah described to him.

Jake put Matty down and nodded as Mikalah entered the room, "Evenin', Mikalah."

"Hi Jake!"

Her father noted the spark that passed between them. It made him a bit uncomfortable but Jake came highly recommended by not only his wife but also Mr. Donaldson. He knew Donaldson wasn't easily impressed.

"Dinner's ready if y'all want to come eat," Mikalah turned toward the kitchen, and they followed her. Hank and Hannah were already seated at the table. Laurana and Mikalah made a large meal for dinner instead of their usual lighter ones. It was a welcome home dinner for Bill, and they put out their best – including Mikalah's apple pie.

"I'm starvin'" Hank moaned.

"You're always starvin' Hank," Jake chuckled.

"Not much has changed around here," Bill laughed as they all sat around the table.

After dinner Jake and Mikalah started to help Laurana wash the dishes, "You two run along. You don't want to miss the movie."

"It doesn't start until seven thirty," Jake continued to clear the dishes from the table.

105

"No, you two run on and have a good evening. Hank and Hannah can help me with these."

Mikalah grabbed her sweater and a blanket, and they walked through the parlor. Bill was seated there, reading his paper. Jake reached out and shook his hand, "Nice meeting you, Sir. I'll have Mikalah back by ten."

Bill nodded, "I'll wait up." His face was serious and it was the first flicker of sternness Jake had seen in the man.

Mikalah grabbed Jake's arm, and they exited the house.

"Boy, he meant business didn't he?" Jake commented as they reached the end of the drive.

Mikalah chuckled, "Daddy can be a bit over protective."

"I would be too if you were my daughter," he winked. "You sure look pretty tonight, Mikalah."

"Thank you. You look extra handsome yourself," she smiled as she slipped her arm in his, and they continued down the street.

"Have you spoken to your mother about you being baptized?" Jake asked.

"Yes, she gave me your book back today," Mikalah related.

"So, did she read it? Did she pray about it?" Jake asked anxiously.

"She read most of it, but she didn't pray about it. It's so sad Jake, I think she's afraid to find out that it's true because then it would hurt worse," Mikalah's eyes glistened.

"What would hurt worse?"

"She says Daddy would never let her change churches and that he would be mad if she gave me permission to be baptized. She thinks it would be best for us not to mention that you're a Latter Day Saint or that I want to become one. She thinks I should wait until after I'm eighteen and just get baptized and not mention it to him. I'll be eighteen Saturday anyway."

"So you have to keep it a secret? That's going to be hard isn't it?" he stopped walking and turned to face her. "I mean how will you go to church without him knowing?"

"I know, but I think Mama's right. I think he would give me grief if he knew that I was getting baptized. If he knew you were the instigator of it, he could make things difficult for us."

106

"You mean, he wouldn't want me to court you – right?"

"Right…"

"I don't like the idea of keeping secrets from your father, but maybe your mother is right. Maybe we can just keep things to ourselves for now and then later on, it may not matter."

"Why wouldn't it matter later on?" she questioned as she looked up into his emerald eyes.

"Let's just take one step at a time, and I'm sure the Lord will provide a way. For now, we know you want to be baptized and next Saturday is your birthday. So let's plan that much and let the Lord take care of the rest."

"I'd love to be baptized on my birthday," she smiled.

"That's what I was hoping you'd say," the dimple in his chin deepened as he smiled. "I was thinking we could have your baptism in the afternoon and then I could take you somewhere special for your birthday."

"Really? Where?"

"Oh, it's a surprise," a teasing grin played at the corners of his mouth. "How about I pick you up around noon and we have your baptism down on the Tennessee River? I'll let the people at church know tomorrow so some of them will come. You'll need a white dress. Do you have one?"

"Hmm.. not a solid white one. But I can make one," she was getting excited just thinking about how close it was.

"Bring an extra set of clothes – the nicest dress you have and some towels. Sister Karrick lives near the river, and we can change at her house and go out for your birthday after that."

"Oh, this sounds fun! I can't wait!" she put her arm in his, and they continued walking toward the hill where the movie was shown. Every Saturday night, a man who sold tonic would put up a screen on the side of the hill by the clay pit and show a movie.

"Mikalah! So good to see you!" a dark-headed young woman with a sickening sweet grin approached them, "I see you've moved on to your next conquest." The girl tossed her head with an air of superiority, "I'm here with Hal." She looked around and pointed to where Hal stood with several other young men, one of which was the girl's sickening brother, Jeb Bailey. At the sight of the two Baileys, nausea churned in Mikalah's stomach, and an eerie feeling jarred her composure. The memory of Jake's blood on her hands as he lay wounded flashed into Mikalah's mind. The police suspected the Bailey's involvement in the shooting, and now Mikalah forced herself to make pleasant conversation with the moonshiner's daughter.

"I'm sure you and Hal will be very happy together," Mikalah tried to act cordial, but Jake noticed Mikalah's clenched jaw and deduced that these two girls were not the best of friends.

"Hal, honey, look who's here!" the girl called out, and Hal joined them, putting his arm around her.

"Hangin' out with the Mormon boy – eh, Micky?" Hal crinkled his nose in distaste. "Better watch out, he's probably got three or four wives spread across the country. He'll be wantin' to add you to his harem."

Jake stood still, clenching and unclenching his fist but told himself to remain calm because Hal wasn't worth his energy.

"If anyone's a womanizer, Hal, you are," Mikalah tightened her grip on Jake's arm. "You better watch out for him, Emmaline. Hal's not exactly the gentleman he purports to be. And you may not be as lucky as I was to have someone strong and kind to protect you."

"If you'll excuse us, we'd like to find a seat before the movie," Jake tipped his hat, smiled at Emmaline and guided Mikalah to a spot on the grass where he helped her spread out a blanket.

"That's a perfect pair. Emmaline Bailey has always been after Hal. She dated him before I did and has been scheming and plotting to get him back ever since. I'm happy to let her have him," Mikalah stood watching them, and Jake plopped down on the blanket.

He tugged her hand indicating that she should join him, "Don't worry about him anymore, Mikalah. Hating him is a waste of energy."

She sat next to him. "Oh I don't hate him – or her. I just think they're a match made in – well – I'd say heaven, but it's more likely the other direction," she rolled her eyes. "I'm just glad he's found someone else so he'll leave me alone."

"Her last name is Bailey? Is she related to the moonshiners?" he asked.

"Yes, she's the daughter of Ed Bailey who shot Pop Richards. So like I said, she and Hal make a perfect match." Mikalah shuddered involuntarily.

Jake reached into the inside pockets of his jacket and pulled out a bottle of orange soda from each side and a small bag of peppermint sticks, "Here, I brought us some snacks for the movie."

"Thank you! I haven't had a soda in months. This is a real treat!" she took the bottle and a peppermint stick. The cartoons started, followed by the serial and then the movie.

Halfway through the movie at the most suspenseful point, the person manning the projector stopped it, and his partner stood to explain about a tonic that he claimed was good for your horse, your cow or even your children. It solved every ailment and cured every malady.

"Watch, Jake, I'll bet you Hal buys at least four bottles of that stuff," Mikalah nudged him with her elbow.

"Really? Why?"

"It's nothing but moonshine. He always buys enough to get whoever he's dating a little tipsy," Mikalah realized she'd said too much when she noticed Jake's startled expression. It didn't take him a second to wonder if Mikalah had learned this about Hal from sad experience.

"So have you tried it?" he asked.

"I'm sorry to say I have. I was out here with Hal last summer, and I had this horrible headache. So Hal says, 'Come on, Micky, I'll get you some tonic, and that'll get rid of your headache.' It didn't get rid of my headache, so Hal kept telling me to drink more and more of it. I realize now that he probably had other things on his mind. But it made me so sick to my stomach, that I made him take me home." She chuckled as she thought about it.

"Guess that backfired on him."

"It sure did, I never would try it again."

"Look," Jake nodded toward Hal who was buying four bottles of tonic from the man. "You were right. It would be funny, but I feel sorry for Emmaline." He shook his head in disgust.

"Oh, don't feel sorry for Emmaline. She can hold her liquor. That moonshiner's daughter can drink any man under the table." Mikalah noticed

Jake's somewhat shocked expression, "I'm sorry, Jake. I'm making you uncomfortable. I guess this is a totally different world than what you're used to in Utah?"

"It is, but I've seen a lot over the last few years. It's just sad to see what people do to each other and what women, in particular, have to put up with," he shook his head.

"We learn to hold our own," she sighed as the movie started again. "Not all men are like Hal. There are lots of nice boys I grew up with who would never treat women like he does."

After the movie, they folded up their blanket. Jake noted Hal standing with his friends and guided Mikalah in the opposite direction toward the main road.

"So do you want to go to church with me tomorrow? Mr. Donaldson said I could borrow his car again."

Mikalah winced, "Oh, I'm sorry, Jake, but I can't."

"Why not?"

"It's Daddy's first Sunday back, and he wants us to go to the Baptist church with him. He's not too pleased that Mama has been taking us to the Methodist church. I'll need to go with them this one Sunday, and then after I'm eighteen I can do what I want."

Jake was disappointed, but he understood that it was important to stay in her father's good graces – at least until after her birthday.

"You could go with us," she suggested.

"I really need to go to our church to arrange for your baptism and also because they need me there so they can have the sacrament."

"That's right. They're going to think I'm horrible not going to church the Sunday before I'm baptized. Not incredibly dedicated of me is it?" Mikalah felt bad.

"It's important that we don't alienate your father. I understand that. They will too," Jake didn't want her to berate herself over something she couldn't do much about.

"It does make me wonder how I'll be able to go to church afterward," a worried expression crossed her face.

110

Jake squeezed her hand, "Don't worry. I have some ideas. Let's just get past Saturday, and you'll be fine."

"You're just full of mysteries tonight," a smile followed her puzzled expression.

"Everythin's going to be all right, I know that. We just need to be faithful and obedient and it will all fall into place."

"You say that with such certainty. How do you know?" she looked up at him as they walked.

"I – I'll tell you someday, but for now, just trust me," he smiled.

"I've gone and found me a man who's tall, dark, handsome *and* mysterious," she chuckled. Jake rolled his eyes and laughed.

As they reached the door to her house, Mikalah could see her father sitting in his favorite chair reading by lantern light.

"Thank you, Jake, that was fun," she shifted nervously and moved until they were out of her father's view. "Why don't you come for lunch tomorrow after church?"

"You sure that will be all right with your parents?"

"Sure, we always have enough. You know that," she smiled.

"That's true," he nodded as he still held her left hand in his, "I guess I should let you get some rest. Thanks for coming out with me," Jake stared at her mouth and leaned his head down toward her lips when …

"Uh-hum," they instantly turned their heads toward the doorway where Mr. Ford stood staring at them.

"Thank you for getting Mikalah home by ten, Mr. Elliot."

"Yes sir," Jake nodded, a bit embarrassed.

"Good night, Mr. Elliot," Bill stood motionless in the door. "Time to come in, Mikalah."

"Yes sir," she turned back to Jake, "Thank you for a wonderful evening, Jake." She quickly put her hands around his neck, tugged him forward and kissed his cheek. "I'll see you tomorrow," she whispered in his ear. Jake was surprised that she would be so bold in front of her father. He watched, somewhat shocked as she walked around Bill, and into the house, "Goodnight, Daddy."

"Goodnight Mr. Ford" Jake nodded and stepped off the porch. His feet felt lighter than air as he strode home. He wondered at Mikalah's daring behavior in front of her father, but realized that it was her way of letting Jake – and her father – know that she wasn't going to let other people make her decisions for her.

~*~

Jake stepped briskly up the Ford's driveway, excited to tell Mikalah about the plans he'd arranged for her baptism. He stepped up onto the front porch and lifted his hand to knock when Mr. Ford opened the door with a rifle in his hands. Jake stepped backward to give the man room to step outside.

Bill's angry eyes bore into Jake as the wiry man's chest heaved. He pointed the gun toward Jake's shoulder.

"Daddy, let me talk to him," Mikalah begged from behind her father.

"Get in the house Mikalah," he growled.

"Is there something wrong, Sir?" Jake asked and looked questioningly past the man toward Mikalah.

Mr. Ford turned back and slammed the door in Mikalah's face so Jake couldn't see inside the house, "Mr. Elliot, I don't want you seeing my daughter anymore, and I kindly ask that you don't come back around my family again."

Kindly, this is kindly? Jake thought to himself. "Why? What's wrong?"

"I don't want you comin' around fillin' my daughter's head with your satanic beliefs," he growled.

"Satanic beliefs? I don't have satanic beliefs." Jake's heart pounded, and an all-to-familiar sick nausea thickened in the pit of his stomach.

"Why you don't even believe in Jesus or the Bible. You worship some fella named Joe Smith and read his golden bible."

"Sir, I don't know who told you this, but they don't know what they're talking about," Jake defended.

"Are you callin' my preacher a liar, boy?"

"No sir, but he has been misinformed. We do believe in the Bible, and the name of our church is The Church of *Jesus Christ* of Latter-day Saints, and the

Book of Mormon is another testament of Jesus Christ. It's obvious we believe in and worship Jesus Christ."

"Get off o' my property boy. I don't need you pumpin' my family's heads full o' your nonsense," Bill took a step forward and adjusted the rifle in his hands.

Jake stood unflinching, "But, sir, surely you're a fair-minded man and will at least give me a chance to tell my side of it." Laurana stepped out onto the porch and put her hand on her husband's shoulder.

"I don't need to hear your side of it," Bill steamed like an angry bull ready to charge.

"Honey, you don't need to threaten violence. Jake's not going to hurt anybody. He saved Mikalah's life less than two weeks ago. You can't treat him like this. It's not right!"

"Get inside, Laurana. I've heard enough of you defendin' him. He's got you brainwashed like he's done Mikalah. He's probably in with those moonshiners and had it comin' to him."

"Mormons don't even drink, Bill. That doesn't make a bit o' sense," she reasoned. Noting her husband's anger rising, Laurana turned to Jake, a sympathetic expression washed over her kind features, "Jake, dear, run along now."

"Yes, ma'am," he hung his head, turned and walked back to the street, all the while the blood pumped through his veins like a racehorse on its final lap of the Kentucky Derby.

He looked back toward the house before turning onto the highway. Matty stood with her nose pressed to the parlor window, tears streaming down her rosy cheeks, and Hannah watched forlornly from the upstairs bedroom window.

Inside the house, Mikalah grabbed her brother by the shoulders, "Hank, cover for me. Tell Daddy I'm upstairs in my room."

"Ok," Hank nodded.

Her heart pounding, Mikalah snuck out the kitchen door, waited until she heard the front door slam, and slipped along the side of the house, cut through the neighbor's field and ran toward the highway to meet Jake. Hank slipped upstairs and locked Mikalah's door, put the skeleton key in his pocket, and returned downstairs.

113

"Jake!" she whispered from behind a tree in a thicket alongside the highway.

Jake peered around and then saw her head peeking out from behind the tree. He stepped off the road and met her in the wooded area.

"Are you all right?" He put one hand on her shoulder and with his other wiped away the tears that streamed from her eyes.

"I had no idea he could be so hard headed and cruel!" she brushed her angry tears and flung her arms around his waist, burying her head in his shoulder. He held her, stroking her strawberry blonde curls with his hand, and let her cry for several minutes.

"What happened?" Jake finally asked when her tears subsided.

"Oh, that preacher got wind that we were courtin' and flew off the handle, tellin' Daddy a bunch of lies. Of course Daddy believed him and not us. Daddy came home all in a huff after church this morning and started telling me I couldn't see you anymore and repeating all these lies about the Church. I tried to explain to him, even Mama tried to explain, but he wouldn't listen."

"People won't listen when they get like that. It's best to not waste your energy," Jake ran his hand through his hair in frustration. He sighed, "What do we do now?"

"We continue as planned," she stated resolutely. "I'm getting baptized on Saturday no matter what."

Jake chuckled at her spunk, "So what do you have in mind?"

"Meet me down by the creek bridge at noon. If I'm late, wait for me. I'll be there no matter what. I'll slip out somehow and meet you. We'll do everything just as we planned. I'll be eighteen, and he can't stop me. He can't tell me what I can or can't do then," nothing was going to shake her determination.

"All right. I'll be there," he couldn't help but be proud of her. He'd seen grown men cower under less threatening circumstances. "I'm so proud of you Mikalah!" he beamed.

"I know it's true, and nobody's going to stop me from having the blessings. They're mine now – mine to take," she became more resolved as she said it.

"You better go back before they notice you're missing," he suggested.

"I know," she reached up on her tip toes, pulled his head toward her and kissed his cheek, "I'll see you Saturday." She turned and ran back toward the house in the direction she'd come. Jake's heart ached for her. The persecution had started, and he wished they could just get past it. He was used to it, but his heart broke for Mikalah. He couldn't bare the thought of her suffering.

~*~

The chilly night air hit his face, and Jake pulled his scarf over his ears as he exited the tile factory for the evening.

"Psst"

Jake searched to see who was trying to get his attention.

"Psst... over here."

Jake looked to his left where a man stood next to a tree. "Elliot, over here." Jake strained to make out the man's face. It was Eddie Richards who worked on the same manufacturing line with Jake. Jake approached him, "What's up, Eddie?"

"Shh- come here a minute," Eddie tugged Jake's arm, pulled him aside and led him a few steps into the woods.

"I need to tell ya somethin'. You know that mornin' you were shot in front of Donaldson's Home Store?"

"Yes."

"That wasn't no accident," Eddie whispered.

"Of course it wasn't an accident. Why would someone shoot a submachine gun out the back of a car by accident," Jake quipped.

"No, I mean they meant to shoot at you and the Ford girl. They weren't shootin' at nobody else," Eddie clarified.

"What? Why would anyone want to shoot at Mikalah and me?" an ominous sensation ascended Jake's spine.

"They was shootin' at one o' ya in particular," Eddie added.

"Which one of us? Who was it? Why were they shooting at us?" Jake fired one question after another.

"I've done said too much already. But watch your back, Jake. I like ya, and well, just watch your back, and keep an eye on that girl. She ain't safe."

Jake grabbed Eddie by the shoulders, "Come on now, you can't just tell me something like this and leave me hanging! What's going on here?"

"I can't say no more, but you and Miss Ford watch your backs. I gotta go," Eddie wiggled free and darted into the darkness.

All the way home, Jake's mind flurried with questions. How was he supposed to watch Mikalah's back if he wasn't allowed around the Ford house anymore? Who in the world would want to harm Mikalah? Why would they want to harm her or him for that matter? Eddie's one of Pop Richard's sons. Does that mean that one of the moonshine factions is after him and Mikalah for some reason? Why? Whatever the answers to those questions, the answer to another dilemma that had been weighing on his mind was now crystallizing into only one solution.

Donaldson counted the register as Jake entered the Home Store, "Evenin' Jake, how was your day?"

"Creepy," Jake stood in front of Donaldson placing both palms on the counter. "Can I help you with anything?"

"Yeah, tell me why your day was creepy," Donaldson studied Jake.

"My day was fine, but as I was leaving the factory…" Jake related his experience with Eddie Richards as Donaldson listened intently.

"You reckon he's just pullin' your leg, Jake? We're comin' up on Halloween next week. People like to play tricks around here at Halloween," Donaldson suggested.

"Halloween's not 'til next Monday. Why wouldn't he save it for then if he was just tricking me?"

"Hmm… Reckon you're right about that. Just doesn't make any sense is all."

"I know," Jake yawned, stretched and went to his room at the back of the store.

"I'm closin' up for the evenin', Jake. I'll see ya tomorrow," Donaldson called out.

"Goodnight!"

~*~

Jake took some money from a sack that he kept hidden under his mattress and put a few bills in his wallet. He looked forward to spending the day and evening with Mikalah. He'd spent some time fasting and praying that week that everything would go well and that Mikalah's baptism would be a special experience for her that she'd always remember.

Jake tossed his folded white pants and shirt into the back of the car along with a brown package. He went back into the store and brought out a picnic basket and set it in the trunk. He peered up at the horizon, thankful for the blue skies and the warm sunny day. It was perfect for a baptism and a picnic.

Jake sat behind the wheel and started up the road toward the creek bridge where he was to meet Mikalah at noon. He arrived a few minutes early and parked on the side of the road to wait.

~*~

Mikalah bundled her best dress, a towel and the white dress she'd made that week into a clean flour sack and let the bag drop out her bedroom window. If she hadn't been afraid of drawing attention to herself, she would have worn her best dress or her white one. But she couldn't take the chance so she wore an everyday dress as she descended the stairs and went into the kitchen.

"Mama," she whispered so her father couldn't hear from the parlor. "I'm goin' now. I'll be back tonight."

Her mother hugged her and kissed her cheek. "Have a good time, dear," she whispered.

Mikalah exited the kitchen door as if she were going for a walk in the yard, went around to the back of the house where her bag lay, picked it up and headed briskly to the main road and toward the creek.

Jake sat in the car, his head tilted back, and his eyes closed. Mikalah tapped on the back window of the car, and he jumped, "Hi!" he greeted as he opened the car door and walked around to let her in the passenger side. "I can put your bag in the trunk."

Mikalah's hands were trembling as she sat in the car waiting for him to join her. The excitement of sneaking out, meeting the man she loved and getting baptized against her father's approval was a bit nerve wracking.

"You nervous?" he reached out to squeeze her hand when he got in the car.

"A little," she grinned.

"You still want to do this?" he asked.

"Of course!"

"Great!" Jake started the car and drove South toward Hixson and the river.

"So are you going to tell me what we're doing tonight?"

"Nope, still a surprise," he winked. "Did you have a hard time getting away?"

"No, it was really easy. I told Mama what I was going to do so she knows where I am, but Daddy will think I just went out with friends – which is true – right?"

"Yes, it is!" he agreed.

"Mama's been so supportive. I wouldn't be able to do this if she wasn't."

"Your mother is a wonderful woman." Mrs. Ford helped ease Jake's homesickness for his own mother.

~*~

Jake parked near the river, stepped out of the car and around to open Mikalah's door.

"Hello Brother Elliot, Sister Ford!" Fanny waved. The large woman stepped out of the driver's side of her car as her sister Lillian opened the passenger side door.

"We're so happy for you, dear!" Lillian stood, and Fanny nodded in agreement.

"I thought this spot over here would be good," Fanny pointed to a cove where it would be easy for them to enter the water.

"That looks perfect," Jake opened the trunk and took out Mikalah's bag and gathered his clothes and towel.

"Hmmm… I need to put on my white dress," Mikalah looked around for somewhere to change.

"Oh, we came prepared," Fanny nodded at her sister, and the two walked to the back of their car and pulled out three large quilts and several yards of rope. They walked to a group of trees and tied the rope around a trunk. Jake and Mikalah followed them; helping them secure the rope around three trees and then hung the quilts over the ropes to form a little dressing area.

"Ladies first," Jake gestured toward the makeshift dressing room. Mikalah moved the quilt aside and stepped in with her bag. Momentarily she emerged, dressed in white, barefoot with her hair pulled back.

Mikalah decided she'd never seen Jake look as handsome as he did when he stepped outside in his bare feet, white shirt and white pants.

Fanny offered a prayer, and the little group sang *I Know that My Redeemer Lives*. Jake took Mikalah by the hand and led her into the water. As she emerged from the cold water, she felt pure, clean, and full of love. She sensed that her Savior was near and that He was smiling in approval. With her strawberry blonde hair swept back glistening in the sun, she wiped the water from her eyes and turned to embrace Jake. Radiant smiles on their faces, they made their way back to shore, and Fanny and Lillian each put an arm around her, patting her back gently.

Pure joy filled her heart as she dried her long curls with her towel and changed from her wet clothes into her best dress. Anxiously she stepped outside and allowed Jake to enter, then joined Fanny and Lillian on the grassy river bank.

"Have a seat here, dear," Fanny pointed to a stump on which they'd laid a blanket.

"You two have the most beautiful quilts!" Mikalah ran her hand along the cloth, admiring the pattern.

"Fanny makes them. Aren't they beautiful? She's an amazing seamstress too," Lillian patted her sister's back and hugged her gently.

119

Mikalah sat down on the stump, and the two ladies sat next to her on a blanket spread out on the ground.

"I should let one of you sit up here," Mikalah rose.

"No dear, you sit there. Brother Elliot will need to stand behind you to confirm you. Are you familiar with how this works?" Fanny asked as Mikalah sat back down.

"Yes, Jake told me that he'll lay his hands on my head and confirm me a member of the Church and give me the Gift of the Holy Ghost," Mikalah answered.

"It's a wonderful feeling Mikalah, to have the Gift of the Holy Ghost," Fanny smiled.

"Oh yes, before I was baptized, I only felt the Spirit occasionally, but afterwards, I feel it so much throughout the day, guiding me and prompting me," Lillian agreed.

"Answers come so much easier than they did before, don't you think Lillian?" Fanny turned to her sister who nodded in agreement.

"It's why I wanted to be baptized. I really want to have that constant companionship of the Spirit. I'm hopin' I'll make better choices with it to guide me on a daily basis," Mikalah explained.

"You will, dear. Be obedient, and the Spirit will be there to show you the way and warn you in dangerous or harmful situations. Listen carefully to the feelings and impressions you receive and don't second guess them. Act immediately when you're prompted," Lillian advised.

"I will!" Mikalah thrilled at the opportunity to learn from these women who knew so much about the gospel and how to discern the voice of the Spirit.

"Best of all it's the abiding peace and assurance you have with the Holy Spirit as your guide," Fanny added.

"Most definitely, I don't worry near as much as I used to," Lillian agreed.

"I'm so excited about this!" Mikalah lifted her gaze, and her heart thrilled to see Jake walking toward them in his best suit. She wasn't entirely sure whether her heart beat so furiously because she was about to receive a precious gift from God or whether it was because Jake, looking so handsome, was the one who would bestow it. She realized at that moment that what made Jake so irresistible in her eyes was not only that he was handsome, strong and kind, but mostly the comfort and peace he carried with him. It was the power of the priesthood that he quietly held and the Spirit's presence that emanated from him, setting everyone at ease. It was what made being in his company so comforting and reassuring. She always felt safe with him.

"You ready?" he smiled.

"Oh yes!" Mikalah beamed as Jake stepped behind her.

"It's Mikalah Allison Ford, right?" he leaned down to ask.

"Yes," she answered, somewhat surprised that he knew her middle name.

Jake placed his hands on her head and confirmed her as a member of The Church of Jesus Christ of Latter-day Saints and commanded her to receive the Holy Ghost. A flood of tingling warmth spread throughout her body, starting at her heart and extending throughout her limbs as tears welled in her eyes. The feeling was like nothing she'd ever experienced, and she hung on every word of the blessing that he pronounced upon her.

He blessed her with the ability to discern truth from error, to find peace in unsettling circumstances, and that one day she would enter the temple of the Lord to be sealed to her husband and that together they would raise a righteous posterity who would rise up and call her blessed for being true and faithful in spite of opposition and strife.

Tears flowed from each person's eyes as the Spirit spread over them like a warm blanket on a cold morning. Mikalah stood, and Fanny and Lillian rose to their feet. Mikalah turned and threw her arms around Jake's waist and nestled her head into his shoulder. He put his arms around her and held her close. Mikalah leaned her head back and looked up into his eyes as he wiped away her tears with the back of his hand.

"Thank you, Jake!"

The look that passed between them did not go unnoticed by Lillian and Fanny. Fanny winked at her sister and smiled as Mikalah turned around to shake each of their hands and embraced them.

"Welcome to the Church, my dear!" Fanny exclaimed.

"Yes, welcome, Sister Ford!" Lillian smiled.

"Thank you so much, ladies. You both have been so wonderful to be here for me," Mikalah's heart was full of gratitude for everyone and for everything in her life. *Surely there could be no more perfect moment than this*, she thought to herself.

The little group took down the rope and the blankets, folded them up and carried them to Sister Snodgrass' car. Jake shut the trunk after the last blanket was loaded and shook the ladies' hands before they turned to enter their car.

"Thank you, sisters! You've been so kind," Jake waved as the two ladies got in their automobile and drove away. He turned to Mikalah who stood next to him waving, "So how do you feel?"

"Wonderful! Clean, peaceful, as if all my worries have melted away," she laced her arm with his.

He turned to face her, caressing her cheek with his hand, "Are you ready for the second half of this day?"

She smiled up at him, "I can't wait!"

"Well this is just as good a spot to start as any," he turned back toward his car, opened the trunk and pulled out a picnic basket and a blanket. He handed the blanket to Mikalah, and they strolled back to a grassy area on the river bank. Mikalah spread out the blanket, and Jake set down the basket.

"Wait here, I need to get one more thing," he ran back to the car and pulled the brown package from the rear seat and trotted back to where Mikalah sat.

"What's that?" she asked.

"It's your birthday present," he smiled.

"Oh, you shouldn't have gotten me anything. The baptism was enough!" she knew he didn't have much money and didn't want him to feel obligated to buy her anything.

"I ordered this for you several weeks ago," he handed her the package. She stared at the Salt Lake City, Utah return address.

"What is it?" she looked up at him.

"Open it and see," he smiled and sat down next to her on the blanket.

Mikalah untied the package, tore open the paper and opened the box, "It's my very own Book of Mormon and Doctrine and Covenants with my name engraved on the outside of them! She traced her fingers over her name, *Mikalah Allison Ford.* "How did you know my middle name?"

"I asked your mother," he winked.

"I love it!" she leaned forward, hugged his neck and kissed his cheek, "Thank you!"

As she moved back, he held her head in his hands, gazing into her eyes, "You're welcome." He lowered his eyes to her lips. Mikalah held her breath, so intense was his gaze. Slowly he leaned forward and gently kissed her apple red lips. Her mouth melted into his, and her heart leapt in exhilaration at his touch. She'd begun to wonder if she'd ever feel it again, but now, it was so deliciously hers that she sighed reluctantly when his lips broke from hers, and he pulled her close. Jake kissed her hair, and his low masculine voice whispered into her ear, "I love you, Mikalah."

She leaned back, searched his eyes, and putting her hand to his cheek, her thumb toyed with the dimple in his chin. Her eyes fell to his lips, "I love you, Jake, more than anything." She leaned forward, and her lips met his once more. All the feelings she had for him poured out in her kiss – a kiss that she never would, never could give to any other man. She knew at that moment she was born for him, and it was no wonder that she'd never felt anything like this before. He was the other half of her that had always been missing. Now that she'd found him, she felt whole and complete in his arms, utterly safe and filled with joy.

Reluctantly, Jake forced himself away from her. In his whole life, he'd never taken a drink or smoked a cigarette, but he felt certain that there could be nothing as addictive as Mikalah's kiss. His heart pounding in his chest, he reached for the picnic basket and started rummaging through it.

Mikalah looked down at her books that lay on her lap, "How did you afford these?"

"Huh?" he turned back to see her staring at the books. "Oh, I've socked some money away over the last few years," he answered casually.

"Ah, so you're not as broke as you led us to believe?" she teased.

"I never said I was broke," he smiled, turned back around and handed Mikalah a plate of fried chicken, mashed potatoes and corn on the cob.

"Did you make this?" she was surprised because she knew he didn't have a kitchen in his little room at the back of Donaldson's store.

"No, you'd be disappointed if I had," he chuckled. "I'm not much of a cook. Mrs. Donaldson was kind enough to cook this for us when I told her about the afternoon we had planned." Jake sat with his plate on his knee and opened a bottle of orange soda and handed it to her, then opened one for him and set it on the ground beside him.

"This looks delicious! Please thank her for me!" she waited for him to say the prayer.

"Why don't you bless the food this time, Mikalah," he suggested.

"Oh, ok," she set her plate down on the blanket in front of her, folded her arms and offered a prayer.

They each took a bite of fried chicken. "This is really good!" they both said simultaneously and began to laugh.

The warmth of the sun shone down on them as a gentle breeze blew a few autumn leaves from the trees. "This is so much fun!" Mikalah's eyes turned out to the river. "I think it's the most perfect day of my life."

When they'd finished their plates of food, Jake asked, "Do you want your desert now or later?"

"Oh, I'm stuffed. I'd like to wait a little while," she rubbed her stomach.

"All right," Jake gathered up their plates and set them back into the basket and shut the lid. He shifted the basket off the blanket and leaned back, resting his head on his hands and crossed his legs. "We've got some time to spare," he pulled his watch from his pocket, noted the time, put it back and then returned his hand behind his head.

"What time is it?" she studied him sprawled out next to her.

"It's about three. We've got about three hours before we need to be anywhere," he closed his eyes. She sat with her knees curled up under her as she watched the ducks fly over the river. She marveled at the warmth of the day and the blue skies. When she glanced back at Jake, he'd already dozed off. She opened her Doctrine and Covenants and began reading. After reading several sections she leaned back on her side facing him, resting her head on her elbow as she

124

continued reading. Soon her eyes were heavy, and she drifted off to sleep, her books lying between them.

Jake woke up and noticed that the sun had shifted significantly. He pulled his arm out from behind his head and looked at his watch. It was shortly after five. He sat up and noticed Mikalah asleep next to him, her Doctrine and Covenants lying open in front of her. He picked up the book and thumbing through the pages noticed that Mikalah had already marked a passage in section 6 verses 33-37:

"Fear not to do good, my sons, for whatsoever ye sow, that shall ye also reap; therefore, if ye sow good ye shall also reap good for your reward. Therefore, fear not, little flock; do good; let earth and hell combine against you, for if ye are built upon my rock, they cannot prevail. Look unto me in every thought; doubt not, fear not."

He leaned on his side, propped up on his elbow facing her. He gently brushed a stray curl back, feeling the softness of her hair as she slept. She was so beautiful. He could hardly believe that life could have brought him such a sweet reward as this young woman who was smart, faithful and beautiful. He leaned over and gently kissed her lips as she slept. She stirred slightly as he sat back up and ran his fingers through her silky hair.

Her eyes fluttered, and she looked up at him, "Did you just kiss me?"

"Who me?" he affected innocence.

"There's no one else around is there?" she chuckled. "If you're going to kiss me, at least let me be awake to enjoy it," she laughed as she sat up and stretched her arms high above her head. "What time is it?"

"A little after five. Would you like some dessert now? Mrs. Donaldson makes some amazing chocolate cake," he winked.

"Oooh, now that sounds good," she yawned.

Jake opened the basket and reached in to pull out a slice of cake for each of them. "Here you go," he handed Mikalah's to her and got one for himself.

Jake took a bite of cake, "Now this is delicious!"

Mikalah set her cake next to her on the blanket and yawned again, "Ugh, I can't seem to wake up."

Jake picked up Mikalah's fork and scooped up a piece of cake and extended it toward her mouth. "Try this, and it'll wake you up," he winked as he fed it to her.

"Mmm.. that is good," she licked her lips.

"I knew you'd like that," he handed her the fork and took another bite of his own cake.

"So where are we going?" she asked.

"Nope, still a secret," he winked.

"When are you going to tell me?"

"You'll know when we get there," he teased and reached out to remove a small piece of chocolate cake from the corner of her mouth.

"Oh great!" she rolled her eyes. "I'll be lucky if I don't have cake all over my dress by the time I'm done."

He chuckled and took his last bite of cake and handed her his handkerchief.

"Thanks," she wiped her mouth and then reached over to clean his chin, "I think you might need this too," she giggled.

"Oh no!" he laughed.

Mikalah rose and brushed her dress making sure she didn't have any cake crumbs on it as Jake packed everything back into the basket and folded up the blanket. She walked closer to the water where she had been baptized earlier in the day, closed her eyes and relived the memory of it.

Suddenly she felt Jake's arms around her waist as he embraced her from behind. "Just one more thing before we go," he whispered into her ear.

She leaned her head back on his shoulder as he kissed her neck, "Yes?"

"Will you marry me?"

Mikalah spun around to face him, "What?" She heard him. She just wanted to hear him say it again because she could hardly believe her ears.

"Will you marry me, Mikalah?"

She was speechless. Her perfect day that she thought could get no better just became something out of a fairy tale. Tears glistened in her blue eyes.

"If you need more time to think about it and pray about it…" he began.

126

"I don't need time to think or to pray. I already know the answer. You're the other half of me, Jake. There's nobody else for me," she put her arms around his neck and held him tight. After several moments, she leaned back and looked into his face.

He put his palms to her cheeks and gazed adoringly into her eyes. "I love you so much, Mikalah," he caressed her cheeks as he kissed her soft lips and remembered his dream. He longed for the moment when he would no longer have to restrain himself where Mikalah was concerned, when he would be free to kiss her as long and as passionately as he liked. But for now.... he reluctantly pulled himself from her lips and took her hand.

"There is one thing we need to pray about." She looked at him expectantly as he spoke. "When and where?" She wasn't sure how to respond so she just waited for him to continue. "See, the thing is, you can't go to the temple for another year – you have to wait a year after you're baptized. The closest temples are in Utah. If we get married and then go to the temple to be sealed, I believe we'll have to wait a year from the time of our marriage to do that. So do you want to marry civilly and then go to the temple or do you want to wait and get married in the temple a year from now?"

"Oh," Mikalah thought it would be wonderful to get married in the perfect place the first time, but she wasn't sure she could stand to wait a year to belong to Jake. "What do you think?"

"If I had my way, I'd marry you tonight, but I'm not so certain that that's what the Lord wants. Plus, I want to be with you forever, not just 'til death do us part."

Mikalah smiled. "I see what you mean."

"So let's spend some time praying about it and see what answer we get," he suggested.

"I was reading in the Doctrine and Covenants and there was a section in there that talked about studying things out in your mind and then asking. So does that mean we need to think on it, come to our own decision and then pray to ask if it's the right one?"

"Yes, that's right. So if we study this out – weighing the pros and cons – and we come to a decision and pray about it, if we get a feeling of peace and comfort, we'll know it's right. If we feel a 'stupor of thought' – which is confusion, darkness or doubt or just forgetting the idea, then we'll know we were wrong."

He led her by the hand back to the picnic area and handed her the blanket. He carried the basket back to the car and loaded it into the trunk. He opened her door, and she got into the car. When he slid behind the wheel she asked, "Maybe we should talk about our options a bit more so we can come to a decision?"

"That sounds like a good idea. We could discuss all the pros and cons of one decision. Which one do you want to choose for discussion purposes?" he started the car.

"How about that we get married soon and then go to the temple in a year," she suggested. "That's what my heart wants to do," she smiled.

"All right, that sounds good to me. So what are the pros for this choice?" he prompted.

"We wouldn't have to wait to be together," Mikalah smiled.

"Right, and there would be less…um… temptation," he nodded and a slight blush rose to her cheeks.

"I have to wait a year to go to the temple anyway, so if we got married soon, it wouldn't make that much difference," she reasoned.

"It would solve the problem of you being able to go to church regularly, because you wouldn't be living under your father's roof."

"Ugh, I forgot about daddy. He'd never give his blessing," Mikalah rubbed her temples with her hands. Just thinking of how her father would react made her head hurt.

"He'll probably never give his blessing – not even a year from now – and the longer we give him to stand in the way, the worse it will be," Jake added.

"You're right. Daddy is all the more reason to marry soon so I can worship as I please without all the fuss." She was aggravated that her father put such a damper on her otherwise perfect day. He should be supportive and loving – not intolerant and overbearing. "At least my mother could be at the wedding this way."

"That's true, that's something to consider," he agreed. Jake added one more pro in his mind, *And I could be with you to protect you and keep you safe.* But he didn't want to spoil her perfect day by bringing up Eddie Richard's warning. "Sounds like there are a lot of pros for going ahead and getting married."

"Sure does!" she smiled. "Now what about the cons?"

"It would be nice to start off on the right foot with an eternal marriage in the temple."

"That's true, being married in the perfect place the first time would be a great blessing to us," Mikalah agreed.

"We'd have to find somewhere to live. We can't live in the back of Mr. Donaldson's store," he chuckled.

"And we sure can't stay at my parent's house!" she rolled her eyes.

"No, maybe we could find a house to rent," Jake suggested.

"Or even a little apartment would be fine," Mikalah added. "I'm afraid I don't have any money to bring into this marriage. So money could be a con – depending upon how much you have."

"I've got some money saved, and I make two dollars a day at the factory. I think we'll be fine," he offered comfortingly.

"So is that all the cons?" she asked.

"I think so. The only other thing I can think of is whether the Lord would want us to wait and get married in the temple to start with. I mean, that's the general procedure… at least out west. But we're not out west, and there's no temple near, and you're a new member who would have to wait anyway. Plus there are all the extenuating circumstances with your father. I mean now more than ever, as a new member, you need to be surrounded by supportive people and attending church as much as possible. You can't sneak out every Sunday for a year. Surely the Lord understands our situation."

"Why don't we take this decision to the Lord now that we've discussed all sides of the situation," she suggested.

"Sounds good," Jake continued to drive toward the city of Chattanooga, and they discussed their plans for the future.

"Oh, look there's the Tivoli Theatre. Isn't it so pretty! I've always wanted to go in there," she stared at the building as they passed it and Jake turned into a parking area.

129

Jake reached into his pocket and pulled out two tickets. "Then maybe tonight is your night," he winked.

"Really? We're going to the Tivoli?" she exclaimed as she took the tickets from his hand, "These are for the Chattanooga Symphony!"

"Rachmaninoff"

Mikalah read the tickets, "Oh I just love his Theme of Paganini!" Mikalah hugged his neck. "You are incredible! Where did you get these?" She handed them back to him.

"I was talking to Mr. Donaldson about the best places in town to take you for your birthday, and one of the places he suggested was the symphony. You seem to enjoy music, and of course you know I love it," he smiled.

"This is perfect!" she exclaimed.

"I'm glad you're pleased," his eyes twinkled. As he extended his arm, she laced hers with his, and they crossed the street toward the Tivoli.

Jake handed the attendant the tickets who tore them and gave him the stubs.

Mikalah sighed as they entered the Tivoli's grand lobby ornamented by lavish chandeliers and finely carved woodwork.

"Just being in here makes me feel rich," she whispered in his ear. "I heard they spent a million dollars building this place in the '20's. It even has air conditioning," her eyes excitedly imbibed the lush decor.

"Impressive," Jake surveyed the lobby from its ceramic tile flooring to the artistry of the gorgeous walls and ceilings. He led her through the elegant foyer and stopped to show an usher their tickets.

"Up the stairs and then back this way and toward the front of the theatre," the usher pointed.

Jake led her as directed up the stairs and to the right upper box seat.

"We have box seats?" she asked incredulously.

Smiling, he guided her to her seat and sat down next to her, "Here, a souvenir," he handed her a ticket stub and slid his left arm around her shoulder.

Mikalah, stunned to actually be sitting in a box seat of the Tivoli theatre, soaked in the atmosphere of the plush surroundings. The symphony members trickled onto the stage and started warming up their instruments. It was the first time Mikalah had ever heard a live orchestra. The closest thing she'd heard was when she and her family gathered around the Morton's radio on summer evenings. Mr. Morton would pull the battery out of his truck and bring it into the house and hook the radio up to it because he didn't have electricity in his home at the time. Neighbors, friends and family would gather around to listen to far away stations from Cincinnati or San Antonio.

She leaned toward him and whispered in his ear, "If I forget to tell you later, thank you for the most incredible day of my life."

For two hours, Jake and Mikalah listened to the sweet melodious strains of Rachmaninoff's piano and orchestra compositions. Mikalah had never heard anything like it. When the concert was over, she reluctantly rose from her seat as he took her hand and guided her out of the luxurious building.

They strolled in silence back to the car, still soaking in the beauty of the music and the moment. Jake opened her door. After he entered the car, she slid closer to him, leaning her head on his shoulder as he wrapped his arm around her.

After driving for several minutes in silence, Mikalah spoke, "I don't want to go home."

"Are you nervous about your father?" he asked as he leaned over and kissed her hair. He loved the way her hair dried into perfect curly ringlets.

"A little, but mainly I just don't want this day to end."

"I know what you mean," he held her a little closer.

The drive home passed too quickly for Mikalah. Her stomach twisted in nervous knots as the weight of the situation descended on her upon entering Daisy. Questions started pouring through her mind. How would she tell her parents that she wanted to marry Jake? How would her father react? How was she going to go to church without her father becoming infuriated? How would she even go to church the next day?

"You're awfully quiet. What are you thinking about?" Jake asked.

"I want to go to church tomorrow. I'm trying to figure a way out of the house without incurring Daddy's wrath."

"Any ideas?"

"Maybe a way will be provided for me that I just can't see yet. Will you wait for me by the creek until at least a quarter past eight? If I'm not there by then, you can go on without me. But I'll do my best to find a way to be there."

"All right, I'll wait for you."

"Don't drop me off at the house tonight. Let me out in front of the neighbors', and I'll walk home. I don't want to take a chance on Daddy seeing your car."

"Are you sure?"

"Yes, just stop right up here, and I'll walk the rest of the way."

Jake didn't like the idea of letting her walk home in the dark. He stopped the car, turned off the engine and stepped out to open her door. He popped the trunk and handed her bag to her. "I'll walk you a little ways and make sure you get in all right."

"You don't have to do that."

"I want to," he took her hand, and she led him to a clump of trees on the edge of her yard.

She leaned her back against a tree, reluctant to reenter the reality of her world. She closed her eyes, and a tear rolled down her cheek, "Thank you, Jake. I know I keep saying thank you, but words just can't express how I feel or how grateful I am for everything."

Jake stepped closer to her, brushed the tear from her cheek and pressed his lips to the spot where the tear had fallen. He embraced her and whispered in her ear, "It's all going to work out, Mikalah." She wrapped her arms around his chest, as her hands caressed the muscles in his back.

Her heart pounded, and suddenly she felt breathless being so close to him as his lips moved toward hers and gently kissed the corners of her mouth and toyed with her bottom lip. She completely fell into his embrace as she slid her arms around his neck and ran her fingers through his wavy dark hair, her back brushing against the scratchy bark of the tree. His kiss was so warm and delicious, that it was she who stopped it this time as she moved to rest her head on his shoulder. In an effort to calm her fluttering heart, she took a deep breath and exhaled. She felt too much for him, too much love, gratitude and sheer desire.

At that moment, she knew waiting a year for him would be too dangerous. She wasn't that strong.

"I better go," she moved to the side and started to leave.

"I'm sorry, Mikalah," he had that look of guilt in his eyes again.

"Jake, don't. Don't be sorry. You didn't do anything wrong. I just better go. I'll see you in the morning," she smiled reassuringly. He reluctantly released her hand and rested his head on his hand with his elbow propped against the tree as he watched her run across the yard and into the house.

Chapter 7

Laurana looked up from her sewing as Mikalah quietly crept in the front door

"Mama, I'm so glad it's you," Mikalah put her hand to her chest in relief.

"Your dad has a bad cold, so I sent him to bed and told him I'd wait up for you," Laurana pointed to the clock that read nine fifteen. "You weren't out too late. That's good. So how was your day, dear?"

Mikalah sat down on the loveseat and turned toward her mother, "Perfect, absolutely perfect."

"Tell me about it," Laurana set her sewing aside, leaning anxiously forward.

"Come up to my room, and let me put my things away, and I'll tell you there so no one else can hear," Mikalah whispered. Laurana nodded in understanding.

Mikalah grabbed her bag and crept quietly up the stairs as her mother followed. They went into her room, and Mikalah shut the door as Laurana sat on the bed. Mikalah pulled the clothes from her bag and hung up her things.

"So…" her mother coaxed.

Mikalah sat down next to her mother on the bed and told her about the baptism and the wonderful feeling she had as she came out of the water and as she received the Gift of the Holy Ghost. She described how kind Fanny and Lillian were to her and about the picnic that Jake brought. She showed her the books he'd given her for her birthday.

"It sounds like a beautiful day, Mikalah," Laurana patted her hand. But Laurana sensed that there was something more, "Is there anything else you'd like to tell me? What about your evening?"

"He took me to the Tivoli Theatre to see the symphony! It was Rachmaninoff. It was so beautiful, Mama."

"The Tivoli? How exciting!" her mother was impressed.

"Not just the Tivoli, but box seats in the upper balcony!"

"How did Jake afford something like that?" Laurana wondered allowed.

"He said he's been saving money for years," Mikalah explained as she fell back, rested her head on her pillow and stretched out on her bed.

"Jake sounds like quite a catch," Laurana winked.

"Oh, he is. He's perfect, absolutely perfect," Mikalah had a far off dreamy look in her eye.

"Nobody's perfect dear, but he is a fine young man," Laurana patted Mikalah's arm.

"Oh, I know he's not really perfect, but he's perfect for me anyway," Mikalah sat up suddenly. "Can you keep a secret?"

"Certainly, dear," Laurana anxiously affirmed.

"I mean no one can know this – especially not Daddy," Mikalah's earnest expression caused Laurana a bit of concern.

"Just between you and me, I promise," Laurana watched Mikalah intently.

"Jake asked me to marry him," she beamed.

"He did?" Laurana knew it was coming, but not so soon. "And what did you tell him?"

"I told him 'yes' of course!" Mikalah lay back on her pillow and stared at the ceiling. When her mother didn't respond for several minutes, Mikalah looked at her mother. Her initial joy for her daughter was now replaced with a worrisome expression.

"What is it, Mama?" Mikalah looked at her mother intently.

"I'm truly happy for you dear, but your father," she shook her head, "your father will be furious."

"That's why you can't tell him," Mikalah reminded.

"But he'll have to be told *sometime!*"

"We haven't decided on when the wedding will be, so I have some time to think about how to break it to him. We may just have to elope," Mikalah thought aloud.

"Elope? You can't elope! I've always wanted to plan your wedding!" Laurana's dejected expression forced Mikalah to sit upright and hug her mother.

136

"Don't worry Mama, I'll figure out some way for you to be there," she comforted. "We have time to think about all that. My problem is figuring out how to go to church in the morning," Mikalah muttered.

"Your father is sick so unless he has an overnight recovery, he'll probably sleep in tomorrow morning. I'll just stay home with the children. Most likely, he won't even notice you're missing. I'll cover for you if he does," the thought occurred to Laurana that she was getting a bit too clever in deceiving her husband.

"Oh, Mama! Would you really do that for me?" Mikalah whispered excitedly.

"Of course, dear. I want you to be happy, and it's not like you're doing anything wrong. You're trying to follow your conscience and do the right thing. It's my duty to help you," Laurana reasoned.

Mikalah put her arms around her mother and kissed her cheek, "You are the best mother in the world! Thank you so much!"

"You're welcome, dear. You better get some sleep now," Laurana rose from the bed.

"Good night, Mama."

"Good night, dear," Laurana walked to the door and slipped out, closing the door quietly behind her.

Mikalah stood, locked the door and descended to her knees and offered a prayer of gratitude for the day and everything that had transpired. Her heart was so full of joy and gratitude that she could contain her emotions no longer. Upon concluding her prayer, she dried her eyes with a handkerchief, slipped out of her clothes, into her nightgown and hopped into bed.

She replayed the events of the day in her mind. One thing troubled her and that was that last kiss of the evening. She wondered why she felt such a strong impression to pull away from Jake. It wasn't like he was kissing her any more intimately than he had earlier in the day. He wasn't crossing any lines or acting improperly, but the emotions that swelled within her let her know she needed to say goodnight. Mikalah pondered on the event over and over again. She wanted to learn from it, because she had definitely felt a need to pull away. She remembered what Fanny and Lillian had told her earlier in the day about listening to the Spirit and acting immediately. She felt good about herself for doing just that, but she wondered why she felt so weak at that moment when earlier in the day she hadn't.

Maybe it was because I was different by the end of the day? After such a romantic evening, knowing we're going to be married, not wanting to go back home, not wanting to leave him, the darkness, maybe that is why my emotions were so intense? She pondered the situation and decided that she would remember this in the future and be more aware of when her resolve began to weaken. She didn't want to cross any lines. She didn't even want to get close to any of them. She loved Jake too much to risk anything. She wanted that temple marriage.

This train of thought reminded her that she needed to pray about when and where they should be married. She knelt once more and explained their decision to go ahead and be married. That evening had shown her that she didn't feel confident that she could wait a whole year. Plus, her father wouldn't be sick every Sunday. If she were with Jake, she could go to church whenever she pleased. It made sense, and she told her Heavenly Father about it all and asked if it was right. Was she making the right decision?

She closed her prayer and knelt there listening for an answer. She didn't feel anything either way. There was no darkness or doubt, but there was no joy or peace. If she were to be honest with herself, she felt nothing.

Resolving to ask again the next day, she stood up, climbed into her bed and soon drifted off to sleep with Jake on her mind.

~*~

Mikalah woke up early, said her morning prayers, dressed and then crept down the stairs carrying her scriptures and Jake's Book of Mormon under her arm. She looked at the clock in the parlor. It was quarter 'til eight. Her mother was rummaging through the storage room looking for something. Mikalah walked in behind her and shut the door.

"Is Daddy staying home today?" she whispered.

"Yes, he's still asleep. I'll bring him his breakfast in bed so he stays there," Laurana planned.

Mikalah hugged her mother quickly and whispered, "Thank you!"

Laurana opened the storage room door and walked into the kitchen. Mikalah followed her, "Mikalah, there are some sausage biscuits here."

"No thank you, Jake and I are fasting about when to get married. I think I'll go while I can. See you a little later," she waved and walked out the kitchen door, her scriptures tucked under her arm.

When she was about a quarter mile from the creek bridge, she felt a sudden uneasiness as if she were being watched. She turned and looked around in all directions but saw no one. She traveled a little further and felt the same eerie sensation. Again she peered around to see if she was being followed, but she appeared to be all alone.

Jake stepped out of the Chevrolet when he saw her coming and greeted her with a hug, "I'm so glad you were able to get away! How did you do it?"

"Daddy's sleeping. He's sick. So Mama said I could go on to church, and she'd cover for me."

Jake opened her door, "Looks like you were right last night... the Lord provided a way."

When he got in the car, she handed him his Book of Mormon and thanked him for the use of it.

"Sure!"

As they drove away, Hal Craig peered out from behind a tree. He'd been following Mikalah for some time. Once their car was out of sight, he stepped onto the road and headed back into Daisy. Pulling a piece of gum from his pocket, he unwrapped it and popped it in his mouth. Just as he was about to toss the wrapper to the ground, he stopped, "Hmmm..."

He stared down at the wrapper and tugged on it to straighten out the folds. He looked around on the side of the road until he found a flat rock and stooped down next to it. Pulling a pencil from his pocket, he began scribbling on the gum wrapper. He stood, opened his wallet and pulled out a dollar bill and folded the gum wrapper inside of the bill and put it in his shirt pocket with the pencil.

Hal traveled until he came to the Baptist church that Mr. Ford belonged to. He walked in the door and peered around the congregation. Spotting Emmaline sitting midway up the right side of the building, he strode to her pew and slid in next to her.

"Hi, Hal!" she radiated infatuation.

"Hey" he seemed preoccupied.

The meeting started and when they passed the plate around for collections, Hal pulled the folded dollar bill from his pocket and dropped it into the plate. Emmaline's eyes widened, and she leaned toward him and whispered in his ear, "Are you crazy? A whole dollar!"

Hal just shrugged his shoulders and put his arm tightly around her to distract her. He didn't want anyone calling attention to who put the dollar in the plate.

When the meeting ended, people streamed out of the chapel. Hal took Emmaline's hand and led her from the building and accompanied her home.

Back in the church, Reverend Arnold poured the three collection plates into one. He noted the one dollar bill in the plate amongst a myriad of nickels, dimes and quarters. He reached in, pulled it out and spread it open. The gum wrapper fell into the plate, and he picked it up, unfolded it and his anger rose as he read:

Mikalah Ford's still running around with that Mormon. You think that's wise?

He'd talked with Bill just last Sunday about this, and Bill said he'd taken care of it. Reverend Arnold quickly put all the money into the treasury box and locked it, placing his keys in his pants pocket and the note and the dollar in his shirt pocket. He grabbed his coat, headed for the door and locked up.

Surprised by a knock on the door, Laurana crossed into the parlor and peered out the window. She saw Reverend Arnold outside and released an aggravated sigh. She mustered her resolve to at least pretend cordiality. She opened the door, "Good morning, Reverend."

"Good morning, Mrs. Ford. Is your husband home?"

"He's asleep. He's been sick. Perhaps you could come back later this afternoon," Laurana suggested.

"I need to speak with him about a pressing matter," the Reverend stated sternly.

"Couldn't it wait a few hours until he's up and about?" she suggested.

"No, I really need to speak with him."

Reluctantly Laurana stepped aside to allow him to enter, "Please have a seat." She pointed to a chair, but the Reverend began to pace around the parlor instead.

Laurana went to the kitchen where Hank and Hannah sat at the table.

"What does *he* want?" Hank whispered in obvious irritation. Reverend Arnold was no longer a popular individual in the Ford household after last Sunday. Only Bill still respected the man.

"He wants to speak with your father – says it's urgent," Laurana quietly related.

Hannah rolled her eyes. "Oh brother," she mumbled.

Laurana took her time ascending the stairs and quietly moved down the hallway toward their bedroom. She slowly opened the door and peered in to find Bill putting on his trousers, "What are you doin' up?"

"I heard the preacher's car drive up," he answered.

"Uh, yes, I told him you were resting, but he insisted upon seeing you."

"Tell him I'll be right down."

Laurana walked out of the room, shut the door behind her and quickly closed Mikalah's door as she passed her room.

Laurana had a sickening feeling. Her heart beat like a drum, and her palms grew clammy. She just knew that the preacher was there to cause problems. She joined the children in the kitchen, "Hannah, will you please take Matty outside to play for a while. Help her with her coat."

"Yes, Ma'am."

Laurana opened the kitchen door for Hannah and Matty and whispered in Hannah's ear, "Keep a look out for Mikalah. I've got a bad feeling about this."

Hannah nodded her head in understanding.

141

Bill sneezed violently into his handkerchief as he descended the stairs, went to the kitchen, and washed his hands and poured himself a drink. Hank sat quietly staring at his father as he met the preacher in the parlor. Laurana followed at a distance.

"Good mornin', Reverend," Bill shook the man's hand. "Please have a seat."

Bill sat in his favorite chair, and the preacher reluctantly sat on the edge of a chair opposite him.

"What can I do for you, Reverend?"

Reverend Arnold pulled the dollar bill and the gum wrapper from his shirt pocket, "Someone put this dollar bill in the collection plate with this note folded inside of it." He reached forward and handed the wrapper to Bill who read it.

"Laurana do you know anything about this?" Bill handed the note to his wife.

She felt hot all over as she read the words. She knew her face must be beet red and that she'd just betrayed Mikalah without even trying, "Since when do we take gum wrappers as gospel truth?"

"It was wrapped up in this," the preacher held up the dollar as if it proved validity.

"So gossip wrapped in money is truth?" Laurana's anger seethed but she held it in restraint. "I really don't see what business it is of yours or anyone else's who our daughter spends her time with."

"Laurana!" Bill scolded, "Reverend Arnold has nothing but Mikalah's best interest at heart."

"Is that so?" she glared at the minister. "I think perhaps all he cares about is how many of those bills make their way into his collection plate," she knew she'd said too much.

The minister rose from his seat, "Ma'am, your daughter is mixed up with a man who has some villainous beliefs. He's fillin' her head with all kinds of things that will damn her soul to hell. Do you want your daughter to go to hell, Mrs. Ford?"

"I believe the Savior said judge not lest ye be judged, sir. Mikalah's a good girl who loves her Savior very much. She would be the last person in this town to be doomed to hell." Laurana became more infuriated by the minute. She knew she had to watch her words for Mikalah's sake, so she breathed deeply, her heart pounding as she fought to regain control.

"Laurana, has Mikalah been with Mr. Elliot since I told her to stay away from him?" Bill asked calmly.

Laurana ignored the question and turned to the minister, "Tell me something, Reverend. You seem to know so much about these 'villainous beliefs' of the Mormons. Have you ever read the Book of Mormon?"

"I've read about the book, and it's a horrible thing, filled with lies," the Reverend answered.

"But have you read the book itself?" Laurana pressed. The man just stared at her blankly. "Sir, you couldn't possibly have read that book or you wouldn't be standing here saying the things you're saying."

"Why's that?" Bill asked.

"Because I've read it, that's why," she retorted boldly.

The Reverend gasped in such a manner that Bill startled and looked toward him.

"You read that book, Laurana?" Bill asked incredulously.

"Of course I did. You think I'm going to just blindly judge my daughter or an innocent man based on what other people tell me they believe? I went straight to the source. I asked to read it so I would know what she was looking into. I read it nearly cover to cover."

"What did it say?" Bill asked.

The Reverend stopped his ears, "I'm not going to listen to the blasphemy contained within that satanic book."

Laurana rolled her eyes in disgust at the preacher's melodrama, "Almost on every page – at least in every chapter – it testifies of Jesus Christ. It admonishes us to follow Him, to call upon Him, to live by His teachings and to live uprightly before God. Now I ask you – you are two reasonably intelligent gentlemen – at least I think the man I married is – how could something that persuades you to believe in Christ and to do good be evil? Why would Satan write a book that told

143

you to follow Christ's example? Even Jesus said that 'a house divided against itself cannot stand.'"

Perplexed, Bill turned to the minister, "I thought you said you read it?"

"I read all about it. I didn't need to read the thing when so many professional scholars had and wrote about its evils," he defended.

Bill stood, "Thank you, Reverend for stopping by. I – I have some thinking to do."

"That young man needs to be run out of town. Do you want me to talk to the town council?" the minister offered.

"No, no need to do that. Let me think this through, and I'll deal with it." Bill walked toward the door indicating the minister should leave.

Reluctantly, Reverend Arnold stepped outside and walked to his car. Bill shut the door and turned to face Laurana, "Where's Mikalah?"

"She's around somewhere," Laurana stalled. She could tell by the clock that Mikalah should be returning home soon. She hoped she didn't pass the minister on the way in.

~*~

Mikalah stepped out of Jake's car in front of the neighbor's house and saw the Reverend driving away. Her heart pounding, she ran around to the barn to hide her scriptures in the loft. She hopped down. Putting on a calm exterior, she breathed deeply to slow the palpitations of her heart and stepped coolly through the kitchen door.

Laurana and Bill turned to watch her enter.

"Hi, Daddy! You feelin' any better?"

"Where have you been, Mikalah?" her father asked sternly.

"Out," she pointed her thumb over her shoulder toward the door.

"I'd like to speak with you for a minute," he waved for her to come into the parlor. She walked casually as if nothing were going on, and sat down on the love seat.

"Somebody put this into the collection plate at church," he handed the wrapper to Mikalah.

144

Her heart started to pound. She recognized the script. She'd burned a stack of love notes that matched that handwriting only a few weeks ago, "This is Hal's handwriting," Mikalah handed the wrapper back to her dad.

A light bulb went on over Laurana's head, "Oh, that makes sense. Hal's jealous."

"What? What's going on?" Bill looked back and forth between his daughter and wife.

Mikalah leaned forward, "Mama, Daddy, will you please sit down. I need to explain something."

Her parents stared at her and slowly seated themselves.

"It all started at the county fair," Mikalah began. Her mother's expression grew puzzled. This sounded like new information. "Daddy, I had been dating Hal Craig while you were gone, but I broke up with him when he pressed me to … uh…" How was she going to say this to her father? "He was getting too familiar." Bill and Laurana's eyes widened.

"Why didn't you ever tell me this?" Laurana scolded.

"It's not the kind of thing you want to talk with your parents about."

"You should have told your mother, Mikalah," Bill's brow furrowed.

"Anyway… at the fair, Hal pulled me into a storage tent and really started harassing me. I screamed for help, and Jake came in and punched him in the nose and threw him out of the tent."

"Good for Jake!" Laurana was in no mood for anyone to mess with her family anymore.

"Now that I think about it, besides us, Hal's the only person who even knew that Jake is Mormon." Mikalah turned to her mother, "Did you tell anyone?"

"No, I didn't say anything about it." Laurana turned to her husband, "See, this all started because of an indecent boy who's jealous of a good man." Laurana suddenly stood and flung her arms in the air. "You didn't bother to listen to Mikalah's side of it. You wouldn't even learn about what she believed. Instead you jumped to conclusions and let that preacher fill your head full of lies." Laurana was getting angrier by the minute.

145

Mikalah could see her father's frustration rising. She stood and took her mother by the shoulders, "Mama, calm down. Daddy thought I was in danger. He didn't know better. He was just looking out for me."

Bill stood, "You're right. I am looking out for you. And just because Hal's jealous and acted improperly doesn't mean Jake's innocent."

"And how, pray tell, would he be guilty?" Laurana barked. "Was it when he saved our daughter's virtue? Or maybe it was when he saved her life and took a bullet for her? Oh, or perhaps it was when he painted our house with a wounded shoulder? Or when he prayed over Matty and she was healed? When? When was he guilty, Bill?" She stared at him with such consternation that he actually backed down.

"All right, all right. Perhaps I misjudged the man," Bill relented. "But I want to know where this relationship stands, Mikalah. How involved are you with Mr. Elliot?"

"I think we better all sit back down," Laurana suggested.

Bill looked at the two women and then slowly sat, "Are you going to be honest with me, Mikalah?"

"Yes sir."

Laurana took a deep breath and sighed. Bill looked at his wife. He knew she was aware of what Mikalah was about to share.

Mikalah prayed silently in her heart for strength and wisdom to know how to relate what she knew had to be said, "Daddy, first off I want to say that I'm eighteen now. I'm an adult, and I can make my own decisions, but I do care what you think of me. And I want you to try to understand that a lot has gone on while you were away. You've been blind sided by all this, and I can understand why you're having a hard time understanding what's happening. You don't know Jake like we do. You haven't read the Book of Mormon like Mama and I have. You haven't prayed and gained a witness from God about it like I have. I know you love me and that you want what's best for me. And if you really do – if you really love me – you'll hear me out. If you promise to hear me out, I'll tell you all of it."

Bill stared at his daughter. He had to admit she'd turned into quite an intelligent young woman, "All right. I'll listen to what you have to say."

Mikalah began at the beginning with the night Hal pressured her and Jake introduced her to the Book of Mormon. She told him about reading it, what she felt, what she learned, how it impacted her life and how she received her answer from God. She told of the day Matty fell and the beautiful blessing Jake gave Matty and how it made her feel inside. She described the first time she went to church with Jake and about her mother giving Jake permission to court her. Mikalah made it clear that Jake was always a perfect gentleman and never pressed her to change her beliefs for him.

When she told him about her baptism Bill shifted uncomfortably, but remained quiet. He'd promised to listen to her. She continued with her story about the picnic, the symphony and even that she'd been to church with Jake that morning. Then she paused.

"Is that everything?" he smiled.

"Well," she hesitated, "There's one more thing. Jake asked me to marry him."

Bill stood, crossed to the fire place and ran his right hand through his salt and pepper hair as he stared into the flame. "What did you tell him?"

"I love him, Daddy. I told him yes."

It seemed like an eternity that Bill stood silently studying the flame. Mikalah's heart felt like it was going to burst with anticipation as she looked to her mother for reassurance. Laurana shrugged her shoulders. Finally, he slowly turned around, "Mikalah, I want to read the book."

"You want to read the Book of Mormon?" she could hardly believe her ears.

"Yes, you and your mother have made it clear to me that I've jumped to judgment when I should have listened and studied first. I want to read what you and your mother read so I can understand you better."

Mikalah rushed to her father and threw her arms around his neck, "Oh thank you, Daddy! Thank you!"

"Now I'm not making any promises. If I read it and I see that it's bad, I'm going to have to put my foot down."

"Just promise me you'll read it with an open mind and really ask God whether it's true or not. If you're going to read it just to find fault then I'd prefer

147

you never even read it at all." Bill just stared at her. "Daddy, do you really want to know if it's true?" she asked.

"I want to believe in you, Mikalah. I want to be happy for you," Bill felt beat down, as if these two women in his life had managed to break his will. "I'm tired. I'm going to go lie down. Bring me that book whenever you can." He walked between them and trudged up the stairs rubbing his temples with his hands.

Mikalah looked at her mother, "Can you believe that?"

"I'm stunned," Laurana whispered.

"You were great, mother! If I didn't know better I'd have thought you had a testimony of the book yourself!" Mikalah laughed as she plopped down on the love seat breathing a sigh of relief.

"I do," Laurana whispered.

Mikalah leaned forward excitedly, "You do? Since when?"

"Since last night. When you told me about your baptism… I felt something. You were so happy and joyous and it seemed like such a good thing. So last night before I went to bed, I came down here, and I prayed about it and asked if it was true, and I had such an indescribable feeling of peace and comfort - a sweet assurance that it was true and that I needed to help you in any way I could."

"So that's why you fought so hard for me this afternoon?" Mikalah smiled.

"Yes. If truth be told, I was fighting for both of us."

Mikalah rushed to her mother and put her arms around her neck, "Oh Mama! I'm so happy for you!" Mikalah pulled back and looked into her mother's eyes, "Now we just need to pray that Daddy asks with a sincere heart with a true desire to know." Mikalah walked toward the kitchen, "I've got to tell Jake about this! Would you mind if I went to see him for a little while?"

"Um… I guess that would be fine."

"I'll go give Daddy my Book of Mormon before I leave," she walked out the kitchen door and to the barn where she'd hidden her scriptures. As she climbed into the loft, Matty walked up behind her.

"Watcha doin' Micky?"

148

Mikalah jumped, "Oh you startled me Matty! I'm just getting something." She carried her books down from the loft and took Matty by the hand. "You outside by yourself?"

"No, Hannah is right over there," Matty pointed to where Hannah sat under a tree reading a book.

"Hannah, I'm taking Matty inside with me," Mikalah called.

"All right," Hannah waved, and Mikalah led Matty into the house.

"Hi Matty! You want to help me make lunch?" Laurana asked.

"Yes, Ma'am," Matty nodded and climbed up on a stool next to the counter.

Mikalah ascended the stairs, put her Doctrine and Covenants in her bedroom, walked down the hallway to her father's room and knocked gently on the door, "Daddy, may I come in?"

"Yes," he answered. He was lying in bed, his covers wrapped up to his neck. She felt his head with the back of her hand, "Daddy, you're hot. You want me to bring you a cool wet wash cloth?"

"Thank you, that would be nice... and a drink of water too, please, if you could."

"All right, I'll get those for you. This is the Book of Mormon you asked for. I'll be right back with your cool cloth and water."

While Mikalah was gone, Bill opened the book and started reading the introduction. When she returned to find him reading, she put the wash cloth on his head and handed him the glass of water. "Would you like me to tell you a bit about the book so that it makes more sense?"

"I guess," he sipped his drink.

She grabbed the Bible off his dresser and showed him the same two verses Jake had showed her and rehearsed to him the explanation Jake had given her. "Now I know it sounds totally bizarre at first, Daddy. I thought he was crazy or pulling my leg. But the more I read, the more it made sense, and I started to ask myself, 'What if? What if it's true? Could a mortal man really have written this?' Try reading it that way and then pray and ask God if it's true. He'll give you an answer if you really want to know."

Bill didn't know what to think, but he was too tired to discuss it further, "All right. I'm going to take a nap now and maybe I'll read some later." He closed the book and noticed Mikalah's name engraved on the front, "I'm not a fast reader, Mikalah. Is this your only copy?"

"That's ok, I can borrow another one from Jake if I need it," she smiled and leaned down to kiss her father's cheek. "Thank you, Daddy."

She gently shut his door and descended the stairs where Hannah, Hank and Matty where helping their mother make lunch. "You want to eat something before you go to Jake's?" Laurana asked.

"No thanks. I'm still fasting. I'll eat dinner later," Mikalah was getting weak, but the miracle of her father's softening convinced her that fasting worked, and she wanted to complete a full twenty-four hours.

Mikalah walked into town toward the Home Store. All the shops were closed on Sunday so she crossed the street and peered through the front window. A light flickered in the back room. She tapped on the window, but there was no movement inside, so she knocked a little louder. When she saw Jake's head behind the rows of shelves coming toward her she waved.

As he realized who it was, he sped up his pace and fumbled with his keys to unlock the front door. He'd obviously been napping, for his shirt was unbuttoned revealing his undershirt beneath. He wiped the sleep from his eyes and shoved his shirt into his pants, "Mikalah, what a pleasant surprise!" He could tell by the smile on her face that there was nothing wrong. "You seem happy. What's happened?"

"Can you lock up and take a walk with me?"

Jake looked down at his socks, "Sure, let me grab my shoes and a coat." He opened the door wider for her to enter the store and trotted back to his room, slid on his boots and grabbed his coat. He opened the door for her and locked it behind them.

"I've got some good news," she beamed.

He chuckled at her enthusiasm, "What is it?" He held her hand, "Who let you escape again anyway?"

She grinned, "Daddy's reading the Book of Mormon!"

"No!" disbelief filled his eyes.

"Yes!" she related the events of the morning as they walked. They turned toward the clay pits where little boys were playing in the caverns and crevices of red earth. Throughout the week, men filled carts with clay, rolled them out on a track, and dumped the clay into a shoot with a collecting bin below. Then they loaded the clay into trucks and took it to the tile factory where Jake worked. Mikalah and Jake sat down on a grassy spot overlooking the pit.

"Looks like they're having fun," Jake nodded.

"This is one of the favorite spots for boys to play."

"So your dad really agreed to read the Book of Mormon? I'm amazed," Jake shook his head in wonder.

"This sort of adds a new dimension to our decision about when to get married, doesn't it? I mean, if Daddy's on our side, then that eliminates one of our concerns," she studied Jake for his reaction. "Have you gotten any kind of answer yet?"

"Have you?" he countered.

She chuckled, "Are you avoiding my question?"

"I have an answer, but I don't want to tell you what it is until you have yours so we can compare."

She sighed, "I prayed about it last night, but I didn't feel anything either way. Of course, I've been fasting today, and I've been praying in my mind, but with all the excitement, I haven't had a chance to really kneel and pray or to read the scriptures."

"I want you to get your own answer, Mikalah. We both need to be certain we're doing the right thing," he squeezed her hand and looked down at the boys playing on the tracks. She leaned over on his shoulder and wrapped her hand around his arm.

They sat quietly together for several minutes, and then she broke the silence, "Jake."

"Uh hum"

"I don't want to wait a year. Maybe that's why I haven't gotten an answer. My heart wants one answer so badly that maybe I'm not listening."

151

He turned to look into her eyes, "Let it go, Mikalah. Give it to Him. Tell the Lord that you are willing to wait if you have to. Tell Him that even though you don't want to wait, you will if He tells you to. Give up your heart's desire to Him, and you'll get your answer."

"How do you know?" she whispered.

"Because that's what I had to do to get mine," his eyes twinkled as he brushed a lock of her hair back into place. He stood up and put out his hand to help her up. "Why don't we stop by the store, and I'll get my extra Book of Mormon so you'll have one while your dad is reading yours."

They walked for a while when Jake asked, "So how many children do you want, Mikalah?"

"Where did that come from?" she chuckled.

"It's the kind of thing we should know about each other, don't ya think?"

"I suppose so. Oh, I don't know, five or six?" She looked at him expectantly, "How 'bout you?"

"That sounds about right," he nodded. "I'll take whatever the Lord wants to send, then again I'm not the one who has to give birth to them," he chuckled as he looked at her with an expression of compassion.

"I suppose you know twins run in my family. Are you ready for that?" she gave him a doubtful grin.

"Twins, ugh, maybe I don't want to get married after all!" he released her hand and scratched his head as if he'd changed his mind.

She huffed, rolled her eyes and elbowed him in the ribs.

He put his arm around her shoulder and laughed as he pulled her close, "I suppose I can handle twins if you can."

When they reached the store, Jake opened the door, and she waited outside as he went to the back to retrieve his extra Book of Mormon and brought it to her.

"I guess I'll be getting' home," she prepared to leave.

"Oh, let me walk you," he turned to lock the door.

"You don't have to," she really wanted him to, but knew that if he was as weak from hunger as she was by now, walking would be the last thing he'd want to do.

"I want to," he grinned, "You think I'd pass up a minute of being with you?"

"You are so sweet!" she grabbed his hand and started walking. "I bet you're starvin'. I'll see if I can sneak you out some food or maybe we can even sneak you into the house for dinner."

"I don't want to push our luck," he winked.

"This is a day for miracles, why not?" she smiled.

They cut through the neighbor's yard so they wouldn't be seen by anyone within the house, and she left him by the side of the house, "Wait here, and I'll see what it's like inside." He leaned against the house as she quietly opened the kitchen door and looked around. Mikalah noticed that her mother had left a plate of lunch for her on the counter. She went further into the house and saw Hannah and Hank playing checkers.

"Where is everybody?" Mikalah asked.

"Mama's taking a nap with Matty. Dad's still asleep I guess," Hannah answered.

"What's up, Micky?" Hank asked.

"Jake's outside. I was going to get him some food, and I'm trying to decide if I should let him inside," she whispered.

"Uh... I don't know about that," Hank didn't think it was too wise of an idea. "Why don't you just take him a plate of food outside? That way if Dad wakes up and comes downstairs you won't get caught."

"Yeah, I guess you're right." Mikalah reentered the kitchen, set her Book of Mormon down on the kitchen table and scrounged around looking for leftovers to make another plate of food. There wasn't much. There never were many leftovers with Hank around. She took the plate her mother had set aside for her and added a few rolls and another mound of mashed potatoes and grabbed a couple forks and a quilt from the storeroom.

She went out the kitchen door and met Jake outside, "Here, take this, and I'll get us some drinks." She walked briskly back into the house and poured them two glasses of milk from the icebox, tucked the Book of Mormon under her arm, picked up the glasses and went outside to meet Jake.

Mikalah passed him and looked back over her shoulder, "Follow me, I have an idea." He followed her to the barn and watched her climb up into the hay loft. "Come on up here. This is my favorite place to hide."

Jake handed her the blanket and carried the plate of food and forks up the ladder to where Mikalah spread out the blanket.

"Sorry there wasn't more food. We'll have to share a plate because Hank is a human piglet," she rolled her eyes in frustration. "We're lucky Mama set a plate aside for me."

"This is fine. It's a lot better than the bowl of beans I was going to heat for dinner." They sat next to each other with their backs leaning against the barn wall and the plate on Jake's knee.

Mikalah sighed in frustration.

"What?" he asked.

"I really wanted my answer before I broke this fast," she answered.

Jake set the plate aside. "Why don't we just pray together now."

They knelt next to each other, and Jake motioned to her, "Go ahead."

"Oh, ok," she was nervous about praying aloud in front of him. A prayer for food was one thing, but a prayer about a personal issue was different, "I'm a little nervous."

"Don't be. It's not like you can mess up," he smiled and took her hand.

Mikalah started hesitantly but as she prayed she began to pour out her heart and let the Lord know that she really wanted to marry Jake soon, but that if He wanted them to wait, she would submit to His will on the matter. She just wanted to be obedient and faithful and do what Heavenly Father wanted them to do. She thanked her Heavenly Father for her father's softened heart, for Jake, for the gospel in her life and concluded by asking for a feeling of peace if their decision to marry soon was right or a bad feeling if it was the wrong decision. She blessed the food and closed in the name of Jesus Christ. The pair continued to kneel and listen for an answer.

After several minutes of silence, Mikalah finally opened her baby blue eyes that were a deeper blue when tears streamed from them as they were at that moment. She looked into Jake's handsome face which was filled with love for her as the tears glistened in his own eyes.

"Did you feel that," she asked?

"Yes, I did," he squeezed her hand, and she put her arms around him joyfully.

"Funny how so many times when we give it up, He gives it back," Jake whispered.

Mikalah pulled a handkerchief from her pocket and dried the tears from her eyes, "Jake, God has given me so much more than I ever dreamed I could have – beyond what I even knew was possible."

"Me too," he smiled, letting his fingers caress the softness of her curls. "I don't know about you, but I'm starving," he leaned back against the barn wall, grabbed the plate and patted the spot next to him for her to join him. They each took a fork and shared the plate of food.

"Mmm... I've missed your Mama's cookin'" he relished in the flavor of it. "Can't wait until we get our own place, and I get to eat like this all the time," he winked.

"Oh, you think my cookin's as good as Mama's?"

"If it's all as good as your pies, it's better than hers!" he smiled.

"Flattery will get you everywhere with me, Jake Elliot," she teased. "So where do you want to live?"

"I saw a little house for rent along the creek. Would you want to go take a look at it with me tomorrow evening?"

"Yes! I'd love to!" she squeezed his arm. "This is so exciting! I just love making decisions knowing that God is on our side. It takes so much of the fear away." His eyes twinkled, and he kissed her cheek.

"So should we set a date?" Jake asked.

She thought for a minute, "I'd love to get married on Thanksgiving," she suggested, "We've been so blessed, and I think it would be a great way to always remember how much we have to be grateful for."

"That's a wonderful idea! It's perfect! Of course, our anniversary won't always fall on Thanksgiving, but it will every once in a while. What's the date for Thanksgiving this year?"

"I believe it's the 24th. That gives us twenty-five days to plan," she estimated.

Mikalah and Jake spent the afternoon in the hayloft planning their wedding and studying the Book of Mormon together while inside the house, Bill Ford lay in his bed reading the introduction and the entire book of 1 Nephi. When the sun started to set, Jake turned to Mikalah, "It's starting to get dark. I better get home before I can't see where I'm going."

Jake helped her fold the blanket and carried it and the book down the ladder and placed them on a barrel.

"You want me to help you carry these things in?" he asked.

"No, that's all right. I'll get them. You better run along."

Jake looked around and made sure they were out of the doorway as he moved closer to kiss her goodnight. He put his hand on her cheek and felt the softness of her hair, "I love you."

"I love you," she whispered as she kissed him one more time.

"I'll see you tomorrow," he turned, looked around to make sure no one observed from the upstairs window or anywhere on the grounds and ran toward the road.

Chapter 8

Mikalah pulled her jacket tightly around her shoulders as she slipped out of the house. She stared up at the yellow, orange and red foliage covering the trees, carpeting the mountains and the lawn. The blustery afternoon was turning into a chilly Halloween evening. To keep warm, she sped up her pace, traveling toward town. She kept an eye out for Jake who said he'd meet her on his way from the store. Butterflies danced in her stomach, and her pulse quickened as she caught sight of him coming down the road. He waved and caught up with her.

Mikalah slid her arms around his waist, "How was your day?"

"Great," he gave her a quick kiss, "People sure like to play tricks around here on Halloween, don't they?" he asked as she turned and fell into stride beside him, her hand entwined with his.

"Yes, they do. What happened?"

"Someone took my jacket and hung it to a fan in one of the highest vaulted ceilings at work. Took me twenty minutes to figure out where they hid the ladder so I could get it down. I thought I was going to be late meeting you."

Mikalah chuckled, "That's mild. I've seen them tip over outhouses while poor folks were using them. Last year, they put Mr. Middleton's wagon on top of his house!"

"You're kidding!"

"No, they really did! Matter of fact, I think we better get our house hunting done early and get back indoors before dark. Some of their pranks can get downright mean."

Jake remembered Eddie's warning about watching their backs and an eerie feeling rattled his bones. "Then, let's step up the pace. Hank says you're a fast runner. Prove it. I'll race you to the creek bridge," Jake chuckled.

"All right, you're on!" she took off running, and Jake followed after her.

"False start!" he teased as he passed her.

157

"You better pace yourself! You've got a ways to go," she called after him. Mikalah was right. About a half mile before the creek, Jake ran out of steam, and Mikalah passed him in one last burst. He struggled to catch up, but she was too fast for him and reached the bridge a full half-minute before he arrived.

Her hands on her hips, she panted, watching him approach, "I told you to pace yourself!"

He bent over holding his sides, breathing heavily, as he wound down, "You started before I did," he panted.

"Oh gimme a break!" she rolled her eyes, "You were ahead of me until that last stretch!"

He laughed as he stood upright, and his breathing slowed, "I want a rematch someday."

"Any time," she giggled.

He grabbed her hand and pointed, "Mr. Morton said it was back in there."

"Oh, is it Mr. Morton's old house?" she asked.

"Yes, that's it. He lived there in exchange for keeping it up and working the land. He said that some folks in New York own the property. His brother-in-law, Frank Springfield, manages it. Do you know where it is?"

"Sure, we just need to go down this little road here and cross the old bridge," she pointed.

She led him down a small dirt road that ran along the South side of the creek to a metal bridge with wooden planks. Their footsteps rattled noisily as they crossed the bridge and made their way to the little house.

"He said it would be unlocked and to feel free to look around," Jake explained as they stepped onto the wooden porch. Jake took hold of the doorknob and twisted it, opening it slowly as he held Mikalah's hand behind him. He peeked in and looked around.

"What're you doin'?" she asked.

"Making sure we don't have any surprises waiting inside," he whispered.

The house was divided into two sections, the kitchen and living room area on the right separated by a small passageway to three bedrooms on the left. The house was dark and empty, but light streamed in through the open door. A large wood burning cook stove set in the corner. Jake's boots shuffled across the wood floor as Mikalah followed him holding his hand.

Mikalah examined the little house. It wasn't much, but it would do she guessed. She inspected the kitchen. She'd miss the sunlight that always came through the windows in her mother's kitchen.

"I think there are some more rooms through here," he pointed to a door that led out into a passageway with an overhang that shielded the area from the weather. Jake thought he saw something move out of the corner of his eye as they stepped outside and toward the other building. His attention darted toward the movement but he saw nothing. He opened the door for Mikalah, and they found three small bedrooms, one of which had a dirt floor.

"Hmmm… I bet it gets cold back in these bedrooms in the winter with nothing to heat them," she observed.

"It's just the two of us. It's really more space than we need. We could just stay in the other part of the house where the stove is most of the time," he suggested.

"That's true…" Mikalah tried to imagine herself living in the little house with Jake, snuggled up with him next to the fire. She liked the feeling it gave her. Of course, being with Jake anywhere gave her a good feeling. Jake on the other hand, felt uneasy. He couldn't decide if it was the house or the eerie feeling that had started even before they arrived. Jake shook the sensation aside, assuming that it came from Eddie Richard's strange warning. He'd been slightly unnerved ever since.

"It would only be temporary," he turned to face her, "At least we don't have to pay money for it. We just need to keep it up and farm the land. That way we can save the money I make at the factory and get a better place."

"Let's do it. I like being close to the creek like this. And the neighbors are nice," she added.

159

"All right, I'll go see Mr. Springfield in the morning," he clasped her hand. "Want to go outside and look around a little?"

"Sure," she followed him out. "You know what we didn't think about is furniture."

"I'll ask Mr. Donaldson. He might have some ideas on how we can get some reasonably."

After looking around the property, they went back to the bridge. As they started to step up on the bridge, flour sacks flew over each of their heads, and someone tied ropes around their arms. Jake struggled, fighting in the dark. He could tell he successfully kneed someone in the stomach from the yelp of pain. But they retaliated by hitting him across the back with something that felt like a wooden rod. Jake fell onto his knees. He swayed dizzily, from his head slamming into the hardwood planks.

"Jake! Are you there?" Mikalah screamed as someone flung her over their shoulder and tied her legs together. She could hear the pounding of footsteps across the wooden planks of the bridge as her kidnapper carried her roughly on his shoulders.

"Mikalah, are you all right?" Jake called as someone bound his hands and yanked him forward across the wooden bridge.

"Jake!" Mikalah's voice got further away from him. Whoever carried her put some distance between them. Jake's arms and shoulder's ached from being drug forward, off the bridge and yanked to the right. Under his feet there were no stones or grass, so he assumed he was being led down the road until suddenly his captor jerked him to the left. The ground grew soft underfoot and occasionally he tripped on a protruding stone.

An unexpected gust of cool air blew through his clothes and the temperature dropped instantly by at least ten degrees as he shuffled across a dirt floor. Jake tried to pay attention to where he was being taken. "Mikalah! Can you hear me?" His voice echoed.

"Shut up!" an angry male voice exclaimed as Jake felt another searing blow across his back, and he fell forward. Someone yanked him back just before he would have landed face first on the ground.

Mikalah was freezing. She knew where she was by the sudden drop in temperature. Someone was taking her into the Blowin' Hole. She kicked and screamed, "Let me go! Jake, are you there?" She knew that once they reached the deepest recesses of the cave, no one would be able to hear her.

"All right, I'll let ya go," came a sneering masculine voice as the person carrying her flung her down on the ground. She fell into the dirt and hit her head on the cave wall. She struggled to sit up, but her hands were tied securely behind her back, and her head throbbed.

"Jake, are you there?" she called, but heard no reply.

Jake continued to be drug by his roped hands until another person behind him shoved him forward, and he landed squarely on his previously injured shoulder. Jake groaned in pain.

"Jake, is that you?" Mikalah called.

"Mikalah, it's me."

"We shoulda gagged these two," a masculine voice remarked in irritation.

"Pull the sacks off their heads," a female instructed.

"You sure?" a man questioned.

"Yes," the woman answered.

Mikalah felt the hood being pulled from her shoulders and raked across her head. A torch lit the interior room of the cave. She squinted, trying to discern who held her captive, "Emmaline!" Mikalah struggled with the ropes that bound her hands behind her. "Is this some kind of joke?"

As the bag lifted from Jake's face he searched the dimly lit cavern for Mikalah. She wasn't that far from him, perhaps twelve feet away, "Mikalah, are you all right?"

"I'm fine. Are you ok?" she studied him.

"I'm all right," he reassured.

"Not for long," Emmaline's mad giggle sent shivers up Jake's spine.

"What do you want, Emmaline?" Mikalah looked toward her old schoolmate.

"Hal," Emmaline replied bluntly.

"Then you've got the wrong people," Jake quipped.

161

"What do you mean?" Mikalah asked in confusion.

"I want Hal for myself," she answered.

"You've got Hal, Emmaline. He's all yours. Take him away!" Mikalah reassured.

"No, I might have his body, but his heart is still yours. I want all of him," Emmaline pulled a knife from a sheath and walked closer to Mikalah, placing the point of the blade to Mikalah's throat. Mikalah held her breath, her heart drumming in her ears.

Jake jerked, trying to get closer to Mikalah but a rough bearded man in his early twenties kicked him in the stomach. Jake doubled over, leaning his head into the floor.

Mikalah winced. "Emmaline, Hal and I broke up," she hurriedly explained in hopes that she could spare Jake from further anguish.

"His mind is still on you. I've caught him following you around town when you don't even know it," Emmaline gritted her teeth angrily.

"I can't help that, Emmaline. As far as I'm concerned, you can have him. What do you want me to do?" Mikalah reasoned.

"I want you gone," Emmaline's evil grin crinkled across her brown eyes.

Mikalah's eyes widened. She could tell Emmaline didn't just mean she wanted her to leave town, she wanted her dead. Jake continued to struggle and inch his way toward Mikalah until the man standing in front of him put the heel of his boot on his chest and shoved him, holding him down.

"You have me then," Mikalah answered. "Let Jake go. You don't need him."

"Yeah, right," Emmaline rolled her eyes. "You must think I'm a fool. Plus, he's my gift to Hal."

"What do you mean, 'your gift to Hal'?" Mikalah stared.

"I'm killin' two birds with one stone here this evenin'. I'm riddin' the world of a sappy, pampered brat and a goody-two-shoes Mormon at the same time. It's really quite ingenious, you'll see. It's not quite as clean as the shootin' I planned, but since that didn't work out, this'll have to do," Emmaline spun around and joined two men who stood lurking in the shadows.

162

"Emmaline arranged the shooting?" Mikalah whispered to Jake.

"I think she's insane," Jake whispered to Mikalah. The man holding his boot to Jake's chest shoved him, "You better not talk 'bout my sister like 'at." The man spit a wad of chewing tobacco onto Jake's jacket.

Emmaline returned holding a bottle of moonshine, handing it to her brother, "Here, get him to drink this."

"Open your mouth, boy. You get the fun part o' this ride," the man leaned over Jake and put the bottle of moonshine to his mouth. Jake pursed his lips and turned his head. The man grabbed Jake's chin, attempting to pry his mouth open and force in the nauseating liquid. Jake put up such a fight that the other two men emerged from the shadows and pinned Jake to the ground as Emmaline's brother tried to force the moonshine down Jake's throat.

"Goodness fella, this is Pappy's best shine. I doubt there's even any wood in this batch. Open your mouth an' enjoy it," the man managed to get Jake's mouth open enough to pour some onto his teeth and gums. Jake spit the fiery liquid out onto the man's pants.

"Oh, just forget it, Jeb, and pour it on his clothes. He doesn't have to really be drunk, just look it," Emmaline impatiently instructed. Jeb pulled open Jake's jacket and poured the liquid all over his shirt. Jake kicked at his arm, knocking the bottle from Jeb's hands, and it shattered as it struck a rock.

"Let him go!" Mikalah cried, "You want me, not him!"

"Oh, it's a shame, but this Mormon fella turned out to be such a scoundrel. He's gonna take advantage of ya and leave ya here to die," Emmaline pointed to a tall lanky blonde man with a week's beard growth. "Earl, you were the one wantin' to make this look authentic, weren't ya?"

Earl approached Emmaline who handed him the knife, "Here ya go; she's all yours. Do what you will and finish her off. Jeb, knock that Mormon trash unconscious and come along with me. Let's give Earl and Mikalah their privacy." Emmaline gestured for the third man and Jeb to follow her as she exited the cave. "We'll see ya at the house when you've finished the job, Earl."

Jeb punched Jake across the side of the face and flung him onto his side as Earl crouched in front of Mikalah and held the knife to her chin. Jeb kicked at Jake with his boot and satisfied that he was unconscious, left the cavern. "Have fun, Earl" he called back over his shoulder.

"I will," his evil grin spread across his whiskered face. He sat down in front of her and stared at her for some time, alternatively drinking a swig of moonshine and spitting out a wad of tobacco. Mikalah couldn't understand why he waited. Why didn't he just get the horrible deed over with and put her out of her misery? Yet, grateful for the time, she began pleading, praying for help, praying that Jake would wake up and somehow come to her rescue.

Periodically the villain checked his watch as if he were waiting for the bewitching hour to start his cruelty. The time drug by relentlessly, and she squirmed, attempting to free herself from her knots. Her actions only served to whet the villain's appetite. He chuckled evilly, "Ya ain't gettin' out o' those knots, girly."

"Let me go. You don't have to do this," Mikalah pleaded.

"Ah, but I want to," he used his knife blade to pick the tobacco from his teeth.

Mikalah looked at Jake, but he remained motionless, unconscious from the blow to his head.

The villain checked his watch one last time and smiling with some secret knowledge, rose onto his knees before her. "Let's see here, first thing that's gotta go is this dress." He took the knife and sadistically popped the buttons one by one from Mikalah's dress.

She held her breath as he leaned forward into her face, the smell of liquor and tobacco permeating the air. She turned her head from him, "Jake wake up!"

"Your feller can't save ya. You're wastin' your breath," the sickening man took the blade of the knife and ran it along her throat.

Jake opened his blurry eyes to see Earl hovering over Mikalah, his mouth on her neck as he pulled her coat from her shoulders and Mikalah squirmed to avoid him. Remembering that he'd shattered the bottle of moonshine, Jake searched in the dim light for a fragment of glass. He found one piece that looked like it might cut through the ropes and quietly maneuvered his tied hands toward it, picked it up between his fingers and began sawing at the rope.

"We gotta make this look like your fella took advantage of ya," the filthy man tore the shoulder from her dress and left it hanging in shreds along her arms.

"Please stop, you don't have to do what Emmaline says," Mikalah tried to reason with him.

"I ain't doin' this for Emmaline. I'm doin' this fur me," the man salivated, spit a wad of tobacco onto the ground beside her, and wiped the brown juice onto his sleeve.

Jake continued to saw at the rope around his wrists. He was half-way through it when Earl began running his filthy paws along her legs. Unwilling to wait any longer to intervene, Jake closed his eyes, wincing as he lunged onto his knees. He hurled his body at the man, knocking him sideways away from Mikalah. Jake was so angry that he pulled his arms apart as hard as he could and burst the remaining cords that bound him, flying at the man in a rage.

Earl swiped at Jake with the knife slicing his shirt and cutting into his chest. Jake grabbed Earl's arm and slammed his wrist repeatedly against a rock until he dropped the blade. Jake curled up his fist and punched Earl several times across the face, leaving him unconscious. Jake kicked the knife across the floor of the cavern and into a crevice in the cave wall. He turned to Mikalah and quickly untied her ropes, and she flung her arms around his neck.

"Are you all right," he put his hands on her cheeks, searching her eyes, and then pulled her coat up around her bare shoulders and began buttoning it for her.

"I'm all right. Are you ok?" she pulled a handkerchief from her pocket and dabbed at the blood trickling from the wound on his chest.

"It's just a scratch. Let's get out of here before he wakes up," Jake crossed to the cavern wall and grabbed the blazing torch, put his free arm comfortingly around Mikalah and led her out of the cave. As they approached the mouth of the cave, they peered around making sure no one waited for them. They quickly worked their way to the main road, still carrying the torch to light their path.

"How in the world are we going to explain this?" Jake looked down at his shirt and jacket that were soaked with moonshine.

Mikalah looked at herself. Fortunately her coat covered her mutilated dress. "I think I can sneak in the house without anyone realizing what's happened to me, but you smell somethin' awful! Should we report this to someone?"

"Let's stop by Mr. Donaldson's, and ask him what he thinks we should do," Jake turned up the road leading to Mr. Donaldson's, still holding the torch in one hand and his other arm around Mikalah. When they reached Donaldson's house, he handed the torch to Mikalah who stood back a few feet as Jake approached the door and knocked.

"Jake," Donaldson opened the door and then stepped back for the stench of liquor filled the air. "Boy, what have you been into?"

"I'm sorry to bother you Mr. Donaldson," Jake motioned for Mikalah to join him, and she came forward.

"Emmaline Bailey, her brother Jeb and a man named Earl abducted us and carried us to the Blowin' Hole," Mikalah began. "They poured moonshine all over Jake and… and…"

"Earl was going to take advantage of her and make everyone think I did it," Jake blurted out so Mikalah wouldn't have to finish the sentence.

"What!" Mrs. Donaldson exclaimed as she heard the conversation from behind her husband's shoulder.

"They planned to kill me and make it look like Jake did it," Mikalah added.

"Why? Why would Emmaline and the others want to do that?" Donaldson opened the door wider, "Come inside out of the cold."

"What about this torch?" Mikalah asked.

"There's a bucket of water over yonder, douse it," Donaldson pointed.

"Go on in, Mikalah," Jake took the torch from her and turned it upside down into the bucket. Satisfied that the flame extinguished, he turned to join Mikalah in the house.

"Come in dear," Mrs. Donaldson took Mikalah by the shoulder.

166

"I thought perhaps Mikalah could stay here, and we could call the police from your store and go return to the cave and see if Earl is still there," Jake suggested

"No, Jake, you can't go back there. It's not safe!" Mikalah exclaimed.

"You said the police take ages to get here from Chattanooga. If we wait, it may be too late," Jake reasoned.

"Hmm… Jake's probably right about that," Donaldson agreed. "Honey, go get Jake one of Henry's jackets and shirts. You can't go anywhere reeking like that!"

Mrs. Donaldson returned with one of her son's shirts and a jacket, "You're a might bigger than Henry, but maybe it'll fit." She handed it to him, and Jake pulled off his jacket and unbuttoned his shirt.

"Get rid o' that t-shirt too, it's soaked." Donaldson pointed. Jake pulled the t-shirt over his head. "Get him a wet wash cloth to get rid of that stench."

Donaldson's wife went into another room and returned with the wet cloth, and Jake washed down his chest and arms as Mrs. Donaldson led Mikalah into a bedroom to help her find another dress.

"Keep all their clothing as proof," Donaldson instructed as he took the cloth from Jake and cleaned his wound. "It's not deep enough for stitches, I don't believe." He grabbed some gauze and wrapped it around Jake's chest to stop the bleeding.

"We really need to hurry," Jake insisted as he started putting on the shirt, flung on the jacket and started out the door before his shirt was fully buttoned. Donaldson got in his truck, and Jake finished buttoning the shirt and coat as Donaldson drove toward his store. Donaldson called the police and explained what happened and told them that they'd meet them at the Blowing Hole.

"And hurry this time! This has nothin' to do with moonshinin'. This is an innocent couple o' kids who've nearly been killed," Donaldson demanded.

He and Jake closed up the store, drove toward the creek and the Blowing Hole. Donaldson parked his truck on the side of the road, stepped out of the truck and grabbed a piece of wood from the back of the truck. He tied old rags around it, struck a match along the bottom of his boot and lit the torch. He pulled out two rifles from the back of his truck and handed one to Jake. The pair entered the cave and back through the small passageway that led to the open room beyond.

Upon reaching the cavern, they peered around and found Earl still lying unconscious on the ground. Donaldson crossed to the man and pointed the barrel of the rifle at him, "I'm surprised he's still here. You must o' walloped him pretty good."

"I was mad," Jake stared at the man hoping he hadn't killed him. He knelt down and put his fingers to his neck. He looked up to Donaldson, "He's still alive." Jake rose to his feet, "I think he was pretty drunk to start with."

"We'll just stay here and guard him until the police arrive," Donaldson suggested.

"You think the others will come back lookin' for him?" Jake wondered aloud.

"If they do, we'll be ready for 'em. I'll guard him, and you watch the entrance," Donaldson suggested.

Jake turned and leaned his back against the cave wall, "How long do you think it'll be before the police arrive."

"It could take anywhere from thirty minutes to a couple hours. Ya never know with them county police," Donaldson shook his head disgusted.

"Emmaline's the one who had us shot outside your store," Jake suddenly remembered.

"Really? What's all this about, Jake? You never have explained what they're after," Donaldson prodded.

"Emmaline's in love with Hal, Mikalah's old boyfriend, but Hal's still stuck on Mikalah – or at least Emmaline thinks he is. She thinks if she gets rid of Mikalah, then Hal will forget about her and focus on Emmaline. I think she's got some mental problems," Jake explained. "She looked crazy out of her eyes tonight."

"And what do they want with you?" Donaldson asked.

"Hal hates me 'cause I stopped him when he tried to take advantage of Mikalah at the fair. Emmaline was trying to get rid of me for Hal's benefit, and also I suppose 'cause she needed someone to blame for what was going to happen to Mikalah tonight. She called it 'killin' two birds with one stone.'"

"She *is* insane," Donaldson agreed. "I always thought there was somethin' not quite right about that girl. Probably all the moonshine that family guzzles has gotten to their minds."

Jake and Mr. Donaldson waited for nearly an hour before the police arrived. Earl still lay in a drunken stupor until the police lifted him and he woke up.

"We'll need you and the Ford girl to come make a statement," the sheriff told Jake.

"All right," Jake nodded.

"I'll drive you two there so you don't get stuck there all night," Donaldson offered.

"Thank you, sir," Jake followed the police.

The Sheriff turned to them, "Mr. Donaldson, take Mr. Elliot and Miss Ford and leave a statement yourself since they came to you first. We'll send Earl here to jail in one of the squad cars, and the rest of us will head up the mountain and see what we can get out of the Bailey girl."

"Good luck," Donaldson offered doubtfully. The moonshiners didn't think twice about shooting anyone, not even policemen.

Jake and Donaldson picked up Mikalah and drove to the police station. By the time Mikalah got home it was nearly eleven o'clock. Donaldson stopped at the end of the Ford's driveway to let Mikalah out.

"I better go with you to explain to your parents," Jake suggested.

"You want me to come in and vouch for ya?" Donaldson offered.

"That might actually be a good idea, Mr. Donaldson. Jake and I are already skating on thin ice with Daddy. Would you mind?" Mikalah asked.

"Sure, no problem," he turned the truck into the driveway and shut off the motor.

Mikalah's father stepped out on the porch as the three walked up the drive.

"Where in the world have you been, Mikalah?" Bill scolded, and Laurana joined him on the porch.

169

"It's a bit of a long story, Bill. Why don't we go inside," Mr. Donaldson offered in his calming tone as he shook Bill's hand.

Everyone entered the house and sat down in the parlor. Donaldson rehearsed the events of the evening to Mikalah's wide-eyed parents. Mikalah knew that her father never would have believed their story if Mr. Donaldson hadn't been the one to tell it. It frightened her to think what would have happened to Jake had he not been able to stop Earl. Emmaline's plan was ingenious because no one would have believed Jake had he stood alone. At that moment, she was very grateful for Mr. Donaldson because she knew that neither the police nor her father would have believed them without his support. He was too well respected in the community to ignore.

When Mr. Donaldson rose to leave, he gestured to Jake, "Come on, Jake, let's get you home."

Jake stood and walked to the door. Mikalah accompanied them to the truck, "Thank you so much, Mr. Donaldson. I don't know what we would have done without you and your wife," Mikalah shook his hand. "Please thank her for me."

"You're welcome, Miss."

Mr. Donaldson got into the truck as Mikalah accompanied Jake to the passenger side, "Promise me that you'll stay close to home until we find out if they got Emmaline and the others," Jake leaned over and kissed her lips softly as Mr. Ford watched from the parlor window. Jake held Mikalah's face in his hands, "I don't know what I would have done if anything had happened to you."

"Don't even think about it," she kissed him once more. "Be careful, Jake."

"I will. I'll see you tomorrow," he opened the truck door, climbed in and watched as Mikalah entered the house.

Her father just stared at her as she passed him and climbed the stairs to her bedroom. She was exhausted and relieved that he didn't stop her to discuss anything further.

~*~

The old rooster behind Mr. Donaldson's store crowed, and Jake restlessly rolled over in his cot. He groped for his pocket watch that he'd left lying on the night table. Lifting one eyelid he read the time. Yawning, he sat up in bed and set his sock feet to the floor. Jake rubbed his eyes, stood and leaned over a wash basin, splashing cool water on his face and rubbing it with a towel.

He pulled off his shirt, peeled back the gauze and examined the wound. Carefully he removed the dressing, cleansed it and applied fresh gauze from the supply that Donaldson had given him the night before.

Hearing the rustling of keys at the front door, he quickly slid his arms into a clean shirt and buttoned it as he went toward the door. Mr. Donaldson entered the building just as Jake reached the checkout counter.

"Mornin' Jake," Donaldson waved.

"You're here early, sir," Jake greeted.

"I was hopin' I could get you to help me with somethin' before you go into work," Donaldson scratched his head.

"Sure, I have a bit of time before I have to leave. What do you need?" Jake buttoned his shirt sleeves.

"Some prankster moved my cows into Mr. Millsap's horse pasture and put his horses in my cow pasture. I could use another hand switchin' 'em back," Donaldson explained.

"Oh," Jake rubbed his mouth with his hand in an effort to conceal the smile that stole across his handsome face. He quickly turned from Mr. Donaldson to hide his humor, "I'll go get my jacket and throw on my boots." Jake walked back to his room to gather his things.

"I sure wish these kids would find somethin' better to do on Halloween," Donaldson stretched his arms above his head and yawned. He was tired. It was nearly midnight before he'd returned home, and he was aggravated that now he had to get up at the crack of dawn to do work that he shouldn't have to be doing.

Jake went out to the truck while Mr. Donaldson locked up and then joined him.

"Jake, I've been thinkin'," Donaldson's expression grew more serious.

"Yes."

"That Bailey family ain't gonna let you get away with puttin' Emmaline Bailey and her brother behind bars without some sort o' retaliation. If the police really picked those two up last night, then Mr. Bailey won't sit idly by and let you get away Scott free. And if they don't get Emmaline and her brother, she's bound to try somethin' again. Either way you and Mikalah are sittin' ducks," Donaldson's worried expression made Jake uneasy.

"You really think they'll try to harm us if the police take in Emmaline, Jeb and the other fellow?" Jake asked.

"Those Baileys are vengeful. They *always* get even, Jake - *always*. I hate to say it, but I think you should take Mikalah and get out of town."

"Really?"

"When we get back from roundin' up these cows, I'll call the police station and see whether they pulled 'em in. You're almost safer if they didn't arrest her."

"You've got to be kidding me?" Jake couldn't believe that he and Mikalah, who were completely innocent, would need to leave town just because their assailants were taken into police custody.

"I'm not kiddin', Jake. These folks strike back. They'd just soon shoot an enemy as look at 'im."

"Mikalah and I aren't even married yet. How could we just up and leave town together?" Jake was having trouble processing what Donaldson was telling him.

"Elope, go into Ringgold and get married. It's the only place around you can get married the same day. Then, I've got a friend in Ooltewah that has a farm that he can't work. He got work on the railroad makin' nearly six dollars a day and doesn't have time to fool with a farm since he's travelin' so much. His kids are grown, and he and his wife are lookin' at a smaller place with less for her to keep up with, but he needs to do somethin' with the farm. I bet I could talk to him and get him to let you live there in exchange for workin' the place," Donaldson turned the truck into Mr. Millsap's property.

"Now I know why you've got those bags under your eyes," Jake noted dryly.

"How's that?"

"Cause you've been up all night scheming and plotting!" Jake rubbed the whiskers on his chin and realized he hadn't shaved.

Donaldson parked the truck. His two sons were already out in Mr. Millsap's field rounding up cattle. "Jake I'll help you. I think either way you need to get out of town. I asked my wife and son to work the store today, and I'll take you to the factory. You can let 'em know you need to quit and collect your pay. Then we'll stop by Mikalah's, and I'll take you two to the court house in Ringgold to get married. Then we'll go talk with my friend. I think we can get all this done today." Donaldson had everything planned.

"Good grief, my friend. You really think we need to get in this big of a rush?"

"Yes I do… especially if those police got hold of the Bailey youngins last night!"

"Let me think on it while we round up these cattle. But I'm not quitting my job until I talk with Mikalah and see if she wants to do this," Jake stepped through the gate and Donaldson closed it behind them.

"Fair 'nough," Donaldson and Jake helped Donaldson's two oldest sons round up the cattle and drive them through the gate that adjoined his property with Mr. Millsaps'. As soon as the last cow crossed through the gate, Mr. Millsaps and his sons led their eleven horses back into their property.

Jake pondered the situation quietly as he and Mr. Donaldson rode back to the store in silence. He wondered what Mikalah would think of the idea. Donaldson was making a lot of sense and working a farm instead of working in a tile factory was more what Jake enjoyed doing. But Mikalah would miss her family.

Jake and Donaldson stepped into the store, "I'll be in the back." Jake walked past the isles of merchandise, into the little back room and shut the door. He knelt and prayed. Meanwhile, Mr. Donaldson picked up the phone and called the county police department to learn the latest news on the case.

After several minutes Jake heard a tap at his door. "Jake, can I come in?" Mr. Donaldson asked from the other side.

Jake rose to his feet and answered affirmatively.

"Those police surprised me. They took all three of 'em in last night. Emmaline is in custody along with her brother and that other fella. I'm tellin' you

Jake, you need to get Mikalah out of Daisy. Those Baileys are fine with everybody but the Richards clan. Normally, they are as harmless as doves with the rest of us in town, but mess with one o' their kin, and they're plum meaner than snakes. Mr. Bailey ain't gonna take too kindly to two of his youngins landin' in jail. Whether they're guilty or not, doesn't matter. You and Mikalah are the ones they're gonna blame."

After praying on the matter, Jake felt certain that Mr. Donaldson knew what he was talking about. It was time for him and Mikalah to leave. He turned and began packing his things into his bag, "You'll help us get married and find somewhere to stay?"

"Yes, this will help out my friend too. He's been needin' a good honest couple to watch his farm," Donaldson went into his store and began pulling household supplies from his shelves and loading them into his truck.

"What are you doing?" Jake looked at him perplexed as he carried his bag out of the room.

"Gettin' a few things you'll need," Donaldson kept loading items in the truck.

"But, but," Jake reached into his wallet and pulled out some money, "How much do I owe you?" Jake held out some cash.

"Your money's no good here," Donaldson turned and walked out to the truck, refusing to take the cash. "Come on, let me lock up," Donaldson motioned for Jake to leave the building.

Jake quietly slid some money next to the register. He knew Donaldson wouldn't take it any other way. He left the store, and Donaldson locked the building.

"Thank you so much for everything, Mr. Donaldson!" Jake had a lump in his throat, "You've been so kind and generous." The two men climbed into the truck.

"Oh, it's nothin'," Donaldson brushed it aside.

"Can I ask you a personal question, sir?" Jake asked hesitantly.

"Sure," Donaldson started the truck, "Where to first?"

"Mikalah's," Jake pointed ahead. "Why are you helping me so much? I mean, I know your minister, Reverend Arnold, is really against Mormons, and he can't be thrilled about you helping me like this."

"Reverend Arnold came to see me Sunday. Did I tell you that?" Donaldson glanced at Jake.

Jake shook his head, "No."

"He told me you had all kinds of blasphemous beliefs, that you worshipped a man named Joe Smith and read a fake Bible. Started rantin' and ravin' about you pollutin' the Ford family's minds, and that I needed to kick you out," Donaldson studied Jake's reaction. "Wanna know what I told him?"

"What *did* you tell him?" Jake looked at his friend.

"I told him I didn't care if you worshipped Santa Claus and read his Christmas list like it was scripture," he chuckled. "You're a good man, Jake Elliot, and you've done nothin' but make this town a better place and bring a smile to those Ford children's faces that I hadn't seen there since their Daddy left."

Jake smiled, "Thank you, sir."

"I told him that if he wanted me to keep bringin' my family to his church, he better leave you and Mikalah alone and let you worship any way you please – cause that's why we live in America instead of over there in Nazi Germany with that Hitler fella we see on the news reels."

Jake chuckled, "What did he do?"

"He shut his mouth, turned and left my house," Donaldson turned into Mikalah's driveway.

Jake's heart started pounding as he stepped out of the car. He really had no idea what to expect. He opened his door, and Donaldson accompanied him to the Ford's porch. Jake hesitantly knocked on the door. He turned to Donaldson, "You think she'll go with me?"

"Of course," Donaldson stated matter-of-factly.

"I'm glad you're so confident," Jake chuckled nervously.

The door opened, and Laurana stood before them, "Jake, dear, come in." She extended her hand and motioned for them to enter.

"Is Mikalah around?" Jake asked.

175

"Yes, she's in here in the kitchen washin' dishes. Come on in."

Jake and Mr. Donaldson walked through the parlor and into the kitchen. Mikalah turned from her work and looked twice before she realized it was him standing there, "Jake!" She dried her hands on her apron and hurried to his side.

"How're you feelin'?" she asked.

"My back's really sore and my chest doesn't feel much better, but I'll live," he grinned. "How about you?"

"I'm no worse for the wear," she stepped back and motioned for him to sit down. "What are you two doin' here this mornin'?"

About that time Matty came running and threw her arms around Jake's knees, "Jake!" Jake lifted her up into his arms, and she kissed his cheek.

"How's my sweetheart?" he tweaked her little nose.

"I'm gweat!" she smiled. "I've missed you!"

"I've missed you too, sweetie," he kissed her cheek. Donaldson pulled out a chair and sat down. Jake sat next to him with Matty on his lap.

Mr. Donaldson began, "Mrs. Ford, would you please sit down here with us. There's something we need to discuss." Donaldson looked around, "Is your husband home?"

"No, he's already left for work," she answered. Jake was a bit relieved. This would be easier without her father interfering.

"I called the police station this mornin', and they've arrested Emmaline and Jeb Bailey and Frank Bevins for what they did to Mikalah and Jake last night."

"Thank heavens!" Mrs. Ford held her hand to her chest and sat down in a vacant chair.

"While it's a good thing that they've come to justice, I'm afraid it isn't that great a thing for Mikalah and Jake," Mr. Donaldson shook his head.

"What do you mean?" Mikalah asked. "Why wouldn't it be a good thing?"

"You know what those Baileys are like when someone crosses 'em. They're gonna seek revenge on you and Jake, no doubt about that." Donaldson's serious expression made Mikalah and Laurana look at each other nervously.

"What are we going to do?" Laurana asked him.

"I think it would be best if I took Jake and Mikalah into Ringgold to be married today."

"What?" Laurana exclaimed.

"I have a friend who needs someone to watch his farm. They could live there, and we'll keep quiet about where they are so that the Baileys can't find 'em."

It was all happening so suddenly that Mikalah looked to Jake in confusion. He reached out his hand and held hers across the table.

"What do you think about this Jake?" Mikalah asked nervously.

Jake stood up and handed Matty to her mother, "Mikalah, maybe we should talk alone for a few minutes."

She rose from her chair and followed him into the parlor. Laurana turned to Mr. Donaldson as the pair left, "Are you sure this is necessary?"

"Yes, I'm really worried for their safety, Mrs. Ford. I think this is the only way. It's not like they weren't plannin' to get married this month anyway."

Laurana's eyebrows rose, "Oh really?"

"Yep, they were hopin' to get married on Thanksgiving. You didn't know?" Donaldson asked.

"I knew they were planning to get married, but I didn't know they'd set a date." Mikalah hadn't told anyone about them setting a wedding date.

In the parlor, Jake and Mikalah stood in front of the fireplace. The roaring fire popped and crackled as Jake held both her hands in his.

"Do you think he's right? Do you think we need to leave town today?" Mikalah asked.

"I took a little time this morning to think and pray, and I think he's right. I think we'll be in danger if we stay here."

Mikalah stared into the fire for a few minutes. Everything was happening so fast. The thought of marrying Jake today filled her with a combination of elation and nervous excitement. Having their own farm to work and him being at her side instead of at a tile factory all day sounded wonderful, but leaving her

177

parents and Matty, Hannah and Hank filled her with sadness. Then, she thought of the moonshiners and the horror of the previous night. She realized that Mr. Donaldson was right. The Baileys would seek revenge. They always did.

She looked into Jake's emerald eyes, "I think it's the best thing." She smiled but there was sadness in her eyes.

"Are you sure? I don't want to push you to do something you're not ready to do."

"Jake, the idea of marrying you today is – it's just unbelievably wonderful, but leaving the town I grew up in, starting somewhere totally new and never knowing when I'm going to see my family again is – well, it's terrifying."

"If you don't want to do this…"

"We don't have a choice. Anyway, it's not like I'll be alone," she smiled and tightened her grip on his hands. "I'll be with you!" At that moment she determined to make the best of the situation. It was really going to be an exciting adventure, and she'd focus on finding the good in it.

"You're certain?" he studied her eyes.

"I'm certain. I want to marry you today," she slid her arms around his neck, pulled him forward and kissed him. "I already have my white dress," she winked, grabbed his hand and the pair returned to the kitchen.

"Mama, will you come to Ringgold for the wedding?" Mikalah asked.

"So you're going to go?" Laurana rose and put her arms around her daughter. "I can't believe you're leaving!" Laurana brushed tears from her eyes.

"Me either," Mikalah held her mother tightly and wiped the tears from her own eyes.

"I'll help you pack," Laurana took her hand and led her upstairs.

"I'll go give my notice at work and be back for you in about thirty minutes," Jake told her.

Mikalah turned to wave at him and smiled, "All right. I'll be ready."

Chapter 9

Laurana looked down into the hope chest, a tear streaming down the corner of her eye, as her daughter tossed clothes on top of her childhood memories, her grandmother's doilies and tablecloth. She could feel a lump welling up in her throat that threatened to erupt into a shower of tears. But she swallowed hard, determined to hold her composure.

Mikalah glanced up to see her mother's back as she walked out of the room. Mikalah's baptism dress lay out on the bed while virtually everything she owned she stuffed into the trunk. Shortly, Laurana entered the room carrying a large garment bag. Laurana brushed at the tears and pulled up the cloth to reveal a beautiful white wedding dress beneath.

Mikalah gasped, "Oh mother!"

"This was my wedding dress. I want you to wear it today," Laurana handed the dress to Mikalah who threw her arms around her mother and kissed her tear-stained cheeks.

Mikalah finished unveiling the dress and held it snugly to her waist, "It's gorgeous, Mama! Are you sure?"

"Of course! I've waited for this day since you were born. I'd just hoped to make more of a celebration of it than we'll have time for. The least you can have is the dress," Laurana felt a mixture of profound sadness and exquisite joy at that moment. It was such an unexpected combination for her that she began to laugh and cry simultaneously.

Laurana put her arms around Mikalah, "I'm so happy for you that you're marrying Jake, but I'm terrified for you both at the same time."

"I know, Mama, but God is on our side. We have to have faith in that. It'll all work out for the best, and we'll be together again soon," Mikalah comforted.

"That's true," Laurana put her hands to her daughter's cheeks, "Not even those blasted Baileys can keep us apart!"

"Ooltewah isn't that far. You can always come to visit us, even if we can't come here," Mikalah brushed a tear from her face.

"That's right," Laurana smiled, "We'll look for the good in this. You're marrying the best man I've ever met, and you'll be able to worship as you please. Plus Mr. Donaldson told me about his friend's farm. It sounds beautiful."

"Oh really?"

"Yes, it has a duck pond and streams running through the property, orchards, cows, pigs, and lots of chickens. The house is big and even has indoor plumbing. It'll be a lot of work for the two of you, but working side-by-side always makes you closer," Laurana smiled.

"It's really going to be an adventure, isn't it Mama?" Mikalah looked out her bedroom window and felt an intense melancholy for the home of her childhood.

"Yes, it is dear, a good one," Laurana ran her hand along Mikalah's back and patted her shoulder. "I hear a car door. That's probably Mr. Donaldson and Jake."

Mikalah put the dress back in the bag and followed her mother downstairs. Jake tapped at the door, and Laurana opened it, "Come on in, Jake, Mikalah's gonna need a hand with her trunk."

Jake had evidently stopped somewhere to change. He'd shaved, wore his best suit and looked so handsome that Mikalah felt suddenly inexplicably shy as she met his gaze. He and Mr. Donaldson followed her up the stairs.

She stopped in the doorway of her room and pointed to the chest on the floor, "It's at the foot of the bed."

Jake took one end, and Mr. Donaldson hefted the other. She followed them down the stairs carrying her wedding dress in the garment bag. The men loaded the chest into the back of Mr. Donaldson's car, and Mikalah laid her dress across the back.

"You comin' with us, Mrs. Ford?" Donaldson asked as the three reentered the house.

"Yes, Matty and I are comin'. I'm just leavin' a note here for Hank and Hannah just in case they get home before I do."

"No specifics now, remember, Mrs. Ford. We don't want to take any chances," Donaldson warned.

"You think they'd come in our house while we're gone?" Laurana's eyebrows rose in alarm.

"I doubt it, but let's just all make a practice of bein' as cautious as we can in what we say and do. Won't do us any good to hide these youngins if the Baileys find out where they are," Donaldson patted Jake on the back. "You two ready ta get hitched?" he chuckled.

Jake took Mikalah's hand, "I guess we're as ready as we're going to be on such short notice."

Donaldson checked his watch, "It's only about half past eight now. I figure if we arrive at the weddin' chapel a little after nine, we can have you two married and on your way to your new house before lunch time." He turned to Laurana, "Mrs. Ford, I can bring you and your daughter home after we settle them in. The hardest part's gonna be findin' my friend. I'm not sure if he's already left the farm or not. But we'll figure somethin' out."

Mikalah inhaled deeply and exhaled, "I'm ready if everyone else is."

"All right, let's go," Donaldson opened the door for them, and everyone walked out of the house. Matty climbed in the back with Jake and Mikalah, and Mrs. Ford sat up front with Mr. Donaldson.

"It's very kind of you to help us like this, Mr. Donaldson," Laurana thanked him as he started the car and backed out of the driveway.

"You're welcome," Donaldson waved his hand as if it were all in a day's work.

Mikalah's stomach churned with more butterflies than she believed she'd ever experienced. She felt almost nauseated. Matty spent the entire ride to Ringgold playing finger puppet games with Jake in the back seat as Mikalah sat quietly gazing out the window. In a whirlwind of a month her world went from playing on the creek with her friends and younger siblings and dating Hal to being baptized into the Church, marrying this incredible man she'd just met and moving at least forty miles from home with him. She didn't know when she'd see her family or her home again. If someone had told her two months ago that this would be happening to her, she would have said they were crazy.

181

Jake reached to clasp her hand, "You ok?"

She glanced up at him, "Oh, I'm fine. Just trying to soak it all in."

He gave her a knowing smile and her hand a reassuring squeeze.

Mr. Donaldson pulled his Chevrolet into a vacant lot next to the little Ringgold wedding chapel. Everyone came from miles around to get married in Ringgold because you didn't have to wait for three days like you did in Chattanooga. They married couples at the little wedding chapel every thirty minutes all day long - providing everything from a dressing room and music to the minister and witnesses.

Mr. Donaldson opened the trunk. Matty skipped out of the car following at Jake's heels as he opened Laurana's door and then went around, opening Mikalah's for her.

Mr. Donaldson handed Mikalah the dress, "Here you go, Miss. There's a changing room inside."

Jake took her hand, and they ascended the chapel steps as Laurana led Matty by the hand. A little old lady greeted them at the door, took their information and helped them with the marriage license. Jake paid the fees, and the lady showed Mikalah, her mother and Matty to a little dressing room.

Mikalah felt as if her heart was going to pound out of her chest. Her hands were shaking so severely that Laurana grabbed them, "Calm down, dear. It's not like you weren't going to marry him eventually."

"I know, but it's all so sudden, I guess I'm just nervous 'cause I haven't had time to digest the whole idea of being married."

"You don't *have* to do this. We could think of something else if you're not ready to get married," Laurana arranged a ringlet of Mikalah's hair in place.

"Oh, I'm ready, I'm just nervous," Mikalah smiled, rubbed her hands together and wiped them on her skirt. She undressed and turned to pull the wedding dress from the hook and removed the bag.

"I'll help you with that, dear," Laurana lifted the dress over Mikalah's head and helped her with the arms.

"I should have tried this on before we got here to make sure it would even fit," Mikalah chuckled.

"It will fit. You're built just like I was at your age," Laurana spun her around, fastened the buttons that went up the back of the dress and fluffed Mikalah's curls. "Turn around."

Mikalah turned to face her mother. Laurana's eyes welled with tears, "Oh Mikalah, you're just beautiful!"

"Oh don't cry, Mama or I'm gonna start," Mikalah leaned forward and hugged her mother.

Laurana reluctantly broke their embrace, holding her handkerchief to her eyes, "All right, this is a happy occasion. We can't have Jake seeing you all teary eyed. He'll think it means you're sorry to be marrying him," she chuckled. "All right, my dress is something old and borrowed. Here's something new and blue. I just made this blue handkerchief the other day."

Mikalah chuckled, "Thank you, Mama."

"You ready, dear?" the little old lady tapped at the dressing room door.

Mikalah took a deep breath and smiled, "I'm ready."

Laurana opened the door, took Matty's hand, and the little old lady pointed, "Ma'am would you like to go ahead and be seated?" Laurana led Matty into the chapel and took a seat up front. At that moment, Mikalah realized that her father wasn't there to give her away. She wished he weren't working out of town. The little old lady handed her a bouquet of artificial flowers, and Mikalah looked up at the ceiling in an effort to hold back the tears.

Noticing Mikalah's uneasiness, Mr. Donaldson came toward her from within the chapel and held out his arm, "I know I'm not your Daddy, Miss Mikalah, but you can pretend I am."

Mikalah took his arm and kissed the kind man's cheek, "Thank you, Mr. Donaldson. I know you're not my daddy, but you feel like you're Jake's."

He patted her hand, and the pair stood at the end of the isle as the organist began the wedding march. Jake stood facing her as they stepped down the isle. He couldn't believe how beautiful she was in the wedding dress with her hair hanging in perfect ringlets around her face. It was a moment he knew he'd never forget, but there was a sadness in his heart that it wasn't perfect for her. He knew she would have preferred her entire family there. He also felt a twinge of regret that they were about to be joined together as man and wife, only until death

183

did them part. Jake wanted so much more for them. He wanted Mikalah to be his for all eternity. The dream of them being in front of the St. George temple flashed into his mind. At that moment he realized that she was wearing the same dress from his dream. He held onto the vision of it. It wouldn't happen today, but it would happen someday, and this moment brought them that much closer.

He smiled, took her arm and whispered in her ear, "You take my breath away, Mikalah."

She blushed and looked ahead to the minister who began the ceremony. When it was time to exchange rings, Jake reached into his coat pocket and pulled out a diamond studded gold band.

Mikalah stared at him, stunned that he actually had a ring, and especially one as spectacular as the one he held. She extended her hand, and he slipped the ring on her finger.

"You may now kiss the bride," the minister concluded.

Mikalah held the bouquet behind his neck as he held her tightly around her waist and kissed her. The organist began to play, and Donaldson and Laurana stood to congratulate them. Laurana hugged them both, tears trickling from her eyes as she wiped at them furiously with her handkerchief.

"That was so beautiful!" Laurana whispered in Mikalah's ear. "I just wish your Daddy was here to see it."

"I know, me too," Mikalah hugged her mother. "Look," Mikalah held out her hand.

Laurana studied the ring, "Jake, this is gorgeous! Where did you get it?"

"It was my grandmother's. She left it to me when she passed away," he put his arm around Mikalah.

"It's beautiful, Jake," Mikalah stood on her tip toes to kiss his cheek. "I love you," she whispered into his ear.

"I love you too, Mrs. Elliot," he grinned.

"A photograph's included with the weddin' package," the little old lady motioned for them to pose, and a man behind a camera took a picture. "We'll mail this to you when it's ready, Mr. and Mrs. Elliot."

Laurana gathered Mikalah's things from the little dressing room as the couple walked out of the church. Matty threw rice from a little bag and then hurriedly jumped in the center of the back of the car and patted the seat with both hands indicating that they should join her on either side.

Jake chuckled as Laurana reached into the back and pulled her out, "You ride up front with me. Let the happy couple enjoy the ride together without you aggravatin' 'em." She set Matty in the front seat and slid in next to Mr. Donaldson as Jake helped Mikalah into the back seat.

"I'm so glad you mawied Micky, Jake. I knew you would!" Matty exclaimed as she turned around facing them.

Jake grabbed her hand, "You sure did, didn't you, sweetie?" Mikalah put her arm around Jake's and leaned on his shoulder as Mr. Donaldson pulled out of the wedding chapel and turned onto Ooltewah-Ringgold Road.

"You're gonna have to come stay with us on the farm, Matty," Mikalah smiled.

"I can stay today!" Matty beamed excitedly.

"Let us get settled in, and once we know what we're doing on the farm, you can come stay with us," Mikalah tweaked her little sister's nose.

"Your daddy's savin' up for a car. When he gets it we can visit a lot," Laurana explained.

"Oh, won't that be fun!" Mikalah felt better thinking that her family might be able to visit.

"So what is Ooltewah like, Mr. Donaldson?" Jake asked.

"It's mainly farming community. Lots of big farms - cotton, sugar cane, cattle farms and tobacco fields," he looked at Jake through the rear view mirror.

"Is there a store?" Mikalah asked.

"Not in Ooltewah, but there's one in McDonald that isn't too far away," he explained.

"Mama said this is a nice farm. What's the main crop?" Mikalah asked.

"It's primarily sugar cane. He's also got hogs, cattle and lots of chickens. There's an apple orchard, blueberry bushes and cherry trees. It's one of the

185

prettiest farms I've every seen. You're gonna love it. Lots of fresh streams and a pond."

"Sounds like a dream," Mikalah smiled.

"It really is. It'll be a lot of work for the two of you. But Henry's two sons live nearby and can help out when it's time to slaughter hogs or harvest the sugar cane. Henry usually takes on laborers when the apples and the sugar cane comes in," Donaldson explained. "You just missed the sugar cane harvest. A man comes around with a machine in October and turns the sugar cane into molasses."

"Sounds like we've got a lot to learn," Mikalah looked at Jake, "Or at least I do."

"I'm familiar with some of it, but I'm sure I'll be learning a lot too," Jake was excited for the opportunity. He loved working outside on a farm and learning new things.

Donaldson turned into a road with a wooden sign that read *Shady Brook Farm.*

"Is this it?" Laurana asked, "It has its own name?"

"Yep, this is it, *Shady Brook Farm.* Henry named it that because there's so many shade trees and the brook runs through them," Donaldson explained.

The farm was sixty acres of the most beautiful rolling hills and fenced in pastures that Jake had ever seen. As they drove into the property Jake counted at least three dozen cattle in the pasture, a hog pen with a couple dozen pigs and a large chicken house with at least a hundred chickens pecking around in the yard.

Mikalah gasped as she saw the two story white farmhouse with a wrap around porch, "Surely this isn't it?" she whispered as she looked to Jake in astonishment.

Laurana turned to Mr. Donaldson, "Why would someone leave this property?"

"Henry's gettin' up in years. He's fifty-nine, and all his kids are grown. He injured his knees a while back and just can't work it. He took a job on the railroad that isn't as strenuous." Donaldson parked in front of the house and stepped out of the car and up on the porch. He knocked, and a woman came to the door with a small child clinging to her hip.

"Howdy, Ma'am, I'm lookin' for Henry Taylor. Is he around?" Donaldson asked.

"No, my father and mother-in-law have moved closer to Chattanooga where he's workin' on the railroad."

"Oh, are you livin' here now?" Donaldson asked.

"No, my husband, Frank, is workin' out here today until we can find someone to take care of the place," the young woman answered as she shifted the dark headed baby boy on her hip.

"I'm Mr. Donaldson from Daisy, and your father-in-law's a friend of mine. I think I've found a good, honest, hard-workin' couple to help out with the place," Donaldson pointed his thumb over his shoulder toward the car.

The lady moved her head to see around him and peered toward the car with her hand shielding her eyes from the sun's glare, "Frank will be thrilled to hear that. He's around back in the barn if you want to go speak with him."

Donaldson turned and motioned for Jake to join him, "Jake, come on over."

"You wanna come?" Jake asked Mikalah.

Mikalah felt suddenly self conscious in her wedding gown, "Uh, I'll just sit here with Mama and Matty and let you men figure this out."

"All right," Jake stepped out of the car, shut the door behind him, and joined Donaldson as he walked around back to the barn.

"This is amazing," Jake surveyed the orchards, and the tidy picket fences. "You sure must have a lot of faith in me to recommend me for this!"

"I do," Donaldson slapped Jake's back.

They stepped into the barn. "Hey Frank, how ya been, fella?" Donaldson waved to a man standing in the hayloft. He looked about Jake's age, blonde straight hair with a mustache, and beard. Frank tossed down a bail of hay that landed directly in front of them and then hopped down and shook Donaldson's hand, "Good to see you again, Mr. Donaldson! Pa's not here. He's off workin' on the railroad." Frank was Mr. Donaldson's height, so he was about six inches shorter than Jake.

"That's what I heard. He said he was lookin' for some hard workin' people to live in the house and take care of things. I believe I've found just the couple to do that," Donaldson slapped Jake on the back.

"Frank Taylor, this is my good friend Jake Elliot. Jake, this is Henry's boy Frank."

"Nice to meet you, sir," Jake shook Frank's gloved hand.

"Good to meet you too. So you think you and your wife can keep up this place?"

Jake looked around, "Looks like a heap of work, but we're up for the challenge."

"I take it you think Mr. Elliot's up for it, Mr. Donaldson, or you wouldn't have brought him out here?"

"Yep, Jake's a hard worker. Tell him about your experience, Jake," Donaldson nudged him.

"Let's see, I can fix about anything around the house – repairs and painting. I've picked cotton, worked a cotton gin, cured meat and herded cattle. I've picked and put up apples, corn and most other crops. I've harvested sugar cane and helped in molasses making – never been in charge of it, but have helped with it."

"We don't do that ourselves anyway. Paul Rivers has a contraption that does that, and he comes 'round, turns it into molasses and takes some of what he makes as payment. Matter of fact, we just finished the last of the molasses makin' last week. You'll find some jars inside," Frank pointed to the house.

"Ah, I see," Jake nodded his head in understanding.

"What kind of arrangement was your father wantin' to make?" Donaldson asked.

"Pa was lookin' for someone to live here and keep up the house and help with the various crops and animals. In exchange, whoever lives here can use what they need of the crops and livestock and the surplus we'll sell or trade. I'm supposed to oversee the sale and trade of the surplus and make sure you have laborers and such when you need them. I'll be checkin' in every week to make sure things are runnin' smoothly and help out."

"That sound fair to you?" Donaldson scratched his head and looked toward Jake.

"Sounds fair to me," Jake nodded.

"If Mr. Donaldson recommends you then I know my Pa would trust his judgment," Frank extended his hand to shake Jake's. Let me show you 'round the place."

"You mind if my wife looks around with us?" Jake asked.

"Sure, go get her," Frank motioned toward the car.

"Uh, we just got married about an hour ago, and she still has on her wedding dress," Jake grinned. "Would your wife mind if she went in the house and changed before we look around?"

"Oh, newlyweds – eh?" Frank rubbed his whiskers and grinned. "Sure, have her go on in."

Jake walked to the car and opened Mikalah's door, "We've worked out a deal. He's going to show us around the place, but I thought you might like to change out of your wedding gown before we do that. He said you could go in the house and change."

"Oh, good idea," Mikalah smiled.

Laurana stepped out of the car with Matty and handed Mikalah her dress. Jake escorted Mikalah to the front door. Frank's wife saw them coming and opened the door.

"Hello, Ma'am. I'm Jake Elliot, and this is my wife, Mikalah and her mother, Mrs. Ford, and her little sister, Matty. As you can tell, we've just come from our wedding, and your husband's hired us to live here and work the land. He said my wife could come inside and change out of her dress."

"Oh, certainly! So you just got married today?" Frank's wife extended her hand, "Congratulations! How exciting!"

Mikalah smiled at the lady as she shook her hand. She could tell already that she was going to like Mrs. Taylor, "Nice to meet you, Ma'am."

"Oh, don't call me Ma'am. I'm not much older than you, Mrs. Elliot. Please call me Ruth."

"Nice to meet you, Ruth. Please call me Mikalah."

"All right," Ruth motioned for Mikalah to follow her back into a master bedroom on the first floor, "Here, this will be your room. Make yourself at home."

"Thank you! Mama, would you come help me with these buttons?" Mikalah motioned for her mother, and Matty followed on her mother's heels.

"Your wife makes a beautiful bride, Mr. Elliot," Ruth smiled and picked up her little boy who clung to her legs.

"She sure does, doesn't she?" Jake smiled.

Mr. Donaldson and Frank stepped into the house and began talking with Jake while Laurana helped Mikalah with her dress.

"Mama, are you believin' this place?" Mikalah marveled. "It's amazing."

"I know. It's almost worth having those crazy Baileys after ya to get to live in a dream place like this. Just look at this bedroom!"

"Mikalah looked around at the oak bedroom furniture and the homey drapes that hung in the window. There was even a back door that went out from the bedroom onto the wrap around porch. Mikalah snooped around and discovered a closet and a bathroom off the bedroom. "Look at this, Mama! Indoor plumbin'! No more runnin' to the outhouse in the middle of the freezing winter nights!"

"Oooh," Laurana was envious.

"I just can't understand why anyone would want to leave this!" Mikalah shook her head dumbfounded.

"It looks like a lot of work. I suppose if you were gettin' older and had joint problems, this all would be a lot to keep up with. Plus those folks on the railroad make nearly three times what a normal man makes," Laurana looked around the room as Mikalah finished changing.

"I'm ready for the tour," Mikalah stepped out of the room and joined Jake.

"What do you want to see first – inside the house or out?" Frank asked.

"Inside," they answered in unison.

"All right, inside it is." Frank began, "This is the living room. This is my Mama's piano. Her new place didn't have room for it. Of course there's the fire place in here, and there's another one in the master bedroom. In the kitchen you've got lots of storage cabinets and indoor plumbin' here at the sink. There's the wood stove. The master bedroom's in here to the right. There's a bathroom in there."

Frank walked to the other side of the house, "Over here there's a dining room and a study. These are Pa's books, but you're welcome to read 'em. Pa's always fiddling with gadgets, always got to have the latest inventions so there's a telephone in his study and a second bathroom right here under the staircase."

Mikalah's eyebrows rose as she looked up at Jake. Frank started up the staircase and motioned for them to follow, "Up here, there's four bedrooms. You probably won't need to do much up here since it's just the two of you, unless your family comes to visit." They quickly looked around and came back downstairs.

"Your parents have a lovely home," Mikalah marveled.

"My dad built this house about ten years ago and has tinkered with it a lot addin' the indoor plumbin' and telephone over the last few years. Then he had a hay bailin' accident a couple years back and tore the ligaments in his knees. He's just not been able to do much farm work since, and my mother couldn't keep up with the place by herself without us boys at home. So when he got the job on the railroad, he took it and asked me to help him find someone to work the place," Frank explained.

"We just feel blessed that Mr. Donaldson brought you two around. It was gettin' too much on us to try to keep up with this place and ours," Ruth shook her head.

"We feel blessed to be here!" Jake smiled and tightened his arm around Mikalah's shoulder.

"We sure do!" she agreed.

"All right, let's take a look outside," Frank walked out the front door, and everyone followed him.

When they finished the tour of the farm, they carried their things into the house, and Mr. Donaldson turned to Laurana, "Mrs. Ford, it's about noon. We better be gettin' you home before your other youngins get home from school."

"Yes, I guess you're right," Laurana turned to Mikalah and Jake and gave them a hug, "Call Mr. Donaldson's store if you need anything dear - or just to talk."

"Why don't you call each other every Monday evening around six thirty," Mr. Donaldson suggested. "You can come up to the store, and Mikalah can call you there. You know the number, Jake, don't you?"

"Yes sir. Thank you for everything Mr. Donaldson," Jake shook Mr. Donaldson's hand and gave him a hug.

"Glad to help, my boy. Enjoy this place!" Donaldson smiled.

"We will!" Jake waved as Mr. Donaldson stepped toward his car.

Mikalah hugged Matty, and then embraced her mother one last time, "Send Daddy my love."

"I will, dear. I'm so glad I got to see where you'll be livin' and that you'll be well cared for. Takes a load off my mind!"

Mikalah and Jake waved as the others got into the car and drove away.

"Ok, Mr. Elliot, here's the keys to the tractor and the truck. You'll need the truck to take the butter and eggs into town. Be sure to fill up the tank whenever you go to McDonald 'cause that's the closest gas station for miles around. You can swap butter and eggs for gas."

"I've got a phone at my house if you need anything. We're just the next farm over, and our phone is tied into this one. Just pick up the phone and crank two shorts and a long and that's us. My brother John is two longs," Frank explained as he motioned for his wife to join him, "Come on Ruth, we need to get goin'."

"Thanks for everything," Jake shook Frank's hand, and he and his wife and child waved good-bye as they got into the truck and drove away.

Jake turned to Mikalah; put his arms around her, lifting her off the ground, "Are you believin' this?"

"I feel like I died and went to heaven," Mikalah smiled down into his face.

"I know. I mean it's going to be a lot of work, but it's just incredible," Jake set her back down on the ground.

"I'm starvin', let's go find somethin' to eat," Mikalah suggested.

"Just one matter to tend to first," a mischievous grin twinkled in Jake's emerald eyes as the dimple in his chin deepened. He put his palm to her cheek, letting his fingers vanish into her soft curls. The mischievous expression fled his handsome face, replaced with the loving gaze of a man who adored his wife. Mikalah's arms encircled his waist as he kissed her lips softly. She trembled at his touch and her heart hammered wildly. She wished she had more time to prepare for this moment, then again, maybe it was best that it all happened in a whirlwind. Suddenly, he scooped her up into his arms and the playful grin returned. He carried her up the porch steps, across the threshold, nudged the front door closed with his boot, and entered the bedroom.

~*~

Mikalah stood on the back porch overlooking the pond and the barn. A chilly breeze wafted through her hair as she pulled the blanket around her shoulders. She could hear Jake's bare feet crossing the hardwood bedroom floor as he ambled out the open door holding a sandwich in his hand. He put his left arm around her waist and kissed her neck as his right hand reached around, offering the sandwich.

"Thank you," she took a bite and held his bare arm at her waist.

She turned to face him. He stood before her in his trousers and bare chest. "It's cool out here. Aren't you cold?" she asked.

"Why? You wanna share that blanket with me?" he winked.

"Sure," she opened the blanket and extended it to encompass him.

"You want to go for a walk?"

"Yes, I'd love to get a better look at the springs and the pond," she smiled as he kissed her lips briefly.

"All right," he led her by the hand back into the house, "We'll go for a walk, and then we've got at least six cows to milk and a hundred chickens to feed."

~*~

Since she'd only cooked a light lunch after arriving home, Laurana prepared a large dinner. As Bill stepped into the house he found his wife in the kitchen and put his arm around her waist, "Somethin' sure smells good."

193

She thanked her husband, but her heart raced nervously. "I didn't expect you'd be back in town until tomorrow." She wasn't looking forward to breaking the news to him about Mikalah and Jake. While he was warming up to the idea of the two getting married, he hadn't completely come to a verdict on what he thought about it.

Hank and Hannah still didn't know about Mikalah. Laurana had sworn Matty to silence – which was incredibly difficult for the chatty five-year-old. As everyone gathered round the table, Bill turned to Hannah, "Where's your sister?"

"Don't know, I haven't seen her around since I've been home," Hannah looked to her mother hoping she'd shed some light on Mikalah's disappearance.

Laurana took a deep breath, "Mr. Donaldson stopped by this morning, said that the police had arrested Emmaline and Jeb Bailey for what they did to Jake and Mikalah last night."

"Oh, good!" Bill clapped his hands. "I wasn't sure they'd do much about it."

"They're in custody along with the other two fellas. Mr. Donaldson felt very strongly that Mr. Bailey would retaliate and take it out on Jake and Mikalah," Laurana looked to her husband.

"I hadn't thought about that," his face fell. "He's probably right about that." He looked around, "Where is Mikalah?"

"You know that Jake and Mikalah were planning to get married – right?"

"Uh … yeah," Bill felt the urge to brace himself for a jolt.

"Donaldson thought it best if they go ahead and get married today and …"

"What?" Bill exclaimed incredulously.

"Donaldson has a friend with a farm that they're going to live on. It's a good ways from here, and the Baileys won't be able to find them."

"Laurana, are you telling me you let our daughter run off and get married today without telling me?"

"It was all such a rush, and you were out of town. It just felt like we didn't have much choice – knowin' how rash those Baileys are. I swear I've seen someone lurkin' out in the shadows all afternoon."

Bill stood up quickly, crossed to the window and peered out. He walked back into the kitchen, "So you're saying Mikalah is married now?" he just wanted her to say it outright.

"Yes, Bill, Mikalah married Jake this morning," Laurana's eyes looked as if she where bracing herself for a tongue lashing.

"Hot dog!" Hank clapped his hands and looked at Hannah who smiled broadly.

"You two think this is funny?" Bill eyes darted furiously in their direction.

"No, Pa, we don't think it's funny. We're just happy for Mikalah and Jake," Hank defended.

"They're just so in love," Hannah clasped her hands together with a dreamy far away look in her eyes.

Bill rolled his eyes, "Oh brother!"

"Well, they are, Bill," Laurana chuckled.

Bill flopped down in his chair, "But I missed my daughter's wedding!"

"Oh, I'm so sorry, Bill. I know Mikalah wanted you there." Laurana felt horrible. "I just had no way of reachin' you, and it was all just a whirlwind. But on the bright side, she's livin' in a dream house. It's the prettiest farmhouse and farm I believe I've ever seen."

Laurana went on to explain to her husband how they came to find the place and described it in detail to her enraptured family. "I was thinking we might be able to go visit her at Thanksgiving," Laurana suggested.

"I'll put in tomorrow for the time off," Bill stood and walked into the parlor to add a few more logs to the fire.

"How romantic!" Hannah had that far off look in her eyes.

"Don't be gettin' any ideas!" Laurana rolled her eyes. "I'm expecting a big wedding for you. I only let Mikalah do this 'cause of the danger to her and Jake."

Chapter 10

The sun began to set in the western sky as Mikalah tossed chicken feed out onto the ground. At the sound of the corn scattering, the chickens scurried forward, pecking frantically. She picked up a bucket of water, poured it into the feeders and returned to the house to wash her hands. Drying her hands on a towel, she peered out the window observing Jake as he milked a cow in the barn. She wondered how she managed to live nearly eighteen years without him. She seemed unable to look at him long enough or quench her thirst for his companionship in the smallest of tasks. He'd become the very air she breathed and the light that illuminated her way. She neatly folded the towel, placed it on the counter and went out the back door.

They had lived in the farmhouse for four days now and had developed a routine for working all the chores together. Jake's eyes lit up as Mikalah entered the barn. She approached him from behind and massaged his shoulders as he milked.

"Dinner will be ready soon. When you finish, come on in," she kissed his cheek and rubbed his shoulder.

"Thanks, I'll be right in," his gaze followed her back to the house.

Mikalah prepared two plates of dinner and placed them on the table next to two glasses of milk. She struck a match and lit a candle in the center of the table, giving a luminous glow to the room which had started to grow dark as the sun sank lower behind the hills.

Jake carried two pails of milk inside the house and placed them in the ice box, "That sure smells good, Honey." Jake rubbed his stomach as he crossed to the sink and washed his hands.

"It's your favorite – fried chicken, mashed potatoes, gravy, biscuits and corn," she smiled as he approached her and put his hands to her waist.

197

"Thank you!" he kissed her quickly, pulled out a chair for her and sat down.

As they were finishing up the last of their meal, Jake's expression grew puzzled, "Do you hear that?"

"What?"

"Listen," Jake and Mikalah sat quietly, listening to a fiddler playing in the distance. Jake rose and crossed to the door, opened it and stepped out on the back porch. The sun had set and a full moon lit up the sky as the stars burst one-by-one through the deep blue blanket of night. Jake motioned for Mikalah to join him on the porch. She rose, took his hand, and he shut the door to keep the cool November air from chilling the house.

"Turkey in the Straw," the corners of Mikalah's mouth curled upward as she recognized the melody.

"Sounds like it's coming from Frank's place," Jake smiled and began to tap his foot to the melody.

"He's really good," Mikalah listened happily as Frank finished the song and started another one – a slower waltz.

Jake bowed exaggeratedly and held out his hand to her, "May I have this dance, Mrs. Elliot?"

She put her hand in his as he led her down the back porch steps into the yard. He took her in his arms and the pair waltzed in the moonlight to the faint but melodious fiddle. Mikalah found it interesting that she would feel butterflies with the man she'd been married to for nearly a week, but nonetheless they were there as he held her closer to him than what would have been appropriate in public.

"We've never danced together before," she thought aloud as the realization struck her.

"No we haven't, but we should more often," he gazed lovingly into her eyes as the song concluded and another began. The pair danced throughout the evening as if the heavenly lights shone and the fiddler played only for them.

~*~

Mikalah stood next to Jake holding a board in place as he repaired the broken fence. It was an unseasonably warm afternoon for mid-November. Jake wiped the perspiration from his brow as he hunkered down, hammering the last nail into place. Jake rose and fixed his eyes on the property entrance. From the expression of dread on his face, Mikalah knew something was wrong.

"What is it Jake?" she asked and then turned to follow his gaze. A police car coming up the drive passed them and parked in front of the house. Mikalah could feel a sinking feeling in the pit of her stomach. What they both knew was coming had finally arrived.

Jake didn't say a word, but hopped over to Mikalah's side of the fence, put his arm around her, and the couple ventured back toward the house.

Three men stepped out of the car. Two wore uniforms and a stocky man in a brown suit emerged from the backseat of the squad car. As Mikalah and Jake drew closer, a tall lanky officer removed his hat, "Are you Mr. and Mrs. Jake Elliot?"

Jake extended his right hand, still holding Mikalah close to him with his left, "Yes, I'm Jake Elliot, and this is my wife Mikalah. How can I help you gentlemen?"

"I'm Officer Anderson, this is my partner Officer McClendon, and this is Mr. Becket. He's the District Attorney prosecuting the Bailey case. Mrs. Elliot's parents told us you were here. We need to speak with you both about what happened on the night of October 31st."

Mikalah glanced quickly to Jake whose expression remained emotionless.

"We were just on our way into the house for a cool drink. Why don't you gentlemen come inside and join us?" Jake didn't wait for a reply but turned to the house, still holding Mikalah protectively as they ascended the porch steps, and the three men followed them.

Jake motioned for them to be seated in the living room as he released Mikalah, and she pulled five glasses from the kitchen cupboard, set them on the counter and began filling them with cool water from the icebox.

Jake helped her carry the glasses to the gentlemen, "How can we help you?"

The brown-haired attorney took a sip of his drink and stroked the corners of his mustache with his thumb and forefinger, "We need you to testify against the Baileys, Frank Bevins and Earl Henderson."

Mikalah sat down on the piano bench, lowered her drink from her lips and stared expectantly at Jake who stood beside her.

"We kinda figured you'd ask us to do that," Jake met Mikalah's gaze, "We've already thought about it and discussed it, and we're willing to testify upon one condition."

"What's that?" asked the District Attorney, straightening his posture.

"We've gone to great lengths to make sure the Baileys don't know where we are. We need your word that they won't find us and that we'll be protected from them the day we testify."

Officer Anderson replied, "We've already discussed that with your parents. They refused to tell us where you were unless we agreed to the same conditions. We'll escort you to the courthouse and make sure you get home safely without being followed. We'll also provide police protection the entire time you're in court."

"So do we have a deal?" the District Attorney asked.

Jake looked to Mikalah, and she nodded in agreement. Jake extended his hand to the District Attorney, "Yes, we do. When will we need to go to court?"

"The exact date hasn't been set yet, but we're expecting it will be sometime in January. We can let you know exactly once we find out," answered Mr. Becket. "Would you mind if we went over your account of the events so I have a good grasp of everything and can do a thorough job of prosecuting the case?"

Jake turned and pulled a kitchen chair into the living room and sat on it backwards leaning his arms on the back of the chair, "That's fine with us."

The District Attorney began asking them questions, and Mikalah and Jake related their remembrances from the frightful evening. After an hour of questions and answers, the District Attorney rose and approached Jake. Jake and Mikalah stood and shook his hand, "Thank you so much. With your testimony I believe we can put these criminals away for life," Mr. Becket stated.

"Really?" Mikalah was surprised that the penalty would be so severe.

"The law doesn't leave much tolerance for kidnapping, especially in combination with the infliction of bodily harm," Mr. Becket explained. Jake' eyebrows rose as he glanced at Mikalah.

The two officers shook their hands and followed Mr. Becket out the front door. Jake stood on the porch with his arms folded across his chest.

"We'll be in touch with you soon," Officer Anderson placed his cap back on his head and nodded to Jake.

Jake watched the men drive away and joined Mikalah in the kitchen. He walked up behind her as she made lunch. Putting his arms around her waist, he kissed her cheek, "Are you all right?"

"I'm fine. You?" she asked.

"I'm just glad we thought and prayed about our decision before today. Sure made it a lot easier to deal with, don't you think?"

"Yes," she sighed, "But I'm still not lookin' forward to it."

"I know, neither am I," he kissed the top of her head and tightened his embrace.

~*~

Jake carried three medium pie pumpkins into the house and set them on the kitchen table, "This going to be enough for your pies, honey?"

Mikalah turned from the counter where she rolled out pie crusts, "Oh, those look perfect. Thank you, dear."

Jake stood beside her, leaning sideways against the kitchen counter as he twirled a stray ringlet of her hair, "You've sure been working hard in the kitchen today." He pushed the ringlet back behind her ear.

"I've got a lot to get done before everyone gets here tomorrow. Can you believe it's already Thanksgiving?"

"I know!" he looked down at her pie dough, "Is there anything I can do to help you in here?"

"No, I believe I have everything under control. Have you had any luck shootin' us a big turkey?"

"I saw a wild flock cutting through the south pasture, but I didn't have my rifle with me. If you don't need any help here, I'll get my rifle, head over there and see if I can get us one."

"Sure, run along. I'm fine here." She patted his arm and kissed him, "Good luck!"

He thanked her and retrieved a rifle from the gun rack. "I'll see you in a little bit with the biggest turkey you ever saw." With a wink and a smile he exited the kitchen door.

"I hope his aim is better at shootin' turkeys than it is at the rabbits nibblin' on my garden," she chuckled. Mikalah was already thinking that they may have to serve chicken instead of turkey. Jake wasn't the best shot in the world. Hunting just wasn't his thing. Mikalah figured it was because he was so kind hearted that animals, plants and people flourished under his care, but killin' just wasn't in him. She smiled to herself just thinking about how he soft-heartedly took the rabbit he'd trapped in the garden out to the edge of their property and set it free. Her brother Hank would have killed it, skinned it for a hat, kept the feet for good luck and made their mother cook it for dinner.

Some time later, Mikalah jumped from her reverie as a shot rent the air. "Well at least he got up the nerve to pull the trigger this time," she chuckled aloud to herself. Mikalah pinched the edges of her pie crust making a pretty frill around the edges. Setting the pie crusts aside she grabbed the pumpkins from the kitchen table, removed their stems, cut them in half, scraped out the seeds and placed two halves face down on a baking sheet and slid them in the oven. She washed the pumpkin seeds and set them aside in a bowl. They'd make a good snack for later.

Mikalah washed her hands and dried them on her apron. *I need a little break* she thought to herself as she sat down at the piano and began picking out a song that Jake had taught her to play. Every night they would play the piano and sing together, and he would give her a piano lesson using his copy of the Church hymn book.

As Mikalah played the third verse of *Lead Kindly Light* Jake proudly tromped in the back door holding a huge turkey upside down by its feet. Mikalah ceased playing, and her mouth dropped open at the sight.

"Bet you thought I couldn't do it, didn't ya," he beamed.

She slapped her hands to her thighs, "You do surprise me every day, Jake Elliot!" She rose to her feet and examined the bird. "This is perfect, Jake!" She looked up at him flirtatiously, "So are you gonna skin it for me?"

"Uh," he winced, "To be honest with you, it took all the effort I could muster to pick it up."

She chuckled, "You better get used to it Jake. We're comin' up on hog killin' time and cleanin' a turkey is nothing compared to hog killin'"

Jake's face fell a little as he thought about it.

She patted him on the arm and took the bird from him. "One step at a time, dear. You've killed your first turkey, and that's quite an accomplishment. We won't get ahead of ourselves," she winked and took the bird to the sink.

"It is a big one, isn't it?" Jake stated proudly.

"Yes it is. You did great! And it only took you one shot! I'm impressed!" she smiled as his pride returned. "Could you please go dig me a dozen each of potatoes and sweet potatoes?"

"Now *that* I'd be happy to help you with," Jake smiled and went out the kitchen door. He peeked his head back in and winked, "You have fun with that bird."

"Jake, sometimes I think you just fake squeamish so you don't have to do the dirty work!" she complained to him even though she knew he couldn't hear her.

~*~

The farmhouse felt warm and toasty from the oven and roaring fires in the two fireplaces. The aroma of pumpkin pies and turkey roasting filled the air. Mikalah stood proudly in the living room admiring her handiwork. She'd decorated the house with colorful leaf, pumpkin and squash arrangements, giving the home a warm country autumn feel.

Jake flung open the kitchen door, stomping his feet on the mat outside the door, "It looks and smells delicious in here, Mikalah! You've really outdone yourself!"

"Thanks," she still stood admiring her handiwork.

"What time are your parents supposed to arrive?" he asked as he washed his hands at the kitchen sink.

"They said around eleven," she glanced at the clock on the wall.

"We've still got a couple hours before they get here. Have you got anything left to do?" he dried his hands on a towel.

"Let's see the turkey's in the oven and has a couple hours left. The pies are all made. The rolls are risin'. I made the sweet potato casserole and just need to warm it after they arrive. The house is all decorated. I believe that I have everything taken care of," she studied the room as if she might be forgetting something.

"It sounds like you've got it all under control with two hours to spare," he said as he walked flirtatiously toward her and put his hands to her waist. "Sounds like you might need a little diversion after all that work," he winked.

She slapped his chest, "You beat everythin' Jake."

"Why?" he asked.

"What if I forgot somethin'?"

"You didn't."

"What if I burn somethin' while...?"

"What's in the oven?" he asked.

"The turkey," she replied.

"It's not gonna burn for three more hours," he winked.

"What if my parents are early?" she retorted.

"Then they can wait outside until we're ready to open the door," he chuckled.

"What if..."

Jake picked her up and carried her toward the bedroom. "What if you stop frettin' and enjoy yourself," he chuckled as he kicked the door shut behind them.

~*~

Mikalah stood at the mirror fixing her hair. She lifted it up and swirled it on top of her head, turning her head this way and that trying to decide the best way to arrange her long strawberry blonde curls.

Jake's bare feet approached her from behind as he pulled a single suspender over his bare torso, "I like it better down." He gestured for her to release the hair she held above her head, and he ran his fingers through her curls, carrying strands from the left and right sides of her head, holding them together loosely at the back.

"I like it when you fix it this way." He leaned over and placed loving kisses on her neck. He released her hair, picked his shirt up from the floor, and sat on the edge of the bed dressing as he watched her fix her hair.

"Like this?" she looked at his reflection questioningly in the mirror.

"Yep, that's it," he smiled. He stood and pulled his suspenders back atop his shoulders. Enveloping her in his arms he admired her face in the mirror, "You get more beautiful every day, Mikalah." She smiled as he reached for one of his boots that lay at her feet and walked to the other side of the room to retrieve its mate. "I'm gonna go check on the cattle before your parents get here."

As he walked past her she grabbed his suspender with her finger, and he stopped to keep it from snapping back. She gently released it and grabbed his hand as he turned to face her, "What?"

"I love you Jake," she smiled.

"I love you too," he winked.

She loved that dimple in his chin. She put her finger to it and then kissed him warm and passionately, playing with the thick dark locks of his hair behind his head.

He took her arms and moved them to her sides, "What are you up to?" he grinned. "Keep that up, and your parents *will* be standin' out in the cold for a while."

"Go check on the cattle," she winked and popped his suspender. As he turned to leave the room she slapped him on the rear.

She giggled as he spun around and shook his finger. "You better watch it, girl!" he teased as he walked backwards out of the room.

205

Mikalah checked the turkey and basted it, then examined the house to see if she'd forgotten anything. She loved holidays, and they would be all the more special this year spending them with Jake in their own house and her family coming to visit. She couldn't wait to see her family again and fidgeted nervously dusting and straightening as she waited for them.

A little before eleven, she heard a car coming up the drive and peered out the window to see a 37 Ford approach, "That must be Daddy's car," she mumbled excitedly. She stepped out on the front porch and waved as Jake hopped over the fence and trotted toward the car. Matty stepped out of the back seat and looked toward Jake and then toward Mikalah. She put her hands to her hips briefly as if she were deciding who to run to and then made her decision. Jake pulled her up into his arms, kissed her cheek and carried her toward the house.

"Well!" Mikalah put her hands to her hips, "I guess I'm just old hat now, Matty?"

Hannah approached her sister and gave her a big hug, "I still love you best, Micky." Hannah walked into the house as Mikalah hugged her parents, and even Hank embraced her briefly.

"Oh, this is gorgeous!" Hannah exuded excitedly as she looked around the house.

"You've really done a wonderful job decorating and something smells fabulous!" Laurana gazed around.

"Duck, sweetie," Jake stepped into the house carrying Matty on his shoulders. Matty lowered her head, and Mikalah snapped Jake's suspenders teasingly. "Hey, it's not my fault that she likes me best."

"Micky!" Matty squealed delightedly, outstretching her arms.

Jake let Mikalah pull Matty from his shoulders.

"Did you miss me?" Mikalah asked.

"More than life!" Matty kissed Mikalah's cheek dramatically and held her little hands to Mikalah's face. "You look bootiful, Micky!"

"Keep talkin' like that pumpkin', and I won't let you go home," Mikalah set the child down. "I swear you look like you've grown!"

Jake shut the door and pointed to the sofa, "Have a seat, Mr. Ford. Everybody just make yourselves at home."

206

Hank went straight for the kitchen, eyeing the food, "Mmmm, pumpkin pie! And rolls!"

"I brought one of my pecan pies," Laurana placed her pie on the table.

"Oh, I was hopin' you'd make one of those. I just love your pecan pies! I've been braggin' on 'em to Jake all week."

"She sure has! I would have been awfully disappointed if I hadn't had a chance to taste one," Jake hugged his mother-in-law and kissed her cheek. "We're so glad you were able to come."

"Jake, dear, can you please help me get this turkey out of the oven?" Mikalah asked.

He picked up two potholders, pulled the heavy bird from the oven and placed it atop the stove.

"Wow! What a bird!" Hank exclaimed.

"We might actually have enough to fill you up!" Mikalah teased as she mussed her brother's hair.

Mikalah slid the rolls into the oven, "Everything will be ready in a few minutes."

"Here, I'll help you with the gravy, dear," her mother offered.

While the women put the finishing touches on the meal, Jake sat in a chair next to his father-in-law, "How have you been, sir?"

"Just fine. Workin' hard. Looks like you have been too from the size o' this place," Bill noted.

"It is a lot of work, but Mikalah works as hard as any man I've ever seen. We manage just fine together," Jake smiled.

"Mikalah has always been a hard worker," Bill nodded.

Jake leaned forward, and his voice dropped sympathetically lower, "Sir, I'm so sorry you couldn't be at the wedding. I know Mikalah really missed having you there."

"She looks happy and healthy and that's what matters to me," Bill's sad eyes smiled briefly. Jake took Bill's brief comment as a compliment and realized it was Bill's way of saying that he was at peace with the fact that Mikalah had married Jake in such a rush.

207

"We are very happy together, sir," Jake smiled. "But I don't know anyone who couldn't get along with your daughter. Now me... she's a saint to put up with me," he grinned.

Mikalah put her hands on his shoulders, "Now what kind of lies are you tellin' my Daddy?"

Jake looked up into her face as she stood behind him, "I'm not tellin' your Daddy lies. I just said you were easy to live with but you were a saint to put up with me."

"Yeah, like I said, you're tellin' my daddy lies. Jake's easy to get along with Daddy. Why even the rabbits love ya, don't they honey?" she winked and returned to the kitchen

"But there's a turkey in there that doesn't!" Jake noted proudly nodding his head in the affirmative.

The family gathered around the dinner table, and Jake offered the prayer. Mikalah's world was perfect. There was so much to be grateful for, and her heart felt near to exploding with the joy of it all. She felt like she was living a dream. Even her father and Jake seemed to be getting along fine. She'd worried that her father still might be upset about the wedding, but it looked like he'd made his peace with the situation.

Jake pushed his chair back from the table and rubbed his stomach, "I'm stuffed! That was delicious, Mikalah!"

"Save room for some pie!" Laurana instructed.

"Too late for that," Bill rubbed his stomach. "I'll have to have mine later."

"Me too," Jake agreed.

"I want mine now!" Hank excitedly rose from his chair and eyed the pies on the counter. Mikalah rose and cut her brother a piece of pie, handed it to him and started clearing the table to do the dishes.

Laurana put her arms to Mikalah's shoulders, "No dish duty for you, Mikalah. The least we can do is do the dishes for you. Come on, Hannah."

"I won't complain about that!" Mikalah was suddenly tired after all the work, excitement and the heavy meal. "Thank you!"

"Can I look around the house?" Matty tugged on the hem of Mikalah's dress.

"Sure honey, just be careful not to touch anything breakable." She took Matty's hand, "Maybe I better show you around." Mikalah gave Matty a tour of the house while Jake sat on the couch and propped his long legs up on the coffee table as Mr. Ford relaxed in a chair. By the time Mikalah returned with Matty, the two men had drifted off to sleep.

"What is it about turkey that always puts a man to sleep?" Mikalah asked her mother as she sat at the clean kitchen table.

"Don't know, but it does it to your daddy every year," Laurana chuckled.

"It's so good to have y'all here!" Mikalah exuded suddenly.

"Oh, it's wonderful to be here, Mikalah! You did such a great job with the dinner! It was delicious!"

"Thank you, Mama," Mikalah smiled.

"Hank and Hannah, why don't you two take Matty and go outside to play. It's a pretty day out," Laurana suggested, and the three darted out the kitchen door.

Laurana sat at the kitchen table next to Mikalah, "So how do you like married life, dear?"

"Oh, I love it!" Mikalah beamed.

"You two gettin' along all right?" Laurana studied Mikalah's reaction, "Marriage isn't always cherry blossoms and roses."

"We get along great. He's a good man," she hesitated, "a bit sloppy at times – but a good man."

"Socks all over the room – eh?" Laurana shook her head knowingly.

"Yes! And his trousers and shirts never manage to make it into the hamper. He just drops them wherever he is. I moved the couch the other day to clean under there and found four of Jake's smelly old socks – the ones he claimed I'd lost doing laundry, I might add!"

Laurana giggled, "Your daddy's the same way. I used to really let it exasperate me until I decided that it wasn't worth all the fuss. He does so many other kind things for me that the least I can do is help him pick up his socks."

"That's true, Jake is very thoughtful," Mikalah squeezed her mother's hand across the table. "I'll remember that the next time I'm cursin' his dirty socks," she chuckled.

"The police and the D.A. stopped by the house a few weeks back…" Laurana began with concern.

"Yes, they stopped by here too. We have to testify… sometime in January they think," Mikalah had forgotten all about it in the holiday bustle, and she wished her mother hadn't reminded her.

"Oh my!" Laurana threw her hand to her heart.

"It's ok, Mama. Jake and I thought and prayed about it, and we'll be all right. They assured us that we'd be kept safe and that the Baileys wouldn't know where we live," Mikalah patted her mother's hand.

"I'll just be glad when this is all over!" Laurana shook her head, worry wrinkling her brow.

"I know, but I'm just tryin' to enjoy everything we have now. I'll leave all that stuff I can't control to the Lord," Mikalah stated resolutely. "So how have you all been? Anything new in Daisy?"

"Not much. The Mortons finally moved into their new house. Took longer than they thought, but it's so nice!"

"Oh that's wonderful!" Mikalah smiled as she thought about little Jack and wondered if he ever found a stump at his new house.

"There was a bit of a calamity when they were diggin' the well. You know Mr. Morton; he's not known for his plannin' abilities." Mikalah nodded and Laurana continued, "He built the house with the well only partially dug in the basement of the house. The Mortons finished the house and moved in and were still digging the well. They got down about forty feet and hit a sheet of limestone. Only way to bust it up was to use dynamite!"

"Wouldn't that destroy the house?" Mikalah asked in astonishment.

"You'd think so, but it was so far down in the well, I guess that it just rattled the house. Of course, they had everyone get out of it when they blasted. Anyway, one of the poor men who helped dig the well fell in and nearly drowned because they couldn't get to him with the house in the way!"

"Oh my!" Mikalah put her hand to her chest.

"It was a big commotion, but everyone was all right in the end."

"Thank heavens! I bet poor Mrs. Morton was aggravated about that!" Mikalah chuckled.

"She was! Sherman drives Edna crazy sometimes with the way he does things backwards," Laurana chuckled.

Mikalah looked at Jake who started to stir from his slumber, "Jake's teaching me how to play the piano."

"Oh, you always wanted to learn to play! How's it going?"

"I can play a few hymns. It'll probably be years before I can hold a candle to Jake's playin', but I enjoy it," she smiled.

"You'll have to play somethin' for me," Laurana pointed, "Go play somethin'."

"Oh, I'm not that good, and the men are sleepin' anyway," Mikalah shook her head.

"They don't need to be sleepin' the day away. Go play for me," Laurana insisted.

"All right," Mikalah reluctantly rose and sat down at the piano. Laurana followed her into the living room and sat on the couch next to Jake.

Mikalah began to play *Lead Kindly Light*. Bill slept through the first verse, but Jake woke immediately. "She's good isn't she?" Jake grinned proudly, and Laurana nodded in agreement.

When she concluded, Bill asked, "Since when do you play the piano, Mikalah?"

"Jake's been teachin' me," she smiled.

"She's really picking it up fast. I think she's got a talent for it," Jake stated proudly.

"Oh, I'm just learnin'. Y'all are just tryin' to make me feel good."

Jake rose from his seat and stood behind her, placing his hands on her shoulders, "No, honey, you're really good. It took me months to learn to play what you've learned in just a few weeks." He bent toward her and kissed her cheek.

"Thanks," she patted his hand that rested on her shoulder.

Hank, Hannah and Matty stumbled in the back door. Their cheeks were rosy from the cold outdoors, "This place is great!" Hank exclaimed.

"You'll have to stay with us some during the summer," Jake suggested.

"Could we Mama?" Hannah asked.

"I suppose, but not all of you at once. I need help around our house, and Jake and Mikalah wouldn't want all of you underfoot at once anyway. We'll see," Laurana answered.

"Jake, why don't you play us some Christmas songs," Mikalah suggested. "It would be fun to sing along." She rose from her seat and pointed for Jake to play.

"That sounds fun!" Laurana agreed.

Jake sat down, "What do you want to sing?"

"I always liked *O Holy Night*," Mikalah requested, "And you play it so beautifully."

"All right, you lead," Jake played, and the family sang along. As they requested song after song, Jake played some from memory and others from the book. They laughed and talked between songs, and before they knew it, sunset was upon them.

Bill stood and stretched his hands above his head, "It's about time for us to go."

"Not already!" Matty whined.

"Can't we stay a little while longer?" Hannah begged. "We don't have school tomorrow."

"Why don't you let the children stay with us for a few days," Mikalah suggested.

"Oh, that would be too much trouble," Laurana shook her head.

"No, they wouldn't be a bit of trouble," Jake insisted. "They can sleep in the bedrooms upstairs. Matter of fact, we've got enough rooms for everyone if you'd all like to stay."

"We have the animals to feed and cows to milk," Bill reminded, "But if you feel up to havin' the kids, I'm off for the next few days and can handle the chores around the house. How long would you want 'em to stay?

"Why don't you let them stay with us until Sunday? Matter of fact, we'd love to have you all join us for church on Sunday," Jake offered. "You could meet us at the church and get the kids from there. It wouldn't be as long of a drive for you that way."

"Oh, I'd like that," Laurana smiled. She'd never been to the LDS church, but she'd been reading the Book of Mormon that Jake and Mikalah left at the house, and she anxiously wanted to learn more.

"Hum, I don't know," Bill hesitated.

"Oh, come on Bill, wouldn't you like to see what their church is like now that you've been reading the book?" Laurana nudged him in the ribs.

"Well…" he was still thinking.

"How much have you read of the book, Mr. Ford?" Jake asked.

"I'm in Alma," he answered.

"So what do you think about it?" Mikalah studied her father for a response.

"I haven't decided yet. I certainly don't find it to be the blasphemous work that Reverend Arnold claims it to be. But I'm not finished with it yet."

"So will you come to church on Sunday, Daddy?" Mikalah patted her father's arm.

"Oh, I suppose we can do that," he turned, and Laurana smiled. "Are you sure you're up to keeping these three until Sunday?"

"No problem. We'd love to have them," Jake lifted Matty up into his arms.

Bill took Laurana by the arm, "Let's get goin' before they change their minds!" He was happy to have a few days alone with his wife and no children underfoot. He couldn't remember the last time that happened.

The children hugged their parents good-bye and waved cheerfully as they drove away. Just as they were out of sight, Mikalah turned to Jake, "Oh no! How are we going to get everyone into the truck to go to church?"

Jake chuckled, "I guess we'll all have to cram in and sit on each other's laps. It's a good thing all of y'all are skinny." He mussed Hank's hair, "Or we can make Hank ride in the back."

"He'd freeze!" Mikalah protested.

"Let's just see if we can all fit. Everyone run out to the truck. First one there doesn't have to hold anyone on his lap, except me of course, I have to drive." Jake chuckled and started for the door, carrying Matty with him. Everyone scrambled out of the house to the truck. Jake was the first one there and slid in the driver's seat with Matty on his lap. The other three crammed in beside him. It was a tight fit, but the four could smush in across the seat.

"Somebody's gotta hold Matty," Jake shifted Matty for someone to take her. Mikalah pulled Matty onto her lap. "Think we can tolerate this togetherness for a thirty minute drive?"

"Yep, we can take it," Hank boasted and then opened the door and fell out onto the ground. Hannah started laughing at her brother, and everyone else joined her. He stood up, dusted himself off, "I meant to do that."

"Yeah – right!" Hannah rolled her eyes

"Just for that *you* can sit by the door!" Hank shook his finger at Hannah and ran back into the house for another piece of pie.

~*~

Sunday morning arrived, and everyone piled in the front of the truck. Hank straddled the gear shift as Jake drove. Hannah sat next to Hank, and Mikalah held Matty on her lap by the door. They were cramped, but relieved when they arrived. They were glad that they wouldn't be riding home from church in the same condition. Jake carefully opened the door for Mikalah so that she wouldn't land on the ground as Hank had a few days earlier. Bill and Laurana pulled in next to them and parked.

"We're so glad you could make it!" Jake shook Bill's hand and hugged Laurana.

"Me too! I wasn't lookin' forward to Hannah squashin' me to death all the way back to Ooltewah!" relief spread across Hank's face, and Hannah darted an irritated scowl.

214

As they were entering the front door of the building a little four-year-old boy greeted them, "Welcome!" He extended his hand as if he were a grown man and the official door greeter.

Jake shook the little boy's hand, "Who all's here, Freddie?"

"Just my mama and the pillows of the church so far," the little boy answered seriously.

"The pillows of the church?" Mikalah tried not to chuckle.

Jake's eyes transformed from confusion to illumination. "Ah, the *pillars* of the church! That's what everybody calls Sister Karrick and Sister Snodgrass," he winked at Mikalah who bit her lip, placing her hand to her mouth.

The group passed the little boy and took their seats in the auditorium. Sister Snodgrass and Sister Karrick greeted them, and Jake introduced his in-laws.

After the meeting, the Fords, Jake and Mikalah sat in the auditorium and talked while Jake and Mikalah answered her parents' questions.

"So you have a woman preacher?" Bill scratched his head.

"We don't have preachers, sir. No one is paid to preach in our church. We all chip in and teach and help where we can. Right now our little group is just a Sunday school so we don't have a branch president or a bishop to lead us. Out west where we have more members, each congregation, called a ward, has a bishop who leads and cares for the group. In smaller areas, the congregations are called branches, and they have a branch president. But we're just too tiny here and don't have enough priesthood leaders to even be a branch. Even where they are large enough to have bishops or branch presidents, they don't do all the teaching and speaking. The members of the congregation share in those duties." Jake explained.

"Interesting. So you don't get paid to do what you do?"

"No sir."

"Not even your bishops or branch presidents?"

"No sir." Jake shook his head.

"Very interesting. I kind of like that. Eliminates the greed for power, I'd imagine," Bill rubbed his chin thoughtfully.

"I suppose it does," Jake nodded.

215

Sister Snodgrass approached Laurana, "We're so happy that your family was able to attend today! As you can imagine, we just love having visitors."

"We enjoyed being here," Laurana smiled. Bill rose from his seat and touched Laurana's arm indicating she should stand. She rose and stood next to her husband facing Sister Snodgrass.

"We hope you'll visit with us again," Sister Snodgrass' smile was contagious.

"We just might do that, ma'am," Bill nodded and started out of the isle. He turned back toward his children who had risen and were following them. "I guess we better get going kids."

The family members exited the building and walked to their cars.

"We'll see you at Christmas, dear," Laurana hugged Mikalah tightly.

Bill shook Jake's hand, "You keep takin' good care o' my girl, Jake."

"I will sir," Jake smiled and Bill hugged Mikalah goodbye.

~*~

John and Frank Taylor leaned their arms against the white fence. Jake's forearms lay across the post in front of him, his hands clasped and his cheeks chapped the shade of red apples in autumn from the cold mid-December air.

"That brown one's big enough," Frank pointed.

"The white shoat and the calico will make some good meat." John pointed.

"Yeah, I'd say they're about two hundred and twenty-five pounds apiece. And of course that big boar is ready," Jake indicated.

"So that gives us four," John tallied. "Reckon' we can get 'em all slaughtered today?"

Frank nodded and turned to John and then Jake, "I think we can do it. We'll get the women to help."

Jake felt a bit queasy. Of all the aspects of farming, killing the animals was his least favorite. Even as a boy he managed to sneak off when it was hog killin' time. His brothers loved to hunt, fish and skin animals, but Jake just didn't have the heart to join in or even watch. He knew it made him appear weak, so he planned to put on a good front for the Taylors. He wasn't about to show his squeamishness to them today. They needed to see that he was fit to run the property in every way. Only Mikalah knew of his dislike for killing, and he'd sworn her to secrecy on the matter.

"Which one first?" Jake asked.

"Let's just get this brown sow that's here handy," John pointed.

"I'll get it," Jake hopped over the fence and put a rope around the hog's neck and led it to where they'd set up a large platform next to a big boiling kettle of water. Mikalah, Ruth and John's wife, Harriett, stoked the fire, bringing the water to a rolling boil.

Jake led the hog up the ramp to the platform. Frank handed him a pistol. Jake cocked it and looked to Mikalah who nodded assuring but subtly. He held the pistol to the animal's head while he still held the sow tightly by the rope with this left hand. He closed his eyes and pulled the trigger. The animal staggered but did not fall.

"Shoot her again, Jake. Sometimes it takes two or three," John instructed.

Jake thought he was going to be sick, and Mikalah noted the pale expression on her husband's face, *You can do it Jake. You can do it!* She encouraged him as if he could read her thoughts. He quickly fired two more bullets into the animal's head, and it fell over. He barely moved his foot in time to avert it landing on his toe. He thrust the gun into his pocket, and Frank and John joined him on the platform.

"Here," Frank handed Jake a large knife.

"Let it bleed good or the meat'll be tough," John instructed.

After the hog had bled sufficiently, the three men lowered it into the boiling water. Mikalah rinsed the platform with a bucket of water.

After some time, Frank poked the animal's flesh with a stick, "I believe it's about ready to scrape." Jake and John climbed onto the platform and helped Frank extricate the hog from the boiling water and laid it up onto the planks.

The women gathered around to scrape all the hair off. Jake looked down at the project and decided he needed a break, "Looks like you fine ladies have this in hand. I'm gonna go get a drink of water. Anyone want something?"

"How 'bout a cup o' coffee?" John asked.

"Oh, I'm sorry, I don't think we have any coffee in the house," Jake shook his head.

"What? No coffee in the house? You two need to get to the store," John suggested.

"We don't drink coffee," Jake answered.

"How in the world do you keep warm in the winter?" Frank asked.

"They have each other," Ruth winked at her husband and giggled. "Jake, I believe Frank's parents' left some coffee in the pantry on the top left shelf."

"I'll go look, but I've got no notion as to how to make it," Jake called back over his shoulder as he sauntered toward the house.

"Just set some water boilin', and I'll make my own." John put his hands to his hips and turned to Mikalah, "You need to get that fella fendin' for himself a bit more."

"Like you're one to talk!" Harriett rolled her eyes. "You *never* make so much as a sandwich for yourself."

"But I'd know how to make a pot o' coffee if I had to," John defended.

"Jake can actually cook rather well, and he makes delicious hot chocolate. He's just never drank coffee, and neither did his parents," Mikalah explained.

"I can't imagine never drinkin' coffee!" John exclaimed. "Ain't natural!"

Mikalah just chuckled. She didn't feel like explaining anything further. "We're almost done with this side, we're gonna need this animal turned over in a few minutes."

Jake stepped out on the porch and called out, "Water will be boiling in a few minutes."

"Come help us flip this hog," Frank instructed.

After all the hair had been cleaned from the hog, Jake and John held it while Frank ran a hook through the tendons of the hind legs, and they hoisted the carcass upside down from a tree. Mikalah and Harriett carried a tub and placed it directly under the hog.

Jake was glad no one saw him suddenly turn away as Frank slit the animal open, and the innards drained into the tub. The women carried hot water forward and rinsed the carcass. John's son Amos and little Matthew ran from the field as fast as they could. The pair had been off playing all morning, but knew when it was time for the fun to begin.

John picked up the bladder and washed it in a tub of water, put it to his mouth and began to blow. It inflated into a large ball, slightly bigger than a basketball. He pulled a piece of twine from his pocket, tied the end and handed it to his son, "Here you go. This is what you're waitin' for isn't it, Amos?"

The eight-year-old delightedly grabbed the ball from his father's hands, "Thanks Dad! Let's go, Matt! Let's go play some ball!" Matthew toddled after his older cousin as he skipped off into the field with their prize.

The ladies began cutting the meat from the first hog into pieces and preparing it to be cured while the men continued with the other animals. It was an all day affair of slaughtering, cleaning, butchering and salt curing the meat to be hung in the salt house.

The women cooked pork chops, mashed potatoes and gravy for dinner and called the men in when it was ready. Jake came in the front door first, "I'm gonna go wash up." He headed straight for the master bathroom, stripped off his blood stained clothes and washed himself at the sink. As he stood splashing water on his face, Mikalah entered the bedroom, shut the door behind her and peeked in the bathroom door.

"You did great, Jake," she caressed his muscular back with her hand.

"That has to be the most sickening thing I've ever done in my life," he splashed more cool water onto his face and chest.

Mikalah chuckled, "You'll get used to it in time. No one else would have known you even had a problem with it." She pulled a towel from a rack and dried the water from his back.

He turned to face her "You must have been prayin' for me."

She continued to dry his chest, "I was."

He took the towel from her and held it to his face, "Thank you!" He hung up the towel with his right hand and pulled her to him with his left, kissing her briefly. "I'm starving and that food smells wonderful!" Jake stepped around and pulled a clean shirt from his drawer, and her hand traced lazily along his back as she left the room.

~*~

A light blanket of snow covered the ground as the sun set behind the hills. Jake parked the truck, and Mikalah scooted out the driver's side behind him. She pulled her scarf tightly around her neck and chin and adjusted her gloves before sliding her arm around Jake's waist. He put his right arm around her shoulder, and the pair began their search for the perfect Christmas tree.

After fifteen minutes of searching through a forest, Jake stopped in front of a well-formed six-foot pine tree, "What about this one honey? It looks about right."

Mikalah studied the tree, "I like it." She stepped back, and Jake chopped the base of the tree with his ax. The trunk wasn't very thick so it soon fell along the snowy ground. He picked up the base of the trunk and drug the tree back to the truck. Mikalah helped him guide it into the truck bed, and they headed back to the farm house.

"I just love Christmas!" Mikalah exclaimed as Jake's deep voice belted out Christmas carols. She'd spent most of the afternoon making colored paper chains, making Christmas ornaments from hollow egg shells, and stringing popcorn. She'd even designed a special tree topper. When they arrived back home, she set up the tree stand that she'd found in the Taylor's attic while Jake brought the tree into the house. He set it up, and Mikalah watered the pine.

"It's beautiful," she observed.

"It is a quite handsome tree," he admired as he picked up a paper chain. They sang Christmas carols, decorated the tree and drank hot apple cider with cinnamon. When everything was decorated but the top of the tree, she went into the bedroom and emerged with her tree topper.

"Here you go, I made us something special for the top," Mikalah turned the topper around for him to see.

"Ah, an angel Moroni like my mom has! Except I believe yours is prettier than Mom's," he smiled as she handed it to him, and he placed it atop the tree. He stepped back and stared at the pine, a hint of melancholy in his expression.

Mikalah slid her arm around him, "You feelin' homesick?"

"A bit," he nodded. "But I can't get too homesick with you at my side now, can I?" he chuckled and pulled her over, flopping down lengthwise on the couch with her on top of him. She adjusted her position until she lay beside him, resting her head on his chest. He held her in his arms, and they enjoyed the tree and the crackling fire until they both drifted off to sleep.

~*~

Christmas Eve morning, Mikalah woke in Jake's arms. They'd slept all night on the couch, and he was still sleeping soundly. She carefully extricated herself from his arms and lit a lamp in the kitchen. She had lots of work to do. The house was already decorated, but she had food to prepare before her family arrived that afternoon. It was still dark outside. She tried to work quietly so as not to awaken Jake.

She set her dough to rising and slipped out the back door to retrieve a chicken. She selected the biggest bird from the yard and quickly wrung its neck and carried it into the house to clean it. She would make chicken and dressing with dumplings for their Christmas Eve dinner.

As Mikalah prepared the bird, Jake shifted to his side, leaned on his elbow rubbing the sleep from his eyes, "What time is it, honey?"

Mikalah looked at the clock on the wall, "It's nearly six."

Jake sat up and stretched his arms high above his head and stood, "Let's say our morning prayers so I can go feed the animals."

"Just a second, I need to wash this chicken from my hands."

Jake knelt by the couch offering his personal prayers, and Mikalah joined him shortly. She watched him until he finished and then knelt beside him. It was their morning ritual to pray and read their scriptures together and then start their daily chores. It set them off on the right foot, and they felt the practice kept their marriage harmonious. Not to say they didn't have their arguments, but they worked toward reconciling their differences quickly.

After breakfast, Mikalah set the chicken to boiling and joined Jake in the barn to help him milk the cows. Next she fed the chickens while he took care of the cattle. Mikalah spent the remainder of the morning in the kitchen preparing the chicken, pies, rolls and everything for their Christmas Eve dinner.

Around noon, Jake entered the front door, "Sure is smelling good in here, Mikalah!" He walked straight to the hall bathroom and cleaned up for lunch.

Mikalah put two chicken salad sandwiches on the table along with two cups of warm apple cider.

"Hmm... looks good," he pulled out her chair for her, pushed it in and then sat down to his sandwich. After the prayer, Jake asked, "So can I help you with anything in here? Your parents don't get here until three – right?"

"That's what they said – around three or four. You could help me peel some potatoes if you'd like." Mikalah glanced at the clock. She rose from her seat and brought them each a piece of pumpkin pie.

"You mean you're gonna let me have a piece of pie already?" he pretended to be shocked.

"It would be rude to eat a piece without you, and I can't wait any longer," she chuckled as she put a dollop of whipped cream on top of each of their pieces.

"Hmm... nothin' in the world like your pumpkin pie!" he smiled as he finished the last bite. "Other than maybe your kisses," he mischievously swirled his finger in the whipped cream until he had a big blob on his finger. He plopped it on her lips and chin, then leaned over and kissed it off.

"Now none of that, I've got a lot to get done before they get here," she licked her lips and shook a scolding finger at him.

"Then let's get to work and get it done," he winked. "Maybe we'll have some time to spare."

"Oh, I don't know about that," Mikalah shook her head as she stood and carried their dishes to the sink. "There's a lot to be done yet."

"The great thing about you, Mikalah, is that you're so organized that you always complete whatever you're working on early." He strolled up behind her as she dunked plates into sudsy water. He enfolded her in his arms and kissed her soft cheek. "Always leaves time for some fun," he whispered in her ear.

"We won't have time to even get the dinner done, if you don't stop flirtin' around and get to work."

"Yes, Ma'am! I'll get crackin'," he saluted her with a smirk and started pulling potatoes out of the bin. He sat down at the kitchen table and peeled the potatoes into a bucket. Jake whistled as he worked. Mikalah loved the way Jake either sang or whistled through any task. It made working alongside him even more enjoyable.

"Is this enough?" he showed her the potatoes he'd peeled and quartered into a pot.

"That should be fine, thanks dear."

"What do you need me to do now?"

"Why don't you put a couple more logs on the fire, and play us some Christmas carols," she suggested.

"Wow, you're actually going to enjoy yourself while you're working?" he teased.

"I *always* enjoy myself when I'm working. I like to work," she retorted.

"Fair enough. No one could argue with that," he covered the potatoes with water, placed the pot on the stove and turned to put another log on the fire. Jake played, and they both sang as Mikalah worked in the kitchen.

When she'd completed her preparations, she looked to the clock that read a little after two o'clock. "We finished in the nick of time," she noted.

"What are you talking about?" Jake looked at the clock, "You've got nearly an hour, maybe more, to spare."

She tugged his arm seductively, "We still have one more project to complete, don't we?"

~*~

"Ah, love the smell of chicken and dumplin's and pumpkin' pie!" Hank burst through the front door.

223

"Knock before you go bustin' into somebody's house, son," Laurana scolded.

"Ah, it's just Mikalah and Jake," Hank waved his hand as if it were nothing.

Laurana knocked on the open door as Matty ran past her, climbed onto the piano bench and plunked the keys. Hannah inspected the Christmas tree.

Bill placed two presents under the tree and looked around the house, "Where's Mikalah?"

"I don't know. Hank barged in without even knocking," Laurana darted her irritated eyes toward her son.

Jake slid out the bedroom door and closed it quickly behind him, "Merry Christmas!" he bellowed jovially and embraced each of his in-laws. "Mikalah will be out in a few minutes. She's been workin' hard all morning and is just freshening up a bit." Jake scooped Matty up from the piano, "How you doin', sweetheart?"

"Gweat!" she slapped her hands to his cheeks and kissed him.

A few minutes later, Mikalah emerged wearing a forest green dress and a white apron about her waist, her soft curls pulled back loosely the way Jake liked them best, "Merry Christmas everybody!"

Laurana ran to her, grabbed both of Mikalah's hands and inspected her, "Why, don't you just look simply radiant, Mikalah!" She turned to her husband, "Bill, doesn't Mikalah look simply radiant?"

"Yes she does. I believe farm life is agreein' with ya, Micky," Bill nodded.

"Maybe it's married life that's agreein' with her," Laurana winked at her daughter, and Mikalah's rosy cheeks turned a deeper shade.

Noting Mikalah's embarrassment, Jake patted his stomach dramatically, "I don't know about Mikalah, but married life's agreein' with me. I'm starting to get a pooch."

Mikalah rolled her eyes melodramatically, slapping the air with her right hand, "Oh, you are *not*." She turned to the kitchen to slide her rolls in the oven and called back over her shoulder, "He works too hard around here to get a pooch."

The family spent the afternoon catching up with each other and the latest events in their lives. Mikalah resisted the uncontrollable urge to brag on Jake for his stone composure at hog killin' time. They ate dinner, sang carols, and Laurana made Jake and Mikalah open their presents from the family. She wanted to see their expressions. She'd made Mikalah a new red dress and knitted Jake a blue scarf. Mikalah and Jake gave each of their family members a small gift that they'd made for them. Jake whittled wooden flutes for Matty and Hannah. Mikalah knitted Hank and her father scarves, and she made an angel Moroni tree topper for her mother.

Before they knew it, the evening had grown late, and it was time for the Fords to leave. Reluctantly, they parted company, and Mikalah and Jake curled up on the couch and read the Christmas story from both the Bible and Book of Mormon before retiring for the evening. Mikalah was convinced that life could get no better than this. But there was a twinge inside her that made her wonder if there weren't dark clouds forming in the distance.

Chapter 11

"Are you all right, Mikalah? You look plum green!" Jake held Mikalah's shoulders firmly and peered into her eyes as she emerged from the bathroom.

"Oh, I just feel sick to my stomach. I'm sure it's just nerves about the trial today," she mumbled. "I've been dreadin' it all week, and my stomach's been botherin' me for days."

"Are you sure you're going to feel up for this?" he stroked her strawberry blonde curls.

She sighed, "Oh, I just want to get it over with. It won't do me any good to put it off 'til another day. I'll just feel sick that day too."

"Can I get you anything? Do you want to eat a little something before we go? I can make breakfast," Jake offered.

"Oh no!" she put her hand to her stomach and then softened her voice, "No thank you dear, I just can't eat anything."

Jake guided her to the bed and gestured for her to lie down. He tucked the covers around her shoulders and knelt beside her, "You rest for a while then, and I'll take care of the animals." Normally Mikalah would have lost herself in her work. That's what she'd done every other morning this week when the nausea hit, but this morning she felt weakened in addition to the nausea. She decided with the long day ahead of her she'd take Jake's suggestion and lie down for a while.

Jake kissed her cheek, "I'll pack you a sandwich for later. There's no telling how long we'll be in court, and you're bound to get hungry ."

"I doubt it," she mumbled as he walked out of the bedroom.

A couple hours later, Jake quietly opened the bedroom door carrying a plate of toast. He set the plate on the nightstand and gently sat beside Mikalah's curled up sleeping body. He gently caressed her cheek with the back of his hand and kissed it lightly. Mikalah's eyes fluttered, and she looked up at him.

"How you feeling, honey?" Jake asked.

Mikalah sat up slightly, "I think I feel quite a bit better."

"Good," relief registered on Jake's face, "I brought you a piece of toast. If you feel up to it, you should probably try to eat something so you have enough energy for the trial."

Mikalah picked up the plate and placed it on her lap, breaking tiny pieces of toast and nibbling them. She was afraid to eat too much too fast. Yesterday she'd gotten sick doing that when she thought she felt well enough to eat. "What time is it?"

"It's half past eight. They'll be here in about an hour. I drew you a hot bath. I thought that might make you feel better," he rubbed her shoulder soothingly.

"How thoughtful of you, Jake! You're just too good to me," she smiled weakly.

"I'm just trying to pay you back for everything you do for me," he winked, leaning his hand on the bed beside her.

She set the plate aside and gently put her feet to the floor. Carefully she stood for a few moments to make sure her head wasn't going to spin.

"You all right?" he put his hands to her hips to steady her.

"I'm fine. I'm just takin' it slowly," she gently held her hand to his cheek and kissed the other one. "Thank you, Jake."

After her bath, Mikalah felt much better and quickly dressed. As she finished styling her hair, Jake popped his head in the bedroom, "They're here. You ready?"

"I guess," she breathed deeply, trying to calm her nerves. Jake handed her a sack of sandwiches and locked up the house.

Two officers stood outside their squad car. Jake opened the rear door for Mikalah, closed it behind her and walked around to the other side and slid in next to her.

"You two ready to go?" Officer Anderson peeked in the back seat.

"We're ready," Jake shook his head, and they were on their way. The trip to the courthouse was uneventful, except for Mikalah's stomach which felt as if a bunny were flip-flopping inside of it. She'd never seen so many uniforms in one place. A throng of police officers formed a sheltered passageway for Jake and Mikalah as they emerged from the squad car and entered the courthouse.

"You better keep your mouths shut if ya know what's good for ya!" an older man's voice threatened from behind, and Jake pulled Mikalah tighter to him.

"Get 'im!" an officer shouted while another motioned for Jake and Mikalah to run quickly into the building. Mikalah could hear a scuffle and voices yelling as they entered the courthouse. The officer quickly led them into a room with a small wooden table, one chair and a wooden bench. A single light fixture hung from the center of the ceiling, and the walls were bare.

"Wait right here Mr. & Mrs. Elliot." We'll come for you when it's time."

Mikalah's heart still raced as she collapsed on the wooden bench. Jake sat next to her and pulled her head onto his shoulder, gently stroking her hair, "Are you all right?" He bent his head to the side to study her pale face.

"That scared me half to death!" she stretched her arm across his chest and nestled her head into his shoulder. She was grateful that the nausea had fled, but she felt suddenly weak as her pulse began to slow.

Jake tossed their sack of sandwiches on the table, "I wonder if they got him?"

"I hope so," she sighed heavily.

After about half an hour, the doorknob jiggled, and Mikalah jumped to an upright position as the door creaked open.

"Just thought you'd like to know that we apprehended the man who threatened you - one of the Baileys. Not sure how long we can hold 'im, but we'll at least keep him locked up 'til after you two are safely home today," the officer explained.

Mikalah breathed a sigh of relief.

"When do you think we'll testify?" Jake asked.

"Not sure. You never know 'bout these things. With the threats, the District Attorney thought it best for y'all to stay clear of the courtroom until he needs ya." The officer started to close the door and then peeked his head back in, "Can I get y'all a cup o' coffee?"

"No thank you," Jake shook his head, "But how about a couple cups of water?"

"Will do," the officer nodded and closed the door behind him. He returned shortly carrying two white paper cups. "Anything else?" he asked.

"No thank you. Thanks for the water," Mikalah smiled at the young officer.

"You're welcome. If y'all need anything else, I'll be standin' guard outside. Might want to just relax. It's probably gonna be a while," the officer smiled and shut the door.

Mikalah took a sip of her water, then placed it on the table and leaned forward resting her head in her hands.

"Honey, are you all right?" Jake lightly placed his hand on her back.

"I'm startin' to feel hot and clammy all of a sudden, and my stomach's getting queasy again," her face grew pale.

"I think this is more than nerves, Mikalah. Maybe you're sick," he crouched in front of her anxiously studying her eyes. "Do you want me to give you a blessing?"

"Oh would you, please?" she raised her head from her hands. "I don't think I can make it through this with the way I'm feeling right now," her eyes betrayed the conflicting emotions of panic and gratitude.

"Sure, I brought my oil with me, just in case. I had a feeling…" he pulled the chair to the center of the room and motioned for her to sit in it. As Mikalah shifted to the chair and folded her arms in front of her, Jake removed a small vial of oil from his pocket. He stood behind her, cleared his throat, and placed a small drop of oil on her head. She could feel the warm comfort of his hands on her head as he began. He blessed her with sufficient health, comfort and energy to withstand the rigors of the day. As he blessed her with safety and peace of mind, she felt that warm tingly comfort of the Spirit, the sweet assurance that all would be right, and her nervousness subsided from that moment forward.

When he concluded she stood and wrapped her arms around Jake's waist, burying her head in his shoulder, "Thank you, you have no idea how badly I needed that." Tears welled in her eyes as her heart filled with gratitude to God for him. Not only did she love him more than life, but also it seemed as if he were a conduit carrying God's love and light directly into the darkest, most frightening recesses of her soul. The power of the Priesthood that he held seemed to extend around them both like a warm protective blanket on a cold winter's night.

Mikalah grew progressively better as the day wore on, and she felt grateful that she had some time to build up her strength to face the Baileys and Earl Henderson. Shortly before two o'clock the judge summoned them to the courtroom. The prosecution called Mikalah to testify first and then be cross examined by the defense. In spite of the defense attorney's efforts to rattle her, Mikalah remained cool, calm and unruffled. She identified her attackers, and her composure remained resolute in spite of their insidious stares.

Jake followed. He too remained in control as he faced the defense's relentless questioning and subtle slurs on his character. The defense claimed that the Bailey's plot was simply a Halloween prank and that Jake and Mikalah had blown it all out of proportion in order to obtain her parent's permission to marry the vagabond Mormon.

The prosecution countered with the fact that Mikalah was already eighteen and needed no one's permission to marry Jake. Photos of Jake's slashed chest and the bruises on his back were submitted as evidence along with Mikalah's mutilated clothing and Jake's moonshine soaked shirt and jacket.

Three hours later, Mikalah and Jake emerged from the courtroom, escorted by six police officers who shielded them as they quickly made their way to a squad car just outside the courthouse steps. Mikalah entered the car first and slid over. As Jake ducked his head to enter, a gunshot fired, and one of the officers shoved Jake into the car. He fell forward with his chest on Mikalah's lap, and his head hit the opposite door. The car door slammed, and Mikalah registered the loud squeal of tires burning as the car sped forward.

"Get down!" Officer McClendon commanded as he observed the commotion they had just left behind them. One officer was down on the sidewalk, and a crowd had gathered around him.

Mikalah knelt in the floor and met Jake's gaze, "Are you all right?"

"I'm fine. They missed me," he crouched in the floorboard behind the front passenger seat.

"There's a man down, and we're being tailed," Officer McClendon warned his partner.

"Time for our backup plan," Anderson took a hard right and gunned the gas. They sped through a narrow one-way street, and just as they went through an intersection another squad car pulled out sideways behind them, blocking their assailant's path. The Bailey's 36 Ford screeched to a halt and nearly missed slamming into the squad car.

The Baileys started to turn their car around but two more squad cars appeared at their rear, completely surrounding them. Officers poured out of their vehicles, pointing rifles at the 36 Ford. Soon two men were handcuffed and their car impounded as Officer Anderson took Mikalah and Jake home through a series of back roads to insure that they arrived home untraced. Satisfied that they were no longer being followed, Officer Anderson took them home.

"Thanks for everything you did, officers. We really appreciate your protection," Jake thanked the two men, shaking their hands from the back seat. He opened his door and extended his hand to help Mikalah out of the car.

They walked a few steps toward the house when Mikalah's legs gave way. Inches before she would have landed face first, Jake scooped her up into his strong arms and carried her into the house. The two officers hopped out of the car and followed him. Jake carried her into the bedroom and sat down next to her on the bed. She was out cold. Jake put the back of his hand to her cold, clammy, pale forehead.

"Can you run for a doctor please?" Jake begged.

"Sure, where does he live?" Officer Anderson asked.

"He's just three farms over. Go out our property, turn left, and look for the third farm you come to on the right. His mailbox says Doc Phillips on it." The officers ran out of the house to retrieve the doctor.

"Mikalah, honey, wake up," Jake patted her cheek and draped over her body a quilt that Sister Snodgrass had given them as a wedding present.

She started to stir and moan, "Jake, what's wrong with me?"

"I don't know, honey. The officers have gone for Doc Phillips. He'll be here soon. Can I get you anything?"

"No thank you. I just feel so weak," Mikalah put both her hands to her cheeks.

"You haven't eaten anything all day. It's no wonder," Jake tried not to show the worry he felt. "I think there's still some of that left over chicken noodle soup in there. How about I bring you some of that?"

"That's the first thing that's sounded appetizing all day, thank you," she agreed.

"I'll go put it on the stove and will be right back," Jake lit the stove and threw in a log, poured some soup in a pot and set it on top. He'd barely returned to the room when the officers knocked at the door.

Jake let the elderly doctor and the officers in, "She's in here Doc. She's been green all day – been sick to her stomach for several days, but it's the worst today. She thought it was just nerves over somethin' she's been worrying about, but I think it's more than that."

Jake showed the doctor to their room, "Officers, you can go on if you need to. I can take the doctor home."

"I guess we should be gettin' back." Officer Anderson extended his hand, "I hope your wife's all right."

"I'm sure she'll be fine. It's probably just a stomach ailment." Jake shook his hand and then Officer McClendon's. "Thank you both for everything. We really do appreciate your kindness."

"You're welcome. We or the District Attorney will keep you posted on what the jury decides," Officer Anderson tipped his hat, and they left. Jake returned to the bedroom where the doctor examined Mikalah.

After he completed his examination, Jake asked, "So is she going to be all right?"

"Oh, she'll be all right in about seven or eight months," the doctor smiled.

"Seven or eight months?" Mikalah asked quizzically.

The doctor patted Mikalah's hand, "You're expectin' a baby, Mrs. Elliot."

Mikalah looked to Jake. They both wore the same shocked expression, which for Jake soon transformed into relieved adoration.

"But you haven't been takin' good care of yourself," the elderly doctor observed. "You need to rest more and eat better. You're pale as a ghost. I want you to eat a biscuit or a piece of toast before you ever set foot to the floor in the mornin's. Lay there and let it settle a bit before you rise. You can also drink a cup o' ginger tea each mornin' to help settle your stomach. My wife grows ginger." He turned to Jake, "Mr. Elliot, if you'll give me a ride home, I'll give you some."

"Thanks, Doc," Jake shook his hand.

"Y'all take a few minutes to talk. I'm gonna step outside an' smoke my pipe while you two adjust to the idea," Doc Phillips nodded his gray head and left the room, pulling his pipe from his vest as he went.

Jake sat on the edge of the bed next to Mikalah, "A baby! Can you believe we're havin' a baby?"

She sat up and put her arms around his neck, "It's wonderful, isn't it?" She pulled back, studying his eyes, "You are happy about it, aren't you Jake?"

"Why of course I am! What do you think this big silly grin's about?" he chuckled.

"You'll make a great Daddy, Jake!" she gazed lovingly into his emerald eyes.

"And of course you'll be the best mother," Jake swept a stray lock of her hair into place. "I'll go get you some of that soup. I'm sure it's hot now." He left the room, and Mikalah lay there with her hand to her stomach. She could hardly believe Jake's baby was growing inside her. Together they would bring a lovable spirit from their Heavenly Father into the world. She marveled at the difference the gospel had made in her life. Now she understood what life was about and the importance of her role as a mother to spirit sons and daughters of her Heavenly Father. Most of all she felt an intense gratitude that their children would always benefit from knowing the fullness of the gospel throughout their lives. They wouldn't feel the confusion, fear or uncertainty that she had once experienced. They would walk in the light from the day of their birth!

Jake entered the room and handed Mikalah a bowl of soup. Noting the grateful tear streaming down her face, he pulled his handkerchief from his pocket, "Are you ok, Mikalah?"

"Oh, I'm just perfect Jake, absolutely perfect," she smiled as she dabbed the corners of her eyes.

He bent toward her and gently kissed her lips, "Will you be all right while I take the doctor home and get that ginger?"

"I'll be just fine. I feel better already just knowing what all of this has been about," she sighed heavily and squeezed his hand.

"All right, I'll be right back," he kissed her again and left her to continue to ponder on the miracles of their life together.

~*~

Mikalah and Jake received word that the Baileys and the others involved in Halloween night's cruelty had been sentenced to twenty years in prison. The retaliating Baileys had been charged with murdering the police officer whom they shot outside the courthouse. Mikalah and Jake breathed a sigh of relief knowing that their enemies had come to justice, but mourned for the officer who had saved them. His heroic act left them free to enjoy their lives on the farm and the baby that would soon join their little family.

Mikalah fought morning sickness until well into spring, and she felt bad that Jake had to take on extra chores due to her weakness. But he insisted upon her resting and letting him handle all the milking and feeding the chickens. Mikalah concentrated on working inside the house – cooking, cleaning and sewing while Jake tended to the outdoors. By April her energy returned, and she helped with planting the garden. She anxiously planned for the birth of their baby in August by sewing baby t-shirts, sleepers and diapers.

~*~

The hot June sun beat against Jake's back as he yanked a handful of weeds from around the staked tomatoes and wiped his brow with the back of his forearm. He selected two large ripe tomatoes from the plant and started for the open back door. He stepped into the kitchen, placed the tomatoes on the table and plopped down in a chair to pull off his boots. He dropped them by the door and crossed to the sink in his sock feet. Putting his arms around Mikalah's belly as she washed dishes, he snuggled against her cheek, "How's my little mama this morning?" He chuckled as the baby kicked him, "He's gettin' strong."

"He? Why do you think the baby's a *he*, Jake? Could be a girl ya know," she suggested.

"It's such a big baby, and you seem to be carryin' it low. Mom always said you carry boys low," he explained.

"Ah" she nodded.

"You excited about Hannah coming today?" he leaned back against the counter as she continued washing the dishes.

"Oh I'm thrilled! It'll be nice to have the help now that I'm gettin' so big that I can hardly bend over or stand on my feet for long without achin'."

"She should be here soon – eh?" Jake looked at the clock on the wall.

"Anytime now," Mikalah dried her hands on her apron, put her arms around Jake's neck and leaned her head on his shoulder.

Jake returned her embrace and then studied her face, "Are you all right, honey?" She looked as if there were something weighing on her mind.

"Oh, I'm fine, I just needed a hug." She didn't want to tell him what she was really thinking. She wasn't sure yet, but she just had a feeling…

A car door slammed outside, and Mikalah lifted her head from his shoulder, "They're here." Kissing his lips briefly, she slid her arms from around his shoulders, put her hand in his, and the pair went out the front door to greet her family.

"Why, Mrs. Ford! I didn't know you could drive?" Jake jovially slapped his hand to his thigh and studied Laurana as she helped Matty out of the back seat.

"Bill taught me," she grinned proudly.

Matty ran straight to Jake who lifted her up into his arms and shifted her onto his hip. Mikalah descended the porch steps carefully, approaching her mother.

"My word, Mikalah! You're about to pop!" Laurana exclaimed. It had been nearly two full months since she'd seen her daughter last, and she was astonished by the change. "Are you sure your doctor has your due date right? I don't see how you're gonna last until mid-August."

"Well, it couldn't be much sooner than that, Mama," at her mother's suggestion, Mikalah stared incredulously. *Anyone who can do simple math would know that,* she thought to herself.

"Oh, I know, but you're just so big!" Laurana put her hands to Mikalah's belly. She felt the baby kick both her hands within moments. "Mikalah, when was the last time you saw the doctor?" Laurana's eyes reflected a combination of anxiety and understanding.

"It's been over a month. He's been out of town for the last couple weeks," Mikalah explained but felt compelled to probe her mother's thoughts, "Why Mama?"

"You've got twins in there, Mikalah. No doubt about it!" Laurana stated authoritatively, as if the fact were as evident as knowing that rain would follow threatening dark clouds on the horizon.

"Twins?" Jake's eyebrows rose, and his mouth dropped wide open.

"How can you be sure, Mama?" Mikalah didn't appear fazed by the information. Jake observed his wife, wondering why she was not as thrown by this suggestion as he was.

"Besides the fact that she's enormous for seven months, you can tell by the kicks. See, put your hand here, and put another one over here." Laurana put Mikalah's hands on either side of her belly. "That's two heads, sweetie."

Mikalah nodded knowingly, "I had a feeling, but I wasn't sure. I knew you could tell me for sure."

"You mean you suspected this?" Jake was still in shock. "Why didn't you tell me?"

"I wasn't sure. I wanted to know for sure before ..." Mikalah studied Jake's reaction. "I wasn't sure how you'd take it, and I just began to suspect it over the last couple weeks. I knew Mama was coming and that she'd know."

"Twins!" Jake put his fist to his hip and stomped his foot, "What about that! Two babies!" Jake was as proud of himself as if he'd bagged two Thanksgiving turkeys with one shot.

Mikalah couldn't help but chuckle at his reaction, "I take it you're happy about this?"

"Why sure! Nervous as all get out, but yeah," he nodded. "I'm happy about it."

"Poor babies," Hannah rolled her eyes, and everyone turned to see if she were serious or joking. "Think about it. Y'all aren't twins so you don't know what it's like to always have someone around to pester you, share your room, share your mother's lap, always in your same classes at school, getting' in your way!"

"Oh, it can't be all that bad," Laurana chuckled, tossing her head as if Hannah were overreacting.

"And I'm one of the lucky ones. At least my twin is a boy, and I don't have someone wearing my same clothes, sharing my face, constantly a mirror of my own imperfections and flaws."

Laurana's frustration poured through the glare she shot in Hannah's direction, "Hannah!" Laurana turned to Mikalah and Jake, "Don't pay her any mind. She's been in a grouchy mood all mornin'. Are you sure you want to put up with her?"

"That's ok, Mama." Mikalah put her arm through Hannah's and led her to the house, "Hannah and I will have great fun. Sounds like she just needs a break from Hank." Mikalah glanced at her sister sympathetically, "Am I right, Hannah?"

"Yes, I could definitely use a break from Hank!"

"Where is Hank, anyway?" Jake asked.

"He went fishin' with some friends from school." Laurana took Jake's arm and whispered into his ear as they approached the house, "Hannah and Hank got into a big argument this mornin', and I think they just need some time apart. Y'all needin' her here couldn't have come at a better time."

"Ah," Jake shook his head understandingly as he set Matty down. "Run along to the barn, Matty. You'll find a surprise in there." Matty skipped off, her curly blonde locks bouncing as she anxiously set off to search the barn. Jake followed the women into the house.

They sat down in the living room and caught up on the latest news and events in Daisy and their lives. Shortly, Matty trotted in the kitchen door carrying a fuzzy white ball in her arms, "Can I have this one?" she pleaded.

"What is that you have there, Matty?" Laurana scolded.

Matty ran to her mother, "Lookie, Mama! Micky's cat had kittens, and this one's my favowite! It looks like a snowball." She held the small snowy white kitten out for her mother to examine.

"Be careful with it. It's too tiny to leave its mama yet," Laurana gestured for her to carry the creature carefully back to the barn.

"Can I have it when it's big enough? Please?" she begged, focusing on Jake.

"Sure, you can have it, sweetheart – if your mama says it's ok," Jake chuckled at the curly headed child's delight. "But she won't be ready to leave her mama for another couple weeks." He imagined that Mikalah must have looked a lot like Matty when she was a child and hoped their babies would be as beautiful.

"Can I have it, Mama? Please?"

Laurana scratched her head and thought it over. "I suppose so – when it's big enough," she relented, unable to deny the little cherub any good thing.

"You should probably take her back to the barn, Matty. Kittens need to stay with their mama," Mikalah suggested.

"Thank you!" she scurried off to return the bundle of fur to its mother.

"We won't be stayin' long. I need to get on home," Laurana explained. "Too much cannin' to get done."

"Oh, you can't leave this soon! I haven't seen you in two months, Mama!" Mikalah begged.

"Maybe we can stay for a few more minutes," she smiled at her daughter. She turned to Jake, "You realize these babies will be here very soon, don't you? Twins come early."

"How much longer do you think it will be?" he asked.

She turned back to Mikalah, "You could have these babies any day, Mikalah. You've already dropped. You're getting' very uncomfortable, aren't you?"

"Yes, I feel like it's close," Mikalah confided.

Jake wondered why she had kept what she was feeling from him. She could read the confusion in his eyes, "Honey, I didn't want you to worry about somethin' that I wasn't really sure about."

"I'm supposed to worry. You should have told me," he reached for her hand. "We're in this together. If I don't know what you're feeling then how will I know when to help you?"

"Jake's right, Mikalah. You need to keep him informed of how you're feelin'. You could go any time and when you do, he really should take you to the hospital. Twins are harder to deliver and sometimes they have to take them by cesarean. If they're too early, they'll need special attention."

"Oh, I don't want to have a cesarean!" Mikalah protested.

"Mikalah, you've got to prepare yourself for the fact that anything can happen with twins. You need to be at the hospital," Laurana insisted and addressed Jake, "The minute, I mean the minute her water breaks or she starts having uncomfortable contractions you get her to Erlanger Hospital in Chattanooga. Have Hannah either call Donaldson's store or the Morton's and have them send for me. I'll meet you there."

Jake nodded, "I will. I'll make sure Hannah knows the numbers to call so that if I'm helping next door she can call for me and call you too."

Mikalah grew more nervous by the minute. She hadn't thought about the possible complications with twins. She just figured Doc Phillips would be back in a week or two and that she'd have the twins at home as planned. Her mother had Hank and Hannah at home without much trouble.

"Hannah, please go get Matty. We really need to go," Laurana pointed to the kitchen door, and Hannah rose from her seat to retrieve her little sister.

"So tell me, did Mikalah look like Matty when she was little?" Jake asked Laurana.

"She sure did. Matty's just about the spittin' image of Mikalah as a little girl. They've got different temperaments but they look alike." Jake took Mikalah's hand again, "Reckon we'll have a little curly headed blonde that looks like you?"

Mikalah smiled, "I thought you wanted a boy?"

"Oh, well, now I can have both!" he smiled.

"Funny how men always think they want a son, but once the children start arriving, they're always partial to their daughters," Laurana teased. "You'll be no different, Jake. Just look how you took right to Matty and she to you. She's got you wrapped right around her little finger," Laurana laughed and turned to Mikalah, "You better hope these are boys, cause Jake's gonna spoil your girls plum rotten!" Jake feigned innocence.

"You will!" Mikalah laughed, "And you know it!"

Matty came trotting back in the living room, "Let me know when that kitten's ready to take home! Mama and I'll come get her!"

"Oh we will, will we?" Laurana ran her fingers through Matty's blonde curls. "I'll be surprised if Mikalah doesn't have those babies before that kitten's ready to leave its Mama."

"Oh goodie! Babies!" Matty squealed. "I can't wait!" She climbed up on the couch and put her arms around Mikalah's neck and kissed her goodbye.

Mikalah started to get up when Laurana stood, "Oh no, Mikalah, you sit down and rest. No need walkin' me to the door. I can see my way out." She turned to Hannah, "Now you help around here like you do for me at home. Keep an eye on Mikalah and don't let her work too hard. I know how she is. I'm sure she's pushin' it to the limits!"

"Oh please, Mother!" Mikalah rolled her eyes.

"You're right!" Jake chimed in. "She does push it to the limit. I have to watch her like a hawk or she'll work herself to death. I'm counting on Hannah here to keep her in line while I'm out working in the fields."

"Hannah, I didn't ask you to come spy on me now, just to help out a little here and there and keep me company," Mikalah told her sister.

Hannah laughed, "Guess I'll do a bit of both." She liked the idea of bossing her older sister instead of the other way around.

Two weeks passed and Doc Phillips stopped by to check on Mikalah. He confirmed Laurana's diagnosis that Mikalah was indeed expecting twins and instructed her to call him immediately at the first symptom of labor. He would ride with them to the hospital when the time arrived.

Hannah was a big help to Mikalah. She picked vegetables, canned, and cleaned. Jake and Mikalah were surprised that a thirteen-year-old girl could work so hard and accomplish so much in such an efficient manner.

They invited her to join them in their morning and evening prayers and their scripture study and to attend church with them on Sundays. Hannah was an intelligent young woman who asked lots of questions. Upon Mikalah's suggestion, she started reading the Book of Mormon while Mikalah napped during the afternoon thunderstorms that so frequently interrupted otherwise sunny afternoons. It was enjoyably easy to sleep with the comforting sound of the rain dancing on the roof and the rolling thunder's soothing rumble.

Sometimes Jake joined her and watched her sleep or napped himself. He wanted to be near her as much as possible for he expected that she could go into labor at any time. He harbored an unspoken fear that when the time came he wouldn't be with her. So he always kept Hannah informed of where he was at any given time.

One sunny morning in early July, Mikalah decided that she wanted to pick blueberries for a pie and to bottle for jam. Hannah, who was her perpetual shadow, joined her. They swung their buckets as they traipsed through the fields to the blueberries. The cultivated blueberry bushes looked more like trees than bushes. They were nearly seven feet tall and heavy laden with delicious sweet berries.

"I just love blueberries!" Hannah exclaimed.

"Me too!" Mikalah popped a large blueberry in her mouth. "And these are the best I've ever tasted. Mr. Taylor must have really known what he was doin' when he planted these." By noon, they had picked nearly six gallons of the sweet delicious fruit.

"I'll carry some of these back to the house and come back to help you carry the rest," Hannah picked up three buckets and started back home, leaving Mikalah brimming the last bucket. Hannah put the three buckets of berries on the counter, poured two glasses of water and sipped one as she walked through the living room and onto the front porch.

She stood in the shade of the big wraparound porch sipping her drink, gazing over the lush green property. Her eyes turned to Mikalah who reached up, pulling a high limb down so she could pluck the large sweet fruit in the highest limbs. Suddenly Mikalah doubled over and fell to the ground.

"Mikalah!" Hannah screamed and set the glasses down on the railing. She started down the steps toward her sister and then realized that it would be a more effective use of time to run in the house and call Jake and then run to Mikalah's aid. She flew back up the steps and to the study to ring Frank Taylor's house.

Ruth answered, "Hello?"

"Mikalah's having the baby! Send Jake home immediately. She's collapsed out by the blueberries!"

"I'll send him. He's right out here working on the fence with Frank. You run back to her."

"I will," Hannah hung up the phone and ran as fast as she could to Mikalah's side. "Mikalah!" she screamed repeatedly as she approached her sister.

Mikalah knelt on the ground holding her stomach with one hand and her back with the other, "It's time, Hannah. Go call Jake!" she gritted her teeth and closed her eyes obviously in excruciating pain.

"I already did. I saw you collapse from the porch and ran in to call next door. Mrs. Taylor's sending him home." Hannah put her hand lightly on Mikalah's back. "Is there anything I can do?" Mikalah just shook her head and doubled over as another wave hit.

"The contractions are so close, Hannah," she said as the wave passed, and she began to catch her breath.

"Here comes Jake!" Hannah pointed. Jake flew up the dirt road, the old truck bouncing on the ruts and veering off the road, cutting through the grass and

243

screeching to a halt beside them. He flung the door open and without saying a word, picked Mikalah up and carried her to the truck.

"How close are the pains?" he asked her once he had her settled.

"Really close," she wrapped her arms around her stomach in anguish.

"Hannah, please go back to the house, and call Doc Phillips, and tell him to meet us at the hospital in Chattanooga," he hopped in the truck. "Then call your Mama, and tell her to meet us there. I'm not sure how long it will be before we're back. So, lock up tonight, and if you need anything, call the Taylors. They said they would help you while we're away."

"I will," Hannah took off running to the house to call the doctor and her mother. She was nervous about staying in the big house by herself, but she needed to be there to take care of the animals while Jake and Mikalah were at the hospital.

Mikalah's water broke half way to the hospital and Jake rummaged through the bag they'd packed for the hospital with his right hand trying to find a towel as he drove with his left, "Here, honey, here's a towel."

Her contractions grew more intense afterwards, "Jake! How much farther? I don't think I'm gonna make it!" Mikalah cried as she clutched his arm and bent over, leaning her head on the dashboard.

"It's maybe fifteen more minutes. I'll try to drive a little faster. I just hate jostling you all over going so fast," he pushed on the accelerator, and the engine roared.

Jake's anxiety increased as Mikalah's pains grew intensely worse, but she managed to hold on until they reached the hospital. He parked the old truck in front of the hospital and lifted Mikalah out, carrying her as quickly as he could to the front door. An orderly opened the door and ran for a wheel chair.

"My wife needs to be seen immediately," Jake demanded as they reached the front desk of the maternity ward. "She's having twins, her water's broke, she's in horrible pain, and her contractions are back-to-back!"

A nurse walked around to check on her, "We'll find her a room immediately. Who's her doctor?"

"Doc Phillips from Ooltewah. He's meeting us here," Jake explained. The nurse handed Jake a clipboard and asked him to fill it out. The last thing Jake wanted to think about was filling out a form. Unable to hide his anxiety, he crouched in front of Mikalah, the clipboard sandwiched between his thigh and elbow.

"Sir, I realize you're worried about your wife, but we need that form filled out before we can put her in a room," the nurse behind the desk instructed.

Jake ran his hand through his hair in frustration. His hand shaking, he began filling out the form as he knelt in front of Mikalah by the reception desk. "Here, here's your form," the clipboard clamored on the desktop and the pen dangled off the desk swinging from its chain.

Doc Phillips arrived as they were about to put her in a room. "Mikalah," he panted. The old man had run from his car as fast as his short legs could carry him. Realizing that Mikalah was in no condition to talk, Doc Phillips turned to Jake, "How is she. What's happened? Has her water broken?"

"Yes, it broke on the way over. She's in horrible pain, and the contractions are continuous. I think somethin's wrong!" Jake was the third oldest of ten children, and he'd seen his mother in labor. It was never like this. This was frightening.

"Let's get her in here so I can examine her and see," a nurse wheeled Mikalah into a room.

Two nurses stepped in front of Jake at the door, "I'm sorry, Mr. Elliot. This is as far as you go."

"What? I'm not leaving her!" his voice was frantic.

The two women stepped closer to block the doorway, and a nurse from inside the room shut the door.

"You don't understand, I'm not leaving my wife," he demanded and pushed past them.

"Sir, you can't go in there!" one of the nurses insisted.

Jake managed to get by them, pushing the door open and rushed to Mikalah's side. The doctor was already examining her. Mikalah's pain-filled eyes pled with Jake as she reached out for his hand.

"Jake, we're gonna have to get her to surgery. She's hemorrhaging, and I'm afraid we'll lose the babies if we don't operate immediately," Doc Phillip's eyes were filled with such sympathy that Jake's heart seized with an intense fear that threatened his ability to breathe. He felt as if someone had stabbed a knife through his lungs.

"Is she gonna be all right, Doc?"

"I don't know - not if we don't act now. Nurse! Get this woman to pre-op now!" Nurses and orderlies scurried around like bees at a hive. For Jake, everything seemed to be happening in slow motion as they lifted Mikalah onto a gurney and sped off to surgery. Still holding her hand, he jogged along beside her.

"You're gonna be all right, Mikalah. I love you!" Jake's eyes brimmed with tears as she reluctantly released the tight grip she held on his hand, and the gurney disappeared into the operating room.

"I love you Jake!" she called out to him as the operating room doors swung shut.

Jake stood stunned staring at the doors through which everything he loved in life had vanished. He turned and slammed his fist against the cinderblock wall, leaning his head into the cold concrete as tears slowly trickled down his tan cheeks. He began to pray frantically in his mind, pleading for Mikalah's life and the lives of their babies. He didn't know how long he stood there praying before he felt a hand grasp his arm and rub it softly.

"Jake, honey, are you all right?" Laurana asked soothingly. "They told us at the desk that they took Mikalah in for emergency surgery."

Jake lifted his gaze and found Bill standing next to Laurana, "She's hemorrhaging." He wiped his moistened cheeks on his arm. "I should have stayed with her. I should have told Frank that I couldn't help him with the fence. We could've gotten here faster!"

"Jake, don't even talk that way. You got here as fast as you could. Hannah said you were there in a flash and that you even had her bag packed in the truck. You couldn't have done anything more," Laurana tried to console him.

Suddenly Jake threw his arms around his mother-in-law, closing his eyes tightly as he fought to control his emotions. Laurana heard his low sobs. "I can't lose her. I can't live without her!"

"You're not going to lose her, son," Jake felt Bill's comforting hand on his shoulder as the three embraced. "She's gonna be fine. Mikalah's a fighter. She never quits. You've gotta know that by now, son."

Jake lifted his gaze to his father-in-law, the first ray of hope shining through to him since that horrible moment in the examining room. "You're right, Mikalah never quits, does she? Not until the job's done," he chuckled and pulled a handkerchief from his pocket to dry his eyes.

The three found a bench on which to sit outside the operating room and waited... and waited. Finally, a nurse carried a small baby wrapped in a pink blanket out of the operating room. Jake leapt to his feet, followed by Mikalah's parents.

"Is that... is that our baby?" Jake asked the nurse. She stopped in front of him and held the baby out for him to see.

"This is your baby girl. Your baby boy has had complications, and the doctors are working with him now. They'll probably take him ..." The operating room door burst open, and a nurse ran out carrying a small blue bundle across the hall and into another room. "They're taking him to ICU," the nurse continued.

Jake took the woman by the shoulders, "What about Mikalah? What about my wife?" he asked frantically.

"She... uh....she," the woman began, and Jake thought his heart would stop beating. "She's lost a lot of blood, Mr. Elliot."

"Is she gonna be all right?" he stared into the woman's eyes, oblivious to Mikalah's parents whose attention remained riveted on the short dark-haired nurse.

"We don't know yet. It doesn't look good," the woman looked as if she might start crying.

"I've got to see her!" Jake demanded.

"Mr. Elliot, you can't right now," her kind eyes seemed to weep with him.

"Please, please let me see my wife," he begged.

"Here," she held the baby out to him, "Would you like to hold your daughter for a minute while I go ask the doctor if you can see her?"

Jake held out his arms to take the baby. It had been a while since he'd held one of his younger siblings as babies, but it came back to him quickly as he took the little bundle in his arms. He gazed lovingly into the baby's blue eyes and gently ran his finger along the light blonde fuzz on her pretty round head. He looked up at Laurana and Bill, "She... she looks just like Mikalah," he began to weep, tears falling from his eyes onto the little pink blanket.

He knew at that moment that this child would always be a reminder to him of the wife he'd lost. The day she learned to walk, her first word, her first day of school, her high school graduation and her wedding day, would all be searing, stabbing knives in his heart, tearing at his soul and reminding him of the woman he loved. How could he endure it? They'd never even been able to go to the temple! The thought sent panic through him. Would God make allowances? Could they still be together for eternity? Surely Heavenly Father would make allowances! After all He was the one who told them to go ahead and get married, and it hadn't even been a year since Mikalah was baptized. God knew that they never meant to settle for a civil ceremony and that the temple was always their goal. They had been working, planning and saving to go for their wedding anniversary.

As their time together flashed through his mind, Jake caught hold on the dream of kissing her in front of the St. George temple. That dream hadn't been fulfilled yet, and he knew... he just *knew* it meant something. Taking courage, he held onto the vision and wiped the tears from his eyes with his handkerchief, handing the baby to Laurana.

"I've got to see Mikalah now," he strode resolutely to the operating room where an orderly stood outside the door. "Please tell Doc Phillips that I'd like to see my wife now."

"Sir, you can't..." the orderly held up his hand to stop him.

"Please, a nurse just went in and said she'd ask," Jake began. At that moment, the operating doors opened, and two nurses pushed Mikalah's gurney out of the room. They stopped momentarily, allowing him to see her for only a second. He stood over her, caressing her forehead and the soft curls that fell around her sleeping face. Then, the gurney moved again as they took her across the hall and behind another door.

"Jake, she'll be unconscious for a while. We're taking her to recovery," Doc Phillips explained.

"Is she gonna be all right?" Jake's eyes pled with the elderly gentleman.

"We'll just have to wait and see. We had to give her a transfusion. She's lost a lot of blood. It's really a miracle we stopped the bleeding at all," he explained.

"Can I please sit with her in the recovery room? Please?" he begged.

"Sure, Jake. They'll give me fits about it, but I'll insist," Doc Phillips didn't expect Mikalah to make it through the night, but knew that if there was any way for her to pull through, it may very well be because she had Jake beside her to help her hold on. "Give me a few minutes, and I'll come get you."

The nurse took the baby back from Laurana and carried her to the nursery.

"They're gonna let me sit with her in recovery," Jake smiled weakly. Laurana buried her head in her husband's chest as the seriousness of the situation seemed to catch up with her. She was trying to be strong for Jake, but after seeing the expression on Doc Phillips' face, she knew the situation was dire.

"Jake, you can come in now," Doc Phillips held the door open for Jake to enter, and Bill and Laurana peeked through the door catching one more glimpse of their dying daughter.

As the door shut, Laurana sobbed into her husband's shoulder, "Oh Bill! This can't be happening!"

"It's not gonna happen!" he insisted but his voice faltered. "Mikalah's a fighter"

Jake sat beside Mikalah's bed and held her limp hand in his. She still lay unconscious.

"Stay with her and make her fight, Jake," Doc Phillips nodded and left the room.

Jake stood and pulled a small vial of oil from his pocket, anointed her head and gave her a blessing. He commanded her to fight. He told her she hadn't finished her work — that she had the temple ahead of her and her babies to raise.

249

He told her he loved her and that Heavenly Father wanted them to be together, to go to the temple and raise their children together in the gospel.

Closing the prayer, he collapsed onto the chair next to her and sobbed bitterly into his hands. He had no idea if the blessing he just gave her was what the Lord wanted for her or only what he so desperately needed himself. In all the prayers he'd offered that day, Jake couldn't bring himself to say, "Thy will be done." He'd learned from experience that in such circumstances one must surrender one's will to God's. But this time he couldn't take the chance. Surrendering Mikalah was not an option that his heart could withstand.

Jake clasped her hand in his as she slept, and nurses came in at fifteen minute intervals to take her pulse and her temperature. Finally after about an hour she stirred.

"Jake, where are my babies?" her blue eyes groggily pled with his.

"They're in the nursery, honey. They're beautiful – a little girl and a little boy." He, of course, hadn't seen their son, but he felt it best to keep the seriousness of his condition from her.

"I'm not gonna make it am I, Jake?" she mumbled.

"Why of course you are! What a silly thing to say!" he tried to hide his fear but Mikalah could tell by his eyes that he'd been crying heavily.

"I love you Jake. Always remember that I loved you more than anything." her voice weakened to a whisper.

"Stop talking past tense, Mikalah! You've got more work to do! We have to go to the temple and be sealed together with our babies. You've got to help me raise this little boy and girl in the gospel."

"I'm too weak, Jake. I don't know if I can..."

Jake sat next to her on the bed holding her hand in his as he bent down to kiss her forehead. "You never quit, Mikalah. You know you never quit," he whispered, his lips pressed against her forehead.

He lifted his head and gently stroked her curls, hoping and praying that she would hold onto life in spite of the odds.

"Do you see that light, Jake? It's so warm and feels so comforting," her eyes were fixed above her, her smile growing peaceful and calm.

WALTZING WITH THE LIGHT

"No, Mikalah! Stay away from the light! Hold on, Mikalah! You have to fight!" he demanded. He leaned his head into her pillow and sobbed, his voice growing softer as he pleaded, "Please Mikalah fight for me, fight for us… for the babies. I can't do this alone."

He knew they had come to the end of all hope, and he finally surrendered and began to plead, "Dear Heavenly Father, if there is any way possible that she can be spared, please I beg of Thee to let me keep her at my side all my days. But, if you must take her, please give me the strength to carry on. I can't do this without Thee. My heart is in Thy hands. Thy will be done…"

Several moments after he concluded his prayer, Jake felt Mikalah's familiar fingers through his thick brown hair, "Please don't cry, Jake. I'll fight for us. I'll hang on."

Jake's bloodshot emerald eyes gazed into hers until she drifted off to sleep, a peaceful smile on her lips. Afraid that she was gone, he quickly felt her pulse, breathing a sigh of relief to find it still there.

Shortly, a nurse entered the room and checked her blood pressure and temperature once again. "Her blood pressure is looking better, Mr. Elliot. I'll send Doctor Phillips in to check on her."

"Thank you!"

Jake didn't sleep much, but what little rest he allowed himself was in the chair beside Mikalah's bed. The next morning, Doctor Phillips came in to assess her condition, "I'd say she's out of the woods, Jake. She's gonna make it."

Jake breathed a sigh of relief, "Oh thank the Lord!" He took the doctor's hand and shook it vigorously, "Thank you so much, Doc! Thanks for everything you did and for letting me stay with her!"

"She's lucky to have you, Jake. It must have been your love that pulled her through, 'cause I wasn't holdin' much hope."

"It was God that pulled her through," Jake smiled.

"I won't argue with you on that point," Doc Phillips turned toward the door. "I'll be back to check on her later this afternoon. Why don't you come see your babies?" He motioned for Jake to follow him, and patted Jake's back as he led him to the nursery. "Your little man is a fighter like his mother. They released him from ICU this morning. He's doin' just fine. Would you like to see him?"

The nurse brought out a little bundle of blue and handed him to Jake. Laurana and Bill turned the corner and approached quickly as Jake pulled back the blanket and felt the downy brown fuzz on his son's head.

"He looks like you, Jake," Laurana smiled. "How's Mikalah?"

"Doc says she's gonna make it," he beamed as he kissed his son's soft little head.

Chapter 12

Mikalah awoke to Frank's faint fiddle playing wafting through the open window. She recognized Johann Strauss' *Beautiful Blue Danube*, and reached for Jake, but only felt the warm reminder of his former presence. She opened her eyes to find that he no longer lay in bed next to her. She sat up and turned to the two cradles that Jake had made for the twins. With the aid of the moonlight streaming through the window, she could see little Hayden sleeping in his, but Hope was not in hers. Mikalah put her feet to the hardwood floor and stepped to the bedroom window where a cool breeze gave respite to the hot, humid night. Out on the lawn, Jake held his little girl to his chest, dancing with her in the moonlight. He supported the two-month-old's curly blonde head in his large hand as her striking blue eyes gazed up into her father's handsome adoring face.

Mikalah folded her arms, watching Hope's eyelids grow heavy as the music and the movement lulled her to a sweet slumber. Jake rested Hope's little head against his shoulder and continued the waltz until Frank completed the piece. He lowered his chin to see her face, assuring that she slept soundly and started up the porch steps. Mikalah opened the door for him, and he gently placed the sleeping babe in her crib. He held his hand softly to her back to assure her of his presence and then quietly crept back. He turned to find the door still open and Mikalah standing in her nightgown on the back porch, her arms folded around her waist as she stared at the moon, listening to Frank's rendition of Strauss' *Tales from the Vienna Woods*.

Jake gently closed the door and joined her on the porch. He stood behind her, enfolding her in his arms and kissed her shoulder.

"I just love it when he plays Strauss," Mikalah tilted her head as Jake softly kissed her neck.

He turned her around to face him, "May I have this waltz, Madam?"

"I'd love to, kind sir," she curtsied and put her hand in his. They stepped onto the lawn where he led her in an elegant box step to the rhythmic melody of the violin. The birds in the trees sang along and the crickets kept time with the music. Mikalah gazed up into the trees as the pair spun around to the waltz.

Jake chuckled at the owl that seemed to be hooting in time with the melody, "We've got an orchestra tonight."

"I know!" Mikalah loved waltzing with Jake in the moonlight. It was as if no matter what threatening hand hung over them, they could still find safety in each other's arms in the tranquil moments when heaven's illuminating light so dramatically broke through the darkness of the world. Tonight there were no threats, no dangers nor worries. Even though Europe was at war and Germany had just invaded Poland, Mikalah's soul rested, nestled in a little pocket of personal peace so sorely needed after the trauma of recent events.

She wouldn't borrow trouble by worrying about world politics. Mikalah's world centered on her children, her adoring husband and the family she grew up in. In this moment, those she loved were safe and happy, and she was incredibly grateful for that. It had taken some time for her to recover fully, and she was just now getting the babies into a routine. She couldn't have done it without Jake. He seemed to know instinctively what to do to assist with the babies. He said it was because he had so many brothers and sisters that he couldn't help but know how to soothe their troubles. But, Mikalah knew it was more than that. It was one of his gifts.

Mikalah had also come to rely heavily upon Hannah who stayed the entire summer and would be going back home in a few days. She wished Hannah could stay with her all the time and felt tempted to ask her mother to let her live with them, but she didn't want to take Hannah away from her friends and school.

The song ended, and Frank put his fiddle away for the evening. Jake took Mikalah by the hand and led her back to their room. They took one last peek at their sleeping babies and went to bed.

~*~

Oak and maple trees burst open with bright red, orange, and yellow foliage against a backdrop of clear blue skies. Jake, Mikalah and the Taylors had just finished up the sorghum harvest and jars of sweet sticky molasses filled their pantry. A gentle breeze blew as Laurana and Bill stepped from their car and approached the house.

Jake opened the door, holding Hayden on his hip, "Hi, come on in. Mikalah's in the bedroom." Laurana took Hayden from Jake's arms and went in search of Mikalah. "Bill, go to the pantry, and get a few jars of molasses to take home with you."

"Thanks," Bill smiled and passed Jake.

Laurana knocked lightly on the open bedroom door.

"Hi Mama!" Mikalah greeted as she closed her suitcase.

"Hello dear! Looks like you're just about ready to go," she shifted Hayden onto her hip. "Do you have everything?"

"I've got everything for the babies here. This is Jake's bag, and this is mine. The Taylors kindly agreed to watch the farm while we're gone. I believe that's everything," Mikalah nodded.

Jake strode into the room, "Are these bags ready?"

"Yes, thank you."

He hefted the two bags and carried them out to the trunk of the Ford's car. Bill stepped into the bedroom, "Anything you want me to take to the car?"

"Yes, Daddy, could you please carry this bag?" Mikalah handed him her suitcase.

"Sure, anything else?"

"No I believe that's it," Mikalah gently lifted Hope from her crib and cradled the sleeping baby in her arms. She grabbed Hope's blanket and tossed it over her shoulder so that it draped over the sleeping baby's body.

Mikalah took one last look around the room, "I believe that's everything."

The women walked out to the car, and Laurana slid in the open front door while Mikalah got in the back. Bill shut their doors while Jake locked up the house.

"I bet y'all are so excited!" Laurana bubbled as she turned sideways to talk with Mikalah over the seat.

"Oh we are!" She lowered her voice slightly as Jake approached the car, "I'm a bit nervous about meeting Jake's parents though."

"At least they won't pull a gun on you," Laurana chuckled and looked at Bill as he slid behind the wheel.

"No I guess they won't!" Mikalah laughed. Bill nodded and laughed at himself.

"I guess I made a real horse's rear end out of myself that day – didn't I?" he chuckled.

Jake slid into the car and shut the door. "I'm sorry about that Jake," Bill said as he met Jake's gaze through the rear view mirror.

"Sorry about what?" Jake looked around wondering what they were referring to and why everyone had been laughing.

"I'm sorry I pulled that rifle on you last year when you came for Mikalah," Bill's expression grew more serious. He really meant to apologize.

"That's ok, sir," Jake was surprised that this should come up now. "I know you were just trying to protect Mikalah." He let his fingers gently play with the soft curls on Hope's head. "I'd probably do the same thing if some smelly old fella came to court my Hope," he chuckled.

"So are you ready to go?" Bill asked.

"Let's go," Mikalah nodded.

Bill started the car and drove them to the railway station. Jake and Mikalah spent most of their savings on the hospital bill, so Jake's parents sent money to help pay for the tickets. Jake gave Bill the money, and he purchased the tickets for them at a discount. Laurana and Bill stood outside the train with them and hugged them goodbye.

Reluctantly, Laurana handed baby Hayden to Jake, "We're gonna miss y'all!" A burst of steam lingered like fog around the base of the train as the engineer blew the whistle for everyone to board.

Mikalah hugged her mother, "We'll miss you too, but we'll be back before you know it."

"A month isn't that long," Jake shook Bill's hand, but Bill pulled Jake to him and patted his back.

"Have a good trip," Bill and Laurana waved as Jake handed the conductor their tickets, and they boarded the train.

They found their compartment, opened the door and stowed their luggage except for a small bag that Mikalah kept for the babies. Mikalah peered out the window and saw her parents standing outside arm-in-arm. She opened the window and waved, "I love you both!"

"We love you too, sweetheart!" Laurana called, and the train eased forward. As her parents faded from sight, her heart ached for them. She wanted them to be there in the temple with her when she and Jake were sealed together for all time and eternity and when their little babies were placed on the altar and sealed to them, never to be separated. With all her heart she longed to be bound to her parents and her brother and sisters, but her father was still hesitant, still unsure. As long as he remained so, Mikalah knew her mother would wait to receive the blessings. But Mikalah resolved to hold the faith for them, that one day her father's eyes would be opened and he would see. She thought of the words to *Lead Kindly Light,*

> *Lead, kindly Light, amid the encircling gloom;*
> *Lead thou me on!*
> *The night is dark, and I am far from home;*
> *Lead thou me on!*
> *Keep thou my feet;*
> *I do not ask to see the distant scene –*
> *One step enough for me.*

One step enough for me. Mikalah and Jake would take the first step, and someday her family would follow. She would hold the faith for them. She thought of Moroni's teachings on faith found in Ether 12:14-15, "*Behold it was the faith of Nephi and Lehi that wrought the change upon the Lamanites, that they were baptized with fire and with the Holy Ghost. Behold it was the faith of Ammon and his brethren which wrought so great a miracle among the Lamanites.*"

One day, she envisioned it being written in heaven, *"Behold it was the faith of Jake Elliot that wrought the change upon Mikalah Ford that she was baptized with fire and with the Holy Ghost. Behold it was their faith together which wrought so great a miracle among her family."*

One day she would be sealed to her family, and they would spend the eternities together. The binding chain of the temple would extend through time tying them to each other, to their ancestors, to their children, and to their Father in Heaven.

"Honey, you all right?" Jake had one leg crossed over the other with Hayden sitting on his legs. The baby boy smiled and clutched his father's finger with his fist. Mikalah still stood at the open window, holding Hope as the train station became simply a speck on the horizon.

"Oh, I'm fine. I'm just... I'm just holding Hope," she smiled wistfully and sat down next to him.

The trip took several days by train, but finally they arrived in St. George on a chilly late-October afternoon. Jake held Hope in his right arm while he secured one bag under his arm and held another in his hand. Mikalah carried Hayden in her right arm with a bag in her left. They carefully exited the train, and Jake scanned the area for his parents.

"There they are!" he nodded toward his right. His parents stood about twenty feet away. Mikalah searched in the direction Jake was staring and saw a tall grey haired man who looked incredibly like Jake. His wife, who was about five foot six, grey-haired and a little plump waved eagerly in their direction. She and her husband hurried toward them. Jake took a few steps forward and dropped his bags, putting his arm around his mother as he still clutched Hope. Mikalah joined them, released her bag, and shifted Hayden to her left hip. Jake's mother embraced her as if she'd known her forever.

Constance Elliot examined her daughter-in-law, clutching her hand in hers, "Oh Jake, she's just beautiful. You're beautiful dear!" She turned to her husband, "Isn't she just gorgeous!"

Edward Elliot nodded and smiled at Mikalah.

"Thank you, Ma'am" Mikalah was a bit embarrassed about all the fuss.

"And let me see these babies!" she took Hope from Jake's arms. "Oh this one looks just like you, Mikalah!" She put the baby to her hip and caressed Hayden's chubby cheek. "And your little boy looks just like you did when you were a baby, Jake! I'll show you some baby pictures when we get back to the house, Mikalah," she patted Mikalah's arm.

"Oh, Mom, not the old photos!" Jake rolled his eyes.

"Oh, yes, the photographs! Your wife wants to see what you looked like as a lad," she chuckled. "Don't you dear?"

"I'd love to, yes Ma'am!"

"Is this everything?" Edward pointed to their bags.

"Yes, this is all of it," Jake nodded. Edward lifted the bag that Mikalah had released, and Jake picked up the other two as Mikalah and Constance carried the babies.

"Oh, I'm just so excited to have you both here!" Constance exclaimed.

"It's all your mother has thought about for months," Edward opened the door for everyone to enter the train station. They cut through the building and out the other side where the Elliot's car was parked. Jake and Edward loaded the bags in the car, and Jake and Mikalah sat in the back seat with Hayden while Constance held Hope in the front with her.

"I don't think we told you, Jake, but we were able to repurchase the house! We moved back in a couple weeks ago!" his father announced excitedly.

"Really? How wonderful!" Jake put his arm around Mikalah's shoulder. "You'll love this place. It's where I grew up." He could hardly wait to show her around his old stomping grounds.

"I assume you two need temple recommends?" Edward asked.

"Uh, yes, we do. I hope that won't be difficult to arrange. But there just aren't too many priesthood leaders out our way."

"I've already set up an appointment for you both. It's tomorrow at noon," Edward peered at them through the rear view mirror.

"Thanks, Dad, we really appreciate you helping with that," Jake smiled.

"And we've let the temple know you're coming on Wednesday too and arranged for someone to watch the babies until it's time for them to be brought in for the sealing," Constance explained.

"Thank you so much! I was wondering what we'd do about the babies," Mikalah liked Jake's parents already. They put her at ease.

"Mikalah brought some of her family names with her, and we'd like to go to the temple several times during our visit so that we can do their temple ordinances," Jake told his parents.

"That's wonderful, dear!" Constance turned around in the seat to smile at Mikalah.

"We usually go to the temple two or three times each week. We'd love the company," Edward Elliot's happy eyes met Mikalah's through the rear view mirror. Mikalah couldn't get over how much Jake looked like his father and was rather pleased that her husband would keep his handsome looks as he grew older.

"If you're up to it in a couple weeks – after you've had some time to rest - we thought we might take a trip to Salt Lake so you can see the temple there and the Tabernacle. Having us along to help with the twins might make traveling a little easier," Constance looked at Jake who smiled at Mikalah.

Mikalah nodded happily, "I'd love that!"

~*~

Mikalah opened the bedroom drawer and held up a little white dress and a white shirt and pants. She laid them out on the bed and looked up at Jake, "If you'll dress Hayden, I'll dress Hope."

She lifted Hope from her crib and kissed her rosy chubby cheek, "Good morning baby girl. Are you ready to go to the temple this morning?"

Jake lifted their son from his crib and nestled his lips to the baby's fuzzy head and then kissed the child's cheek. Mikalah grabbed two diapers and handed one to Jake. They each laid a baby out on the bed, changed their diapers and dressed them in the little white clothes that Mikalah had made for the occasion.

"Don't they look adorable?" Mikalah grinned.

"They sure do!" he sat on the bed and pulled a baby onto each knee. "You get dressed, and I'll put my suit on when you're finished."

Mikalah pulled her wedding dress out of the closet and hung it in the doorway, then found her green dress to wear. She'd change into her wedding dress later at the temple.

Jake played with the babies while Mikalah dressed. Then she sat on the bed tickling them and making them laugh while Jake put on his suit. Mikalah handed Hope to Jake and lifted Hayden onto her hip as she grabbed her covered wedding dress from the closet doorway. Jake picked up the diaper bag.

"Do we have everything?" she asked.

"I believe so," he patted his suit pocket. "I've got the recommends."

They turned out the lights and walked down the stairs to meet Jake's parents.

"Oh, don't you all look so pretty and handsome!" Constance cooed as she took Hayden from Mikalah. "Edward, go open the trunk for Mikalah so she can spread out her dress."

It was the first time Mikalah had ever seen a temple. As the beautiful St. George temple came into view, a warm feeling of peace spread throughout her body. She could hardly believe they were finally there. She reached for Jake and squeezed his hand.

Edward parked their car, and they carried the babies to the front of the holy edifice. Two friends of Constance' met them at the door.

"Mikalah and Jake, these are my friends, Sister Abernathy and Sister Hallstead. This is my son Jake and his wife Mikalah and their twins – Hope and Hayden," Constance introduced.

"Nice to meet you," Sister Abernathy shook their hands followed by Sister Hallstead.

"Give us those babies, and we'll watch them while you go through the ordinances. We'll bring them to the sealing room when it's time," Sister Hallstead reached out her hand to take Hayden and Sister Abernathy took Hope from Jake.

261

Hope looked at her daddy and began to whine as her bottom lip quivered, and she reached her arms out to him.

Jake leaned over and kissed her chubby cheek, "Be good now, Hope. Stay with Sister Abernathy and Daddy will see you soon." As he took Mikalah's hand and they entered the temple, Hope followed him with her eyes, her bottom lip still pouting.

Mikalah had never felt anything like the temple. It was as if she had stepped out of the world for a few hours and entered heaven. She wished she could stay there all day and soak in the quiet reverence, feeling the Spirit within those hallowed walls.

After completing the necessary ordinances, she and Jake entered the sealing room in their white clothes. The first faces they met were Jake's parents, some of his brothers and sisters and their spouses who were able to attend. The sealer asked them to kneel across the altar from each other and spoke to them about the importance of eternal families, giving them council and direction. Mikalah's eyes filled with tears of joy as she held her husband's hand across the altar, and the elderly gentleman sealed them together as husband and wife for all time and eternity. Jake offered a silent prayer of gratitude that Mikalah had lived to share this day with him. Ever after he would be grateful that the Lord had heard his prayer and given back to him what he had so reluctantly surrendered that awful night in the recovery room only four months earlier.

Sister Hallstead and Sister Abernathy entered with the babies. The women held Hayden and Hope on the altar as their tiny little hands joined their parents. Mikalah and Jake wept as their little ones were bound to them forever by covenant. As Mikalah and Jake stood with their babies in their arms surrounded by mirrors in front and behind them, Jake pondered on the symbol of eternity which they reflected. He thought about the binding chain that tied them to their forebears and to their posterity. He and Mikalah carried their ancestors with them and their children, grandchildren and great grandchildren for generations to come would carry some of Mikalah's faith and spunk, some of Jake's loyalty and compassion, and both of their hard working integrity. Most of all they would carry their love for each other and for the restored gospel of Jesus Christ that bound them together throughout the eternities.

Reluctantly they left the hallowed corridors of the temple with resolution to return as often as they could. As they stepped outside, the cool autumn breeze blew through Mikalah's hair, and she longed for the warmth and peace that only the temple could bring.

Jake turned to his parents, "Mom, could you and Dad please take the babies to the car. Mikalah and I would like a moment."

"Sure, son," Constance took Hayden and Edward took Hope.

Mikalah quizzically gazed into her husband's emerald eyes as he took her hand, leading her to a point on the grounds that gave them a perfect view of the temple.

He put his arm around her shoulders, and they enjoyed the view, "I've been dreaming of this day since I was shot, lying in your bedroom at your parents' house, Mikalah. I had a dream that you were standing right here," he turned her to face him with her back to the temple. "You looked exactly like you do today - your beautiful curls arranged just the way I love them and wearing your mother's wedding dress. I knew from that day on that you would be my bride and that we would be together forever. That dream got me through the night at the hospital when you almost died, and I feel inspired to fulfill it fully here today."

He slipped his arms about her small waist and pulled her to him, kissing her without reservation or restraint. Her arms slid around his neck, and her fingers lovingly toyed with the locks on the back of his head. He looked up and a feeling of love and warmth filled him as the magnificent structure of the St. George temple stood majestically as a token of their everlasting love, and he knew that this was only just the beginning.

MARNIE L. PEHRSON

Bibliography

James Montgomery, *A Poor Wayfaring Man of Grief*, Hymns of The Church of Jesus Christ of Latter-day Saints, 29.

John Henry Newman, *Lead Kindly Light*, Hymns of the Church of Jesus Christ of Latter-day Saints, 97.

William W. Phelps, *The Spirit of God*, Hymns of the Church of Jesus Christ of Latter-day Saints, 2.

About the Author

Marnie L. Pehrson was born and raised in the Chattanooga, Tennessee area. An avid enthusiast of family history, Marnie integrates elements of the places, people and events of her family's heritage into her historical fiction romances. Marnie's life is steeped in Southern history from the little town of Daisy that she grew up in to the 24 acres bordering the famous Chickamauga Battlefield upon which she, her husband and their six children reside. The Chickamauga Battlefield inspired her book *Rebecca's Reveries* and e-books *Back in Emily's Arms* and *In Love We Trust* available through www.CleanRomanceClub.com or www.MarniePehrson.com.

Marnie is the author of inspirational nonfiction works such as *Lord, Are You Sure?*, and *10 Steps to Fulfilling Your Divine Destiny* as well as historical fiction such as *The Patriot Wore Petticoats* about her heroic 4th great-grandmother, Laodicea "Daring Dicey" Langston. She also writes new ebooks regularly for www.CleanRomanceClub.com with cofounder, Marcia Lynn McClure.

Marnie's family converted to the LDS faith when she was four. Being the only LDS student in her private Christian school class for nine years gave her the unique opportunity to learn about other faiths and how to build on common ground. She continues to draw upon this valuable experience as an author and as founder of multi-denominational SheLovesGod.com. The site hosts the annual SheLovesGod Virtual Women's Conference the 3rd week of October each year. She's also an accomplished Web developer and entrepreneur. You may reach her through www.MarniePehrson.com and www.PWGroup.com or by email at marnie@pwgroup.com or by phone 706-866-2295.

The Patriot Wore Petticoats
Historical fiction, 224, pages, ISBN: 0-9729750-4-7
Daring "Dicey" Langston, the bold and reckless rider and expert shot, saves her family and an entire village during the American Revolution. Having faced British soldiers, rushing swollen rivers, the "Bloody Scouts," and the barrel of a loaded pistol, nothing had quite prepared this valiant heroine for the heart-pounding exhilaration she'd find in the arms of one brave Patriot. Based on a true story about the author's fourth great-grandmother. Learn more at www.DiceyLangston.com

Rebecca's Reveries
Historical Fiction, 224 pages, paperback, ISBN: 0-9729750-2-0
Rebecca Marchant had led a sheltered life until she found herself inexplicably drawn to the home of her father's youth. Surrounded by the historical landscape of the Chickamauga Battlefield in Georgia, Rebecca finds herself plagued by haunting dreams and vivid visions of Civil War events. As Rebecca walks a mile in another girl's moccasins through her visions and dreams she learns about compassion, forgiveness, temptation and the power of true love.

Hannah's Heart
Historical Fiction, 108 pages, paperback, ISBN: 0-9729750-6-3
Hannah Jamison made the mistake of falling for the wrong man. Not only did he find her irritating and troublesome, but also her father had no use for him. All seemed a hopeless infatuation until Mother Nature threw the two together in the perfect time and place. But now what to do about her father?

Beyond the Waterfall
Historical Fiction, 136 pages, paperback ISBN: 0-9729750-7-1
Jillian's feet were precariously planted in two worlds: the Cherokee nation on the brink of extermination, and the world where he belonged. On her first meeting with the charming and handsome merchant, Jesse Whitmore had set her young heart ablaze. Yet, could she trust him? Or was he just like all the other white men she'd encountered? Would he stand beside her while she witnessed her nation ripped apart, or would he join the ranks of the powerful greedy to betray her? Based on family history and local legend.

Lord, Are You Sure?
Inspirational, 152 pages, ISBN 0-9729750-0-4
A roadmap for understanding how Heavenly Father works in your life, helping you understand why certain problems keep repeating themselves, how to break the cycle and unlock the mystery of why you encounter challenges and roadblocks on roads you felt inspired to travel.

10 Steps to Fulfilling Your Divine Destiny:
A Christian Woman's Guide to
Learning & Living God's Plan for Her
Inspirational, 124 pages, ISBN 0-9676162-1-2
Have you ever said to yourself, "I'd love to do great things with my life, but I'm just too busy, too untalented, too ordinary, too afraid, too anything but extraordinary"? Inside this book you'll learn how to reach your full God-given potential.

Packets of Sunlight for Parents
Compiled by: Marnie L. Pehrson
Inspirational, 144 pages, ISBN 0-9676162-4-7
Brighten your day with inspiration for parents of tots to teens! Inspirational quote book.

Packets of Sunlight for American Patriots
Compiled by: Marnie L. Pehrson
Inspirational, 108 pages, ISBN 0-9676162-3-9
Let the founding fathers, reignite your love for freedom! Inspirational quote book.

A Closer Walk with Him
SheLovesGod Study Lessons Volume 1
Inspiraitonal, 212 pages, paperback, ISBN 0-9729750-3-9
A collection of insights and ponderings on the scriptures and how we can apply them to our everyday lives. Great for the faith-lift you need in the morning, just before bed, or whenever you need a quick boost of inspiration. Each lesson is self-contained and independent. Read them in any order the Spirit moves you or read the 52 lessons in order as a yearly study guide - it's up to you.

To order call 800-524-2307 or visit
www.MarniePehrson.com

CPSIA information can be obtained at www.ICGtesting.com
Printed in the USA
LVOW050313080812

293351LV00002B/221/A

9 780972 975056